PERILOUS
JUDGMENT

PERILOUS JUDGMENT

A REAL JUSTICE THRILLER

DENNIS RICCI

Waterfall
PRESS

Text copyright © 2016 Dennis Ricci
All rights reserved.

Published by Waterfall Press, Grand Haven, MI
www.brilliancepublishing.com

Amazon, the Amazon logo, and Waterfall Press are trademarks of Amazon.com, Inc., or its affiliates.

ISBN-13: 9781503934771
ISBN-10: 1503934772

Cover design by Janet Perr

Printed in the United States of America

Jesus, my Lord
You alive in me makes all things possible.

Jill, my Beauty
Your patient love and encouragement helped me
persist through trials and obstacles. I couldn't have
finished this story without you.

One has not only a legal but a moral responsibility to obey just laws. Conversely, one has a moral responsibility to disobey unjust laws.

—Dr. Martin Luther King, Jr.

Never do anything against conscience, even if the state demands it.

—Albert Einstein

PART I

POWERS THAT BE

The devil can cite Scripture for his purpose.

—William Shakespeare, *The Merchant of Venice*

Chapter 1

US District Judge Edward Lamport marched into his chambers and swapped his robe for a bulletproof vest.

"So, another threat on my life," he said to Deputy US Marshal Campbell McCormack. "Why the rush to armor me up?"

"Sorry to interrupt your court session, Your Honor."

"I agreed to such things two weeks ago. After the Ernesto Marroquín threat. You didn't answer my question."

McCormack gave him a stern look. "When you turned down our offer of twenty-four-seven protection."

Edward heard a bit of his younger self in McCormack's irreverence and let it go. "When did you learn of this new threat?"

"Within the last hour."

Edward ran fingers through his hair. "FBI called the threat from Marroquín midlevel. I thought that was a stretch. He's incarcerated, appealing his death sentence. How would having me popped help him?"

McCormack avoided eye contact. He handed Edward a plain navy-blue nylon jacket. "Our raid jacket, without the insignia. See how this fits over the armor."

Edward zipped the jacket to chest level and checked himself out in the mirror on his wardrobe door. He patted his waistline and grimaced. "Makes me look like I need to drop twenty."

"We have three concealable vests on order that'll fit under your shirts."

"Good thing I like mine full cut." Edward removed the jacket and draped it over the back of his desk chair and loosened the vest.

"The first death threat didn't come from Marroquín," McCormack said.

Edward stared at the deputy. "What are you talking about?"

"Marroquín's LA drug ring has gotten more aggressive since his conviction. The threat came from his successor."

"Someone still on the street?" McCormack's revelation amplified Edward's vulnerability—and blind spots. "You were going to tell me this when?"

"FBI waited until they were sure. Got word this morning. It's front burner now. They're working with LAPD to hunt him down."

Edward paced his chambers. "So who made today's threat?"

"Someone from Las Reconquistas."

"That Mexican group who wants to take back the southwest US?" Edward shook his head. "You sure it's not some crazed publicity seeker?"

"Timing's no coincidence. It's why we recommend the body armor. And that you carry a pistol."

Edward put up a hand. "No way. Why do I need a gun if you guys'll be with me around the clock?"

"Because your last, best line of defense is *you*."

Edward studied the deputy's boyish face. "How long have you been in the Marshals Service?"

"Ten years, Your Honor."

"And how long in your current post?"

"Eighteen months."

"So you know how hard it is to get a concealed-carry permit in Los Angeles County, even for federal judges."

"Marshal Hunter is working with the LA County Sheriff's Office to expedite."

Edward crossed his arms. *McCormack is confident. I like that.* "You had this all figured out before you barged into my courtroom."

"Our job, Your Honor. You and I have a date right now at a nearby gun range to get you acquainted with—"

"No can do. I have another hearing in fifteen minutes."

"Chief Judge Marrone has notified the parties that it's been postponed."

Edward and McCormack slipped into The Downtown Gun Club through a nondescript side door. The shooting range was tucked away in a brown stucco building near the LA Wholesale Produce Market, about a mile south of the federal courthouse. McCormack, who frequented the place and had made friends with the owner, had arranged for a private session before the club opened to the public at three p.m.

Edward removed his jacket and unstrapped the bulletproof vest.

"I need you to keep the vest on, Your Honor," McCormack said as he laid his black range bag on a counter opposite the row of fourteen shooting lanes. "You need to get comfortable firing the weapon while wearing your armor." He removed a black pistol encased in a holster and held it up. "Glock twenty-seven. In our opinion the best concealed carry. The holster's called a pancake." He pulled the pistol out and set it on the counter. "You slip it over your pants at the hip." McCormack demonstrated how to place the holster over his waistband and then handed it to Edward. "We're going to practice drawing from the holster today. Next time we'll do it with the concealable vest and the suit jackets you wear to teach you how to break your coat—clear your jacket out of the way and draw the gun in one fluid motion."

Edward knew little about McCormack, but he'd sensed straight-away that the deputy had taken personal ownership of his protection. What had been foretold last year at "baby judges school" had come true—Edward was more vulnerable now to losing his life in service of his country than ever before. His work as a prosecutor in years past had put him in dangerous situations, but this was different. A force he couldn't see. He blew a deep breath, strapped the vest back in place, and slipped the pancake holster over his waistband at his right hip.

The shooting lanes were about six feet wide and separated by plastic dividers a foot taller than him. The targets were maybe twelve feet away.

"I didn't picture this place would be so cramped," Edward said.

"You don't need to be a marksman, Your Honor. We want you to be comfortable with close-range shooting."

"That's an oxymoron if I've ever heard one."

Of course Edward needed to protect himself. He had a responsibility to his wife, Jacqui. To his colleagues on the bench. To the people who depended on him to render justice.

But his family had a deadly history with guns. Which was what had driven him into the criminal justice system in the first place.

And the threats on his life had ripped him away from his most important case. The Justice Department had filed suit last November against the State of California to block Proposition 68, a law passed by California voters that required every resident to carry a special ID card in order to get government services. Its backers had sold it as an invitation for illegal immigrants to come out from the shadows and as sound fiscal policy. Exit polls had shown that more than one in five Latinos who'd voted in the election had voted *for* the law.

Opponents had derided it as backhanded oppression. They accused Proposition 68 supporters of having intent to drive undocumented Latinos out of California.

Edward had thought Prop. 68 was a terrible idea and voted against it. Didn't matter.

His job was to decide whether the law was constitutional, not good policy.

His demonstrated ability to separate his personal feelings from his professional duty had won him praise during his Senate confirmation. He'd confessed to the Judiciary Committee that deportation cases had been hardest on his heart when he was a US Attorney. But the people he'd prosecuted had entered the United States without permission. They'd broken the law. Some were criminals and opportunists, but most had only sought to flee poverty and hopelessness.

Didn't matter.

His job was to ensure that those who came to America illegally were not allowed to stay.

He had learned to disassociate.

He didn't like that about himself.

He snapped his attention back to the business at hand. "I've never used one of those. Wouldn't want to shoot myself by mistake."

McCormack handed him the gun. "Polymer frame, steel slide and barrel." McCormack snapped a magazine into the handle and handed it to him. "Nine rounds in the clip. Keep 'er pointed down. There's no bullet in the chamber yet, but it's good practice."

Edward took the pistol and rotated his wrist right, left. "Lighter than it looks." He handed the gun back to McCormack, barrel sideways. "I trust you'll be the one to maintain this bad boy."

"We'll have a regular check, Your Honor. But you'll still need to know how to keep it clean. The Glock twenty-seven has simple mechanisms." McCormack held the weapon at chest level. "There's a magazine release, slide lock, and a small button to release the slide rail to clean the barrel. That's it." He popped out the clip and pointed to the trigger area. "There's no safety, but the weapon won't fire as long as the slide lock is engaged and the trigger is back in this decocked position." He thumbed the slide lock forward and pulled back on the slide. "Now you see the trigger is forward." He moved the gun closer to Edward. "See this small trigger on top of the main trigger? The main won't move unless you depress that small one, but it's a light touch. Your best safety is to keep your finger out of the trigger guard until you're ready to fire."

"Hmm . . . I can plop this baby next to my nameplate when my courtroom's in session."

McCormack shook his head and smirked. "Your Honor, we're here to acquaint you with safe and correct firearm use. We'll need to spend some time at a tactical range before you get your own." He handed the loaded clip back to Edward.

Edward slid the magazine into the handle and slapped it into place and holstered the weapon. He stepped between the sidewalls of the shooting lane, and McCormack ran him through the basic stance, arm position, and grip. Feet shoulder width apart, left foot a few inches back from the right, knees flexed. Arms extended, elbows bent. Right hand on the grip, left hand wrapped around the right, thumb on top, parallel to but underneath the slide. "Firm grip with your left hand, keep the right hand relaxed."

"Reminds me of breaking down a golf swing," Edward said.

"It's called the Weaver stance. As long as your feet are under you and your knees are bent, you'll have a good base if you need to hold the weapon closer to your chest."

Edward slipped on a pair of electronic ear protectors that allowed him to hear McCormack. He drew the Glock and settled into firing stance. He aimed at the bull's-eye on the target.

"Looking good, Your Honor. Now rack the slide to chamber a round."

Do what to the slide? "Plain English, please."

"Sorry. Pull the slide back until the trigger pops into cocked position."

He did as instructed and then sighted the target. He couldn't steady his hands. He wouldn't have time to steady them or even think about them if confronted at close range.

"When you fire, think press, not pull. A smooth press on the trigger."

He nodded and pointed the gun at the spot on the target that represented a person's heart area.

Press.

His shot struck the lower abdomen area of the target. "Not a complete miss, eh?" he said with a nervous laugh. He upped his concentration, raised the pistol, and this time sighted only with his right eye. He fired another shot.

Outer target ring.

Concentrate. Aim. Press.

A hit in the heart area.

"I'll let you out of here when you can get nine for nine, and then three double taps," McCormack said with a gruff voice.

"What the heck is a double tap?"

"Two shots to the thoracic area, preferably the heart, and one to the head."

"You're on. I won't let *myself* out until I can do it four times."

Edward emptied the magazine and hit the heart on three of the remaining seven rounds. He stepped back three paces and emptied another clip. Six hits out of nine shots.

"Tell your friend to keep the public out of here until I tell you I'm ready," Edward said.

"I'll get you another box of bullets." McCormack stepped to the ammunition counter.

Edward ejected the magazine and fumbled with the loader until he figured out how to press the bullets against the spring-loaded mechanism. He loaded the last nine rounds, slapped the mag into place, racked the slide, and returned to stance.

Press. Chest.

Press. Neck.

Press. Head.

Got him.

McCormack returned with a fresh box of round-point target rounds.

"Gettin' the hang of this quick," Edward said. He reached for the box of bullets and loaded three magazines.

"You figured out loading the mags pretty quick," McCormack said.

"I'm a fast study. Hey, no one takes those Las Reconquistas people seriously, right?"

"No law enforcement agency had until the protesters showed up across the street from the courthouse. Las Reconquistas members have made themselves conspicuous in the crowd."

Edward set the pistol and one of the loaded magazines on the counter and turned toward McCormack. "These death threats make no sense. The jury sentenced Marroquín to death, not me. Fearmongering about Prop. Sixty-Eight is irrational."

"None of that matters," McCormack said. "We take every threat seriously until it's eliminated."

Edward slapped a magazine into the Glock and resumed his practice. The gun felt a little heavier with each shot. He hit one double tap out of three tries on his next mag, and two on the next.

"You've done enough for today," McCormack said. He extended his hand and gestured toward the pistol.

"One miss could be life or death. I need to know I can do it."

"Your Honor, I don't—"

"One more time." Edward yanked on the target holder line and clipped on a fresh sheet. He sent the target back into position and this time set his feet just beyond the edges of the dividing walls. He shook fatigue out of his arms and settled into stance.

Aim. Press.

Miss.

He cursed under his breath.

Edward varied his shooting distance and made six thoracic hits on the next eight shots. His shoulder muscles began to protest. "My respect for weapons training has gone up a few notches." He popped out the magazine and handed it and the Glock to McCormack.

"There's still a round in the chamber," McCormack said. He racked the slide to release the bullet, packed the pistol into its case, and slipped it into his range bag. "We'll break the weapon down back at the station."

Edward and McCormack thanked the proprietor of the gun club and headed for McCormack's black Crown Victoria. Edward pulled his cell phone from his pocket and saw he had missed two calls and a text. He slid into the backseat and listened to the first message. It was Jacqui—she'd be late getting home this evening but would still have dinner ready as planned. He returned her call, got her voice mail, and let her know all was well.

The second missed call and text came from the same number.

It was international.

No voice mail. The text read, *Please call. I need your help*, and included a photo thumbnail he couldn't make out.

Strange.

He brought the phone closer and tapped the image. The picture was grainy and the colors were faded. It was—

Whoa.

A photo of him. And a woman.

Not just any woman.

Alana Walsh.

His first love. The woman he'd been sure was his forever. Until . . .

He stared at the image. Looked like a photo of the photo.

He laid his phone on the seat next to him. Screen-side down. *We were never supposed to have contact again.*

He'd thrown out every trace of their relationship twenty-five years ago. Long before he and Jacqui had met. He'd accepted agony—he would never see her face again—and then had buried it, deep, where no one could access it. Himself included.

Now there she was. The long-repressed hurt of losing her rushed back like it had happened yesterday. He suppressed the urge to groan.

"Everything all right back there, Your Honor?"

Edward was quiet. Memories and images and emotions swirled through his being.

"Something wrong?"

"Huh? Sorry, lost in thought."

"I asked if everything was all right with you, Your Honor."

"I'm fine. Something personal came up."

Chapter 2

Edward managed to stay present with McCormack as he went over how to de-chamber a round from the Glock and disassemble it for cleaning. They left the Marshals Service station on the first floor of the courthouse and headed to Edward's fifth-floor chambers. Edward forced himself to work through some documents to satisfy the law enforcement bureaucracy. McCormack stepped to one of the tall, narrow windows in Edward's chambers on his way out. "Crazy what's going on down there."

Edward joined him and scanned the raucous throng of hundreds crammed into Bowron Square across the street. A line of blue-uniformed Federal Protective Service policemen wearing helmets and vests and pistols on both hips stood guard in front of the courthouse. Several dozen officers from the Los Angeles Police Department dressed in full riot gear guarded the sidewalk around the square. The street was closed to all traffic except official vehicles. Handwritten placards in Spanish and

English that said "STOP THE GREED" and "PROPOSITION 68 IS IMMORAL" faced off against others that read "CUT OFF THE ILLEGAL SPONGES" and "GET IN LINE LIKE MY PARENTS DID." Brown and black and white faces populated both sides of the divide.

"That's not going to make your job any easier," Edward said.

"Or yours, Your Honor."

"If I let that crowd influence me, we'll have even bigger problems on our hands."

McCormack turned to Edward. "How soon will you rule on Proposition Sixty-Eight?"

Edward moved away from the window. "Not soon enough for them. It's a complicated contest." He stepped toward the door, hoping McCormack would catch the cue that it was time for him to leave.

"I haven't paid attention to the issues," McCormack said. "Prop. Sixty-Eight requires *everyone* living in California to get a state services ID card. So what's the beef?"

You picked a great time to be curious, McCormack. "Opponents claim it will force illegal immigrants to go underground."

McCormack crossed his arms. "So what's the process?"

Edward put hands on hips and took a step toward McCormack, straining inside to keep his comportment. "Say you're from Mexico and you're here without papers. You go to a state office, probably DMV, to register for the ID. If you don't have proof of citizenship or legal residence, then you mark 'undocumented' on the form. Sorting people out that way allows California to track how much it spends to give benefits to people who aren't in the US legally."

"But it doesn't turn anyone away."

"Correct. This court settled that question twenty years ago. States may not deny public services to illegal immigrants."

"I don't envy you," McCormack said.

Yeah, no kidding. Edward turned back to his chambers door and opened it. "Will you excuse me, please?"

McCormack nodded and headed out, closing the door behind him.

Edward yanked his phone from his pocket and Googled Alana's number. It was from Hermosillo, Mexico.

She'd stayed home.

He drew a long, quiet breath and exhaled slowly. His conscience allowed him a few moments to linger on their romance, and then he crammed his memories back into their hiding place. Where they belonged. Where he needed to keep them.

What had happened between Edward and Alana's father made it certain she couldn't have shared that picture with anyone. He was shocked it still existed. They were young and passion-filled and they'd lost control and . . .

"How dare you ruin my Alana's life this way?" her father had said through a boiling rage. "You make her pregnant and bring shame on her and my family!"

Those words had been bad enough. But what came next . . .

"I forbid you to ever see Alana again. Go home, you Irish pig! I don't care if you come from the San Patricios. You disgrace their legacy."

After laying Edward out, he'd turned to Alana and grabbed her arm and twisted it behind her. The most hurtful words he'd spoken over her still echoed. "You will not bear a bastard child in my home. I'll send you away to a convent. You have dishonored God and your father."

The bile Edward had tasted in that moment returned. Not because of her father's irrational anger. Not because he still hadn't forgiven him.

But because Edward Lamport had caved.

Instead of fighting for Alana, he'd chosen appeasement. Signed away his paternal rights to their child in exchange for Alana's father not banishing her to that convent. Afterward, her father had vowed Alana would marry Guillermo Alvarez, the son of his business partner.

Edward could have fought him. Could have put his plans on hold, done whatever he needed to do to win her father's approval. But he didn't. He'd thought he was being honorable. Justified it as best for Alana and their child.

And he lost them. Forever.

Now, here she was. Where his cowardice had determined she couldn't be. Where now there wasn't room.

He was supposed to move on with his life as if Alana and their baby had never existed. But he hadn't. They were very much in his heart.

No one else knew. Not even Jacqui.

Out of the blue, Alana had found him.

How would she have gotten his personal cell phone number? His cousin Pato Lamport still lived in the area, as far as he knew, but neither Edward nor his father had received a Christmas card from him this year.

Maybe Pato had sent the text.

Enough questions.

I'm twenty-two all over again.

He drew a deep breath and called the number from his desk phone. Three rings.

"Diga." A female voice.

"Is this Alana Walsh?" Edward said in Spanish.

"Alana Walsh Alvarez."

Her father made good on the shotgun wedding. "This is Edward Lamport."

"Hello, Eduardo."

Alana had called him that, though he'd preferred Ed. Her voice didn't sound like he'd remembered. "Been a long time."

"Thank you for responding to my message."

Edward had no idea what to say next. So he kept quiet. Awkward silence was better than blurting out something stupid.

"I never thought we would speak with each other again," she said in a hushed tone.

"Nor I."

Alana might as well have been standing next to Edward. He felt her presence somehow. She needed help—but what could he possibly do after all this time?

Unless it was about their child. The one he'd abandoned yet longed to know . . . wondering all these years if it was a boy or girl, if Alana had kept the child, or given it up for adoption, or . . .

He asked, "How did you get my number?"

"From Pato Lamport's sister-in-law. We go to church together."

"You know where Pato is? We haven't heard from him in more than a year."

"He moved to Ciudad Obregón last fall. The *narcos* took over his neighborhood."

"My father will be relieved to know he's all right." Edward gazed again at the photo she'd sent to his phone. "I'm surprised your father let you keep that picture."

"I hid it where he could never find it."

It meant that much to her.

"Your message said you needed help. What kind of help?"

"Our son needs it."

She . . . had a boy. I have a son.

He washed down a rising lump with a sip of water. "Our son." Another sip to keep it down. "What's his name?"

"Carlos."

Carlos. Charles. *A name that means strong, manly.*

He and Jacqui had planned to name their first baby Edward Charles. Or Charles Edward. But they'd never had the chance to choose. She'd miscarried after four months. And three more times over the next four years.

He wanted to see Alana. His conscience said no.

He ignored it.

"What kind of cell phone do you have?"

"iPhone."

Perfect. "Would you mind if we switched to FaceTime?"

"*Sí, por supuesto.*"

Yes, of course.

"Give me a few minutes to set up."

Edward had told Jacqui about his relationship with Alana when they were dating. But he'd never told her how things had ended. And why. He'd vowed to Alana's father he wouldn't tell anyone, ever, that he'd fathered her baby. For her sake.

Alana's reappearance forced the issue.

He needed to tell Jacqui.

No. You can't tell her. Think of what it would do to her.

How could she accept such news? So what if it had happened before he and Jacqui had met?

Jacqui had desperately wanted children. Knowing that another woman had borne him a son would devastate her.

Wait and see what kind of help Carlos needs.

Yes, he would wait to hear the full story before he decided whether and when to tell his wife that his first love had reentered his life and that he was a father.

A video call was a good idea. The years had changed Alana, as they had him.

She wore the patina of her life well.

Her smile was delightful. Still. "Eduardo." She fingered the gold chain around her neck. "You look . . . very well."

She was being kind. Life in the criminal justice system had aged him beyond his years.

"What kind of help does Carlos need?"

"Carlos reminds me so much of you. He's a very brave young man." Her voice quavered.

He reminds me so much of you.

Ha. If she meant that literally, then Carlos was running from something he'd done for which he hadn't taken full responsibility.

"You haven't answered my question."

Alana delayed a few more moments. "Carlos works for Bancomex, second-largest bank in Mexico. As do I. He's so smart. After his year in National Military Service, he finished his bachelor's degree in three years. He went straight to EGADE for his MBA."

She still hadn't answered his question, but he was intrigued to know more about Carlos. "Can you show me a picture of him?"

"Oh, yes. *Discúlpeme.*" She looked to her left and her right. "I'll be right back."

"No need to apologize."

She propped her phone and stood, revealing a body fit and shapely for a woman in her midforties.

As was Jacqui's body. She and Edward worked out hard, together, to keep up with their demanding jobs and have energy and strength left over on weekends to play tennis at Hancock Hills Country Club and water ski at Lake Arrowhead.

Alana returned with a picture frame in hand and rotated it toward the camera.

Edward suppressed a gasp.

Carlos had Alana's dark hair, full with a bit of curl. His hairline resembled Edward's in his younger days. The shape of Carlos's face fell between Edward's oval proportions and Alana's rounder contour. He had her chin and jawline. His complexion was a bit ruddy and his eyes were brown. Like Edward's.

His self-control melted. "Carlos gets his good looks from you."

Alana smiled, then quickly turned somber. "Eduardo, his life is in danger."

Her words cut. The son he'd abandoned was back in his life, and he was in danger of losing him again. "From whom?"

"He believes Bancomex is laundering money for drug cartels."

Drug money . . . Edward's pulse quickened.

He'd prosecuted drug-money-laundering cases as a US Attorney. He knew firsthand how multinational banks had acquiesced to the methods and tactics—and ruthlessness—the perpetrators had used to make their dirty enterprises work. He'd seen how they assassinated their enemies.

Brutal savages.

He pictured Carlos meeting such a fate and shuddered. His stomach burned. "Direct or for a middleman?"

"Our largest customer, ALEXA Inversiones. Their primary business lines are real estate development and casino gambling."

"What did he find?"

She recounted what Carlos had told her he'd discovered. Payments to corporations in Nigeria and Madagascar. Electronic transfers to an account owned by the head of Mexico's bank regulation ministry. Suspiciously large daily cash deposits from gambling casinos in the Caribbean.

"He thinks there may be American involvement. ALEXA is an investor in the International Trade Center."

"Oh, that experimental complex that straddles Calexico and Mexicali. Quite controversial here. I know the man whose company built the American side."

"Stanley Gleason. He has become prominent in Mexican business circles through that project and his dealings with the chairman of our bank," Alana said. "How do you know him?"

"When I was a deputy district attorney I prosecuted some gang members who had roughed him up and ransacked his offices. Many years later he recommended me to one of the US senators from California to fill an opening here in the district court."

"So you and he are friends?"

"Acquaintances. Did Carlos report what he found to his boss?"

"He believes his boss is in on it. Carlos downloaded as much information as he could and fled."

"To where?"

Alana shook her head. "All he said was he had a plan and he trusted God to protect him." She leaned closer. "His faith seems so . . . reckless."

Reckless faith . . . some people I know say that's as it should be. "What do you want from me, Alana?" He hoped that didn't sound harsh to her, but her motive for contacting him now seemed vague.

She blinked a few times and bit her lower lip. "Can you bring Carlos into the United States and give him asylum?"

Edward looked away. What was happening here? Alana had married. Another man raised Edward's son as his own. Twenty-five years ago, her family's attitudes would not have allowed this conversation to happen.

"Does your husband know you've reached out to me?"

"Guillermo died two years ago. Accident with a drunk driver."

She's a widow.

A forbidden pang invaded his heart. He relished it a moment and then sent it away.

"I'm so sorry. And your father?"

Alana closed her eyes and shook her head. "Died ten years ago. Lung cancer."

She has no one else.

"Do you have any sense of Carlos's plan?"

"He said there's no one in Mexico he can trust. He was in such a rush I had no chance to ask him anything. I don't know when I will hear from him again."

Edward's mind swirled with the potential complications and implications of what Alana was asking of him. He would have to work the system as a private citizen, not in his official role. Personal relationships were his only leverage.

If he was going to help, then Carlos should know the truth about his father. Maybe he already did.

"Does Carlos know about me?"

"To him, Guillermo is his father."

Her father and husband were dead. And she hadn't told Carlos who his real father was. Why?

"If I help, Carlos should know who I am."

Alana lowered her gaze. "I'm not ready to tell him."

"There won't be a better time than now."

Streaks ran down Alana's cheeks. "I understand. Will you help him, Eduardo?"

Enough with the conditions, Lamport.

He'd been handed an opportunity to atone for his youthful cowardice. A chance to reach back in time and do now what he should have done then.

Of course he would help.

"I'll get started on my end. Call me as soon as you hear from him." A new, stronger wave of emotion swelled and threatened to burst. He drew a deep breath and held himself together. "Alana, he needs to know the truth before this goes much further."

"*Sí*, Eduardo. *Sí.*"

The truth.

Now it was his turn.

Think of what it will do to Jacqui.

Was one life more important than another? Yes, Jacqui was his most important human relationship. Her needs were primary. In all things.

Yet he'd been handed an improbable gift, a second chance to know the son he'd forsaken.

This was no coincidence.

If he chose not to act, it would show that in God he *didn't* trust.

Wouldn't that be the graver risk?

Chapter 3

Edward entered his home through the back door that led to the kitchen. Jacqui was busy spooning some kind of Asian food from brown containers onto plates. Her hair was up in a bun, per usual when she worked in the kitchen. He touched her shoulders from behind and kissed the back of her neck. She cooed at his affection.

"What's for dinner, dear?"

"Thai." She turned and gave him a peck on the lips. "Hope you don't mind. It was the nearest good place for takeout." She handed him a plate of noodles topped with beef and broccoli and an aromatic brown gravy. "Table's set."

He carried his plate to the dining room. She'd set the table with forks and chopsticks and a glass of red wine for each of them. When she set a table like this it meant she wanted to linger in conversation. He always enjoyed these times with her, but not tonight. His news really couldn't wait. It would affect both of them, and had already. As hard as it would be for Jacqui to hear about Carlos, she also needed to know about the second death threat and their twenty-four-seven protection. And that he'd soon be carrying a gun.

She joined him with her plate in one hand and an opened bottle of reserve Pinot Noir in the other. She took her seat and undid her bun, giving her light brown hair a quick flip. She looked extra beautiful and relaxed.

Her serene countenance would soon change.

He kept his eyes low and unfolded his napkin and placed it on his lap. "Pinot should be good with this."

Jacqui took a taste of each. "Mmm, yes." A pause. "Heard about the protesters at the courthouse. Radio news said it was peaceful."

Edward nodded as he finished a bite. He took a sip of wine. "So far."

"Can't say the same about the climate at my office. We got new poll results on Prop. Sixty-Eight today."

"Not what you were hoping for?"

"Forty percent of Latinos said they wouldn't register for the ID card. Way more than we expected."

"Did it say why?"

"Fear of deportation. The survey also said three-quarters of those families would pull their kids out of school. My local district would see the highest rates of unenrollment."

Edward shook his head. "Is this the school board's way of pressuring me to strike it down?" He took another bite of food.

Jacqui sat back. "You know, it's getting harder to be Mrs. Edward Lamport at work."

He squinted at her. "What's that supposed to mean?"

"The board and administration don't like that it's taking you so long."

"Like *you* have anything to do with it." He wiped his mouth with the napkin and sat back.

As much as he wanted to engage Jacqui on what was important to her, he couldn't wait a moment longer to say what needed to be said.

"I know your work stuff is important, but I have news."

"Oh?"

He looked deep into her eyes. "I got another death threat."

Jacqui gasped. "My God . . . who from?"

"Someone who says he's from Las Reconquistas. Heard of 'em?"

"Yeah. They want the Southwest returned to Mexico. Crazy." Jacqui rested her face in her hands a moment. "How are you feeling?"

"Am I scared? I'm concerned, sure." He took a sip of wine. "I went to a gun range this afternoon with a deputy marshal."

"I thought you hated guns."

"Yeah, well, I have more to think about than myself."

The last thing he wanted to do right now was sit around and talk. It was time for action. On all battlefronts. But right now, his wife took priority.

"Okay if we sit in the living room and talk?"

Jacqui sat on the sofa and patted the cushion next to her.

"I'd rather stand," Edward said.

He stepped to the window and pulled back the drapes. McCormack's black Crown Vic and a black Chrysler 300 with four deputies inside were parked on the street in front of the house.

"Deputy marshals are providing twenty-four-hour protection. Five are out there right now. One'll be inside when we're home, the others in front and back."

"So we'll have no privacy?"

"We haven't talked routine yet."

She shifted her weight. "You okay? Your face is flushed."

He took a couple of steps toward her. "There's more." He shoved his hands into his pockets and pulled a deep breath. "Remember I told you about a woman named Alana Walsh when we were dating?"

"Your old girlfriend." She moved her hands to her lap. "What brings her up?"

"Got a text today."

"Uh-huh."

"The number was from Hermosillo. It said, 'Please call. I need your help.' Came with a picture of me and Alana."

"A picture?"

"From when we were together."

Jacqui stood and walked toward him. "Okay. That's more than strange."

"I called back. It was her."

She raised her brows. "You called her? Why?"

"Because she said she needed help."

"And why did she contact *you?*"

"She has no one else."

"No family?"

"Her husband died two years ago in a car accident. Parents are gone, too."

Jacqui walked to the window and looked out. She turned. "What kind of help?"

"She has a son. His life's in danger."

"And why would she contact you?"

"Because he's not only *her* son."

She stepped directly in front of him, eyes wide. "He's yours?"

He was quiet.

"And did you know about this before today?"

"Yes, but—"

"You have a son?" Her face reddened. She looked at him with hard eyes. "How could you not tell me?"

"I'd vowed not to tell anyone. Ever."

She stepped back. Her eyes welled and her hands trembled. "How could . . . how could you . . . keep this from me?" She turned her back on him.

He rubbed his palms together. "Honey, please look at me."

She shook her head.

"Jacqui. Please. Let me explain."

She sat on the arm of the sofa, head down and arms crossed.

"Her father hit the ceiling. All about his reputation. He wanted to ship her off to a convent to have the baby, then give it away. When I heard, I went back to Hermosillo to face him."

Jacqui looked up. "What did he want from you?"

"He kept screaming that his business would be ruined if people knew his daughter got pregnant out of wedlock."

"Family honor's important in Mexican culture. We see it every day in the schools."

"I was twenty-two, she was twenty." He shoved his hands in his pockets and paced the room. "Didn't *you* ever do anything when you were young that you now regret?"

Jacqui slid to the center of the sofa and crossed her legs and folded her arms. Lowered her gaze. Said nothing.

Edward approached, tentatively.

She remained silent.

"Honey?"

She looked up. "Yes. I *did*. Something that affected me in ways I couldn't . . ." She teared up again.

Edward sat at the end of the sofa and extended a hand.

"Not now." She shifted. "Tell me the rest about your son."

"Something else is—"

"I said, not now!"

She bowed her head. Silent moments passed.

"Tell me the rest . . . about your son."

"I renounced my parental rights. Her father had already drawn up the legal documents. I signed, and he relented on sending Alana away."

"What's your son's name?"

"Carlos."

"Why couldn't you tell me? It's not like I would have broadcast it to the world."

"Because I'd given my word. Because my child could never be in my life. If there was even a hair's breadth of a chance Carlos could have been in my life, I would have told you." He reached for her. She stood and walked toward the window.

"What did she want from you?" she said with her back turned.

"Alana asked if I could bring Carlos into the US and get him asylum."

"Why?"

"She and Carlos both work for the second-largest bank in Mexico. He believes they're helping their biggest customer launder drug money. Carlos took some data and fled. People are after him who want him dead."

Jacqui shook her head. "How much can go wrong in one day?"

"There's more going on than we know."

Jacqui took a few more steps, then stopped. "I need a few minutes." She turned and strode toward the hallway. The bedroom door closed.

◆ ◆ ◆

Jacqui returned to the living room ten minutes later, dressed to go out.

"Where are you going?"

"Cynthia Thompson's. I need help to process all this."

"I don't mind you talking with Cynthia about Carlos, but why don't you invite her here?"

She looked away. "I don't feel safe with you right now."

Edward stared at the floor, hands in pockets. A tense minute passed. "One of the deputy marshals will need to escort you."

"Fair enough." She stepped to the closet next to the front door and grabbed her jacket. "What're you going to do about Carlos?"

"I told Alana I'd help get them into the country somehow."

"Them? You're including Alana?"

"If we only help Carlos, the people after him will get her, too."

"We?"

"Yes. We have to help them."

She shifted her weight. "I'm worried. About what could happen."

"To whom?"

"Between you and her. Where are you with that?"

"I'm not anywhere. I can't remember the last time I'd thought about Alana before today. That life, that Edward, is dead." He gave her an exasperated look. "Now's not the time for this. Everything's too raw."

"Too raw. Well. We can agree on that."

◆ ◆ ◆

Silver Lake District, Los Angeles
7:32 p.m.

Jacqui gave Cynthia an extra-long hug.

"Girl, something big is troubling you."

"Some *things.*"

"I have as much time as you need. Glass of wine?"

"Sure, thanks."

Cynthia returned with two glasses of white wine and a small bowl of mixed nuts. "Sauvignon Blanc from Paso Robles. My new favorite."

They settled into plush chairs that faced each other. "So, what things?"

Jacqui ran her finger around the rim of her glass. "The present and past collided big-time tonight." She looked up at Cynthia. "Edward got another death threat today."

"Oh, no. From who?"

"Some radical group who wants to return the southwest US to Mexico." Jacqui pointed at the living room window. "We're on twenty-four-seven protection by the US Marshals. One of them drove me here."

Cynthia hurried to the window. "The black car?"

"Gracious man. Takes his job seriously." Jacqui stood and moved toward Cynthia. "Ed told me he got a text today from an old girlfriend. The one he had in Mexico before we met. She asked for his help."

"What kind?"

Jacqui bit her lower lip. "I'll get to that. Her name is Alana Walsh. He got her pregnant. He has a twenty-five-year-old son named Carlos."

Cynthia's jaw slackened. "A son?" She reached for Jacqui's hands. "Did he say why he never told you?"

Jacqui drew a deep breath. "He'd signed away his parental rights and vowed to tell no one." She lowered her gaze. "I can't believe he never told *me*."

"Had to have a good reason."

"He said he honored his word. I thought . . . what about honoring me?"

Cynthia beckoned her to the chairs. Jacqui took another sip of wine and plucked a few cashews from the bowl. "His son's life is in danger. He figured out the bank he works for is laundering drug money. People want him dead."

Cynthia gave a slow, disbelieving head shake. "What's he going to do?"

"Bring him into this country so he can get asylum."

"Can he do that?"

Jacqui choked back a lump of despair. "He's going to bring both of them over."

"Why her?" Cynthia said.

"He thinks whoever's after Carlos would come after her, too. I have to admit, I agree with that."

Cynthia leaned back and crossed her arms. "Let me ask you something. Does your reaction to Edward's news have anything to do with—?"

"Stop right there. I've told you, I'm not going there. What's done is done. I won't dig up the past anymore. I won't."

"The longer you hide it, the worse it'll get."

Silence.

"Like tonight."

Cynthia's words pierced her heart. "What I . . . what I did was final. The boy I was with couldn't have cared less. I was a scared girl. Totally different."

"You sure?"

Jacqui turned to face her friend. Cynthia looked her up and down. Jacqui asked, "What's going on in that head of yours?"

"Remember our talks about living by faith and not by what we see?"

Jacqui gave a curt nod.

"This is one of those times. I see a bigger purpose in this. Edward is going to do what he has to do to rescue Carlos—and Alana—but more is about to unfold that we can't foresee."

"Ed kind of said the same thing." Jacqui looked up and gave her a wan smile. "Thanks for letting me come over. I couldn't handle this alone."

"You're not supposed to." Cynthia gave her the look she always gave when she was about to challenge her. Jacqui shifted her attention to her wineglass.

"How much *does* Edward know?"

"About?" Jacqui kept her gaze down.

"Don't play with me, sister."

Jacqui set her glass down and folded her hands in her lap. "What the doctor said. Uterine abnormalities."

"Did that doctor know your full history?"

"I was sixteen. They told me I could still have children."

"So you believe it's your fault."

"All I know is we couldn't have babies."

Cynthia smiled. She had a twinkle in her eye. "I think God wants to heal you."

Heal? What good would it do to heal a forty-six-year-old woman's uterus? She waved Cynthia off. "Way too late for that."

Cynthia grabbed Jacqui's forearm and locked eyes with her. "I'm not talking about babies. Edward told you about Carlos because something he thought would never matter to your marriage now does. Do you see?"

"That baby was never in my life. What good would it—?"

A sword sliced through her.

She'd criticized Edward for keeping his child a secret their whole marriage. She felt justified doing so. But when her own hidden past—not even Cynthia knew the full story—threatened to expose itself, the pain of regret and the fear of how Edward might connect it to their infertility was more than she could bear.

She feared his judgment.

Condemnation was her self-assigned lot. The consequence would be delayed, of course, and then she would give an account, and . . . then what?

There would be another time to deal with her issue. Again.

"You've been a big help. I need to get back home."

As long as she focused on Ed's problem, she could keep her own truth locked away. Safe.

She hoped.

Chapter 4

Carlos Alvarez stood in ankle-deep sand, about fifty meters from the irrigation canal he and his friend Gonzalo DeAnza had to swim across. At this spot the canal was wide as a football field. Carlos had researched it online and learned the water was ice-cold and the current was swift and strong. They could get sucked into a diversion gate if they failed to grab hold of the buoy line that lay five hundred meters downstream. Many *emigrantes* from Mexico and points south had died trying to cross these waters.

Once they made it to the other side, they'd have to traverse three more kilometers of sand to reach Highway 98. Then a fifteen-kilometer walk to Calexico, where they hoped to find a like-minded *hombre* who'd help them get to Los Angeles.

Minor obstacles compared to the men chasing them who wanted him dead.

Carlos drew in a breath of cold, dry air. A full moon illuminated the expanse of dunes and scrub around them. A steady breeze peppered fine sand particles on the back of his neck. He blew on his hands, then turned back toward Gonzalo. He was on the ground with legs stretched forward, about ten paces behind. Carlos waved him ahead. *"Vamos."*

Gonzalo staggered upright and stumbled forward. "Sorry, *hombre.* My legs are dead." Clouds of vapor trailed his tired words.

"Have you forgotten what we learned in National Military Service?"

"A year of weekend army school doesn't make you a soldier."

"We learned enough to pull this off. Our legs will tighten if we rest now. It'll only take a few minutes to ride the current to the buoy line."

"Well, that's comforting news."

"Would you rather be at home marinating in your own blood?" Carlos turned and plodded ahead toward the south bank of the canal.

If only he'd questioned sooner what he'd seen at work the last few months.

After they'd earned their MBA degrees, he and Gonzalo had chosen to work for Bancomex because it was an innovative and fast-growing financial services company. But Carlos had discovered that their largest customer, ALEXA Inversiones, had been sending payments to corporations in Nigeria and Madagascar every business day for the last eighteen months. Problem was, they had no operations or suppliers there. Then he found payments to personal accounts of government officials and huge deposits from business operations that couldn't possibly generate that much cash flow.

ALEXA's business had the smell of drug money all over it.

Carlos had made bad judgments and trusted the wrong people. Especially Julio Nardo from the information technology division. He'd asked Nardo about remote access to the core banking system, the same system he used every day in the office, through the Bancomex virtual private network. Carlos had not said a word to Nardo or anyone else of his concerns about ALEXA. Someone had to have tipped off Carlos's boss that he'd downloaded transaction data from home. He'd only been able to grab three months' worth before his system access was cut off. When that happened, he grabbed his computer and some clothes and headed over to Gonzalo's place to show him what he'd found and talk about what to do next. When he returned home in the middle of the night, his house had been ransacked. They'd come for him.

The information he'd been able to grab only showed a partial pattern of what he'd seen and knew in his gut was happening—high-level government bribery and offshore concealment of ill-gotten cash. By itself, his evidence wouldn't be enough to prove ALEXA and Bancomex were laundering drug money. He would need a face-to-face meeting with trustworthy authorities to fill in the missing pieces.

He'd tried WikiLeaks. They hadn't yet responded to his submission. Probably didn't meet their standards.

And he had no more time to wait.

He had to get to Los Angeles somehow and give the data and his explanation to the one man who could move the right people to action—Albert Sanchez, the American TV news reporter. Carlos had to convince Sanchez and count on his credibility to get the attention of the right people, whoever they were. There sure wasn't anyone in Mexico he could trust.

He checked one more time to make sure the data disc was securely taped to his shaved chest. God's favor was on his mission. It had to be.

He plodded to within a few meters of the canal's edge. Gonzalo lumbered alongside and flopped onto a sand mound. "This isn't going to work. How can two *chavos* bring down Bancomex and ALEXA?"

"You still don't get it!" Carlos snapped.

"Get what? We're mosquitoes to them! The big boss will squash us and splatter your evidence into nothing." Gonzalo grabbed a handful of sand and pitched it at the water. "Better if Border Patrol finds us."

Carlos resisted the urge to grab Gonzalo by his slender neck and shake the fear out of him. "We must get to Sanchez."

"Right. You show up at his office looking like a—"

"I'm done with your questions!"

Carlos blew out a breath of frustration. He opened his palms toward Gonzalo. "Sanchez makes his living on stories like ours. When he finds out what's been going down and that the big boss and the head of the banking commission are facilitating it, he'll jump all over it." He extended a hand. "Let's go."

Gonzalo grasped Carlos's wrist and struggled to his feet. Carlos bowed his head and crossed himself, and then they trudged toward the canal's edge.

A voice bellowed from behind. "You got some moxie, Alvarez, I'll give you that."

Carlos pivoted toward the sound. A wiry man dressed in black, his face masked, stood a couple of meters away. With a gun. Aimed at his head.

Carlos's insides churned. He willed his shoulders to relax and stood firm. "Who are you?"

"It's over, Alvarez. We know you stole the transaction data. Give it to me."

Adrenaline surged through Carlos's limbs. His heart galloped. But he measured his breathing and kept still.

He would not surrender the disc.

Gonzalo got down on one knee. Carlos held his breath. *What is he thinking?*

"Get back on your feet," the masked man said. He kept his gun pointed at Carlos.

Gonzalo stayed down.

"I said get up!" The man took a step closer and aimed the pistol at Gonzalo. Gonzalo remained still.

Carlos's mind whirled. If all this guy wanted was the disc, he'd have killed them by now. Maybe he was told to bring them to the big boss alive. *But it's me he wants, not Gonzalo.* This was *his* mission. He didn't want Gonzalo to pay for his mistakes. Gonzalo had asked to join him, but no way could he have realized the cost of his choice. Now Carlos was sorry he hadn't persuaded him to escape the big boss's threats another way.

The intruder stepped in front of Gonzalo and thrust his gun onto his forehead. "One more time, Alvarez. Give me the disc now."

Carlos pointed at Gonzalo. "Let him go. He knows nothing."

"Now, Alvarez!"

Gonzalo stayed down and bowed his head. A steely band tightened around Carlos's heart.

He's willing to die.

If Carlos tried to save his own life, he and Gonzalo would both wind up dead. How could he stop this man from killing his friend?

Carlos took a step toward the intruder. "Let him walk away first."

"I'm not leaving you," Gonzalo said.

The masked man turned his head toward Gonzalo, then back to Carlos. "Your *amigo* has more guts than you, Alvarez."

Fear slithered up Carlos's throat. Had Gonzalo been right about bringing down two big companies? He drew a slow, deep breath through his mouth. God had called him to do this. He was sure. So God would protect him and Gonzalo from this man.

Wouldn't He?

Carlos closed his eyes and kept still. A swirling gust sprayed sand in his face.

"What's it gonna be, Alvarez?" The wind muted the intruder's voice. "The disc or your *amigo*?"

Carlos opened his eyes and locked his gaze on the intruder. "He walks away first."

"Your choice. Not mine." The man fingered the trigger.

"No!" Carlos lunged at his hand. The gun fired. Gonzalo's head jerked back and his body slumped backward.

Carlos grabbed and twisted the intruder's wrist and reached for his other forearm. The man elbowed Carlos's jaw and turned the hand holding the gun toward him. Carlos shifted his weight and wrestled his enemy down. The man landed on his back, Carlos on top. Carlos sucked in air fast and grabbed the gun with both hands and thrust the barrel into the man's chest. He jammed a finger over the trigger and pulled.

◆　◆　◆

Carlos's breathing and pulse slowed after a time. He pushed up with shaky arms into a sitting position.

The masked attacker lay on his back. Gonzalo's crumpled body lay a couple of meters away. A trickle of blood drained from his forehead into thirsty sand.

Carlos buried his face in his hands and heaved a breath. The last words he'd said to Gonzalo hadn't been kind. His friend's questions had been his way of steeling himself for the job ahead.

And Carlos had misunderstood him.

He wiped grit from around his eyes and crawled to his slain *amigo*. "I was wrong about you." The words scoured his parched throat. "Forgive me."

All he could do, knew to do, was stare at Gonzalo's face. He was home now. No way he'd want to come back to this mess. Gonzalo's parents and sister came to mind. Carlos had no idea what, if anything, Gonzalo had told them about this mission.

He'd died for nothing. In the middle of nowhere.

The tape holding the disc to his chest pulled at his skin. He didn't dare remove it.

What now? What about Sanchez?

He grabbed Gonzalo's lifeless arm. "I don't think I can make it alone."

He staggered upright and scanned for a spot where he could hide and recharge a bit. The cluster of bushes at the canal's edge was too close to the water. He turned to his left.

Two points of light appeared.

They steadily grew larger. Then a third light, like a spotlight, swept side to side over the sand.

Think fast! Whoever this is can't be trusted.

Where could he hide? The shrub growth at the bank of the canal was high enough, but the downslope behind them was less than a meter above the waterline. He swept his gaze forward and back. There was no other option.

He struggled to stand and his legs gave out from under him. The lights drew closer, and the moving beam flashed in his eyes. They'd spotted him.

Now what?

The journey to here, the fight, and Gonzalo's death had sapped the last of his reserves. He scrambled through the sand as fast as his depleted muscles would allow. The growl of the vehicle's engine grew louder. He pulled and pulled, his gaze fixed on the shrub line.

"Don't move!"

He kept struggling toward the bank of the canal. A hand grabbed his right ankle.

"Stop right there!"

Chapter 5

Edward offered to make French-style omelets, Jacqui's favorite. She nodded her thanks instead of showing her usual effusive appreciation when he took one of his rare morning turns at the stove.

Not a great start to the day here, Lamport.

"Plain or with Gruyère?" he said.

"Plain." Her eyes stayed locked on her iPad.

He used proper technique as Jacqui had taught him, shaking the pan and whisking the eggs with a fork. Cooking perfectly. Time to fold the edges together.

His phone vibrated on the countertop and broke his concentration. He yanked the pan away from the fire so he wouldn't brown the fluffy egg creation, folded and flipped it, and slid it onto a plate. He added a mini croissant and served Jacqui her *petit déjeuner*.

"Thanks." Her head stayed down.

The ice hasn't melted.

He picked up his phone. Missed call and voice mail from Alana. He called back.

"Alana, it's Edward. What's the latest?"

Jacqui made eye contact, with a stern look.

"Carlos called early this morning," Alana said with alarm in her voice. "He crossed the border into California in the middle of the night, but one of Javier Bernal's *matóns* caught up with him and tried to kill him."

"Who's Javier Bernal?"

"President of Bancomex." Sobs came through the phone.

"Where is he now?"

"The Border Patrol picked him up. They held him for a few hours and sent him back to Mexicali. That's where he called me from. He stole an old pickup truck and now he's on his way to Ciudad Obregón, to stay with Pato Lamport."

"Pato?" He shot a quizzical look Jacqui's way. Jacqui got up from the table and came over to him. Edward turned on his speakerphone.

A pause on the line. "He knows about Carlos," Alana said. "We've stayed in touch over the years, mostly by letter. He doesn't know Carlos is your son."

Jacqui started to speak but stopped herself. She looked Edward in the eye and then returned to the table.

"Did Carlos tell you why he jumped the border?"

"There is a man in Los Angeles he can trust with his evidence, but he wouldn't tell me his name. For my protection and the man's."

Los Angeles . . . does Carlos know now?

By the sound of things, Carlos had street smarts. Still, it was likely he had no plan once he made it to Pato's. "Does he have a phone on him?"

"No. Eduardo, I'm afraid for him."

Jacqui's countenance fell when Alana said "Eduardo."

Not good, Lamport. Think how this is hitting her heart.

He turned off the speakerphone. "Text me when you hear from him. I'll get back to you when I know what I can do on my end."

He grabbed a croissant and poured himself a coffee and joined Jacqui at the kitchen table.

"Eduardo?"

Edward rubbed his eyes. "Never cared for it."

Silence.

A heaviness descended between them. He debated whether to ask how she was coping or wait for her to share her feelings.

You started this . . . pursue her.

"How are you—"

"I'm dealing. Cynthia helped." She reached for his hand. "Carlos means a lot to you." She paused and licked her lips. "Alana worries me."

Edward reached for her other hand. She pulled away.

"She's no threat to you."

"I want to believe you." She dabbed her eye with her napkin. "I want to."

Chapter 6

It wouldn't take much this morning to make Jacqui's heart palpitate and hands tremble. She'd give her last breath if she could rewind the clock to before last night's dinner. Not the best condition to be in before a meeting with Superintendent Ramon Velasquez and her local district superintendent peers.

A familiar face emerged through Velasquez's door as she approached his office suite—Cecilia Gallegos, board of education president. Gallegos walked toward Jacqui with a hand extended.

"Mrs. Lamport, how good to see you." She gave a polite and quick grasp. "How is your husband? I'd have thought he would have ruled on Proposition Sixty-Eight by now. I don't see how a law that shames and ridicules undocumented immigrants so they can educate their kids needs *any* deliberation."

Jacqui wanted to strangle the woman. "Good morning, Ms. Gallegos." It mattered not that she agreed with Gallegos's opinion. Or that Gallegos was her superior. No one took a swipe at her husband to her face and got away with it. "Edward doesn't share his deliberations with me or anyone else. I assure you he is quite sensitive to effects this law will have on the Hispanic community of Los Angeles."

Gallegos tilted her chin and flashed an insincere smile. "You would know best, Mrs. Lamport. Good day." She turned and strode to the elevator.

Jacqui took a deep breath and stilled her hands and walked with her head high into Velasquez's conference room.

She was the second to arrive for the meeting. Velasquez was seated in his customary head-of-table seat, riffling through a short stack of documents. Lenora Soto, Local District East superintendent, was seated at the first chair to his left.

"Good morning, Ramon," Jacqui said.

He kept his face down. "Just had an interesting chat with Gallegos."

So had she. Where should she go with this? "About the budget deficit?"

"About your husband. She and one other board member, whom she wouldn't name, are going to hold a news conference tomorrow morning to voice their displeasure with how long it's taking Judge Lamport to rule on Proposition Sixty-Eight."

Potshots from haughty politicians were nothing new to her husband. She still struggled with them. "I would think patience is called for on such a far-reaching decision. My husband is all about being faithful to the Constitution."

As soon as those words crossed her lips she wished she could retract them. She had no business giving anyone reasons to cast aspersions on Edward.

Velasquez kept silent. Two more of her fellow local district superintendents entered the conference room. Jacqui settled into her seat and ordered her budget option documents in front of her. The last two of her peers filed into the room whispering and making emphatic gestures. They each gave Jacqui a quick glance and took their seats.

"Let's get started," Velasquez said. "I need to shorten this meeting fifteen minutes, so I'm putting the elephant on the table first." He reviewed the timeline and interim deadlines the local district superintendents needed to hit so he could present the first preview budget to the LAUSD board and the public on time.

After he finished he sat back and removed his glasses. "We've heard loud and clear from our community meetings and through the survey responses. People aren't buying the no-discrimination line from the Prop. Sixty-Eight proponents. They're not stupid. They see what will happen—cooked books on how much is being spent to educate illegal immigrants."

Jacqui sat up straight. "What if we beat them at their own game?"

Velasquez turned to her, his eyes narrowed. "What do you mean?"

Jacqui leaned toward Velasquez, filled with hopeful energy. "What if we launch an aggressive education and registration campaign in each of our schools? I volunteer my team to develop it. We'll show the Prop. Sixty-Eight supporters that every LAUSD family is willing to step up and be counted. That they won't be intimidated by fear of deportation. Of course, things would be better for all of us if Sixty-Eight was overturned, but in the event it's not this would be an in-your-face response. Defiance through compliance."

"I *love* that idea," said Lenora Soto. "Talk about unintended consequences." Her comment released faint laughter.

Velasquez's expression was flat. He kept his gaze on Jacqui. The room fell dead silent. "Who else wants to chime in?"

"Wait a minute, Ramon," Lenora Soto said. "Her idea's worth discussing."

Velasquez remained locked on Jacqui. "Any other ideas to engage the community?"

Jacqui scanned the room. Other than Lenora, her peers left her to twist in the wind. Two others offered warmed-over variations of plans discussed at last week's meeting. Velasquez moved on to review the roll-up draft budgets they'd submitted and gave them each specific cuts to fit into the target budget for the whole district, and then dismissed the group.

Jacqui approached Velasquez. He turned and walked away.

She turned to Lenora. "What just happened?"

Lenora waved her to a corner of the conference room. "Velasquez got his backside chewed by Gallegos right before the meeting. She stormed in here and laid into him in front of me. She's got a burr in her butt about your husband and she wants to take it out on you. Makes no sense."

"What does 'take it out on me' mean? Is she trying to get me fired?"

"She knows that wouldn't go down politically. She said they want you on administrative leave until your husband makes his ruling."

Jacqui shook her head and muttered an uncomplimentary word about Gallegos under her breath. "They can't do that. I've got to talk to Ramon. This is beyond ridiculous."

Chapter 7

Guadalajara, México
10:41 a.m. CST

Javier Bernal assembled his inner circle to assess the damage caused by Carlos Alvarez's data theft. As always, he would use this problem to eliminate weaknesses and stay current on who he could trust.

He strode into his war room, jacket buttoned and tie tight. Seated at the large square table were his chief of security and two executive vice presidents and his number-one client—Vicente Salvatierra, CEO of ALEXA Inversiones, S.A.

"Let's make this quick. We don't want to keep the *señoritas* who will entertain us at dinner tonight waiting, do we?"

Tense laughter rose at Bernal's question. He turned to his chief of security, who was seated to his immediate left. "An error in judgment to send only one man to apprehend Alvarez."

"*Sí*, in hindsight."

"Where are we on recovering the stolen data?"

"Alvarez is back inside Mexico. He withdrew money from an ATM in Puebla. We assume he still has a copy of the data in his possession. The second copy is unaccounted for."

"You *assume*." Bernal strode around the table, eyeing each of his leaders, and then stood behind his security chief. "What possibilities are you investigating?"

"Obviously, we need to question his mother, Alana Alvarez. She works in our Hermosillo regional office."

Bernal put his hands on the man's shoulders and gave a firm squeeze. "I don't pay you to do the obvious. What else?"

"We checked with our facilitators in the banking commission. Nothing has turned up as of an hour ago."

Bernal moved to the front of the room. "Who else might Alvarez have sent the data to?"

"We are counting on Señora Alvarez for answers," the security chief said.

"Your powers of persuasion better be strong." He turned to his executive vice presidents. "Are we missing anything?"

The younger of the two, Daniel Canedo, chimed in. "Every Mexican Internet company has blocked access to all WikiLeaks servers."

Vicente Salvatierra smiled and stretched his arms wide. "Leave it to the young ones." He paced around the table and gave Bernal's man a pat on the back. "I could use one like him, Javier. So we keep the dollars flowing through the Mexicali pipeline, yes?"

Heads nodded around the table.

"Do we need to tell *el gran jefe*?" Hector Del Cueto, the other executive vice president, asked.

"I don't wish to trouble him with this now," Bernal said.

"Change of subject," Salvatierra said. "What time Friday is the International Trade Center grand opening?"

"Eleven a.m.," Canedo said.

Bernal turned to Salvatierra. "We fly to Mexicali tomorrow at six thirty p.m."

Bernal adjourned the meeting, and Salvatierra stayed behind.

"I trust Canedo and Del Cueto most among my top executives," Bernal said. "The people I use to keep an eye on all my leaders say their ambitions are aligned with mine. I asked them into this meeting as a test, to see if one of them tries to use this stolen data problem against me."

"You spy on your own people?"

"Let that be a warning to you, Vicente."

Salvatierra stroked his chin. "We must compare methods sometime."

Bernal waved him off. "You old fox." He stepped to the phone and punched the intercom. "Please escort the gentleman waiting outside into the war room."

The door opened and Bernal's secretary, tall and slender with super-model looks, led a thick, gray-haired man dressed in a dark blue suit and red tie to a chair across the table from Bernal and Salvatierra.

"Welcome, Señor Mota," Bernal said. "How was your flight from Mexicali?"

Mota blinked and averted eye contact. "Your Gulfstream is quite comfortable."

"My condolences on the death of your subordinate, Señor DeAnza. Every war has casualties, though we do our best to prevent them."

"His family appreciates that you brought him home for a proper Catholic burial."

"Respect must be shown where it is due. Please, sit."

Mota backpedaled into the chair. His eyes shifted side to side. "I am even more shocked than you by Alvarez's betrayal."

"He's become quite the fugitive." Bernal studied the demeanor of his Mexicali division director. "You hired a capable young man to your staff. It seems we all misjudged his character. And resourcefulness."

"He was . . . like a son to me. I trusted him. Too much as—"

"Did he have help to make his untimely discovery?" Salvatierra asked.

Mota shook his head. "Too smart for his own good."

Salvatierra shrugged. "Since you can't find him, I'd say his smarts and toughness are serving him well."

"We will get him soon enough," Bernal said. "I am disappointed in you, Mota, but I'm not unreasonable. Relax and enjoy yourself as my guest tonight. You and I and Señor Salvatierra will fly to Mexicali together tomorrow."

Fear slithered across Mota's face. "You are coming for the American-side grand opening?"

Bernal moved around the table and sat next to Mota. "We can't let Stanley Gleason and company grab all the glory." He patted Mota's shoulder. "You will have a place of honor at the festivities. My secretary will now escort you to our executive lounge. Partake of anything you like. We leave for dinner in half an hour."

He buzzed his secretary, and she escorted Mota out.

Bernal stood and turned to Salvatierra. "Fear for one's life is a powerful incentive for loyalty. Let that also be a warning to you."

"Are we not partners, Javier? We are bound by opportunity and mutual benefit, not fear." Salvatierra flashed a sinister grin.

Bernal kept his cool. What he liked most about Salvatierra also troubled him most. Their enterprises were inextricably linked, but Salvatierra was his own man, beholden to no one.

Bernal strode to the door. "Let's enjoy our evening."

Chapter 8

Carlos slumped in the driver's seat of the truck he'd stolen in Mexicali. He kept shaking his head at how the US Border Patrol had handled him. Three hours in a holding cell with a dozen other *emigrantes* caught crossing. Then two agents picked him and two other men out of the group and loaded them onto a small bus and drove them back to Mexicali. No questions, no paperwork, no fingerprints.

They had taken his CD when they frisked him in the desert. He'd asked about it at the station, and they told him they'd destroyed it.

He didn't believe them.

The second CD that he'd mailed to his mother's friend, Pato Lamport, should have arrived by now.

Dust coated the dashboard and the inside of his eyelids. Food and fuel stops had been few and far between on his thousand-kilometer drive through scrub-laden desert, past stony mountains, and through sleepy villages. He checked his wallet. Ninety-three pesos remained of the four thousand he'd withdrawn from the ATM in Puebla. He'd left a mark on his trail, but he had no other option.

Pato Lamport's house had been easier to find than expected. He couldn't count on Pato and his wife to hide him for long. The men who wanted him dead wouldn't give up.

The house was wrapped in light-colored stucco with dark trim. The lot wasn't much wider than the house and was surrounded by a wrought-iron fence. Small home for a man who had been successful in business.

He heaved a sigh and shuffled toward the front door. His feet were lead weights. Good thing the porch had no steps. He knocked twice. Soft voices vibrated through the door. A fit, gray-haired *dón* greeted him. He was half a head shorter than Carlos and wore a white T-shirt bearing a small crest of the Mexican national *futból* team, faded jeans, and black sandals.

"*Bienvenido*, Carlos." Pato gave him a strong embrace.

He stepped through the doorway and met a short and slender woman dressed in a plain dark blue dress and black sandals. Her silver hair was up in a bun. His eyes met hers, and her smile revealed a missing tooth on the right side.

"Carlos, this is my wife, Marta."

She opened her arms and beckoned him to hug her. "I have looked forward to this day for many years. Please, sit down and be comfortable. I bring you *horchata* and fruit."

Pato directed Carlos to the couch, then settled into an armchair. "It's a great blessing for both of us to see you."

"You've taken a big risk to let me stay with you."

Marta returned with a tall glass and two watermelon slices. He gulped down all of the cold rice-and-cinnamon beverage without a breath and powered through the fruit.

"There's more," Marta said.

"*Gracias.* This is enough for now."

Pato said, "It's no trouble to have you here. We've seen much terror and death from *los narcos*. You have shown great courage. I believe God is with you and will protect you. And us."

"My mother said she hasn't seen you since before I was born."

Pato's visage was firm. He hesitated. "Your grandfather and I were once friends and business associates. We had a falling-out. We kept in touch with Alana by letter and phone."

Carlos nodded his understanding. "May I use your phone to call Mamá to let her know I made it here?"

Pato pointed to a table at the opposite end of the couch, then left the room. Carlos made the call and assured his mother he was safe and in good hands.

Pato returned with a small package. "We received this yesterday." He opened the padded brown envelope and removed a white envelope containing a CD. "Does this belong to you?"

Energy surged through Carlos's limbs. "¡Dios *mio!* Do you have a computer with Internet connection?"

"In the bedroom. Come with me."

Carlos bounded behind Pato down the hallway.

"Our Internet isn't very fast," Pato said.

"This is perfect." Carlos sat at the keyboard and opened a web browser.

"I'll leave you alone," Pato said. "Give a yell if you need anything."

"It's no bother to get up and ask." Carlos stood and gave Pato a quick hug and returned to the computer.

He typed the WikiLeaks web address. The browser progress indicator crept forward, stopped, then moved again.

The page changed. Server not found.

He repeated the operation. Waited. Same result.

He typed *WikiLeaks* in the search bar. Clicked the first link on the results page. Forty-five seconds passed.

Server not found.

Again. Same result.

E-mail was his only option to reach Albert Sanchez.

He created a Gmail account with a fictitious name. It wasn't secure, and Pato's IP address would be attached to his online session. Easy to intercept if you know what you're looking for.

He had no other option.

He removed the CD from the envelope and lifted it up to God—he knew he was holding a miracle—and then inserted it into the drive. He opened the spreadsheet and scrolled through rows of data. Everything he'd downloaded was there. He saved the file as a PDF document.

Carlos stood for a moment and stretched his aching back and legs. Then he searched for USANews Network. He navigated the website and clicked the link to send Sanchez a message. An e-mail window popped up and he copied the address into a new message on his fictitious e-mail account, then wrote his missive:

> *Dear Señor Sanchez,*
> *I am a concerned citizen of México. I have seen your war on drugs reports on cable TV. They have helped change some things in our country. I have informa-tion I believe you will find valuable in your ongoing reporting. I have reason to believe a large drug money laundering syndicate operating in México is connected to individuals in the US. I have attached some evi-dence to demonstrate this. But it is incomplete. More must be uncovered. I believe you are the one to do it.*
> *Numbers 13:28–30*
> *Saludos,*
> *A. Believer.*

He hoped Sanchez was a Bible reader, or at least would look up the passage. Sanchez's reports showed the same attitude the Israelite Caleb had.

We should be more than able to conquer it.

Carlos attached the PDF, held his breath, and clicked Send. He ejected the CD and stuck it in his back pocket.

God had kept him safe when the *matón* had attacked him at the border. He had to trust it would happen again.

He sent a second e-mail to his mother from his Gmail account so she'd have a way to contact him. Then he opened the sent folder and deleted both messages and trashed the cache on the web browser. Best he could do.

Now, the hard part.

Wait. Hope.

Wait for the message to get through Sanchez's gatekeepers. Hope Sanchez would see the gravity of what Carlos had discovered and, as he'd told Gonzalo, jump all over the story.

God *had* been with him.

Next time?

Chapter 9

Wednesday, February 17
Chambers of Hon. Edward J. Lamport
8:06 a.m.

A text from Alana reached Edward overnight. Carlos had made it to Pato's house. As far as Edward knew, his cousin was still connected with people in Mexico who could move mountains.

Time would tell.

McCormack had showed up half an hour before with Edward's gun permit and his Glock 27 and pancake holster. A lot more to learn about using it. He'd start by getting accustomed to wearing it on his hip. His concealable bulletproof vests would arrive tomorrow.

The intercom sounded. "Chief Judge Marrone is here to see you," his assistant, Rebecca, said with a cheerful air.

"Bring him in."

Edward still had a job to do. He needed Marrone's seasoned perspective on the Prop. 68 case. And he owed Marrone a heads-up on his personal life.

He stepped to the window and studied the teeming mob outside. Bigger than yesterday. The LAPD had sent more officers. The FPS police presence had doubled. The demonstrators were fervent. Las Reconquistas placards were still prominent.

The latch to his chambers door clicked. He turned and waved Marrone to the window. Edward gestured toward the protesters. "Abandon principles for politics long enough and you get this kind of unrest." He stayed focused on the crowd.

"Every side thinks *their* principles are the right ones," Marrone said. He pointed at Edward's hip. "You gonna wear that thing all the time?"

"I have an appointment across town after we meet and I'm supposed to carry it everywhere." He turned back to the window. "I don't tack with prevailing winds. I won't join the herd of judges who fix every legislative shortcoming they see."

"Pretty bold assertion from the new guy around here. And I hope you plan on wearing your jacket when you walk around the courthouse."

"It'll stay locked in my credenza when I'm in the building." Edward motioned to the padded leather armchairs in front of his desk. "Before we talk Prop. Sixty-Eight, a family problem came up yesterday. It's serious and I'll need to take time off to deal with it."

"Sorry to hear that. Illness?"

"It's complicated. Close relatives in Mexico."

"Mexico? I thought you were Irish."

"Irish-Mexican. My great-great-great-grandfather was in the Battalion of St. Patrick, which fought for Mexico during the US invasion."

"You mean the Mexican-American War?"

"My ancestors didn't see it that way."

"We'll have to talk about that over a drink sometime."

"I'd like that."

Edward reached for the eighty-page draft of his opinion sitting on his desk and held it up. "I don't like Proposition Sixty-Eight. It's bad policy. But I don't see anything unconstitutional. It's not my job to judge the policy merits of a law."

Marrone shrugged. "Myself, I think the government's case is compelling."

"It's not unconstitutional for a state to keep track of who consumes what. It passes the test of a compelling state interest."

Edward stepped from his chair to his desk and fired up his laptop. He pulled up a *Los Angeles Times* article about the LAUSD poll Jacqui had told him about the night before. He slid his computer from its docking station and brought it to Marrone.

"Did you see this article in today's *Times*?"

Marrone scanned the screen. "Missed this somehow."

"Forty percent of Hispanic respondents said they wouldn't register for the state services ID for fear of deportation." He closed the laptop and set it on his desk. "There's no way the registrations could be used for that purpose." He grabbed a second copy of his draft opinion and handed it to Marrone. "Turn to page eighteen and read the fourth paragraph."

Marrone thumbed to the page and read, "'As long as the executive branch chooses not to enforce existing immigration laws or enforce them selectively, the effect of Proposition Sixty-Eight will be to make it more, not less, possible for persons who have entered the United States unlawfully to receive state and local government services and benefits.' How do you support that?"

Edward strode to one of his mahogany bookshelves and pulled two volumes—federal court decisions from 1997 and Supreme Court decisions from 1982. He opened each to where he'd bookmarked the cases he used to render his opinion.

"You expect me to read these now?" Marrone said.

"Take them with you. The authors of Prop. Sixty-Eight did their homework. These two decisions show the power in question is regulating access to services and benefits. But they're based on the fact that no state has proven that providing services to illegal immigrants damages a compelling interest."

Marrone stood and handed back the books. "E-mail me the case names and page numbers. I'll get back to you before end of day Friday."

"One more thought."

Marrone checked his watch. "I need to go. Let's walk."

Not the best, but Edward would take it. He yanked the holster off and locked the gun in his credenza, then followed Marrone out. He flagged down McCormack, who was engaged in conversation with Rebecca. "Back in five minutes, then we're off to my meetings."

Marrone led the way to the judges-only elevator. He tapped his security badge on the reader and selected the sixteenth floor.

"My clerks have documented all prior court decisions I believe opened the door to Proposition Sixty-Eight," Edward said. "I want to go on record why they should be reversed."

Marrone narrowed his eyes. "You're kidding, right?"

"I'm dead serious."

Marrone pointed a finger at Edward's chest. "You can't challenge higher court decisions."

"I know that. I want to start a debate."

"To what end?"

"If federal judges want to make law, then shouldn't those laws be subject to repeal?"

The car completed its ascent and the doors opened. "Prop. Sixty-Eight is going to the Supremes no matter what you do. Don't let your zeal cloud your judgment."

Edward hit the fifth-floor button and leaned against the wall of the elevator car. Marrone's response was predictable. Calling for reversals wouldn't win points with his peers.

So what? His job wasn't about popularity.

◆ ◆ ◆

Edward paused at his chambers door and motioned to McCormack. "I need to tell you something before we go."

McCormack followed him in. Edward grabbed a folder and stuffed it into a black leather portfolio case. "I want to grab a coffee on the way out." He retrieved his Glock and slipped it into place, then pulled on his suit jacket.

They rode the judges-only car down to the Main Street lobby. Edward stopped in front of a statue situated at the lobby's east wall. "This is confidential."

"Your Honor, does anything you're about to tell me involve illegal activity?"

Edward tipped his head. "Why do you ask?"

"Because if it does I'm obligated to report what you say to my superiors."

"Good."

McCormack shot him a confused look.

"It's not anything I've done, if that's what you're thinking."

"Your Honor, I never presume—"

"A family member's life's been threatened."

McCormack stared at a plaque mounted on the wall next to the statue. "It would be bad for my career in the Marshals Service to disclose any information that might jeopardize the safety of a federal judge or any of his family members whom I'm assigned to protect."

Edward put a hand on McCormack's shoulder. "Good man." He turned to walk the perimeter of the lobby. The FPS officers manning the security screening station waved a greeting his way. "I had a love affair in Mexico twenty-five years ago," he said as he walked past the entrance to the Clerk of the Court offices. "We have a son. But I've never met him. And I hadn't told my wife about him until Monday evening."

Edward stepped into the café and ordered a double Americano, black, then led McCormack toward the elevators.

"I signed away my paternity. Hadn't spoken to Alana since then. Until two days ago. She contacted me because someone wants our son dead. That was the personal matter that came up when we left the gun range."

"Is this what our excursion is about?"

"First stop is Citizenship and Immigration Services. A law school classmate of mine is the local director. We're also meeting with the FBI in Westwood. Do me a favor and give Special Agent Novack over there a heads-up on what I shared about Carlos while I meet with the CIS director."

"Your Honor, if we're going to other federal facilities I need to let the security personnel know we're coming."

"FBI, yes. But not CIS. That's personal business."

"Your safety is my responsibility and if I don't follow proper protocols—"

"Deputy McCormack. I may be your responsibility, but it's my life. Visiting CIS is not official business. It's personal and sensitive. I can refuse your protection at any time, so either we go together my way or I go alone. End of debate."

Chapter 10

Edward extended a hand to CIS Los Angeles director Ramon Ortiz. He welcomed Edward into his spartan office and brought him a glass of ice water. McCormack remained in Ortiz's waiting area.

"How may I assist you, Judge Lamport?"

"I have family in Mexico who are in danger. I want them here on asylum."

"Your Honor, people seeking asylum must—"

"I know the process, Ramon. It won't do. Time is of the essence."

"May I ask which relatives?"

"My son and his mother."

Ortiz's face turned quizzical. "Your son's not a citizen?"

Edward shared the story of his love affair with Alana.

"How old is Carlos?"

"Twenty-five."

"We could expedite under family reunification—"

"I need them out of Mexico *now*."

"Do they have current passports?"

"If Carlos had one we wouldn't be talking. Your own rules say people can apply for asylum regardless of how they entered the country."

Ortiz crossed his arms. "Are you asking me to aid and abet a crime?"

"I'm asking for a favor. People want my son dead because he saw things at work he wasn't supposed to see. Can you help me?"

Ortiz cleared his throat. "Things might be different if they were in another country. Cooperation between the US and Mexico on these matters has never been good, and it's gotten worse since Proposition Sixty-Eight passed. I've heard through the grapevine that Mexico has threatened to close our consulates."

Close consulates . . . should he knock on the State Department's door instead? "Listen—" He checked himself. "Lives are at stake. Let Carlos and Alana in and put them in detention. All I'm asking for is their safety."

Ortiz looked away. "Not that simple."

"Why not? Between you and Immigration and Customs Enforcement you have the means."

"I'm sorry, Judge Lamport. I can't." Ortiz came out from behind his desk. "I have family in Mexico, too. I know what goes on. If there were anything I could do, I'd do it now. But my hands are tied." Ortiz stepped to his office door. "I'm not at liberty to say why."

Edward and McCormack paced to the elevator and the deputy's black Crown Vic. They both kept quiet. Once inside the car, Edward called FBI Special Agent Frank Novack, who was ready to brief him and McCormack on the second death threat. The federal building in Westwood was a fifteen-mile drive down Wilshire Boulevard from their current location.

"It wasn't so long ago when the favor I asked Ortiz for would have been a slam dunk." He shook his head. "I need more leverage. I need to talk to Carlos."

"A suggestion, Your Honor."

"Fire away."

"Let me and Special Agent Novack question him. It's what we do."

Question Carlos? "He's not a suspect."

"Not what I meant. There are still too many unknowns. I don't want you to take unnecessary risks."

"Appreciate your concern, but no. I need to know why he was compelled to take on this money-laundering thing."

Why, indeed. There were plenty of other ways Carlos could have alerted authorities to what he suspected. Even if he believed every Mexican official was corrupt, he could have talked with Alana about it and figured out a way to get the right people on the case.

What drove him to take such a huge risk? What or whom was he trying to protect?

It had to be more than fresh-faced idealism.

Or maybe that was exactly what it was. Maybe he was naïve enough to believe that doing the right thing, whatever the cost, was its own reward. Maybe the same spirit that had emboldened Edward's Irish ancestor to defect from the US Army and fight alongside his Catholic brothers had been passed down to Carlos.

Whatever his motivation, Carlos had shown great courage at his young age.

Which Edward had not done in his young age.

If Edward was going to get help, he'd need to go to Washington and sell it in person. It would help matters if he took Jacqui with him. From what she'd said the night before, a little time away from the office might be good for her.

Their terse exchange over breakfast that morning had left him little hope she'd go.

One thing at a time.

"Deputy McCormack, will your boss let you travel out of town with me?"

"My assignment is to protect you, Your Honor. What are your plans?"

"Washington, D.C."

Chapter 11

LAUSD Administration Building, downtown Los Angeles
9:58 a.m.

Senior LAUSD staff were expected to attend Cecilia Gallegos's news conference. Jacqui had told Edward last night about her meeting with Velasquez and prepared him for what might happen to her, and she promised to text him as soon as Gallegos's event ended.

Jacqui wanted to avoid contact with Gallegos, so she chose a seat in the back left corner of the last row in the boardroom gallery. About thirty journalists occupied the first three rows of seats, and two television cameras with "TV POOL" stickers affixed flanked the seating area. A blond-wood counter stretched from wall to wall, separating the gallery from the half-circle desk where board members sat during public hearings.

Jacqui hadn't been in this room in a while. It struck her afresh how that wood counter separated the board of education members from the community they served.

The scheduled ten a.m. start time came and went. Seven minutes later, Gallegos entered the boardroom from the right—alone—and sat in her customary center chair. Lenora Soto entered the room and spotted Jacqui. She joined her in the back row of the gallery.

"Thank you all for coming today," Gallegos said, her expression grim. "Today marks the sixtieth day since the United States Justice Department lawsuit to block the implementation of California Proposition Sixty-Eight began, and the forty-second day since the presiding judge, Edward J. Lamport, recessed the trial for his deliberation."

A murmur sprung forth from the media members present. Jacqui turned and shot Lenora a frown. If Jacqui didn't care about her tenure with the district, she'd have stood and corrected Gallegos for not referring to her husband as "The Honorable Edward J. Lamport."

Loudly.

"I'm here today to share with concerned parents and school district administrators around the great State of California how this delay is affecting the ability of the body that I lead to perform its fiduciary duty to the citizens of Los Angeles."

Lenora turned to Jacqui with a smirk on her face. "I've heard her pontificate before, but this is beyond the pale," she whispered. Jacqui noticed a few rolling eyes around the room.

Gallegos blinked rapidly as she turned the page of her prepared remarks. She took a sip of water. "The first, and most damaging, consequence of Proposition Sixty-Eight will be a mass exodus of students. Based on scientific polling by Metrix Research, we expect twenty-five to thirty-five percent of families in our district to withdraw their children from LAUSD schools if Proposition Sixty-Eight is allowed to become law."

"That's not news," Jacqui said to Lenora. "Their polls only validate what was pleaded during the election campaign."

"Second," Gallegos continued, "since state funding for LAUSD is keyed to student enrollment, we will face a catastrophic reduction in the number of teachers, noncredentialed staff, and administrators. Third, the administration and the board will have no choice but to implement the closure of a minimum of thirty percent of our elementary, middle, and high school campuses."

Gallegos droned on about the devastation to Latino families and communities in greater Los Angeles and the moral bankruptcy of Prop. 68.

"In spite of the unfairness and added cost burden this law imposes, I implore all the undocumented residents of Los Angeles and throughout California, if Proposition Sixty-Eight is allowed to stand, to rise and be counted. Show them your numbers and your strength. Overwhelm them with your willingness to comply. Do not let the fearmongering of the proponents of this law keep your children from their destiny."

Jacqui's mouth fell agape. "I don't believe it. She stole my idea."

Lenora grabbed her hand. "It's brilliant. I went back to Velasquez after the meeting and challenged him. He admitted he liked it. Guess she did, too."

"Wonder if she'll call the dogs off me now. Is this why she did the press conference alone?"

Lenora shrugged her shoulders. "Does it matter?"

Jacqui raised steepled fingers to her lips. How could she show gratitude to Gallegos *and* admonish her disrespect of Edward?

"In closing," Gallegos said, "I appeal to United States District Judge Edward Lamport for swift resolution to the uncertainty that hovers over our state. I call on you, Your Honor, to be the man we need who understands the signs of the times and knows what must be done. I will now take your questions."

Jacqui dropped her hands to her lap. She'd hold the gratitude for now.

Chapter 12

Edward studied the suspect board Special Agent Novack had mounted on the briefing room wall while Novack and McCormack huddled at the opposite end. Novack had posted a chart that showed that the total investment in the International Trade Center project was $2.8 billion and the cost to build the US side was 40 percent higher than the Mexican side. Some details he hadn't known grabbed his attention. ALEXA Inversiones was the lead investor for the *Mexican* side of the International Trade Center, and Construcción Sotomayor was the builder. Stanley Gleason's Angeles Development Corporation built the US side and held a 60 percent interest in that portion. The remaining ownership stake was divided between private equity firms and individual investors.

The CEO and majority shareholder of ALEXA was identified by his formal Mexican name—Vicente Salvatierra Obregón.

Obregón. *Español* for O'Brian. Edward's great-grandmother's maiden name was Obregón. A common surname in Mexico. Little chance they shared any common ancestry. Though the possibility creeped him out.

Novack had posted a placeholder for Las Reconquistas, the subject of this meeting, on the board. He'd also posted a picture of Ernesto Marroquín, the LA drug kingpin sentenced to death by the jury in Edward's courtroom, and underneath it, the organization Marroquín had operated before his conviction. The diagram showed that three of Marroquín's five first-level *capitáns* were in custody and about a quarter of his soldiers had been arrested. The man who'd threatened Edward—Marroquín's successor—was not on the board.

Edward's phone chirped a text message alert in his pocket. "Excuse me, gentlemen."

"We're ready when you are, Your Honor," Novack said.

Edward checked his phone. Message from Jacqui.

*Gallegos stole my idea about the Prop.
68 sign-up campaign. Call me when you
can.*

Edward shook his head and chuckled under his breath. He waved the federal agents over to the table, and he and McCormack sat on one side and Novack across. Novack opened a manila folder with a half-inch stack of documents inside, pulled a photograph off the top, and slid it toward Edward and McCormack.

"César Monterrez. He made the threat against you and claimed he was affiliated with Las Reconquistas. So far it looks like he's a solo act."

"On what basis?" McCormack said.

"We asked simple questions about the organization—where it's headquartered, who runs it, who he worked with locally. Nothing he said checks out, so either he's a real good actor—which I doubt—or he's dumb as a sheep. Fidgeted constantly and his Spanish was uneducated. We're pursuing other leads from Homeland Security Investigations."

"So what of Las Reconquistas?" Edward said.

Novack removed a set of documents from his folder and handed them to Edward. "Their leader is Rafael Obregón—"

"The CEO of ALEXA—his mother's family name is Obregón."

"How do you know that?" McCormack said.

Edward pointed to the suspect board. "In Mexican culture, families use two surnames. The first is the father's family name, the second the mother's. Some men prefer to omit the second surname. My grandmother's family name was Obregón."

"Noted," Novack said. "Obregón lives in the Mescalero Reservation in New Mexico."

"Who's backing them?" McCormack said.

Novack shook his head. "Mexican law enforcement refuses to cooperate."

"Bank records?" Edward said.

"We've had a peek. A federal judge in Albuquerque said we didn't have enough cause for a warrant."

Edward stood and paced. "Why isn't the first man who threatened me on your suspect board?"

Novack pulled another photo from his file. "Artúro Mondragón. We believe he's in Mexico right now."

Edward ran a hand through his hair. It felt thinner. "Deputy McCormack has briefed you about my son."

"I didn't want to mention it unless you brought it up."

"I hope to speak with him before day's end. McCormack will relay anything I learn from Carlos and his mother that might help you." He checked his watch. He was due back at the courthouse in forty-five minutes. "I'm going to Washington in the next day or two. McCormack will accompany me. I need as much information as you can dig up on Bancomex, ALEXA, and Las Reconquistas. I need leverage. Lots of leverage."

Chapter 13

Stanley Gleason gathered his public relations team in front of Cal-3, the showcase building on the US side of the International Trade Center. Vicente Salvatierra had built his own premier edifice on the Mexican side, and they'd engaged in a heated competition to make their signature building's architecture the most impressive. Each thought theirs was, of course. But the soured politics between the US and Mexico had rendered their rivalry irrelevant.

The presidents of Mexico and the United States would not appear at the grand opening as originally planned. As of today, three cabinet members had agreed to keep their commitment—Commerce, Homeland Security, and State. Their Mexican counterparts would also attend.

He called his team to attention. Present were Janine Agresta, president of his public relations agency; five of her associates; Gleason's PR director; and Miguel Rodrigues, Gleason's chief operating officer.

"I want to focus the media tour in three areas of the complex. First stop will be the north port of entry, with a demonstration of the security infrastructure and procedures. We need to show how the entry/exit process directs workers back to their respective countries every night."

Gleason led the team in front of a monument set between the Cal-3 and Mex-3 buildings that marked the US-Mexico border. "When we tour these two buildings I want to showcase the electric-vehicle-battery manufacturing and distribution centers—"

A ringing cell phone. It belonged to Rodrigues. He peeled away from the team.

"Anyway," Gleason said, "the big story at this stop is how the borderless labor treaty allows the two electronics manufacturers who've set up shop here to produce battery cells at forty-percent-lower unit cost, making electric cars more affordable, reducing carbon footprint, all that jazz."

Rodrigues returned and waved Gleason over.

"This better be important," Gleason said.

"One of the foremen just told me Albert Sanchez was here checking out the project."

"Sanchez? Why did he wait until now to tell you?"

"Came out in conversation about the grounds cleanup. Sanchez did his thing—man on the street. He spoke with three of our workers."

"We were very clear about keeping prying eyes away until the opening. Were they American or Mexican?"

"From Mexicali."

Gleason shoved his hands into his pockets. "You talk to them?"

"Sanchez asked 'em how the ITC benefits their community and what it was like to work on a high-profile project."

"And you believed them?"

"Why wouldn't I?"

Gleason crossed his arms. "Sanchez is a con man. Get those men here pronto. The foreman, too. I want full details." He returned to the huddle.

"Sorry, folks." He turned to Janine Agresta. "Did we give credentials to Albert Sanchez?"

"Yes, Mr. Gleason."

"You know how I feel about him."

"It would be worse if you didn't invite him."

Gleason grimaced. "Who here has dealt with him?"

A young, athletic-looking man raised his hand. "I pitched a story to USANews last year. The client wanted Sanchez because of his tough reputation. It conflicted with another assignment, and we got Lou Holman instead."

"Holman? He interviewed me five years ago about my downtown LA mixed-use project. He thought I was crazy for building residential on top of thirty floors of office—"

"Excuse me," Agresta said. "We have deadlines."

Gleason and his team reviewed the grand opening event logistics and the draft media release and ended the meeting on time. He returned to his office in the Cal-3 building. Rodrigues met him there five minutes later.

"You round up those men?"

"They've left the site. Neither exit port checked them out."

Gleason's hands shook slightly, and he squeezed them to stay in control. "You find those men! We gotta keep a tight lid on this."

Chapter 14

Edward scanned the half-full dining room at La Ferme. He and Jacqui dined at this country-French restaurant every chance they could, and it was the first place he thought of to meet with Joe Foley, his longtime friend and personal private investigator.

Edward checked in with a statuesque brunette at the host station. Foley hadn't arrived. She escorted him to a booth that overlooked the midday bustle on Grand Avenue.

He sat against the wall so he could see Foley come in. He hadn't heard from Jacqui since he'd left the house that morning. Not a good sign. He pictured how her colleagues must have reacted to her deputy marshal escort. Good thing they'd agreed the deputy would be the one to answer all questions.

The receptionist escorted Foley to Edward's table. He hadn't aged a day in the last four years. Same thick crop of reddish-brown hair. Same taut and muscular build. PI work appeared to suit his friend well. They shared a back-slapping embrace.

"Man, you look good," Edward said.

"Still doing the SEAL workout. Who needs a gym when you can pound your body at Manhattan Beach?"

Edward pinched his own waistline. "I need to have you put me through your paces. Thanks for meeting on short notice."

"Good thing I was in the office today instead of working from home."

They settled in and ordered lunch.

"I need protection for two family members in Mexico," Edward said. It was easier for now to consider Alana family.

"Protection's not my thing. What's going on?"

He shared the full story about Alana and Carlos, about the death threats he'd received, and the tension between him and Jacqui.

"Jacqui's taking it hard," Edward said. "We spoke few words before I left this morning."

Foley nodded. "Understandable. What's your next move?"

"I'm going to Washington to hustle a meeting with Conrad Beverley, secretary of Homeland Security. He owes me one."

"Good to have friends in high places."

"We'll see how good a friend he is. I met with Ramon Ortiz at CIS this morning. Shut me down. Blamed it on bad relations with Mexico." Edward took a sip of water. "He's toeing the party line."

"You think Beverley will be any different?"

Edward shrugged. "I'm not leaving D.C. until somebody does the right thing."

"What do you need from me?"

"Time. You still have contacts in Mexico?"

"Omar Espinosa. Lives near Durango. Tough and crackerjack smart."

"Alana lives in Hermosillo. Carlos is staying with my cousin Pato Lamport in Obregón City, two and a half hours south."

Foley leaned in. "I'll go, too."

"You said protection's not your thing."

"For you I'll make the exception. We've been through too much together."

They had indeed. They were an all-star team at the district attorney's office back in the day. "Your other clients?"

Foley smiled. "I'll make room."

"First thing I need help with is coordinating with Alana. I need to get some work done and get ready to leave."

"Send me the contact info and what you want done and I'll work it through Omar."

Edward pulled out his cell phone and sent Foley Alana's number. "I'll e-mail you details when I get back to my chambers. How well do you think Espinosa can protect them?"

"No guarantees. Too hard to tell the good guys from the bad."

Chapter 15

Edward made quick work of the e-mail to Foley and set an appointment with Chief Judge Marrone for six p.m. to offload his docket. Then he called Jacqui.

"So, dear, you have more influence with the LAUSD brass than you give yourself credit for."

"Yeah, go figure," Jacqui said. "Have you heard any reports on the news conference?"

"Wall-to-wall meetings. Had lunch with Joe Foley today."

"There's a name you haven't mentioned in a while. What was the occasion?"

"I'm sending him to Mexico to protect Carlos and Alana while things get sorted out on this end."

Silence on the line.

"I'm sorry," Edward said. "I haven't heard about Gallegos's news conference. Did she decry me as the man who would allow LAUSD to be ruined?"

"Words to that effect. She implored you to do the right thing. I thought she disrespected you."

"Nothing new. You think the fact that she used your idea will calm her down about having you put on admin leave?"

"Time will tell." A pause. "Ed . . . I'm trying to accept what's happening with your son and Alana. But it's hard."

He grimaced inside. She couldn't say Carlos's name.

He knew this would happen. He knew it would hurt Jacqui. But he owed a debt to the son he'd fathered and the woman who bore him. He had to repay.

He still loved Alana. He struggled with how intense his feelings for her were after all these years. He couldn't act on them, of course. Except to make sure she and Carlos were brought safely into the United States.

"Something great will come out of this. I don't know what, but I believe it will happen." He paused to collect himself. "It has to."

"I'm frightened, Ed. About Alana."

So was he.

They promised each other to work through the pain, then ended the call.

He drew a deep breath and exhaled, then paced his chambers. He peered out the window at the protesters for a few seconds, then rubbed his temples and returned to his desk.

He had to compartmentalize. People's lives depended on his ability to do so.

He forced his thoughts to Conrad Beverley. Longtime US Attorney in the San Francisco district. Their tenures in the US Attorney's Office had overlapped by two years, and they'd collaborated on two noteworthy cases involving domestic terrorism in which Beverley had been the lead prosecutor. Beverley moved on to become Department of

Homeland Security general counsel and had been confirmed for the top job late last year after his predecessor stepped down.

Edward called the secretary's direct line from his cell phone.

"Judge Edward Lamport. To what do I owe the pleasure?"

"I'm coming to D.C. on Friday. Like to see you while I'm in town. Friday evening, if you're open."

"I'll be in California on Friday. I fly in tomorrow night for the International Trade Center event. State and Commerce are coming, too."

Gleason's project. "How long will you stay?"

"There's a private dinner with our Mexican counterparts and the private-sector guys Friday at six. We fly back right after. What brings you to Washington? Aren't you deciding that big California immigration case?"

"A personal emergency. Any chance we can connect while you're on the West Coast?"

"Hardly a minute to spare. We land at El Centro Naval around ten p.m. Thursday and motorcade to Calexico. Breakfast at eight and a preceremony meeting. The event runs from eleven to three."

Edward caught himself pacing too quickly. "How about between the event and dinner? I need a half hour tops."

A pause. "Even if I could, wouldn't it be bad form for you to show up in a sea of media types?"

Carlos's life was too important. "I don't believe judges should isolate themselves. My family's worth any perception risk."

"Let me check the schedule."

Edward paced again and rubbed tension from his eyes.

"I could squeeze you in around four o'clock," Beverley said.

"My wife will be with me. If anyone asks why I'm there it's strictly a show of support for a friend."

"No promises, Judge Lamport. Text me at three fifteen Friday and I'll let you know."

Now Edward had to get himself invited to the event. He left a message for Gleason and then tapped Jacqui's number.

"How was your budget meeting this morning?"

"Strange in many ways." Her tone was flat. "Your time with Ortiz?"

"Fruitless. I want to go down to Calexico tomorrow afternoon for the International Trade Center grand opening Friday morning. Conrad Beverley will be there, and I can talk with him about Carlos. I'd like you with me."

His intercom buzzed. Gleason was on the line. He asked Jacqui to think it over while he took the call.

"Judge Lamport, my office in LA told me you called. I'm in Calexico for our grand opening Friday."

"I'd like to be there. With Jacqui."

"Well . . . I'm honored. But the place will be crawling with media types. I thought judges were supposed to avoid such things."

"Matter of opinion. Besides, it's my turn to repay a good deed."

"Fair enough. I'll have passes for you and your wife. I'm sure you know what you're doing."

He wasn't sure at all. Didn't matter. If things turned wrong he could back out.

That wouldn't do.

He called Jacqui back. She was in. As he'd surmised, a day away from the office met a need. And they'd have time alone. Which they both needed.

Marrone would object. The way to sell it to him—not that he needed to, but it was best for their working relationship—was to disclose everything. He bolted for the door and breezed past Rebecca without a word.

PART II

GAMBITS

He who knows when he can fight and when he cannot will be victorious.

—Sun Tzu, *The Art of War*

Chapter 16

Ciudad Obregón, México
6:07 p.m. MST

"Carlos, your mother is on the phone." Pato brought him a cordless handset.

"Good news, *mijo*," Alana said. "We have people in America who will help us. Pato has a cousin in Los Angeles who is a judge. He's working on getting us asylum. He sent some men to protect us until we can get out."

"How? When?"

"Two men come to my house today. Then we come for you."

"Mamá, this is too slow."

Pato burst into the room. "You must hide. Men out front approaching the house."

Carlos dropped the phone and followed Pato down the hallway into a bedroom across from the master. "There's an attic cutout in the closet. Hide in there."

Carlos pushed aside clothing. "I need a boost!" Pato locked his hands together into a stirrup. Carlos kicked off his shoes, put his right foot in Pato's hands, and then grabbed the closet rod. The right side came loose. He thrust upward and reached for the attic opening. He pushed the board that covered the opening out of the way and pulled himself up enough to poke his head through. Cobwebs blanketed his face. The attic was pitch-dark. He groped around and grabbed a truss board and pulled himself through the opening. Bare studs, no floor. He slid away from the opening, replaced the board, and rolled himself until he bumped into another truss.

He lay still, heart pounding, and fought to keep from coughing.

Muffled voices vibrated through the attic. The tone seemed civil.

Then someone—a man—raised his voice.

Then a second voice rose. And a third.

Carlos counted off seconds. Ten. Twenty. Thirty. The angry conversation continued.

Forty. Fifty. Sixty.

Then it stopped.

He counted more seconds.

Thirty. Sixty. One hundred.

Silence. Did they leave?

Did he dare move? What if someone stayed behind? What if they knew he was up there and were waiting for him to emerge?

The sound of his pounding heart reverberated through his body to his eardrums. He didn't dare take a deep breath for fear he'd cough and give away his hiding place. Pressure from the bare joist under his left hip intensified, throbbed. If he moved, the ceiling would vibrate or a joist would squeak.

A noise. More voices. Shouting.

Someone was in the room below him.

The pain in his hip turned searing. As if his skin had split open. He raised his hand slowly to his mouth, covered it, and drew as much air as he could without giving off a sound.

He heard the closet door slam underneath him. Twice.

His heart pounded harder. Harder.

More yelling. Including his name.

The pounding and shouting underneath him shifted. They'd moved to another room.

Hold, hold.

Still.

Another breath, slow, quiet.

The noises ceased.

Oh, no.

The truck.

If they saw the Baja California license plates they would know he'd been there. They'd wait him out, expecting him to come back. He had to endure the pain and stifling air. He had to wait until their patience wore thin and they moved on.

◆ ◆ ◆

Gen. Ignacio P. Garcia International Airport, Hermosillo, México
8:21 p.m.

Joe Foley double-timed through the general aviation terminal to the ground transportation exit. He approached a dark-haired man of medium height and muscular build, dressed in a navy blazer and gray slacks. The man held a hand-lettered sign that read "Señor José."

Foley extended a hand and exchanged back slaps with Omar Espinosa. "Thanks for getting up here on short notice."

"I gladly accept opportunities to leave Durango. Where are we going first?"

Foley handed Espinosa one of his business cards with Alana Alvarez's address and phone number hand printed on the back.

Omar tapped the number on his phone and handed it to Foley.

"Mrs. Alvarez, Joseph Foley from Los Angeles. I'm at the airport."

"Welcome, Señor Foley. You're about twenty minutes away. My home is in a gated neighborhood. The code is 3572."

Gated. Her husband must have been quite the businessman. "We'll see you soon."

Espinosa made quick work of the compact airport's exit drive and steered his rented black Town Car onto Jesús Garcia Morales Highway. He cruised ten kilometers of city streets to Alana's neighborhood in under fifteen minutes. Espinosa turned left into a driveway flanked by curved stucco walls about three meters high. Three young toughs stood around the entry key panel at the gate.

"What business do you have here?" one of the young men said.

"To visit a friend," Espinosa said.

The young man pulled open his jacket. A holstered pistol interrupted the conversation.

Foley stepped out of the right rear door and strode around to face the three men. Their spokesman put his hand on the grip of his gun. Espinosa rolled his window down.

"Omar, translate," Foley said.

"Sí, señor." Espinosa stayed put, hands on the steering wheel.

Foley looked the gun-toting young man in the eye. "I'm sure you're here to protect these fine homes and their occupants. We are here to visit a family friend. We go way back, from when I worked at the Ford factory across town in the late nineties."

"And who is your friend?" the man with the pistol said. He stepped to within two feet of Foley and drew his gun.

Foley looked the man up and down. "Why do you need to know?"

The spokesman raised his weapon. Foley snatched it from his hand in a blink and snapped a punch into the man's abdomen. The man doubled over and hit the ground, gasping for air. Espinosa slammed the car door into a second man while Foley pistol-whipped the third on the back of his head. Foley pointed the pistol he'd snatched at the spokesman, still doubled over on the ground. Espinosa pulled a Beretta Pico from a leg holster and pointed it at the man he'd door-slammed. The third man lay unconscious.

"We'll be on our way now," Foley said. He kept the snatched gun trained on the three men as he backpedaled to the key panel and punched in Alana's gate code. A double beep sounded and a video screen next to the keypad lit up. Alana's face appeared. Foley spotted the small camera lens above the screen and positioned his face in front of it.

"Who is this?" Alana said.

Foley glanced at Espinosa and the three men, then back to the camera. "Joseph Foley for our scheduled appointment."

The screen went dark and the gate retracted. Foley jogged back to the car, pistol still aimed at the three men, and slid into the backseat. Espinosa backed into the driver's seat and closed the door. They drove through the gate, then stopped and got out of the car. They pointed their pistols at the men until the gate closed. Foley shouted to them, *"Buenos dias."* He turned to Espinosa. "Pretty low-grade security there."

"Must be a small-time *narco* in the neighborhood."

They returned to the car and cruised toward Alana's house. Foley inspected the weapon he'd seized, then tossed it onto the front passenger seat. "Yours now, *amigo.*"

Alana's house was about a quarter mile from the entry gate. It was an elegant two-story villa with cream-colored stucco walls and a multi-level Spanish tile roof. A low, stucco-covered wall topped with a black iron fence about eight feet tall guarded the perimeter.

Foley and Espinosa parked and walked under an archway to the front door. A press on the doorbell button released three chime tones. The door opened about ten seconds later.

Alana wore a pale blue blouse, tan khakis, and brown flats. She gave a tight smile. *"Bienvenido.* Please come in." She escorted Foley and Espinosa to an elegant sitting room.

"Make yourselves comfortable. May I bring you a drink?"

"Cold bottled water would be fine," Foley said.

The sitting room reflected a woman's touch. The floor was travertine, the sofa and chairs cream-colored leather and accented with white-and-blue-striped pillows. An ornate coffee table with carved legs sat atop an embroidered rug in the center of the room.

"You and Mr. Alvarez put a lot of love into this place."

"I won't be here much longer. Too much to maintain. And my new neighbors down the street are drug dealers."

Foley nodded. "We encountered three men at the entry gate. Have you spoken to Carlos?"

Her expression turned grim. "Two hours ago. I heard Pato yell in the background that men were approaching the house." She swallowed. "No word since."

"We need to get you out of here," Espinosa said. "Permanently."

Her eyes widened. "I . . . I'm not prepared."

"Killers will show up here soon," Espinosa said.

Alana looked left and right. She tilted her head up and closed her eyes for a few seconds. Then she bolted to the foyer and up the stairs.

"I'll stand guard outside while she gets ready," Espinosa said.

Foley sent Edward a text.

Leaving hermosillo too hot.

Alana descended the stairs ten minutes later carrying a black nylon suitcase and a beige tote bag slung over her shoulder. Foley grabbed the larger bag.

"Forgot something." She bounded upstairs and returned with an overstuffed manila envelope. "I keep all my records electronically, but I'd been keeping these in the house."

Foley took the envelope from Alana and stuffed it into the suitcase. Alana walked to the front door, then turned back to look around her home.

"Leftovers of a life I no longer live."

Foley opened the door for Alana and guided her into the backseat of the Town Car. Espinosa put Alana's bags in the trunk and slid behind the wheel. Edward sat in back with Alana. Espinosa drew his gun, then handed Foley the pistol he'd snatched from the young toughs at the gate.

"Duck down," Foley said to Alana. She crammed herself into the footwell. Foley covered her with his jacket and laid his backpack on top of her.

Espinosa idled toward the exit until the gate was visible, then stopped. Four men now stood outside. The new guard brandished a rifle. Espinosa grabbed two more pistols from the glove box and passed one back to Foley.

Foley popped the magazine out of the snatched pistol. Eight rounds loaded. He snapped it back in and readied the second gun Espinosa gave him. Espinosa held his Pico in his left hand, rested in his lap, and steered with his right. Foley put on mirrored sunglasses.

They drove to within a few meters of the gate and it opened. Foley kept his head facing directly forward but swept his eyes from side to side. The man with the rifle—older than the others—eyed Espinosa first, then Foley. He lowered the barrel of the rifle in front of the car. Espinosa stopped and kept his right hand on the wheel and his left on the Pico. Foley shoved his two pistols under his right thigh.

The rifle-toting man walked to Foley's window and spoke to him in angry, rapid-fire Spanish. Foley opened the window a crack.

"No comprendo Español. *"* He pointed at Espinosa.

The man shifted to the driver's window. Espinosa rolled it down about an inch. "What do you want?"

He gestured toward the men they'd encountered on the way in. "You beat up my *amigos*. What was your business here?"

"We came to say good-bye to a friend. Ask your people down the street if we disturbed anyone or anything."

The man with the rifle glowered at Espinosa, then pulled a phone from his shirt pocket and tapped a number. He spoke a few words, and with it still to his ear said, *"Puede pasar."*

Espinosa closed both windows and sped away.

After they'd motored two blocks, Foley pulled his jacket off Alana. Then the back window exploded.

Glass pebbles showered Foley and Alana. The car lunged forward and gained speed. "What's the fastest way to the highway from here?"

"Stay on Morales-Peña Road," Alana said. "We're two minutes away."

Chapter 17

Hancock Park, Los Angeles
8:38 p.m.

Edward had missed a text from Foley.

> Leaving hermosillo too hot.

Cold dampness lashed his face and slithered down his body. He called back and got voice mail.

"It's Ed. Everyone all right?"

He hung up and hung his head.

◆ ◆ ◆

Federal Highway 15, Sonora, México
10:08 p.m. MST

Foley's phone woke up, and a voice mail from Edward arrived. He returned the call.

"What happened?" Edward asked.

"Ran into resistance at Alana's place. Had to disarm three drug soldiers-in-training at the gate. Alana told us she had new neighbors who were drug dealers, so we had her grab her essentials and got her out of there. The drug guys brought in reinforcement. They let us out the gate, then shot out our back window after we drove away."

"Where are you now?"

"On our way to Obregón City."

"Do you have help?"

"Half dozen of Espinosa's guys are driving in from Durango. Should get there early tomorrow morning."

"Give the phone to Alana."

A few seconds passed. *"Hola,* Eduardo. *"*

"Thank God you're safe. Have you talked with Pato today?"

"I was on the phone with Carlos when I heard trouble. Pato said men were approaching the house. No word since."

"I have a high-level meeting on Friday to ask for help from our government to get you and Carlos out of there."

"Gracias, Eduardo. I'm so . . . I don't know what I could do to help Carlos."

His pulse quickened. *Keep control.* "I'm glad you reached out. Have you told Carlos about me yet?"

"I fear something horrible has happened to all of them."

So do I. "Carlos is resourceful. Hold on to hope."

◆ ◆ ◆

Foley let ten minutes pass after their talk with Edward.

"Señora . . . what do you know about what Carlos found?"

"Please, Señor Foley. Not now." Alana massaged her brow.

He reached out and touched her arm. "Ed's right. Carlos is a survivor."

Alana pressed her lips together and looked straight ahead. "Money launderers avoid patterns." She mouthed the beginning of a word, then looked down.

"This is hard. But I need to understand why Carlos was willing to risk his life to expose what he saw."

Alana nodded. "From what he said, ALEXA got sloppy. He found deposits and payments between three offshore entities and ALEXA every week for more than a year."

"Is that so unusual for a multinational corporation?"

"One of them is their gaming subsidiary in the Dominican Republic. The other two are corporations in Madagascar and Nigeria. The money was paid direct. Usually people with something to hide flow their funds through countries that have banking privacy laws, like Switzerland or the Cayman Islands."

"Sounds like tax strategy. Mexico has some of the highest corporate rates in the world."

"ALEXA has no operations or suppliers in Madagascar or Nigeria."

Foley turned toward her. "Does that matter?"

"I'm no expert, but it's unusual."

"What else did he find?"

"Payments to government officials in Mexico and the US."

"Bribery?"

"What do you think?"

Foley nodded deliberately. "How large?"

"I don't know."

Foley grimaced, then looked her in the eyes. He didn't want to ask the next question, but he needed to. "You're sure Carlos has the data he downloaded in his possession?"

Alana crossed her arms. "He said he did." She looked away. "Why do you question?"

"In my business I don't presume anything."

Chapter 18

Ciudad Obregón, México
11:16 p.m. MST

Foley and Alana waited in the car while Espinosa surveyed the surroundings. Espinosa returned and signaled them out. Foley scanned Pato Lamport's block. A mix of old beaters and newer cars and pickup trucks populated the dusty asphalt street. A third of the lots were empty. The air was quiet. Light glowed through draped windows of three houses. The rest were dark.

Foley stepped through a black iron gate, Alana a pace behind. They crossed a short walkway onto a small concrete porch. Espinosa stood guard at the edge of the street.

No doorbell button. Foley knocked.

No answer.

He knocked again. Still no answer. He waved Espinosa over.

"I'll take Alana and check the right side. You go left and we meet in back."

The windows were wide and shallow and dressed with drapes inside and iron bars outside. Foley felt for his flashlight but kept it in his pocket. They trod lightly to the rear of the house. Alana gripped Foley's arm as they turned the corner. Dim light radiated through drapes covering a rear window wider and taller than those on the side of the house. Likely the master bedroom.

Espinosa turned the corner on the other side. He'd drawn a pistol. "Looks deserted."

"We need to get in," Foley said.

"Leave that to me," Espinosa said. "I have tools in the trunk." He tiptoed down the side of the house to the street.

Foley turned to Alana. "What did you hear when you were on the phone with Carlos?"

"Pato yelled to hide. Didn't say where. Then I heard bumps and slams and shouts. Couldn't make out the words. Then the line went dead."

Espinosa returned with a black bag about two feet long. The three of them moved across dirt to a small concrete patio situated midway along the back of the house. An iron gate covered a sliding glass door-wall. Espinosa made quick work of picking the locks in both and led the way in, holding his pistol in front of him with both hands. Foley handed Alana one of the guns Espinosa had given him.

"I don't know how to use this," Alana whispered, her voice shaky.

Foley took the gun and checked that the safety was off. "If you need to shoot anyone, aim low. Keep it pointed down in the meantime."

Alana shuddered. "You keep it."

"Take it," Foley said. He handed it back to her, barrel down. She took it in both hands and kept it pointed at the floor as he'd instructed. "Keep your fingers off the trigger until . . ."

The kitchen and table were clean. Sink empty, cabinets and drawers closed. Espinosa led the way into the living room. Small pillows rested against each arm of a three-cushion sofa. Two armchairs sat opposite. A small coffee table between the sofa and chairs had a small crocheted doily and a small vase with flowers. Silk. Nothing disturbed. Their exit had been orderly.

Espinosa turned into a narrow hall lined with family photographs. A closed door at the left end. Dim light peeked out the bottom.

Same room they'd seen from the outside.

Espinosa opened the door, pistol trained forward. Foley followed. A double bed occupied the center of the room, and a small dresser sat against the wall opposite the foot of the bed. A pair of sliding wood doors to the right indicated a closet. A laptop computer, closed and powered off, sat atop a small desk. Foley slid the closet door open. Dresses, blouses, and pants hung neatly. The other side held Pato's clothes, also neat and organized.

They moved to the room across the hall. Only a double bed and small dresser in there. Foley slid open the closet door. The top of the hanging rod bracket hung loose on the wall. He spotted an attic cutout in the closet ceiling. "Omar, grab me a chair."

Foley stood on the chair and turned his flashlight on. The top shelf was dusty. A faint handprint had displaced some of the dust underneath the attic opening. He pushed the board covering the opening out of the way, poked his head through, and swept his flashlight and his gaze around the dark, grimy space. The joists were evenly covered with dust except for a spot next to one of the roof trusses. Someone or something had been there.

Foley climbed down and brushed off. "Where's Omar?"

"Checking the computer."

They stepped to the other bedroom. Espinoza hunched over the laptop. "Internet's off. No browser history. E-mail inbox and sent folder empty. Nothing saved in the last three days."

Foley put his hands on his hips and stared at the floor. "Carlos was in that attic." He pivoted to Alana, who stood at the doorway.

"Can you please take this thing back?" she said.

Foley took the pistol and set the safety, then tucked it in his waist-band. "Let's consider the possibilities. If the killers after Carlos were who showed up, they could be anywhere. Or they took Pato and didn't find Carlos in the attic. Which I find hard to believe. Or they all managed to get away." He ran a hand through his hair. "If Carlos escaped," he said to Alana, "where would he go?"

"His friends live either in Mexicali or Hermosillo."

"Any way to reach him?" Espinosa said.

"Only e-mail. No phone."

"Pato?"

Alana threw up her hands. Foley sat on the edge of the bed.

They'd hit a dead end.

◆ ◆ ◆

Hancock Park, Los Angeles
10:41 p.m.

Chief Judge Marrone and the court executive had been gracious and understanding about Edward's family situation.

What he'd shared, anyway.

All of his current cases except the Prop. 68 decision were now assigned to either a district or a magistrate judge. Edward's clerks would stay with the cases on his docket.

He reached for his coffee. His ringing cell phone stopped him. Call from Foley.

"What do you have?"

"Carlos has disappeared. Pato and Marta, too. Don't know if they left on their own or were captured. Someone had been in the attic. Had to have been Carlos."

Edward's chest tightened. Carlos's face, the picture Alana had shown him, flashed into his mind and then faded to black. "What now?"

"Carlos gave Alana an e-mail address yesterday. We've sent him messages. No response yet."

If Carlos's pursuers had caught up with him, he and Pato and Marta could be anywhere. Finding them would take more resources than Conrad Beverley had charge over.

"How's Alana?"

"How you'd expect." A pause. "She has a current passport. I want to bring her to LA."

"Is that what she wants?"

"Not at the moment. But if we move fast we can keep her from being the next victim."

Chapter 19

Edward paced through the Main Street lobby of the courthouse and spotted McCormack waiting for him outside the US Marshals Command Center. "I need your video conference room to call the secretary of Homeland Security."

"It's in use, Your Honor. The boss is meeting with Arlington."

Edward checked his watch. "Can we wait inside?"

McCormack unlocked the command center door and escorted Edward to an empty meeting room. "Why DHS?"

"I'll get to that. Anything new from Novack?"

"He believes the Las Reconquistas thing is under control. FBI and HSI have questioned local leaders of the organization and they're convinced the guy acted alone. They have close watch on the group in LA and in New Mexico."

"What about Artúro Mondragón?"

"We're monitoring voice traffic to and from Mexico. Nothing yet."

Edward crossed his arms and paced. The death threats were stealing mental cycles he needed for more important matters. Jacqui, too, seemed more concerned with Alana's reentry into his life than with the threats. Perhaps she felt secure enough with the round-the-clock protection.

"When will the room be available?"

"Nine."

Edward checked his watch again: 11:50 in Washington. He dialed Conrad Beverley's private cell, got voice mail, and left an urgent message. Also sent a text.

"Carlos is missing. So are my cousin and his wife."

"That's why the call to Beverley?"

"In part. I sent my PI down there. He and a Mexican associate are with Alana now. Foley's going to fly her to LA today." Edward sat. "Beverley's coming to California tonight for the grand opening of that International Trade Center on the border. Secretary of State Carlisle is traveling with him. We're going there tonight."

"D.C. is off?"

"They'll all be in Calexico, so I got us invited to the event."

McCormack stood and slid his hands into his pockets. "I have an idea about your son."

Edward widened his eyes. "I'm listening."

"The marshals have lead responsibility for tracking and extraditing fugitives in foreign countries. We may be able to use our mandate to track down Carlos."

"Who would approve it?"

"Marshal Hunter has authority. I can arrange a meeting."

"Good. We need to leave for Calexico by noon."

McCormack checked Marshal Hunter's online calendar. His shoulders slumped. "He's booked."

"Keep after it."

Beverley called back.

"Are you somewhere you can access secure video teleconference?"

"I'm in my office."

"May I call you in about ten minutes? It's about my family issue. The game's changed."

"Can this keep until tomorrow?"

"Lives are at stake, Mr. Secretary."

A pause. "Call me in fifteen."

◆ ◆ ◆

McCormack fired up the federal government secure video conference system and entered Beverley's connect information. "Ready to go, Your Honor."

Beverley's face appeared on screen.

"Appreciate you making room for me, Mr. Secretary," Edward said.

"Cut the formality, Lamport. You said lives were at stake."

"My son's in Mexico and he's gone missing. I need to get him into the US now and get him asylum."

Beverley twisted his expression. "Why would your son need asylum?"

Edward kept his face steady. "He's not an American citizen."

"What are you talking about?"

He shared the story of Alana and how their relationship had ended. "Alana reached out to me three days ago. My son discovered evidence that the bank he works for is orchestrating an international money-laundering scheme. The perpetrators want him dead."

Beverley's gaze remained fixed on Edward. "Quite a story, Judge Lamport." He slid his chair back. Silence hung for ten seconds. "You have proof he's your son?"

Proof? Only the truth Alana and I know. "If you mean official documents, his Mexican birth certificate would show he's the son of Guillermo Alvarez."

"So what do you want?"

Edward matched Beverley's intense gaze. "Arrange passage for my son into the United States. Put him in detention if you must. I've got to get him out of Mexico. Now. There's reason to believe government officials are involved in what he's uncovered."

Beverley tilted his head and flashed a condescending smile. "Mexican bureaucrats?"

Edward kept quiet on American involvement. For now.

"Head of the banking commission."

Beverley smirked. "Nothing new there. What else?"

"Alana is traveling to Los Angeles tomorrow and will apply for asylum. I'm asking you to fast-track it for her. And for my son when he gets here."

Beverley narrowed his eyes. Edward kept his shoulders back and his chin up. His next argument for why Beverley should help him was cued and ready.

He hoped he wouldn't need to use it.

Beverley said, "On the surface, what you want is a no-brainer." He laid a hand behind his neck. "But this town has become so blasted predatory. People have lost cabinet jobs and congressional seats for not vetting their housekeepers. Doesn't matter which side of the aisle you're on. The naysayers and obstructionists are ravenous for specks of dirt they can use to embarrass you or force you out." Beverley swiveled his chair to his left and looked out his window. "Sometimes I regret my ambitions, you know?"

Edward knew, all right. Men and women of purpose and zeal answer the call to public service with noble ideals and goals to change things for the better and soon get tamped into molds shaped by ambition and oppositional politics, as if those were impersonal and unstoppable forces rather than attitudes they could influence.

Beverley turned to face the camera. "I'd need to tell the president."

"So he wouldn't be blindsided if it were ever leaked."

Beverley nodded. "Who else have you told?"

"The Marshals Service is seeking approval to get involved."

Beverley reached to his right for a tablet. He tapped a few times, then picked up the handset on his desk phone. "I need CIS and Customs and Border Protection to weigh in."

Edward sat forward. "Before you call, you need to know I met with Ramon Ortiz here in Los Angeles yesterday. He said CIS can't help. Made it sound like relations between the US and Mexico are in the toilet. Is it true Mexico has threatened to close our consulates?"

Beverley's upper lip curled. "Too many competing voices. Hard to see a way it straightens out."

"Ortiz was right?"

"He's a loyal soldier. My predecessor put him in his job. Not a risk taker. Exactly what I need from people in his role."

"I'd gathered as much." Edward shifted in his chair. "Can you help me?"

"Need to figure out how we pull it off. Got to reach out to other departments."

"Can you broker a meeting with Carlisle and us in Calexico?"

Beverley rubbed his chin, then leaned in. "I have too much respect for you and your position to jerk you around." He paused. "This is one of those deals that could blow up real easy. Picture it. We do this in the dark. Then some whistle-blower with an ax to grind finds out and puts it on WikiLeaks. It'll burn up the web and cable nets for weeks, and the immigration hawks will have a royal field day. The last thing I want to do is embarrass the president."

"Are you telling me that the Department of Homeland Security doesn't undertake covert operations to achieve its objectives?" A prickly warmth crept up the back of Edward's neck. "Is my son's life not worth your bother?"

Beverley shook his head. "I'm telling you others are better equipped to handle this sort of thing than we are."

"CIA?"

"Someone who does black ops for a living. Not necessarily CIA."

"What about Carlisle?"

"I'll see what I can do. Good day, Judge Lamport." The screen went dark.

Not a washout. Not a success.

Had he gone to the right man? Had he exposed himself to people who'd throw him under the bus in a heartbeat if it would benefit them?

Chapter 20

The atmosphere in Vicente Salvatierra's conference room in the Mex-3 building shifted from relaxed camaraderie to tense silence. His American counterpart, Stanley Gleason, was about to meet Salvatierra's elite security detail for the first time.

The two dozen six-foot-something muscular men were dressed in crisp long-sleeved tan shirts and olive twill slacks. Salvatierra had equipped them each with a Beretta PX4 pistol, and their side holster belts carried three ten-round magazines.

Salvatierra rapped his knuckles on the conference table. Chatter faded to silence as the uniformed men took seats.

"Gentlemen, tomorrow is a big day for all of us. I want to introduce Señor Stanley Gleason to you. With his cooperation, we built what I will show you in the next hour—a feature of this complex no one else will know exists. It's the most sophisticated system of its kind ever built." Salvatierra scanned the eyes of his charges. "I chose each of you for your skill, strength, and courage. Your mission will be to guard this feature from prying eyes and soon-to-be jealous competitors."

He moved to an easel and uncovered a large display board that had been draped with a black cloth. Two logos, side by side, were on the board. "These companies have completed the setup of their electric-vehicle-battery assembly lines in the International Trade Center. They start test production in a week."

He held up a gray plastic rectangular object, eight by three by three-quarter inches. "This is an EV battery module. It holds twelve lithium-ion cells, each a little larger than a AA battery. Every electric car that gets produced in the United States for at least the next ten years will have battery packs made of these modules. This one's made by GK Electronics of South Korea, housed in this building, Mex-Three." He held up a similarly sized black module. "Here's another, with a little different case design, made by EVTechnical, an American company. They're in the Cal-Three building on the US side."

Salvatierra set the two module housings on the table and from his jacket pocket pulled a slender six-inch metal rod with a twelve-point spline cut into one end. He inserted the spline end of the rod into a hole in one of the battery cases, pushed it in, and turned it counterclockwise, which loosed a rectangular latch. He did the same with the other casing, then removed the top cover from both and pulled a battery cell out of each module. He placed the blunt end of the rod on the positive terminal of one of the cells and pushed down, and the terminal popped up. He repeated the operation on the other cell. Then he lifted both cells and turned them upside down. The terminal tops fell off and fine white powder poured out of each cell.

"That, gentlemen, is influence. Pure, white influence."

The security agents remained stoic.

"On the afternoon of February 26, Señor Gleason will begin shipments of what, to the American customs officers, will look like electric car batteries destined for automobile factories in California,

Tennessee, and Alabama. But they will, in fact, be what I've shown you here. Filled with cocaine and methamphetamine destined for markets throughout the United States. We will now show you how this will be accomplished."

Salvatierra motioned to an assistant to clean the powders from the table. "Dump it into a plastic bag and throw it into the trash chute. Make sure it's well sealed." The assistant gave him a look of disbelief. "It's powdered sugar and cornstarch." A few of the guards laughed nervously. "Follow me. We'll take the stairs."

Salvatierra and Gleason led the parade of guards down eight flights to the lowest level of the Mex-3 building's parking garage. They walked across the empty parking area and through a door marked with a sign that read "DANGER HIGH VOLTAGE AUTHORIZED PERSONNEL ONLY" in Spanish and English. The door opened to reveal a neatly arranged network of galvanized steel conduits ranging from one to six inches in diameter, all connected to a wall of gray metal circuit breaker panels.

"This is the electrical wiring closet for Mex-Three," Salvatierra said. "Look carefully at the ceiling, walls, conduits, breaker panels, and floor. Tell me if you see anything that looks unusual or out of place."

The two dozen guards combed the room. They examined the surfaces of the walls, floor, and ceiling. They inspected every conduit, every electrical panel, every wall and corner.

"Everything looks in order, *señor*," one of the guards said.

"Our engineers designed an efficient layout, and our contractor built it with outstanding fit and finish. Would you agree?"

Heads nodded around the room.

"Gentlemen, it is, as my American friend would say, showtime."

Salvatierra reached into his pocket and pulled out a small black metal device that resembled an electronic key fob for a car. He opened the centermost electrical panel and attached the device to the third breaker switch from the bottom. He opened the top of the device, which exposed a clear LED and a camera lens similar to that of a smartphone. He crouched and positioned his right eye in front of the lens and pushed a small button on its top edge. The LED pulsed twice in less than a second.

The eight-foot-wide wall opposite the doorway to the wiring closet moved back, at a rate of about two centimeters per second. Wire conduits attached to the wall and securely fastened to the circuit breaker panels slid smoothly away, revealing pipes of smaller diameter. Fifteen seconds later, a hallway appeared. The wall continued to move for another minute and a half, then stopped. The opened wall revealed a two-meter-wide, six-meter-long hallway with a vault door at the far end. Salvatierra retrieved the electronic device, closed the breaker panel, and entered the hallway. Gleason and the guards followed.

Salvatierra pulled a second device out of his pocket, this one encased in brushed aluminum. He opened the back of the device and pulled out a hinged connector, then inserted the connector into a slot in the massive stainless-steel door. He opened the front of the fob. Inside was the same LED/lens configuration as on the previous device. Salvatierra scanned his eye, and solenoid switches activated and electric motors whirred. The door opened outward, revealing a concrete pipe two meters in diameter. Two metal rails half a meter apart ran along the bottom.

Salvatierra turned to face the group. "Say hello to *la cloaca*. The sewer."

"Señor Salvatierra," one of the guards said, "this is a tunnel."

"*Exactamente.* But we will not call it that. To anyone. Understood?"

Heads nodded all around.

"*La cloaca* runs underneath the border to the Cal-Three building, where Señor Gleason's crew has built the same access and security setup. We can move a load of high-density cargo from one building to the other in fifteen minutes. This transport system is ninety-nine percent vibration-free, less than the resonant frequency coming from the overall ITC complex, making it undetectable by the underground sensors installed by the US government. The battery housings will be filled at Señor Gleason's manufacturing facility in San Luis and shipped through this tunnel for distribution to American markets. As I said upstairs, to the US customs officers these will appear to be batteries assembled by GK Electronics."

Salvatierra invited the guards one by one to have an up-close look at the pipe. Gleason tapped Salvatierra on the shoulder and pulled him aside. "I'm keeping this under wraps on my side until after the grand opening," Gleason said. "I still think you jumped the gun. This place is going to be crawling with people whose business is being nosy."

"There is a great difference between you and me, Señor Gleason. I hire people who have proven their trustworthiness *before* they come to work for me."

"Don't be so sure of yourself, Vicente."

Chapter 21

Edward needed to put the Prop. 68 decision to bed. Not because of Cecilia Gallegos, but because it was time. He'd sifted and sorted all the blocks of gray served up by both sides. He'd whirled them through his legal centrifuge until the black and white had separated. The proponents of Prop. 68 had managed to convince a slim majority of California citizens to pass a law that obligated all Californians.

He didn't like it. Voted against it.

Yet he could not conclude it was unconstitutional.

But Prop. 68 had given him a rare opportunity. He wanted judges out of the lawmaking business. He would set an example.

Judges were the referees, not the players. A small handful of people shouldn't even have standing to bring lawsuits whose decisions have such broad social impact.

The only justification Edward had to strike down Proposition 68 was that he didn't like it. It offended his Irish-Mexican sensibilities.

Not good enough. Not even close.

Why should one man's opinion change the course of the nation?

There was no timetable he *had* to satisfy, but the moment was fleeting. He couldn't walk away from the opportunity to couple the announcement of his ruling with his personal denouncement of prior court decisions. The spotlight would never be brighter than now. He had to seize the moment. He had to do *something* to make his point.

An idea came.

He'd used the media strategically to advance his cause as a prosecutor. Nine times out of ten, it had worked. Starting this evening he would be in a place crawling with reporters, many of whom he was acquainted with from his deputy DA and US Attorney days.

Of all the journalists who'd interviewed him, one stood out as a possible ally. And given his proclivity for controversy, surely he'd be in Calexico for Gleason's big party.

Chapter 22

Foley's charter flight to Los Angeles would depart in forty-eight minutes. He and Alana pushed to get through customs in enough time to avoid delaying the flight and complicating matters with air traffic control.

A sign posted in the general aviation lobby announced that all luggage for flights to the United States must be inspected by US Customs and Border Protection before being released to aircraft. Alana appeared calm, like she was a veteran of this drill.

Foley asked, "How often have you traveled to the States?"

"To Hawaii twice, San Antonio and Houston once each."

"Los Angeles?"

Her mouth turned downward. "No, *señor*. On purpose."

Ten minutes passed, and then it was their turn in line. Foley gestured for Alana to go first. She handed her passport to a thirty-something male attendant with jet-black hair and a megawatt smile. He tapped keys and then held Alana's passport under a reader. The attendant's smile turned to a frown. He scanned her passport again.

"I am sorry, Señora Alvarez, but there is a problem with your passport. I cannot release you to the boarding gate. You will need to go to the US Customs and Border Protection office at the end of the concourse." He extended his hand to his left. "The sign is over the door."

Alana's expression turned angry. "My passport does not expire for another three years," she said sharply. "I visited the USA two months ago."

The young man's bright smile returned. "I understand, *señora*, but the system is preventing me from clearing you. I'm sure everything will be fine once you go through the secondary customs check."

The attendant handed Alana's passport back to her. *"Señor?"*

Alana nodded at Foley. He gave the attendant his passport and charter manifest. "One bag today?"

Foley placed his bag next to the lectern. The attendant tagged it and returned Foley's documents. "Your gate is to my right, *señor*. Have a pleasant flight home."

"Wait," Foley said. "I'll keep my bag until we get Señora Alvarez's passport cleared." He put his hand on Alana's back and guided her toward the CBP office.

Alana raised her chin. "I was in San Antonio two months ago. Everything was fine."

Foley offered his arm to Alana, and she slipped her hand into the crook of his elbow. She relaxed a bit.

"Any irregularities or run-ins with the law?"

Alana stopped and yanked on Foley's arm. "Absolutely not. Nor anyone who traveled with me."

"Who were you with?"

"Two coworkers. We attended a conference on US-Mexico bank transfers."

Foley smiled. "Must have been a rip-roaring event."

Alana slapped his arm playfully and strode toward the customs office. Foley stayed a step behind as they entered.

A blocky US Customs and Border Protection agent greeted her. She handed the agent her Mexican passport. "The services attendant said he couldn't clear me and to come here."

"This will take a minute or two." The agent scanned her passport. His gaze remained on his monitor for several seconds. The reflection of the screen in the agent's glasses changed. He tapped several keys and shook his head. "I regret to inform you, Señora Alvarez, that you are denied entry into the United States. The Department of Homeland Security has categorized you as inadmissible. I'm very sorry." He handed her passport back.

The blood drained from her face. Her mouth was agape. "I . . . I don't understand. What's the reason?"

The agent tapped a few more keys. "Your record shows you overstayed your visa two months ago."

"That's impossible. I was in San Antonio on business for four days and three nights." She handed him her passport. "Look at the visa stamps."

The agent thumbed through the back pages of her passport and nodded. "I see, right here." He tapped his index finger on the customs stamps from San Antonio International Airport and the Mexico re-entry stamp from Hermosillo Ignacio P. Garcia Airport. He typed a few words, then pointed to his screen. "Your employer is on an illegal commerce watch list."

Alana remained steady. Foley touched her arm and cocked his head toward the door. "Thank you, *señor*," she said. "I will take this up with the Mexican consulate."

The agent nodded and wrote something on a notepad, then handed Alana her passport. Foley led her to a quiet corner of the lobby.

"I'm not surprised Bancomex is being watched," Foley said. "That mistake in your visa record is too coincidental, though. Can you think of any reason someone in the US government would single you out?"

"No. But if Bancomex—" She lowered her voice. "If Bancomex is laundering money, they may have corrupted people with influence."

"Or they're watching one of the people you went to San Antonio with and you're tagged by association."

Alana closed her eyes. "Or Bancomex provided false information to someone they've bought and paid for in your Homeland Security."

Foley checked his watch. "Need to call Ed."

◆ ◆ ◆

Edward's phone interrupted his writing flow.

"Alana and I are at the airport," Foley said. "Customs won't let her board. She's been tagged inadmissible."

As much as he'd tried to avoid negative thoughts, Edward wasn't surprised. "Reason?"

"DHS has Bancomex on watch. And a mistake in her visa record. The stamps on her passport prove the error, but the agent couldn't override it."

Could Beverley be responsible for this? Or did Bancomex own someone in DHS? *So this is how it feels to be a conspiracy theorist.*

"I'll press Beverley. Things don't just happen. If someone in his operation is dirty, then he should be able to override it. What's next?"

"We'll talk it over and get back to you."

It wasn't far-fetched that Bancomex or ALEXA had compromised someone inside DHS.

But friendly fire? Could Beverley have orchestrated it? Were the politics with Mexico so bad his own government would betray him to make a point? If Beverley had anything to do with Alana's predicament, Edward would make sure he lived to regret it.

He flipped his pen onto his desk.

Plan B . . . he needed a fallback. He couldn't put all his chips on two cabinet secretaries. Senator Mitchell Corman would be there, too. Connection with the chairman of the Judiciary Committee had to count for something.

And McCormack's offer was no accident. The FBI might have more resources, but the US Marshals protected federal judges. As far as he was concerned, that extended to his family.

Their citizenship notwithstanding.

Then again . . . a plan C. If Mexico and the United States were hurtling toward confrontation he needed to be ready with his own rescue operation.

It wouldn't be unprecedented.

◆ ◆ ◆

"You go to Los Angeles," Alana said. "Espinosa and I will find Carlos."

Foley grimaced. "Edward needs someone he trusts to be on point."

"Understand." She looked down for a moment. "We go to Guadalajara. I cannot believe all Bancomex executives are corrupt."

"We can't assume anything. I'll ask Espinosa what he thinks."

Foley called him. "Need you back here. They won't accept Alana's passport. I'm staying. We need a home base."

A pause on the line. "I don't know anyone in Obregón. My *hombres* are in town now. I'll ask if they do."

Foley scanned his surroundings for suspicious characters. Clear, as far as he could discern. "Are they well armed?"

"With eight of us we should be able to keep Alana safe. Unless they send a squadron."

They couldn't assume anything.

Chapter 23

La Junta, Chihuahua, México
12:32 p.m. MST

Carlos pounded his frustration into the steering wheel of his stolen truck. The Toyota Tacoma pickup had kept him mobile and out of sight of the *matóns*. Until now. Blue smoke billowed from under the hood. The temperature gauge needle licked the *H*. The engine knocked and lost power every second.

At least he'd made it to a town he could actually find on a map.

He idled the limping truck off Highway 16 onto a side street and into the parking lot of a fried chicken restaurant.

He wondered where Pato and Marta were. It still amazed him that Pato'd had the foresight to change the license plates on this truck. He'd spent the last of his cash to get this far and he didn't dare use his debit card or go to another ATM for more. He'd already left too many bread crumbs on his trail.

Carlos had seen enough to know Pato was smart and mentally tough. He'd enjoyed Pato's stories about working with his grandfather.

He wasn't forthcoming about why they'd had a falling-out. The great sadness in Pato's eyes as he recalled the past had stayed with Carlos.

La Junta was a big enough town to have an American franchise restaurant, so it probably had decent cellular and Internet service. And, hopefully, someone kind enough to let him borrow their phone so he could send his mother a text or e-mail.

Or call her, if they were kind *and* generous.

He slipped out of the overheated truck and smoothed his hair as best he could. He stank of body odor and burnt oil. His rumpled shirt was caked with dust and soaked with sweat.

He strode into the restaurant, chest out and head high. His insides churned like white water. *What am I doing here?*

The smell of *pollo frito* made his mouth water. But communication with Mamá was way more important than food. He made his way to the counter. A round, middle-aged woman asked what he wanted to order.

"I'm not here to eat, *señora*. My truck has broken down. May I borrow your phone to call for help?"

The woman wrinkled her nose and eyed him up and down. *"Un momento."* She waddled through a swinging door into the kitchen.

He turned and scanned the small dining room. Four graying, over-weight men sat at two tables butted together, working through a bucket of chicken and a plate of biscuits.

"I'm sorry, *muchacho*," the woman at the counter said.

Carlos turned and faced her.

"Customers are not allowed in the back of the restaurant."

"Please, *señora*. One quick phone call."

A younger man emerged through the kitchen doorway. "I don't want trouble in my restaurant. Be on your way."

"I'll not be trouble—"

"Look at you, *vagante*. Leave my restaurant. Now!"

Carlos bowed his head. *"Gracias, señor."*

Carlos turned and headed for the door. One of the men stood and took scraps and well-used napkins to a trash receptacle. Carlos followed him.

"Excuse me, *señor*, do you have a cell phone I could borrow to make a call for help?"

The man eyed him up and down. His face wrinkled at Carlos's stench. "Sorry, I do not." The man looked out the window at the truck, then back at him. "Where you from, *muchacho*?"

"I'd rather not say. Any of your friends have one?"

The man shook his head. "Few in this town. We are not very advanced here."

Great.

Where could he go? "Is there a public library?"

One of the man's friends shuffled toward Carlos. "In Ciudad Cuauhtémoc. Fifty kilometers east."

Carlos rammed his hands into his pockets and stared out the window at his truck. "So where *can* I get some help?"

The first man shrugged. "You have money?"

Carlos shook his head. "Anyplace to make a free phone call or send an e-mail?"

"Free phone call?" the second man said. "There's the police station."

The other men laughed. "Yeah, go get yourself arrested, *muchacho*. They'll let you call someone to bail you out. Maybe."

All four men howled. At him.

Carlos wasn't amused. "Where is it?"

The first man looked at him, mouth agape. "We were just messing with you, *hombre*."

Carlos crossed his arms. "Where is the police station?"

The four men traded looks with one another. One pointed out the window. "Walk ten blocks that way and turn right. Go five more blocks."

"Muchas gracias, señores." Carlos bolted out the door in the direction he'd been told.

◆ ◆ ◆

To his surprise, the police station was right where the men at the restaurant had said.

The station occupied half of a building that also housed other city government offices. Carlos relaxed his shoulders and stepped to a messy desk manned by a graying policeman with a weathered face. "May I help you?"

"My truck is broken down. It's in the parking lot of the chicken restaurant on the other end of town. May I use your phone?"

The desk officer looked him over as he rolled a pencil around his fingers. "Let me see your identification, *muchacho*."

Of course a policeman would want his identification. He fished out his wallet and handed the officer his Baja, California, driver's license.

"You're a long way from home. What are you doing here?"

"Running away."

"From what? Or is it who?"

Trust in the truth. "Someone wants to kill me."

"I see." The officer stood. "Wait right here." He disappeared down a hallway to his left.

Was it possible Bancomex's killers had connections here, too? Javier Bernal's money knew no boundaries.

Money.

Between his mother and the American who had come to Hermosillo, he might be able to offer these small-town policemen enough to give him what he wanted.

The officer returned with a taller, younger man in uniform. "This is our *capitán*. He wishes to talk with you. Follow, please."

Carlos reminded himself to trust in the truth as he followed them into a small interview room. It was plain and empty like the one at the Border Patrol station. He sat at the end of a rectangular table. The captain remained standing. "Leave us," he told the older officer.

"Who wants to kill you?"

"I work for Bancomex in Mexicali. Our biggest customer is ALEXA, the conglomerate controlled by Vicente Salvatierra."

"I know of Salvatierra."

"I'm convinced Bancomex and ALEXA are laundering drug money. I have partial evidence in my possession, but I need to explain it in detail for it to make sense."

"Are your superiors aware of your discovery?"

"They're in on it. They cut off my system access shortly after I started downloading data. I took what I had and ran. My friend and I jumped the border fence into the US but we were assaulted by a killer and caught by Border Patrol. They sent me back within hours."

The captain's expression was flat.

He doesn't believe me. Guilt and sadness over Gonzalo's death wormed their way up Carlos's throat. He drew a deep breath and swallowed the emotions down.

"When I got off the bus, another *matón* was there waiting, but I was able to lose him. I stole a truck and drove away as fast as I could."

Did I say too much? Truth was Carlos's only asset. He had to believe God would bless him for using it. And that he would find people who hated evil as much as he did and weren't lashed to one of Bernal's tentacles.

Which kind of man was this *capitán*?

"*Un chavo* fighting an empire is foolish."

"It didn't stop David."

"Ah, you are a Bible-believing man."

"Someone has to stop them. They spread their poison and make billions. And ruin our country."

The captain took a seat at the opposite end of the table. "I once thought as you do. Why did you come to my station?"

"I need to contact my mother. She's with a man from the United States who came to protect us. He was sent by an American federal judge. This judge will get us into the United States and give us asylum."

"Asylum doesn't promise protection."

The captain was right. Bancomex and ALEXA had people in America working for them. "May I use your phone?"

The captain crossed his arms. "What makes you think I can trust you?"

"Well . . . you trust actions, not words. Will you call for me if I give you the number?"

The captain got up from his chair and stood over Carlos. "And why *should* I help you?"

"I'm sure my mother and the American will compensate you well for trusting me."

"Compensate? You want to bribe me, *joven*?"

"I'm sorry, Captain, I thought—"

"You thought my hand was out, ready to sell you my power? On your feet. Now."

Carlos stood and the captain grabbed his wrists, cuffed him, and dragged him out of the interview room and down a hallway that ended at a steel door with a small rectangular window. The captain held Carlos with one arm while he unlocked the door. He flung the door open and shoved him into a jail cell and slammed its iron-barred gate shut.

Chapter 24

"I, Edward Jorge Lamport, do solemnly swear that I will administer justice without respect to persons, and do equal right to the poor and to the rich, and that I will faithfully and impartially discharge and perform all the duties incumbent upon me as a United States District Judge under the Constitution and laws of the United States. So help me God."

So help me God. If he'd invoked God to help him do his job, then shouldn't he do what God says to do with his life?

Echoes of his swearing-in ceremony reverberated. He'd thought he knew what he was getting into when he'd recited that oath. Twenty years of prosecuting criminals in state and federal courtrooms had shown him what judges did and how they did it.

Hardly.

Nine months in the robe had made it clear the *official* job of a judge had little to do with the *reality* of judging. A government of laws, not men, was an ideal that did not exist.

The last three days had taught him another lesson. When the law hits home, keeping your mind and heart severed is a futile effort.

He scanned the walls of his mahogany-paneled chambers—cocoon?—laden with volumes of United States Code and federal case law. *Do equal right to the poor and to the rich.*

While the likelihood of Carlos's death rose with each passing hour. *Faithfully and impartially discharge . . .*

According to whom?

His inner light dimmed. Were saving Carlos and challenging federal judges mutually exclusive goals?

He couldn't throw away the opportunity. He had to go with his gut.

He punched the intercom and asked Rebecca into his chambers.

"I just followed up with the proofreader—"

"I need you to call the court executive's office and ask for the contact information of Albert Sanchez, the reporter from USANews Network."

Rebecca gave him a puzzled look. "What for?"

"I have a story idea. Give people a close look into how judges do their work. If the executive asks why, tell her that. If she presses, refer her to me."

Rebecca's brows drew together. "I thought we weren't supposed to have direct contact with the media."

"A guideline, not a law."

Rebecca returned with the number, and Edward dialed Sanchez's office. He got voice mail. "This is Judge Edward Lamport, United States Central District Court of Los Angeles. I'm calling to discuss an idea for a story I think you'll be very interested in." He left his office number, then called Rebecca back in and told her how to handle Sanchez when he called back.

He returned to his laptop and the statement he would read in open court after he announced his decision on Prop. 68. The Federal

Judiciary codes of conduct weren't binding. There was no reason not to push the limits.

A knock. Rebecca poked her head around the door. "Mr. Sanchez on hold."

He summoned the pitch he'd practiced to mind and picked up the phone.

"Judge Edward Lamport."

"Albert Sanchez from USANews Network returning your call. Sorry I missed you. I was in a prep meeting."

"Thanks for calling back. I have an idea for a grabber story and I want to give you an exclusive."

A pause. "Is it about Proposition Sixty-Eight?"

"Related."

"You have my attention."

"People see judges as mysterious black boxes, insulated from real life. They have no idea how we conduct our business. So I want to tell my story. The attention on Prop. Sixty-Eight makes the timing right. I think it'll play well. The public deserves an opportunity to hear from a sitting judge, speaking on their level."

He drew a deep breath.

"Thanks for your offer, Your Honor. I'm grateful you would bring me a rare opportunity to interview a federal judge."

"I respect your work. You don't shrink from tough issues or questions. I can't think of anyone else I'd rather handle my story."

"I need to sell this to my editor." Another pause. "Straight up, he'll want something on your Prop. Sixty-Eight decision or your views on immigration reform."

"I want people to see the human side. Know why we work alone. I want them to feel what I feel. Walk in my shoes."

"Why do you want this, Your Honor?"

"The judiciary is expected to conduct itself differently from the other branches of government. Many argue we shouldn't engage in public activity outside our courtrooms. Judicial lockjaw, they call it. I don't buy it. Our independence doesn't absolve us of accountability to the people."

"Sounds admirable." A pause. "My audience wants timely, hard-hitting stories on what's happening in their world and how they're affected. I don't want to waste your time. What you're proposing doesn't fit. I'm sorry."

"Hold on a moment, Mr. Sanchez."

He wanted to give Sanchez what he needed. But he couldn't be reckless.

What's the downside?

"We do the interview right after I announce my Prop. Sixty-Eight ruling."

"You'll have the nation's attention. No guarantees, though."

"All I can ask." *Never ask a question you don't know the answer to.* "You'll be covering the International Trade Center grand opening, correct?"

"Headed there now."

"My wife and I will be there as guests of Stanley Gleason. Could you meet me for a drink tonight at the International Hotel? I'd like to show you something that could be part of the story."

"Let me check my itinerary."

Sanchez was well known for protecting his sources. Edward would let him peek at his post-ruling message.

"How about six thirty?"

"Eight's better."

Sanchez agreed.

"Your Honor, pardon my frankness . . . is it a good idea for you to be there?"

Not another one who thinks judges should be cloistered. "My wife and I will be there to support a friend's big moment."

Quiet on the line.

"I'd hate to see you compromise yourself for no good reason."

Chapter 25

Carlos rolled over on the hard, smelly cot in the dank jail cell. His heart and thoughts wrestled. Another bad judgment had bit him hard. The captain's questions were respectful. Carlos should have returned his respect.

The stench of the rotten cell melded with his own and hurled him to the edge of nausea.

All he could do was ask forgiveness. And mercy.

If he ever got the chance.

The cells to his left and his right were empty. He had no idea what time it was. How long would they keep him here?

The handle on the metal door opposite his cell moved. The door opened a crack. The older officer from the desk pushed it open with his rear and backpedaled into the cell area. He held a small metal tray with a short metal cup and a plate with something on it. The officer brought the tray to a slot in the cell bars. "Take this."

Carlos turned his back to the officer. "Can these come off now?"

The officer took the cuffs off and then slid the tray through the slot in the bars.

A cup of water and some beans and one corn tortilla. Carlos took it. Smelled moldy.

He laid the tray next to the cot.

"What you did with the captain was stupid," the officer said. "He's going to keep you here for a while."

Carlos approached the bars. "I need to ask his forgiveness."

"He's out on patrol."

"Let me give you my mother's phone number and e-mail. Maybe you could convince him to reconsider."

The officer was quiet. He looked Carlos up and down, turned, and walked to the door. His hand grabbed the knob, and then he stopped and pivoted around. "I don't think you're a troublemaker." He shook his head. "He would have let you make your call." The officer pulled a small notepad and pen from his pocket and passed them through the bars. Carlos wrote the information and handed them back.

"The captain should be back in an hour."

◆ ◆ ◆

Ciudad Obregón, México
2:32 p.m. MST

Foley and Alana crammed around a table with Espinosa and his six-man Durango crew in a small taqueria near the Ciudad Obregón limits. The restaurant owners, a young husband-and-wife team, barked orders at each other through smoke rising from their grill as they prepared *tacos al carbon* for the famished bunch.

Foley chugged a full glass of ice water—not the best idea to drink tap. He said to Espinosa's men, "Since none of you know anyone here, there's a hotel on the south end of town. We'll stay there while we figure out what's next."

Alana's face was wrapped in worry. "Pato moved here to get away from the *narcos* . . . after he left, he didn't tell anyone where he'd gone for weeks. Maybe he's—"

The door to the taqueria burst open and shouting filled the cramped dining room. Five men brandishing automatic rifles surrounded their table. The men wore black knit caps and black bandanas around their faces. "Hands on the table or you die! All of you!"

The young woman at the grill screamed and grabbed on to her husband.

"*¡Callate!*" one of the gunmen shouted. Her screaming persisted. He fired a burst of bullets at the two of them. Blood splattered on the walls and sizzled on the grill. Their bodies fell together between the grill and counter.

The gunman who'd shouted first grabbed Alana's hair and dragged her from the table.

"Let go of me!"

He yanked her head back and grabbed one of her arms and pulled it around her back. A second man jammed his rifle into her side. "Weapons on the table!"

Foley made quick eye contact with Espinosa. Foley moved his hand under the table, slowly. Espinosa did likewise.

"Weapons on the table now!" another gunman barked as he swept his rifle at Espinosa's men. The gunmen drew their weapons to firing position and fingered the triggers.

Foley and Espinosa lifted their pistols from their laps and set them on the table.

"Throw them on the floor!" the leader said.

Foley tossed his pistol at the man's feet. Espinosa slid his off the table and it hit the floor and bounced into one of the gunmen's shins.

"Stand up. Over here," the leader said.

Foley shuffled sideways to where the lead gunman had ordered him. Espinosa didn't move.

"You, *gordo*, over here!"

Espinosa remained still. So did his six men.

Four gunmen opened fire. The force of the bullets slammed Espinosa and his men against the wall. Their shredded bodies fell in a heap.

Alana screamed. Foley's knees weakened but he remained stoic. The gunmen dragged them out to a military-style transport truck with canvas sides and shoved them in the back compartment. Three of the five gunmen joined them. Doors slammed at the front and the vehicle lurched forward.

Chapter 26

Calexico, California
7:52 p.m.

Edward and Jacqui strode arm in arm into the marble-clad lobby of the American International Hotel. The horseshoe-shaped lounge where they would meet Sanchez echoed the craggy rock formations in the foothills of the Imperial Valley, accented with rough wood posts and beams.

Edward wore a tan golf shirt, forest-green gabardine slacks, his favorite green Donegal tweed jacket, and oxblood loafers. Jacqui had adorned herself in black slacks, teal blouse, and black flats. They asked to be seated in a secluded corner booth. "We're expecting a guest— Mr. Sanchez. Would you bring him to our table when he arrives?"

"My pleasure, sir."

They ordered cocktails and settled in. Jacqui fidgeted with her blouse, then pulled a mirror from her purse. She held it close to one eye, then the other, then put it away.

"You look beautiful, dear, as always."

Jacqui returned a curt nod. "This is some place. Must be sure they'll have a steady stream of business types rolling through here."

"When it comes to real estate, Gleason knows what he's doing."

He held her hand. She didn't return the grasp. The tension that had flared on the drive down remained. Something was different this time, though, from other conflicts they'd had.

The quiet.

He needed to be patient. It was hard.

"I don't like what you're doing with Sanchez," Jacqui said, looking at something other than him.

"I don't have handlers to set up media interviews. This is normal stuff."

"I sure don't like you doing it in the open like this."

The last thing we need is another fight. "I have nothing to hide."

"People always judge appearances," she said. "You can't give them the opportunity."

He didn't like where this was headed. "Transparency is the whole point. When judges hide behind their robes they invite more criticism, not less. One side of the story gets out and the mob mentality kicks in."

"Mm-hmm. Your mob leader is here."

The hostess arrived at their booth with Albert Sanchez at her side. Edward and Jacqui stood to greet him. Sanchez ordered a San Pellegrino with lime and sat to Edward's right.

"We won't take a lot of your time," Edward said. "Tell me if this will close the deal on the interview." He handed Sanchez a letter-sized envelope. Sanchez pulled out a single sheet of plain paper with a bullet point list printed on it. His eyes grew as he read.

"This is a rant against federal judges," Sanchez said.

"Candid, certainly. Legislators and executives speak out all the time. Time for a judge to lead the debate."

Sanchez shifted his gaze between Edward and Jacqui and the paper. He folded it and slipped it back into the envelope. "I don't do softball."

"Who said I wanted softball?"

A server arrived with Sanchez's beverage. Sanchez took a generous sip, then slid the envelope across the table to Edward. "You're a gutsy guy, Judge Lamport."

Edward kept a steady expression. "You can keep that if you want."

Sanchez folded his hands. "I get the gist. This will play."

"We'll work out the details back in LA," Edward said. They shook hands. "You'll have a front-row gallery seat when I announce my ruling."

Sanchez nodded and slid his chair back. "I have an early start. I'll see myself out."

Jacqui sipped her drink. "Can you trust him?"

"His influence may come in handy after we get Carlos and Alana out of Mexico."

"How so?"

"I just handed him a scoop. He'll want to help us when the time comes."

If the time comes.

Foley hadn't checked in since the morning. Calls Edward had made in the last two hours hadn't been returned.

Not like Foley. At all.

Chapter 27

"Let's wait in the lobby," Edward said.

Jacqui frowned. "You want to intercept the secretaries of State and Homeland Security."

"Want to know when they arrive is all. I have Beverley's cell."

"I'm going upstairs." Jacqui turned and left the lounge.

You've put her through enough. He watched her stroll out of the lounge and turn left for the elevators.

The way she moved still moved him.

He called Foley again. Voice mail. He texted McCormack, who stood guard outside the lounge, to let him know he was leaving. He finished his drink and slid out of the booth.

"You can have another on the house." Stanley Gleason stood about ten feet away. "You and the wife enjoying your stay?"

Had he been there the whole time? "This hotel is spectacular."

"Noticed you had a visitor. You know Albert Sanchez?"

Had he been watching from a distance? Or did he have cameras snooping on his customers? "He's considering a feature story on me."

"Watch out, Judge. He's a troublemaker."

"I'm aware of his reputation."

"Suit yourself. Another drink?"

"Jacqui's waiting upstairs."

Gleason flashed a devilish grin. "Well, then, I don't want to get between you."

Edward didn't appreciate the innuendo.

"Check-in tomorrow morning is at Imperial Ballroom A, first floor. Join us for breakfast next door at eight."

Doesn't he have anything better to do? "Appreciate the hospitality."

"Don't mention it. Your presence here matters."

Edward nodded politely. He wanted to shove him aside instead. He turned and walked toward the exit.

"Don't underestimate yourself. Hey, what was in that envelope you and Sanchez passed back and forth?"

No way could Gleason have known about the envelope unless he had cameras all over the lounge. Better Edward found out now. He had to assume Gleason had them in every public space. Maybe the private ones, too. Could that be one of the terms of the treaty that led to this complex? Or was he just paranoid? Or a twisted voyeur?

He turned to answer. "My talking points for the interview."

Gleason chuckled. "You expect him to serve your agenda?"

"I expect him to do a story people will watch."

◆ ◆ ◆

Undisclosed location near Culiacán, México
9:39 p.m. MST

Zip-tie restraints cut into Foley's wrists. His arms were tied behind his back, and his ankles were strapped to the legs of his chair. He couldn't feel his feet. Alana was somewhere behind him, out of eyeshot. The room reeked of spilled tequila and marijuana. No windows. A single bare light bulb overhead showed it was empty, save its two involuntary occupants.

The gunmen had taken his phone. If Edward had tried to call they'd have his number and could figure out who he was.

"Alana. How you holding up?"

"They want to get Carlos through me. How do you think?"

Foley had never served in the military. In the moment he remembered conversations with a friend who'd fought in Vietnam. About torture he'd endured at the hands of the Vietcong.

Not that their present circumstances bore any resemblance.

It was what his friend shared about "the code."

It wasn't about only giving one's captors your name, rank, and serial number. It was about believing. Believing in your country. In the value of liberty. In the men you fought alongside.

And that you never, ever gave in to the enemy. No matter what.

What about Alana? Would she never, ever give in?

How could he stand in for her so she wouldn't need to face the choice?

"Alana."

No response.

Oh. The room was bugged.

"No more questions," he said.

"*Gracias.*"

Whenever their captors came back he would tell them he knew everything Alana did and more about Carlos. He'd spin a fiction so elaborate they'd be chasing leads for weeks.

That would buy them all what they needed most.

Time.

Chapter 28

Friday, February 19
International Trade Center
10:41 a.m.

Stanley Gleason stood next to the stage his team had set up in the central quadrangle of the ITC campus. He surveyed the gathering of reporters and dignitaries. The world was at his doorstep to witness the debut of his masterpiece.

Javier Bernal and Vicente Salvatierra arrived with their usual entourage. Except for one new face. *"Buenos dias,* Señor Gleason,*"* Bernal said, hand extended.

Gleason gave him a firm shake. "End of a long road, Javier."

"This is Señor Mota. He is the director of our Mexicali division."

Gleason shook Mota's hand. "I didn't know you were bringing a guest."

"Come now, do we have to clear every last detail with you? Mota is a key man in the operation."

The man looked terrified.

"He has proven himself reliable." Bernal put an arm around Mota's shoulders. "There will be no risk of detection with him on the team."

"Good to know. May I have a word with you in private?"

Bernal followed Gleason to a spot behind the stage.

"Zip it up about the sewer. What's your hurry?"

Bernal glowered. "You listen to me and listen well. You would not have this big moment without the doors I've opened for you. I don't care what you think about how I'm handling the sewer."

Gleason drilled his gaze into Bernal. "Stuff your greed in your pockets. My business turned your second-rate bank into a global player. We hold the cards together, Javier. You, me, and Salvatierra. Like it or not."

Gleason hated it. He did, however, like the profits this dysfunctional marriage produced.

He also relished the storehouse of political capital he'd accumulated through his association with White House chief of staff Carl Bender, the president's point man on the ITC project. His enterprise certainly benefited from Bender's the-end-justifies-the-means way of getting things done.

Bernal returned a thin smile. "We should take our places. It would not look well for the master of ceremonies to delay his own event."

Gleason strode up the steps and took his seat on the dais, left of the lectern. Bernal and Salvatierra followed and took seats on the opposite side. Gleason opened the portfolio his PR team had prepared for him and reviewed the run sheet one more time. The stage manager gave him his cue. He stepped to the microphone and called the assembly to their seats.

"Good morning, ladies and gentlemen. Thank you for attending what we believe is an event of historic proportions. Before I begin, I'd like to thank the cities of Calexico, California, and Mexicali, Baja California, for their cooperation with this unprecedented venture." Applause and cheers rose from the laborers who'd built the complex. They were seated on the outer ring of the temporary arena.

"I'd also like to thank our distinguished United States senator Mitchell Corman. His tireless efforts in Washington and Mexico City to forge the borderless labor zone pilot project in California gave birth to the idea that became the International Trade Center." Corman, seated to Gleason's right, stood and waved to the crowd. Media members joined the applause.

"Many have paid a high political price to make this happen. Recent events on both sides of the border have conspired to darken the bright light this complex was envisioned to be." Gleason scanned the crowd. Awkwardness hung heavy in the atmosphere.

"This cross-border initiative is an experiment that, if successful, will spawn more such projects and bring new hope to millions of Americans and Mexicans living in our shared border region." More hearty applause and shouts from the outer ring.

Gleason moved through the rest of his briefing seamlessly, just as he and his PR agency had planned.

"Ladies and gentlemen of the media, I invite you to join us for a tour of the center, followed by lunch in the Cal-One atrium."

He gathered his notes and left the dais.

Albert Sanchez, who had been seated second row center, walked toward him.

Gleason intercepted him halfway between the platform and the entrance to Cal-3. He extended his hand. "Good morning, Mr. Sanchez. I'm grateful a journalist of your stature is here to cover the opening of our little project."

"Hardly little, Mr. Gleason. May I ask a few questions?"

"Shoot."

"What impact will Proposition Sixty-Eight have on the ITC if Judge Lamport upholds it?"

"Absolutely none. Mexican guest workers remain residents of Mexicali."

"But what about illegal immigrants living in the US?"

"I can only speak for my company. All of our employees are in the United States legally."

"Can you say the same for your subcontractors and tenants?"

"We comply with all requirements. Our subcontractors had to do the same. If they weren't clean they couldn't have bid on the work. I can't speak to how our tenants manage their enterprises."

"You're not concerned about appearances? Doesn't the visibility of this place increase scrutiny?"

Gleason wanted to punch Sanchez in the mouth. "The borderless labor zone treaty is specific and is the federal government's responsibility to enforce. Our job was to design and build the center to our tenants' and the government's specifications."

"The US side of the center. What about the Mexican side?"

Gleason grinned. "People don't sneak into Mexico from California." He turned to walk away. "If you want to know about scrutiny," he said, looking over his right shoulder, "talk to the officials here. I need to lead the media tour."

He wanted to play smashmouth with Sanchez, but this game called for finesse and flawless execution. He looked over his left shoulder as he neared the first station of the media tour. Sanchez was about ten feet behind.

Gleason kicked off the first round, then stayed close to the reporters from the *Wall Street Journal*, the *Economist*, and *Forbes*. He also gave special attention to the local television and print journalists. At the scheduled twelve-fifteen break, Gleason excused himself to visit the restroom. He ran into Sanchez in the hallway.

"Something else I can do for you?"

"Your briefing was thorough. One of the best I've attended. My compliments."

"You didn't stalk me to the men's room to give out kudos."

"I have a sensitive question I didn't want to ask in front of the others."

They looked each other in the eye. "Well?" Gleason said.

"I spoke to some of your construction workers."

"So I heard. Using it in your report?"

"Haven't decided." Sanchez pulled out a small black notebook. "One of them said they'd heard rumors about the Mexican side of the project."

I was right. They lied to Rodrigues. "What sort?"

"About unusual construction equipment."

Gleason let out a belly laugh. "I knew you were a con man, but you've stooped to a new low. What would three Mexican laborers know about civil engineering?"

"You tell me."

This guy doesn't know what he thinks he knows. "First I'm hearing about it. I'll ask 'em myself."

"Any comment?"

"I run a tight ship, Mr. Sanchez, but I don't know every minute detail of what my construction crew says or does."

"Fair enough. One more question?"

"I need to use the bathroom."

Sanchez bowed slightly from the waist. "My apologies."

Gleason locked himself in a stall and texted Rodrigues.

Have you found the men Sanchez interviewed?

He left the bathroom and Sanchez wasn't around. He heaved a sigh, then walked toward the next tour stop.

"Mr. Gleason. Over here." Sanchez stood around a corner, sipping an iced tea. "Two more questions."

Gleason glowered at him. "You get one."

Sanchez swept his gaze around the plaza and pointed to the now empty dais. "Your partner from ALEXA S.A., Vicente Salvatierra, did not speak. I find that odd."

"ALEXA is an investor and a subcontractor, not a partner. If you'd done your homework, then you'd know the borderless labor treaty specified *Mexican* financing *and* labor for their side of the project. This event was about the American side. You'll need to talk to Salvatierra and Javier Bernal of Bancomex about their plans."

"But Mexican media were here."

"Ask my PR agency about it."

Sanchez raised an eyebrow. "Mr. Gleason, isn't it true you wouldn't have gotten the deal to build this complex without Salvatierra's influence?"

"Time's up."

"Thank you, Mr. Gleason. I'm sure we'll see each other soon."

Gleason extended his hand and gave Sanchez a bone-crusher handshake. "Don't bet on it," he said with a grin.

Chapter 29

Edward had paid little attention to Gleason's talk. Too focused on the conversation he would soon have with Conrad Beverley and Ronald Carlisle. He'd also excused himself from the tour of the complex and the luncheon for the same reason.

He checked his watch. Beverley had confirmed they would meet him in his room at four o'clock. Eight minutes late.

Jacqui had decided to have lunch on her own and shop at the outlet mall next door to the ITC. McCormack insisted on joining her, and she relented rather than settle for room service. Edward had chosen to fast until after he met with the cabinet secretaries.

He took a long pull of bottled water and paced the spacious suite. He'd arranged the furniture so Beverley and Carlisle would take the sofa and he'd be in an armchair facing them.

A knock.

Here we go.

He strode to the door.

Two men in charcoal-gray suits wearing earpieces stood in the hall-way. "Judge Edward Lamport?" one of them said.

"Yes."

"Secretary Beverley and Secretary Carlisle are on their way. We need to inspect your room."

Edward stepped aside. The two men drew their pistols and checked every cubic inch of the three-room suite. They took care of business in five minutes and returned to the main room. One of them raised a hand to his mouth. "All clear." The two then stood shoulder to shoulder with hands in front, each still gripping his pistol.

Beverley and Carlisle strode into the room. Their faces were grim. Edward approached Beverley first to shake his hand. "Secretary Carlisle," Beverley said, "District Judge Edward Lamport from Los Angeles."

Edward shook both men's hands and thanked them. "Can the security detail wait in one of the other rooms?"

Beverley and Carlisle nodded, and the gray-suited agents stepped to the glass-walled bedroom and closed the door. The blinds behind the glass wall remained open.

"Secretary Carlisle, do you have any questions about my situation and my need?" Edward said.

Carlisle said, "Conrad briefed me on the situation. We're barely on speaking terms with the Mexican government right now."

"I'm aware of their threat to close our consulates."

Carlisle frowned. "That's not public knowledge."

"I'm not the public, Secretary Carlisle."

Beverley said, "Ortiz from CIS mentioned it to Judge Lamport. I'm okay with that."

"I respect your position, Judge Lamport," Carlisle said. "That information is classified. As is a long list of discoveries we've made."

"I know foreign policy is your domain," Edward said to Carlisle. "And I have no interest in disclosing anything sensitive. I'd be subject to the same consequences as anyone else."

"Ortiz, Judge Lamport, and I have known each other for many years," Beverley said. "Trust still counts in this business."

"Fair enough," Carlisle said, worry evident in his voice.

"When I first approached Secretary Beverley for help, I knew where Carlos and Alana were. My son was staying with a cousin of mine and his wife in Ciudad Obregón, and his mother was at home in Hermosillo. I sent a private investigator there to pick up Alana and arrange protection for the whole lot of them. By the time my investigator arrived yesterday, Carlos and my cousin and his wife had disappeared. No evidence of a struggle. Can't reach my PI either."

"Who's after them?" Carlisle asked.

"Carlos is sure his employer and their largest customer are laundering drug money. Who else could it be?"

Carlisle stood. "So you have no idea where any of them are."

Edward nodded. "We now have an American citizen and two of my family members missing. Find Foley and you'll find the others." He turned to Beverley. "And I need you to let my son and his mother into this country. Detain them if you must. But let them apply for asylum."

"Judge Lamport," Carlisle said, "the president has made his Mexico objectives clear. Which I'm not at liberty to discuss. Suffice to say we're heading toward confrontation. The border, drugs, systemic corruption, trade . . . you name it, we're at odds. Asking for help with a manhunt for one American and four of their own won't even get an acknowledgment."

Edward's insides boiled. These men could not know that, though. "Back channels?"

"There are ways," Carlisle said. "We have to be judicious with how we use them and what's discussed."

"What could be more important than saving lives?"

"There's a big difference between being a player on the field and a sideline reporter," Carlisle said.

"Hold on, Mr. Secretary," Edward said. "If this were a congressman or member of the White House staff you wouldn't think twice about—"

"The president has to keep the big picture in view. We have to do what's right for the country. Sometimes that means being suboptimal on certain matters."

"Suboptimal?" *What kind of monster was this man?* "Why don't you let the president of the United States speak for himself? I can't believe he would look me in the eye and tell me, 'I'm sorry, Judge Lamport, but your family isn't a priority for the most powerful nation on earth.'"

"I meant no disrespect, Judge Lamport."

"But you're still shutting me down."

The secretary of state stood and walked toward the door. The agents emerged from the master bedroom. "I'm sorry," Carlisle said.

Beverley moved toward Carlisle. "We serve at the pleasure of the president."

"Then I'll take this up with him myself."

The cabinet members left the room, followed by the gray-suited agents.

What Edward couldn't reconcile was that these men *didn't care.* Or if they did, they were well trained to not let it show, probably out of a misapplied negotiating principle.

Carlos was missing.

Foley was unaccounted for.

Alana was with Foley.

Pato and Marta had disappeared without a trace.

And the US government would not help one of its own.

His shot at redemption was looking more like a divine tease. Yes, he was responsible for Carlos. Yes, his moral failure had caused Carlos to be born. So he was responsible for Alana, too. Consequences multiplied by the minute.

Jacqui had assured him during their drive to Calexico that she supported his rescue efforts. He didn't feel she'd been sincere, and he didn't know why. He'd rocked her world. Way beyond anything that had ever come between them.

He couldn't shake it. Something was different this time. And he had no right to ask.

Not now. Maybe not ever.

Three options remained. Persuade Corman to cash in some markers. Convince the marshals to send resources into Mexico.

Or take matters into his own hands.

Chapter 30

Perhaps Beverley and Carlisle would do business with someone who had control over their purse strings.

Senator Mitchell Corman, chairman of the Judiciary Committee and member of the Select Committees on Foreign Relations and Intelligence, had been the one, at Stanley Gleason's urging, to present him to the White House for the open seat in the Central District Court of California. Corman had gone to bat for him. He'd faced off with influential senators who disputed his qualifications—his politics, really—and ended up delivering a 90 percent upvote for his confirmation.

Edward had chatted him up during Gleason's media event, and Corman appreciated the show of support. But now Edward needed to talk to him about his real reason for being there. He dialed the hotel operator and asked for Corman's room.

To his surprise, Corman answered.

"Senator, can you spare half an hour with me on a personal matter?"

"I have a meeting with the chairman of the Permanent Committee of the Mexican Congress in fifteen minutes. It'll go until the formal dinner at six. Will you be there?"

Edward had forgotten about the dinner. "I declined."

"Tell you what, there's room at my table. We'll talk there."

"Thanks, but it's too sensitive for a public setting."

"Why, it's not public at all. Eighteen people coming. Beverley and Carlisle will be sitting with their counterparts, Gleason and a couple of his guys will be with Salvatierra and his crew, and I'll be with Congressman Gilbert, the US trade representative, and the committee chairman and senior deputy of the Mexican Congress."

Everyone in that room could move mountains on his behalf. "Not the right place."

"Then give me the short version now."

Edward's resolve hardened with each retelling.

"Carlisle's right about the state of affairs with Mexico. We're having the dinner to reopen dialogue with them. A year ago the borderless labor zone pilot treaty was the toast of Mexico City. In the last six months it's dropped like a rock."

"And you can't tell me why."

"Prop. Sixty-Eight sure didn't help. Foreign policy is dicey business. When push comes to shove, I support the president. Tell you what. I'll poke around a little bit. Let's connect afterward."

He thanked Corman and ended the call. As soon as the receiver hit the cradle, the door opened. Jacqui was back, McCormack right behind.

"How was lunch?"

"The Japanese restaurant here is outstanding," Jacqui said. "We had the best bento boxes ever. And the outlet mall was way better than I expected. How'd your meeting go?"

"Fruitless."

To say the least.

His first foray with Washington power players was . . . what exactly?

His time inside the Beltway for his confirmation hearings had been professional and cordial. He'd gained a new level of respect for the members of the Senate. Sure, they were masters of obfuscation. His confirmation process was as much about putting on a show for the constituents as it was about vetting his fitness for the job.

Did anyone even watch?

Once the C-SPAN cameras were off he'd sensed a genuine respect and an earnestness about them. They believed in what they were doing.

He didn't get that at all with Carlisle and Beverley. Maybe because his business was personal. What drove these men? What drove their boss?

"Where'd you go, Ed?" Jacqui asked.

"Rehashing the meeting. I talked with Senator Corman right before you walked in. He's gonna nose around some tonight and let me know."

Jacqui kicked her shoes off and rubbed her right heel. "So coming here was a waste of time."

"Not necessarily." Edward turned to McCormack. "You hear back from the marshal on your idea?"

"Didn't say no . . . but he's leery. He's concerned the scope would grow beyond what we're equipped to handle."

"Five people."

"That's not it. When I told him your son had disappeared, the prospect of no cooperation from Mexican law enforcement gave him pause. He'd need to clear a hostile international pursuit with the director. It's not a fugitive hunt."

"They're fleeing from evil."

"But not from United States justice."

"There's nothing in anyone's book for this deal." Edward's remark hung in the air. McCormack and Jacqui averted eye contact.

Edward sat on the sofa and rested his head in his hands. The events of the day had his mind in a spin and his heart in a pit. Diplomats wouldn't help. The president wanted confrontation. Maybe Corman's way was best—schmooze the other side with champagne and promises.

He still couldn't shake Carlisle's "suboptimal" comment. Five people's lives meant nothing in the realm of statecraft. Collateral damage. Pocket change.

The kind no one ever hears about.

Edward made eye contact with Jacqui. "Deputy, would you excuse us?"

"I'll be right outside."

After McCormack closed the door behind him, Edward beckoned Jacqui to come next to him. He sat silent, chin rested on his hands. After a time, she put her arm around his waist and leaned into him. Her touch felt good.

A rare experience, of late.

"I'm thinking . . ." he said, "about Sanchez."

"Have you changed your mind about the interview?"

He faced her. "His network employs some ex-military leaders as news analysts. I want to ask him for a referral to one in particular."

"What for?"

"To find someone who can organize a commando team. No one in the government's going to help. The only option I have left is to get them out myself."

"Are you serious?" She stood and backpedaled toward the bedroom door.

He licked his lips. "No one will help me."

"But what about us? What about our careers? If you got caught we'd be ruined."

He extended his hand toward her.

She faced him, biting her lower lip. Stayed put.

"Please, sit down."

She relaxed. "Is there no other way?" She sat at the far end of the sofa.

"I've been given a second chance." He swallowed a rising lump. "I didn't do right by Carlos. He needs me now."

"So you're choosing him over me?"

"What? Where'd that come from?"

"If what you're doing blows up, it'll ruin my career. Have you thought about that?"

"I've thought about all of it. Our careers, the life we've made. But this—" He willed himself to remain calm. "Jesus said we must love our enemies and do good to them. So how can I turn my back on my own son?"

"And you keep including Alana." She wiped at her nose. "I don't know how else to say it. She threatens me. I'm afraid of the two of you together."

Nothing he could say would help.

The truth was he didn't know how he'd feel in Alana's presence. He feared the temptation he'd face.

He feared he might give in.

He stood and walked across the room. "I'm not going to knee-jerk anything." He crossed his arms. "But I have to do something. I have to."

It wasn't Carlos versus Jacqui. He had more than enough love for both of them. She was in charge of her own feelings and attitude toward this. All he could do was believe he was doing the right thing. Which was its own justification.

He had to see this through.

Jacqui threw up her hands. "Do what you have to do."

Resignation, not support. He understood. "I don't have a choice."

"You always have choices, dear."

"I can't live with Carlos's blood on my hands. I can't live with not doing everything possible to save him."

His phone rang. Sanchez.

"I was about to call you. Still in Calexico?"

"Until tomorrow morning."

"Can you meet us in our hotel room? I need a referral."

"To whom?"

"Not over the phone."

Chapter 31

Sanchez arrived with a room-service waiter in tow who carried three interesting-looking cold beverages into the room and placed them on top of a cabinet. "Nonalcoholic sangria. Had one downstairs at lunch."

"Thoughtful of you," Jacqui said as she picked up a glass. "I'll leave you to talk." She made her way to the bedroom and closed the door and the blinds behind the bedroom's glass wall.

"What do you know about Colonel Steven Jessup?" Edward said.

"Jessup's a fine man. Rare combination of a brilliant military mind and the ability to communicate in ways regular folks understand. I'd say he's the best expert commentator on the network. Why do you ask?"

"I have a huge problem on my hands. My son, Carlos, and his mother live in Mexico. Their lives are in danger and I need to get them into the US."

"They don't have the means to get out on their own?"

"They're not American citizens. My son tried to cross the border on Tuesday and got caught and sent back. His mother tried to fly into Los Angeles, but she's been tagged inadmissible."

"Who's threatening them?"

"They both work for Bancomex. Carlos handles their largest account—"

"And he thinks they're laundering drug money."

Edward widened his eyes. "Excuse me?"

"Someone who self-identified as 'A. Believer' sent an e-mail to my network account. Said they discovered a massive drug-money-laundering scheme in Mexico and it involves Americans."

Could it be? "What else?"

"A spreadsheet with what looked like a series of transactions. Made no sense to me. Our IT guys traced the sending IP address. It's from Mexico, from an Internet account owned by Pato Lamport."

"He's my cousin. You have the spreadsheet with you?"

"In my laptop. He also put a Bible reference in the e-mail. Numbers 13:28–30."

Sanchez got up to retrieve his computer while Edward strode to the bedroom.

Jacqui lay on the bed on her side, eyes closed. He touched her on the shoulder. She rolled on her back. "You look troubled," she said.

"Sanchez has a lead on Carlos. Come join us."

Jacqui rubbed her eyes. "Give me a minute." She bounded up and headed for the bathroom.

Edward trotted around the bed and grabbed his Bible from the nightstand, then returned to the table with Sanchez.

He riffled the pages until he found the passage. He read it aloud:

"But the people living there are powerful, and their towns are large and fortified. We even saw giants there, the descendants of Anak! The Amalekites live in the Negev, and the Hittites, Jebusites, and Amorites live in the hill country. The Canaanites live along the coast of the Mediterranean Sea and along the Jordan Valley.

But Caleb tried to quiet the people as they stood before Moses. 'Let's go at once to take the land,' he said. 'We can certainly conquer it!'"

Sanchez set his laptop on the dining table. "Internet's fast here."

"Careful," Edward said. "Gleason built heavy surveillance into this place. He watched us in the lounge last night."

"No worries. We use an encrypted VPN with two-factor security."

Jacqui entered and sat with them. "You know where Carlos is?" she said to Sanchez.

She said his name.

"I got an e-mail a couple of days ago from someone who said they discovered a big money-laundering scheme that involved Americans. Your husband filled me in."

"The e-mail was sent from Pato's Internet account," Edward said. "It had to be from Carlos."

Jacqui asked, "Should we get McCormack in here?"

"Not yet." Edward turned to Sanchez. "This is why I want to get with Jessup. I came down here to meet with Secretary of State Carlisle and Homeland Security Secretary Beverley. I asked for their help to get Carlos and Alana out of Mexico. They shut me down. Too much bad blood between our government and Mexico's."

Sanchez nodded. "We've been on that story awhile."

"No time to pay attention to that stuff," Edward said. "The deputy marshal you saw in the hallway had suggested they could help, but I'm not counting on it. The only option I have left is to go get Carlos myself."

Sanchez put a hand up. "You want me to hook you up with Colonel Jessup to set up a commando raid into a foreign country?"

"That's precisely what I'm asking. This sort of thing's been done before."

"But not facilitated by a news organization."

"I'm not asking you to facilitate anything. Just get me his phone number."

Sanchez stood. "That's semantics, Judge Lamport."

"Aren't you guys supposed to be defenders of liberty? Watchdogs of democracy?" Edward composed himself. This was getting too personal, which wouldn't help anyone. "I'm not expecting Jessup to do anything other than point me at people he thinks would be qualified and interested. That's all."

"I'd be taking a huge risk, Judge Lamport. What's in it for me?"

Edward slapped the table. "What's in it for you? How about doing the right thing? Isn't that good enough for anyone anymore? Have we totally lost our moral fiber in this country?"

"That's a cheap shot—"

"The only thing cheap around here is talk and there's plenty going around. The only war this can start is a war on cowardice."

Edward caught himself. He was teetering on an emotional precipice. One more out-of-control moment and he'd plunge into a deep crevasse.

From which he might not emerge.

Tough.

"Ed, you all right?" Jacqui asked.

"I'm not all right!" He stood and paced the room. "Nothing's all right." He stopped and lasered his gaze at Sanchez. "You know why I got into criminal justice?"

"Ed, don't," Jacqui said.

His wife didn't want to see him spill his pain.

But he had to. Once and for all, he had to vomit it all out.

"My senior year in high school. I was All-City Section in football and baseball. USC and UCLA were fighting over me for both sports. They let scholarship athletes play more than one back then. Scouts from the Dodgers and Angels and Giants said they wanted to draft me. I was on top of the world. Ready to live my dreams. I'd decided college was the right choice. Two days before letter-of-intent day, I get called to the principal's office. I get there and two cops are in the room."

Edward's pulse approached redline speed. He trembled everywhere. It had been more than twenty years since he'd talked about this.

It was still raw.

He blew a deep breath and looked down.

"The cops tell me my mother's been murdered. In cold blood." He choked up. "They stole her purse."

Jacqui stood. Edward waved her off.

"She and my dad were walking home from lunch at a restaurant a few blocks from our house in Highland Park. They got mugged." He wrung his hands. "Two . . ." He bridled his tongue. "Two gangbangers. They killed her for her purse. For her stupid purse . . ."

He stopped for another deep breath. His chest was on fire. Long-buried grief boiled inside, ready to explode like a geyser. Jacqui moved toward him, and he backed away.

Sanchez was quiet.

"When the cops questioned them, they said my mom tried to fight them off. And my dad froze. He didn't fight for her." Bitter bile rose from his stomach. "I still have a hard time forgiving him."

He sat. Jacqui approached him. This time he extended an arm toward her. She embraced him around his shoulders.

"I was set to be a big leaguer. But I walked away. Worked my way through Cal State LA and got a degree in criminal justice. My first job was with the LA City Attorney's office. Saved enough in three years to go to UCLA Law."

"We have something in common," Sanchez said. "I grew up in the barrio, East LA. Saw my share of gang fights. My best friend from high school ended up joining the MaraVillas. He tried to rope me in, too. Saw him get killed by the Avenues. What a stupid waste."

"Do you get why this refusal upon refusal upon refusal is so maddening?"

"I do." Sanchez stood to make a call, then looked back at Edward. "I'll get you Jessup's number. And count me as part of your team. I'll do whatever I can to help."

Chapter 32

Now that the grand opening festivities and politicking were over, Bernal and Salvatierra got down to important business. His business. Now was the time to reveal the Carlos Alvarez incident to Stanley Gleason along with what Bernal's team was doing in response.

"Shipments to Cal-Three of battery housings filled with your product will begin next Friday, as planned," Salvatierra said.

Gleason scowled. "You could have told me that on the phone."

Bernal said, "Before we begin the movement of cash through the sewer to Señor Salvatierra's casinos, Señor Mota has an update for you."

Mota's eyes darted from side to side. "We are winding down the old process of moving cash across the border, which you know was sporadic and unreliable."

Gleason steepled his fingers and bounced his gaze between Bernal and Salvatierra. "Which is why we built the sewer."

"Señor Gleason, I need to tell you . . . we've encountered an unexpected problem."

Gleason frowned. "Give it to me straight."

"One of my employees figured it out," Mota said.

"Figured what out?"

Bernal leaned toward Gleason. "Tell him, Señor Mota."

"This employee stole three months' worth of transaction records from the Caribbean casinos to the offshore companies and back to Mexico. He tried to jump the border into California but he got caught. The records don't—"

"When did this happen?"

"Three days ago."

Gleason bolted out of his seat. "And you're telling me now?" He scowled at Bernal. "How am I supposed to trust you guys with my money when you keep stuff like this from me?"

"*Our* money, Stanley," Salvatierra said. "Our money."

Gleason waved Salvatierra off. "So who knows about it?"

"We know that this employee made two copies of the data. We have not located either yet," Mota said.

Bernal chimed in. "We have his mother, who works in our Hermosillo regional office. Our security team caught her and an American man she was traveling with yesterday. The timing of events this week, plus the fact we haven't yet found the employee who stole the data, made it difficult to schedule this meeting until now."

"Who did it?" Gleason said.

"His name is Carlos Alvarez," Bernal said. "Since the Border Patrol sent him back to Mexicali he has managed to evade our security operatives here. His mother is Alana Alvarez. She is the widow of Guillermo Alvarez, the former CEO of a large automotive supplier in Hermosillo."

"Those names mean nothing to me," Gleason said. "The American?"

"His name is Joseph Foley," Bernal said. "He claims to be Alana Alvarez's boyfriend. We are putting them through intense interrogation."

"But the data's still loose out there?"

Heads nodded around the room.

Gleason muttered something under his breath. "What are you doing to find Alvarez?"

"He has proven himself resourceful," Bernal said. "His last known location was Ciudad Obregón. We got word he was staying at the home of a man named Pato Lamport. We sent some men there, but they didn't find him."

"Lamport?" Gleason said.

"That name means something to you, Stanley?" Salvatierra asked.

He hesitated. "Unusual name for a Mexican."

"There are at least a half million people of Irish descent living in our country," Salvatierra said. "They first came during the US invasion. Many men from Ireland left the United States Army to fight for Mexico. They were some of our country's greatest heroes."

"Never knew that," Gleason said.

Bernal stood. "We are closely monitoring the media and Internet and are in frequent contact with all our resources in Mexico and the United States. So far nothing has appeared anywhere. Rest assured we can proceed with our shipments as planned. Our venture carries on. The others will not be able to compete and will soon beg to join us."

Gleason stood. "Not before we make some changes." He moved from his seat to the office door. "As of now I'm putting Rodrigues in charge of the sewer operation. No cash or product moves through without his personal authorization. Anyone who tries to circumvent his authority will be eliminated. Permanently."

Bernal bolted from his seat and got nose to nose with Gleason. "You can't unilaterally decide—"

"I just did. My technology built it. My organization takes all the risk. You and Vicente will still get your share. *After* the cleaning cycle is confirmed and the funds are under my control." Gleason pointed at Mota. "And I want this guy gone. Take care of it today or I'll do it myself."

Chapter 33

Saturday, February 20
La Junta Police Station, La Junta, México
10:03 a.m. MST

Carlos had left the desk officer's most recent serving of rancid *frijoles y tortilla* on the floor. His body felt tight from inactivity and lying on the smelly cot. He'd asked the officer to bring him a Bible. They didn't have one in the station. So he had to feed his soul with the words he could remember.

How could this police captain be so merciless?

Why would God forsake him in this place after all He'd done to protect him?

He had to constantly reject the voice in his head that told him he hadn't heard right. That he was never supposed to get involved in stopping Bancomex. That God never asked him to do it and he was on his own, without God's protection.

That wasn't the God he knew.

Carlos would have condoned evil if he hadn't acted. If he died, so be it.

So, where are you, God? Carlos believed to his core that what he'd done was a work of mercy. He'd obeyed the church's teaching.

Ours not to reason why, ours but to do and die.

Those words of the Victorian poet had stayed with him since he'd read them his first year in the university. They'd resonated with truth. Trust God and obey. Even to death.

So there had to be some purpose for being stuck in this jail cell, not knowing what would happen next.

Don't be afraid of those who want to kill your body; they cannot touch your soul.

Jesus had spoken to him. So he confessed everything he could think of that he'd done wrong.

The metal door to the jail opened. The desk officer would surely give him grief for not eating the food he'd brought, which might mean he wouldn't bother when the next mealtime came. Carlos remained on the lumpy cot.

"Alvarez!"

The captain. His abdominal muscles wobbled and strained as he sat up.

"*Sí,* Capitán. "

"I called the number you gave to my officer. There was no answer."

Not good. Had ALEXA's *matóns* caught his mother? "Maybe my handwriting wasn't clear. Do you have the paper I wrote it on?"

The captain pulled the paper from his shirt pocket and handed it to Carlos. He double-checked the number.

It was correct.

"And there was no message?"

The captain shook his head.

The American, Joseph Foley, was with her. And Espinosa. Were they all captured? Were they all dead?

"There are two other people who may be able to help. Both Americans."

The captain pulled a set of keys from his pocket and opened the cell door. "Come with me."

Chapter 34

Arranging the meeting with Colonel Jessup was more complicated than Edward had anticipated. First there was the matter of interrupting Jessup's weekend fishing trip. There were questions upon questions why a sitting federal judge wanted to talk with him about mercenary operations. And then he had to finesse the meeting with the US Marshals hanging around. McCormack in particular pressed him on why Albert Sanchez was coming to his home. Calling it a preinterview prep session had worked. And he managed to keep the identity of the colonel a secret, convincing the deputies he was an old friend from his deputy district attorney days.

All to protect McCormack and the other deputy marshals, of course.

Edward knew which laws he would break if he went ahead with the operation. He realized that prosecutorial discretion at his level would rest more on politics than principle. And politically he was in the "highest vulnerability" class. What better way to look tough on illegal immigration than to put away a federal judge who smuggled two Mexicans into the country?

He'd concluded he could change the world more by going to prison for doing right than by incarcerating thousands from the bench. And saving Carlos and Alana in the process.

Prison. He'd put enough men there to know the realities.

Right. He'd said the same thing about being a judge.

◆　◆　◆

Sanchez and retired Marine Corps colonel Steven J. "Jesse" Jessup arrived on schedule. Col. Jessup had been a leader in the Marine Corps Special Operations Command. His last command billet had landed him at Camp Pendleton, north of San Diego, California, and he had moved to the Los Angeles area after retiring from the Corps four years ago.

McCormack and a second deputy marshal remained outside, respecting Edward's desire for private conversation.

"It's an honor to meet you and have you in our home, Colonel Jessup," Edward said.

"I sense a kindred spirit between us. Tell me more about what you want to do."

The men settled into the living room. "I have a son who lives in Mexico. Carlos is his name. He's a Mexican citizen. And he doesn't know I'm his father."

"And you want to extract him from Mexico and bring him here."

"Right. Him and his mother. He works for a big bank, and he's blown the cover off a drug- money-laundering scheme. The perpetrators want them dead. The problem is I don't know where either of them are."

"You got someone who'll look the other way when they come to the border?" Jessup said.

No. Not him, too. He rubbed his eyes. "That's the whole problem, Colonel Jessup. I've tried asking for permission. I'm out of time."

"I'm not in the business of breaking federal laws. We can secure your people and buy you time. Any access to people who might know where they are?"

Edward shook his head. "I don't know anything about his life other than what I just told you. Or about his mother's. It's been more than twenty-five years, Colonel."

"First thing you'll need is solid intel," Jessup said. "You'll need men with contacts down there who know the dialects, local customs, and routines. And if you're talking drug-money laundering, you'll want some ex-DEA agents who've worked in country and know who's who and what's what in the cartels. That's your biggest hurdle. Once you find them, whoever's got 'em now would be no match for trained American fighters."

"Can you hook me up with some men who might lead it for me?"

"Plenty who are capable. Willing's another story."

"All I need from you are names and numbers."

Jessup looked at Sanchez. "We talked on the way over here. Mr. Sanchez wants to tap into his journalist network to help with intel. I'm willing to facilitate the formation of your team. But it'll take time."

"How much?"

"I've got three Mexican journalists onboard," Sanchez said. "Already tapping into their networks."

Jessup said, "There are four men I'll recommend from my MARSOC company at Pendleton who are now doing contract work. Any of 'em would be great."

"You mentioned ex-DEA. Know anyone?"

Jessup chuckled. "Google. There's an association of ex–narcotics agents."

"Right. I'll work my own Rolodex." *But you've got to wrap up Prop. 68.* "I have a few people who can chase that down. I have a big case to wrap up next week."

Jessup nodded. "Quite a powder keg, that one."

"I'll help with ex-DEA," Sanchez said.

"Thanks, but no," Edward said. "You've already stuck your neck out big-time."

"I have my sources, Your Honor."

"What about our interview? I'm announcing my Prop. Sixty-Eight ruling next Tuesday."

"We're still on. The boss is counting on it."

Chapter 35

Edward and Sanchez and Colonel Jessup responded to Jacqui's invitation to the dining room, where she'd laid out a spread of croissants, brie, fresh berries, and a carafe of fresh-brewed French roast coffee.

"So that's what I've been smelling," Jessup said. "Did you bake these?"

"I wish," Jacqui said.

The men helped themselves and carried on a conversation around the table. Edward spotted Sanchez holding his phone.

"Got another message from A. Believer. Check this out."

Edward hurried over to Sanchez and took his phone. The e-mail was written in Spanish, and he translated it out loud:

> *Dear Señor Sanchez,*
> *I am writing to you from La Junta, Mexico. I escaped*
> *a second attempt by assassins to capture me. Please get*
> *a message to the American judge who is the cousin of*
> *Pato Lamport that I am at the police station and that*
> *the police captain here knows my story and has said he is*
> *willing to help find my mother and Señor Foley from Los*

Angeles. Please have him call the police station at +52
10 609 73585 and ask for Captain Martinez.
Sincerely, A. Believer.

"If that's legit, we grab Carlos right away," Jessup said. "You have yourself a local ally in that Captain Martinez. If he's an honest cop, he should be able to point your team at people who can track the others down."

"If he's in reliable police custody, that buys us time," Edward said. "Let's go to my office so we can call from my computer."

The men followed Edward to his home office. Edward sat at the desk while Sanchez and Jessup stood beside his chair. He opened his VoIP app and dialed the number Carlos had e-mailed to Sanchez.

"Policía de La Junta," a gravelly voice said.

"Judge Edward Lamport from Los Angeles calling for Captain Martinez," Edward said in Spanish.

A brief hold. "This is Captain Martinez, Judge Lamport. Do you know a young man named Carlos Alvarez?"

"I do. I understand you have him in custody."

"He has spent some time in my jail, yes. He and I had a misunderstanding. I'm allowing him to stay here for his safety."

"He's told you about Bancomex and ALEXA?"

"Javier Bernal is a ruthless man. He's well known here. Carlos said you had sent a private investigator to Hermosillo to secure Carlos's mother. They are now missing."

"Yes, Joseph Foley. Haven't heard from him the last two days."

"Carlos said their last known location was Ciudad Obregón. I spoke with the police department there. A brutal massacre happened at a small taqueria not far from the airport. The owners were a young couple, and they were both shot dead. Seven men were also shot dead. The killers used automatic rifles."

"Seven men," Edward said. "Must have been Foley's friend Omar Espinosa and his crew. Any witnesses?"

"The police canvassed the area but found none who could say they saw anything. This was not a typical *narco* attack. They've learned not to do their killings in the cities."

"Any blood evidence other than the bodies at the scene?"

"No. They did find some hair and fiber that did not match the victims."

"What's the crime lab capability like down there?"

"For us we use the one in Chihuahua. I don't know about Obregón."

It was time to talk with his son. The first conversation with him he'd imagined wasn't like this. "Captain Martinez, I'd like to speak with Carlos."

"He's right here."

Breathe, he told himself. His mouth dried like someone had shoved cotton in it. His heart raced like a runaway truck. What would Carlos sound like?

"Señor Lamport, it is good to speak with you."

His voice was labored. "Same for me, Carlos." *More than I can say right now.* "I want you to know we're working hard to get you and your mother out of Mexico as soon as possible."

"Thank you for sending Señor Foley to her. I fear for both of them now. Bernal is ruthless and relentless."

"You're the one they want. You're the only one who can explain the data you obtained. Albert Sanchez has given me the spreadsheet you sent him."

"Please, only give it to someone trustworthy, Señor Lamport. I fear many people in your government are involved."

Based on his experience with Carlisle and Beverley, Edward understood Carlos's fear. "Let me speak with Captain Martinez."

He'd heard the bright, idealistic young man Alana had described to him.

Edward muted the call. "We sit on Carlos's data until we get him and Alana out of there."

"Judge Lamport, are you going to show the money-laundering evidence to your FBI?" Captain Martinez said.

"Not until we get him out of Mexico."

"You should know that Bancomex and ALEXA are very powerful down here. There is a competition between the government, drug cartels, and business conglomerates for control of Mexico. Make sure you know what you're getting involved in."

Is this what Carlisle and Beverley wouldn't tell him? "Thanks for the input, Captain Martinez. My focus is getting our people out safely."

Jessup and Sanchez returned to the living room with him.

"I wonder if a lower-profile way of spiriting Carlos out of Mexico would be better," Sanchez said.

"Like what?" Jessup asked.

Edward made eye contact with Sanchez. They understood each other.

"A coyote," Sanchez said. "Professional smuggler. They know the best routes into the US and how to evade the Border Patrol. The challenge will be finding one who isn't owned by one of the cartels."

"I haven't the first idea how to hire one," Edward said to Sanchez.

"I do. I did a story on *los coyotes* a couple of years ago. I can start with some of the men I interviewed."

Edward asked, "You sure you want to—"

"I'm in, okay? Your story about your mother's murder pulled me back to what's right and worthwhile."

Edward extended his hand to Sanchez. Sanchez returned a firm shake.

He turned to Jessup. "So we bring Carlos in with the coyote and focus the commando op on finding Foley and Alana."

"I concur, Your Honor. But you said it yourself. Those Bancomex thugs will break them to get Carlos. We have a small window to get this done."

PART III

ENGAGEMENTS

The strictest law sometimes becomes the severest injustice.

—Benjamin Franklin

Chapter 36

Sunday, February 21
Chambers of Hon. Edward J. Lamport
10:00 a.m.

Edward wanted to get on with the commando op, but his conscience told him to make one more attempt to work through the authorities instead of taking matters into his own hands. One last shot at convincing the US Marshals Service to launch a manhunt inside Mexico for Foley and Alana. After all, an American citizen was endangered in a foreign country, and the Marshals Service *had* undertaken those types of missions many times before.

Marshal James K. Hunter of the Central District and McCormack sat together and across the table from Edward.

A line of scrimmage.

He claimed home field advantage by holding the meeting in his chambers instead of the US Marshals Command Center. Since he'd kept McCormack out of the loop yesterday, he needed to start with a briefing.

"There are some new developments in my situation since Deputy McCormack approached you," Edward said to Marshal Hunter. "My son, Carlos Alvarez, had been missing since Wednesday. We've found him. He's in protective custody of the La Junta, Mexico, police."

"Great news, Your Honor," McCormack said.

Hunter's expression remained flat.

"I'd sent my private investigator, Joseph Foley, to Hermosillo to protect Carlos's mother while she made arrangements to leave Mexico. He arrived there Wednesday, the day Carlos went missing. US Customs prevented her from entering the country. DHS has tagged her inadmissible for overstaying a visa. Foley and Mrs. Alvarez disappeared shortly thereafter."

"Let me make sure I've got this straight, Your Honor," Marshal Hunter said. "Your son lives in Mexico and isn't an American citizen. In fact, he doesn't even know you're his father."

"That's correct." Edward told Hunter the full story. "I didn't know my child was male, or his name, until last Monday."

"And you want us to send a Special Operations Group unit into Mexico to conduct a manhunt rescue of your investigator and your son's mother."

"And I want to bring Carlos and Mrs. Alvarez into the US so they can apply for asylum."

"Judge Lamport, do you have documented proof Carlos is your son?" Hunter said.

Each time someone asked that question, his guilt stood up front and center. "I signed away my parental rights before he was born. His birth certificate would list Alana Alvarez's late husband, Guillermo Alvarez, as the father."

"So we only have your word."

"I, Alana, and her parents were the only ones who knew about Carlos. And her parents are both dead."

Hunter grimaced and closed his eyes for a moment. "You can't prove Carlos is your son. You were never married to his mother, correct?"

"That's correct."

"His mother is barred from entering this country legally. And your PI, Mr. Foley, isn't a member of your family or there under contract with the federal judiciary." Hunter rolled his chair back from the table. "None of this fits our jurisdiction or mission."

"But *I'm* your mission and jurisdiction. It affects *me*. The death threats against me—both have ties to Mexico and/or Mexican interests. Failure to rescue my people could threaten my survival. If whoever has captured Foley and Alana connects them to me, I'm next. Isn't that reason enough to get your protective intelligence and tactical ops people on this?"

Hunter folded his hands on the table. "I understand your point, but it doesn't fit our mission."

"Sir, the FBI is engaged with us on the threats to Judge Lamport's life," McCormack said. "It wouldn't be a burdensome expansion of scope to do what Judge Lamport has asked."

"Okay, let's roll with this a moment," Hunter said. "We'd then have the matter of what we do with your son and his mother when we find them."

"I've spoken with Secretary Beverley twice about this. Both times he seemed willing to allow Carlos and Alana to enter the country but was concerned with the internal and international politics. Could your director work with the attorney general to give Beverley some cover? All I've asked is that they be allowed to enter the country. Keep them in detention or wherever while they apply for asylum. From there we go to Immigration Court."

Hunter stood. "I feel for you, Your Honor. I don't want to say no, but I can't say yes. I'll need to take this up with the director tomorrow morning. Will you be available to speak with her if she requests it?"

"I'll make sure of it."

"Sorry I can't be more encouraging," Hunter said as he extended a hand to Edward.

"I've gotten used to being turned down."

"Will you be needing me for anything, Your Honor?" McCormack asked.

"Wait for me at Rebecca's desk. I'll be a few minutes."

McCormack walked out. Edward called Jessup.

"I gave it one last try with the Marshals Service. Not holding my breath. Ramp up the recruiting, Colonel."

"I have three men in so far," Jessup said.

"We need twelve to fourteen, correct?"

"The three I have are recruiting the others. I'll have the team formed before end of day tomorrow."

Okay.

Edward drew a deep breath to slow down so he could recap where everything stood. The death threats had been contained, but the Marshals strongly recommended that their twenty-four-hour protection continue indefinitely. On Friday, as a precaution, the other judges in the Central District had been made aware of the threats against Edward. Marshal Hunter had put in a request for six additional deputies to be deployed to his command immediately, but headquarters approval was pending.

Jessup and Sanchez would make progress today. They believed as much as he did that doing the right thing was its own reward.

Still, so many unknowns.

Chapter 37

Albert Sanchez plowed through his video library of investigative reports on human trafficking to the section with his profiles of *la mafia de los coyotes*—the organized-crime groups who controlled the illegal movement of people across America's southern border. He slowed his shuttling as he approached the interview with the man he'd considered his "star subject"—known as M.C. on the air, presented with his face grayed out and his voice altered to an exaggerated baritone. M.C.'s true name was Miguel Carreras de Orozco, but he was known inside the trade as Coropiedro—"heart of stone." M.C. was a stark capitalist. He cared not whether his customers were fleeing poverty, persecution, or bodily harm. If you met his price, he'd move you across the border.

When Sanchez had interviewed M.C. two years ago he lived in Cuencamé, a small municipality in Durango State between the cities of Durango and Torreón. He lived there because that was where his customers were. For the most part, it wasn't people who lived in the border towns who wanted to migrate to the United States. It was the poorest of the poor from the central and southern parts of Mexico and into Central America who were the desperate ones. The ones who would pay his price—which had climbed in the last ten years from two to three thousand American dollars to up to five times that amount. Most got the money from relatives who had already made it to America. He was able to charge a high price because he was one of the best at avoiding *las rinches*—the slang name men of his trade had given Border Patrol agents and other law enforcement officers.

Sanchez watched the edited version of the interview that ran on air first, then pulled up the raw footage from the video archive server. His viewers were not given the opportunity for a fuller measure of the man via facial expression and body language. And even if they had seen those things, the man's presence did not come through the video. On the outside he was all machismo—his rough voice, steely eyes, and imposing physique.

The unedited footage helped Sanchez remember how he'd felt when he interviewed Carreras. He'd sensed a softer heart under the hard veneer that few, if any, had experienced. Every now and then he'd see it in the man's eyes, or the way his body moved before he responded to one of Sanchez's questions about the people he'd trafficked.

Or maybe Sanchez saw what he wanted to see.

Regardless, M.C. was the right man to bring Judge Lamport's son out of Mexico.

Sanchez navigated to the interview archives he kept on his laptop and opened the file containing his notes and voice-over scripts for the Carreras interview. The document with M.C.'s contact information was first on the list.

He made the call.

"Señor Sanchez, you want to put me on television again?"

"I want Coropiedro."

A pause. "You want to bring someone to America?"

"Not me. A friend. Whose identity I will not disclose."

"The only identity I care about is *dólares*."

"Nothing's changed, then."

"I'm not as active as I was two years ago. And my price has gone up."

"How can that be? Fewer people are crossing into the US now with the increase in patrols and more fences."

"You think you know the ways of the coyote because of your reports, Señor Sanchez, but you don't. You are correct that much has changed in the last two years. But it's not just *las rinches*. The *narcos* have swallowed up the old mafia. A few of us have been able to stay independent. We've hardened ourselves and learned new tactics and routes. I pick and choose who I work with."

"I thought you didn't care about who or why as long as you got paid."

"I am not a criminal," Carreras said. "Or a *narco*."

Maybe Sanchez was right after all. Maybe this man was concerned with more than the money. But what did it matter? The more Coropiedro, the better.

"California is the final destination. We want him moved across there."

"Him? Tell me about your cargo."

Cargo. He hadn't heard M.C. use such an impersonal description before. Maybe he was playing hard to get.

"Male, midtwenties. Excellent physical shape, capable fighter."

"If he's all that, why do you need me?"

"Because smuggling people across the border is your business, not his."

"Crossing in California is a bad idea, *señor*. There are better routes through Arizona. My best crossing is the Tohono O'Odham Indian Reservation."

"Tohono is a drug-smuggling corridor. How can it be easier to cross there?"

"Who said anything about easier? Effective, señor. Effective is what counts."

Sanchez stood and paced to the window in his office that overlooked the Hollywood sign. The idea of doing the right thing and the realities of pulling it off were miles apart. "How soon will we know the crossing point?"

A pause. "When I am ready to choose it. Tell your friend he's not in control. I am."

"And how much will this cost?"

"Thirty thousand American dollars."

◆ ◆ ◆

Carreras called back three hours later.

"We are ready, *señor*," he said. "We leave for La Junta in one hour. It will take us about eight hours to make the drive. Tell your friend to have his cargo ready to be picked up at nine o'clock tomorrow morning. From there we drive ten hours to Sáric, about seventy kilometers southwest of Nogales. We rest and resupply in Sáric, then leave for the crossing point about ten at night. From there we reach the border in two hours."

Carreras described the route through which he and his team would lead Carlos, then sent him an e-mail with detailed maps and turn-by-turn directions. The rendezvous spot would be in Chukut Kuk district, south of Tribal Road 2.

Sanchez asked, "When do we meet?"

"One a.m. Tuesday."

Sanchez opened the e-mail Carreras sent him and went straight to the maps. It would take about eleven hours to drive from the rendezvous point in the reservation to downtown Los Angeles, a route that avoided the interstates and Border Patrol checkpoints. From there he could take Carlos straight to the Citizenship and Immigration Services office, where he could apply for asylum. After that it would be up to Edward where to bring him.

Maybe Edward could get the US Marshals to put him in witness protection.

Sanchez ended the conversation with Carreras and called Edward to brief him on the logistics and cost to spirit Carlos out of Mexico. The crossing would take place the morning of Edward's announcement. Sanchez and Carlos would be three-fourths of the way to Los Angeles when he entered his courtroom. They agreed Sanchez would take Carlos up to Edward and Jacqui's Lake Arrowhead chalet after he was finished at CIS, and that Sanchez would stay the night and have his crew come up Wednesday morning for the interview taping.

He sat down to reckon with what he'd committed himself to. He alternated between wanting to call Carreras back to cancel the whole thing and spinning in his mind the possibilities that being on the inside of a story like Carlos's could bring. Then he put the brakes on his imaginings and refocused on harsh reality.

There were no guarantees Carlos would make it to the rendezvous point.

Or him either.

◆　◆　◆

"I just got off with Sanchez," Edward said to Jacqui. "The next twenty-four hours are gonna be a whirlwind. Carlos will cross the border early Tuesday morning. Sanchez will meet him in Arizona and bring him to LA."

"Not to sound crass," Jacqui said, "but how much is it going to cost to get him here?"

"Thirty thousand."

Jacqui grabbed his arm. "Thirty grand? My word . . ."

"What's the price for saving a life?" Edward said.

"I know . . . it's . . . wow, is all."

"Yeah. Sanchez will call us when it's safe to do so." He turned and faced her. "When he gets to LA he'll take Carlos straight to the CIS office. Once he's done there, he'll meet us at Lake Arrowhead. We're still planning to do the interview on Wednesday."

"Oh. Couldn't we have talked about this first?"

"We have to move fast."

"That's not what I mean. You're going to have Carlos in our cabin. With us. And all he will know is that you're the cousin of his mother's friend and you're helping him because you're a good guy. How are you going to handle being together with him and not be able to tell him who you really are?"

Chapter 38

Carlos's spirits were higher than they'd been since he first discovered the money-laundering scheme. He and Captain Martinez were on good terms, and a friendship had begun. The station had taken in a couple of prisoners the day before, so the captain had moved him to an empty office and given him a cot to sleep on. He'd even brought in some of his wife's home-cooked food a few times, like black bean enchiladas and *carnitas sopes*. Carlos felt energetic again and he'd been able to exercise outdoors behind the police building.

Even Officer Garcia from the front desk treated Carlos better now that he was in *el capitán*'s good graces. And he'd brought him a Bible that his priest had given him. Even promised to get his priest to visit Carlos soon.

Carlos reclined on his cot to have a quiet moment of prayer. Garcia interrupted.

"You have a phone call from California. Albert Sanchez."

Sanchez? ¡Dios mio! Carlos bounded up and sprinted from his room to Officer Garcia's desk phone.

"Señor Sanchez! Thank you for calling. And for reading my e-mails. Have you looked at the spreadsheet I sent?"

"You're welcome, Carlos. I have, and as you said you'll need to explain what's in it. But that's not why I'm calling. I have good news—Judge Lamport has arranged to bring you into the US."

"*¡Gracias a Dios!* Who's coming for me? Will he meet me here, too?"

"We've hired a coyote to bring you in through Arizona. One of the best."

Carlos's heart deflated. "Coyote? The drug cartels own all the coyotes. They cannot be trusted." He slumped into a chair next to Officer Garcia's desk.

"We don't have time to wait. You don't have time. It's our fastest and—"

"No. I will not go with a coyote."

Silence on the line.

"Carlos, he's on his way to you now. Don't be foolish."

"You are the ones who are foolish! How can you work with the very people who are trying to kill me?" *God, don't let this happen to me. Please!*

"I know this man. I interviewed him extensively for one of my rep—"

"You don't know him! You can't possibly know him." Carlos's hands shook so much he had to grip the handset with both. "Who knows the heart of any man? Not you. Not anyone."

More silence.

Carlos knew deep in his gut crossing the border with a coyote would be a disaster. Everyone with a brain in México knew *los narcos* had taken over human smuggling years ago. His faith in Sanchez and the American judge fell through the floor.

This was it. He'd overstepped. He hadn't heard God right. He had no choice but to put himself at the mercy of Captain Martinez, hope that La Junta was small enough and remote enough that even Bernal's *matóns* would not think to come for him here.

He was on his own now.

"Carlos?" Sanchez said.

"I will not go with your coyote. I will not."

◆ ◆ ◆

"Judge Lamport, we have a problem," Sanchez said.

Problem. The word hit Edward and bounced off. His emotions stayed flat. Every move thwarted had become his expectation. It was the only way he could rise above his fear. "The coyote change his mind?"

"Carlos refuses to go with him. Thinks we'd be handing him to the enemy."

No way could he have expected *that*. "Maybe he's right. Can you trust the coyote you've chosen?"

"Any other solution will take time you don't have, Judge Lamport."

Sanchez was right. "Then I'll talk to him."

"I don't think that's a good idea, Your Honor. I need to keep you as isolated—"

"I don't care about that! I don't need plausible deniability. I need my son out of Mexico. If I go down, then so be it."

Edward hung up with Sanchez and called Captain Martinez. The captain got Carlos on the line.

And Edward froze. No words came. All of his power, all of his experience . . . and he didn't know how to persuade his son to receive his help.

"Carlos, I know you're skeptical of our solution."

"No one in México can be trusted, Señor Lamport."

Not Mr. Lamport . . . Dad . . . I want to tell him now that I'm Dad, but that would be selfish and unhelpful . . .

"I'm organizing a group of men . . . former soldiers and law enforcement agents . . . to find Alana and Mr. Foley. And I'm working on a way to keep you and them in the US."

"Then I'll wait for the soldiers to get me, too."

"Carlos, we can't wait. The people who have your mother are the ones after you. Their goal is to get to you through her. Foley won't give you up, and I don't think Alana will either. But they won't stop coming for you. We have to take the risk and get you out now. You'll be in Los Angeles within forty-eight hours."

"I want . . . the soldiers."

"They won't do it. Not without government permission. The coyote is the only way."

◆ ◆ ◆

Carlos burned inside. How could these supposedly smart Americans put their faith in *la mafia*? Put his life in the hands of men whose only care was money?

Officer Garcia walked in and waved a hand at him.

"Hold, please, Señor Lamport." He turned to the officer. "What is it?"

"If I were you I'd do what the American judge says."

"You were listening to us?"

"Don't take the captain's hospitality for granted, *muchacho*. It's my business to know everything said and done in this station. It's time for you to move on anyway."

"You're throwing me out?"

"We do as we please, *muchacho*. You can stay until the coyote comes for you. If you refuse, you leave now."

Fear, the same fear he'd felt from the masked intruder at the canal, paid a return visit, slithering up his throat, teasing him, taunting him to give in. What had he done then? He'd stood firm, trusted in his God, kept his focus on the mission and on Gonzalo.

And it had turned out badly.

Really, what choice did he have? If he refused to cross with the coyote, he would be on his own with no transportation, unless he wanted to steal another vehicle. Which would be total disrespect to the *capitán* who'd extended his trust to him when he had no reason to.

He took Señor Lamport's call off hold.

"I'll do it. I'll go with the coyote."

Chapter 39

Edward gave a polite nod to the two colleagues with whom he rode up in the judges-only elevator. His fifth-floor stop was the first, and he gave a wave of the hand and looked straight ahead as he left the car. He skipped his customary stop at the coffee station and strode directly to his chambers. The close call with Carlos had left an indelible mark. Exactly where and when he could least afford it. He had to get Prop. 68 off his back.

"Morning, Rebecca."

She raised her hand as if to tell him something, but he stepped through his chambers door and closed it without a word. He'd make it up to her later.

He dropped his briefcase on his desk, pulled his laptop from its sleeve, and slid it into the docking station. He made a quick e-mail check, then printed his opinion.

While the eighty-three pages streamed out of the printer, he unlocked the bottom drawer of his credenza and pulled out two slim books. He opened the one on top—a leather-bound copy of the US Constitution his father had given him after he graduated from UCLA Law.

"Next to the Bible," his father had said, "this is the most precious document in the world. Guard what it stands for with your life."

Edward opened to the front plate and meditated on the words his father had written there:

> *If the principles from which this document emerged were followed faithfully, the land of our Mexican brothers would not have been stolen from them, and our Irish ancestors would not have been slaughtered and disgraced. Respect these words as you would respect God's word.*

He'd always thought his father's view of the Mexican-American War was a stretch.

Until he was assigned the Prop. 68 trial.

He dissected each word of Article I, unpacking the construction and meaning of the text, then going back over each section to distill the higher principles. He'd read it hundreds of times, but he still needed a deeper understanding of the heart and spirit of the founders.

After an hour of reading and meditation and reflection, he opened the second book—a worn and brittle leather portfolio that held a collection of faded letters written by his ancestor, Padraig Lamport, to his wife, Heather. An envelope inside guarded three faded photographs—one of Padraig and Heather, a second of Padraig with his fellow members of the Battalion of St. Patrick, and a third of Padraig with the letter *D* branded into his right cheek.

He grabbed a napkin from his desk drawer and pulled the seventh letter from the portfolio, careful not to bend the brittle paper or allow the oil from his fingers to touch it. Padraig Lamport had endured disgrace for the sake of honor and put loyalty to God over allegiance to a country, fighting what he believed was an unjust war. He'd laid down his own honor and endured the hate of the "nativists" of the day, second- and third-generation sons of the revolutionaries who'd stolen other men's land, broken away from their colonial rulers, and then vilified those against whom they'd had generational prejudices in the old country.

He settled on two paragraphs in that seventh letter that he'd revisited now and then since his father had handed down these family treasures to him when Edward had graduated from law school.

> *I still fail to understand, my dearest Heather, how our quest to find newness of life and opportunity, to escape the dirty and naked misery olde Erin had become, had turned into a reprise of the hate and oppression we thought we had left behind. My heart is grieved to death over how men who profess the same blessed Savior as we continue to cause our brothers to suffer indignity and lack and, through their indifference, continue to grind us into poverty and then, looking on the fruit of their deeds, crush us for standing for what is just in the eyes of God.*

> *Yet this indignity I now suffer, the scar born of hatred in vile men, pales in the light of what Our Lord endured for me. I wear the scar and the label of dastard and deserter to my grave as but a minor affliction, awaiting the hope we have in Him to be made manifest for us.*

Words a century and a half old sang an anthem for the present.

Endless media blather prophesied a permanent rift between the states and the federal government, even between America and the rest of the world, because of Proposition 68. Yet the question of a state's right to regulate its own affairs, or the federal government's exclusive domain over immigration and naturalization, weren't the real issues.

After 170 years of social progress, technological advancements, wars, and shifted borders, the fundamental issue was the same as it ever was.

The same as Padraig Lamport encountered.

We are here now, and we don't want to share what we have with you.

That the parents or grandparents of most Americans were immigrants from every corner of the world mattered not.

Edward pulled a well-worn Bible from his credenza, thumbed to the center, and searched for wisdom as he grappled with longings and regrets and hopes.

◆ ◆ ◆

"This is Judge Lamport," he said to the clerk of the court. "I will announce my decision on *United States v. Robison and Johnson* tomorrow morning at ten thirty. Please issue a media release immediately."

"Any special instructions?" the clerk asked.

"Judge Kenworth is allowing me to use Courtroom Five for the announcement. Reserve half the gallery seats for reporters. The rest will be available to the public. Both the media and the public need to contact your office to reserve a seat, first come, first served. I'm permitting credentialed media to use audio recording devices, but no video or live transmission will be allowed."

He ended the call and dialed Chief Judge Marrone's chambers.

"What do you need, Judge Lamport?" Marrone said tersely.

"I've informed the court executive and the clerk of the court that I'm announcing my decision on Prop. Sixty-Eight tomorrow morning. Media release goes out in an hour."

"Good. Look forward to it."

Something hadn't agreed with him that morning. "Do you have fifteen minutes this afternoon? I'd like to review how I'm handling the announcement with the media."

A pause. "No. Come at nine thirty. You're doing this by the book, right?"

"You know my track record, Michael."

"That's what concerns me."

◆ ◆ ◆

Chambers of Hon. Michael Marrone
9:30 a.m.

A storm swirled around the chief judge. "Sit down, Judge Lamport." Marrone settled into his desk chair. "The court executive just informed me you're allowing the media to have audio recording equipment in your courtroom tomorrow morning."

"That's correct."

"But no live broadcast."

"Also correct."

"Then what are you doing with Albert Sanchez from USANews Network?"

"That's why I wanted to see you. The attention on me and my decision is a rare platform to show the public how we judges do our jobs. I want to set an example with my story."

"You know what the code—"

"This isn't the first time I've worked with the media." *You shouldn't have cut him off.* "My apologies for interrupting."

Marrone raised his chin. "Go on."

"I want to open the window and show people how I look at cases and apply my judicial philosophy. I want to be accessible to ordinary people. Our independence and autonomy is a sacred trust, and I don't believe we should be above scrutiny."

"You're giving him an exclusive. Why not make the rounds?"

"I'm not selling anything. I offered Sanchez an exclusive because he's the only journalist I trust with the story. There is one caveat, though."

Marrone narrowed his eyes. "Which is?"

"Sanchez wants to ask me questions about my decision process on Proposition Sixty-Eight. I can address—"

"You can't talk about an active case!"

"I have no intention of doing so. I'll talk only about process."

Marrone stood and crossed his arms. "You're walking on a thin, sharp blade."

Like I haven't done that before. "I have discretion over the affairs of my court. I know the boundaries and what's at stake."

"I'm glad about that. Because I'm telling you right now if you so much as nick your toe on that blade, I'll bring you up for sanctions myself."

Sanctions? Where'd that come from?

"Excuse me, Michael, but if a judge speaking his mind is cause for sanctions, take a number. There are Supreme Court justices and court of appeals judges way ahead of me in line."

"You still act like you're in front of the bench." Marrone pointed a finger at him. "You've got a lot to learn about how to function within the federal court system."

Why is he gunning for me like this?

"Do you *really* think anything I have to say will warrant the attention of the judicial council?"

"You'll be smart not to test me."

◆ ◆ ◆

Edward figured Marrone's distress over his interview with Sanchez had more to do with his past than anything he'd done as a judge.

That would soon change, of course.

Edward had accepted the nomination to the bench because he wanted to make a difference, not lord it over people. Same reason he'd laid down his pro baseball dreams for a life in criminal justice. His mother's senseless murder had propelled him to seek justice, uncompromising justice, against all the killers and thieves and drug dealers and gangbangers he could get his hands on.

Uncompromising.

Without mercy.

You gave no mercy, yet you want it for your son. With the measure you give, it will be given to you . . .

His phone's ringtone yanked him out of his contemplations. It was Albert Sanchez.

"Didn't expect to hear from you so soon."

"No updates on Carlos. I need to cover some details on the interview. I'd like to push it to Thursday."

Edward had spent his life suppressing his emotions to do his job. But doing this interview with Carlos in their presence, that would be unprecedented. To say the least. "Fine. When your crew comes in, I'd prefer they arrive in an unmarked vehicle. I don't want to call attention to what we're doing."

The timing of this interview was becoming less and less attractive by the hour.

Chapter 40

Tuesday, February 23
Arroyo Seco, Sonora, México, one kilometer south of the US border
12:19 a.m. MST

Carlos asked God to forgive him for the twentieth time for not trusting Sanchez and Judge Lamport. Carreras—*el coyote*—had treated him with respect on their journey from La Junta and had prepared him well for the crossing.

He guessed the light of the waning moon gave them about twenty meters forward visibility. At best. Carreras had said he'd traveled the dry creek bed multiple times and would get them through to the rendezvous point without incident.

"The winds in the canyon are unpredictable." Carreras handed him a large bandana and clear safety goggles. "Wear these as we travel. Make sure you cover your ears if the sand blows."

Carlos looked Carreras up and down. In spite of how well the journey with him had gone to this point, something in Carreras's spirit did not seem right. How many of the hundreds of thousands who'd crossed into America here with nothing but the clothes on their back and worn-out huaraches on their feet had Carreras profited from?

All was not as it seemed. Should he confront him? Should he risk angering him and jeopardize his escape, just because he had a hunch the man was not of clean heart?

No. He couldn't trust his own judgment. Not after what he'd done with the captain at the police station.

Carlos accepted his reality. Carreras was one of the few coyotes who hadn't sold out to the drug cartels. He said the Tohono were sympathetic to the cause of the Mexican people. Their nation—the nation of their fathers—existed on *both* sides of the US-Mexico border.

"Time to move," Carreras said. Carlos tied the bandana around his neck, then pulled the goggle strap over his head and let the eyewear dangle on his neck. He patted the front pocket where he'd slipped the CD with the transaction data. He'd thought about destroying it now that he knew Sanchez and Judge Lamport had the PDF copy, but changed his mind.

Carreras led the way, and his two men guarded the rear. Their pistols remained holstered as they began their trek. The rocky sand did not give as much under Carlos's feet as he'd expected, a pleasant surprise. A mild breeze chilled his face, and the air smelled earthy and sweet. He knew nothing about desert vegetation except the tall saguaro cactus and didn't think the spiny trees gave off any aroma.

"I've not smelled the sage and creosote plants like this in a long time," Carreras said.

Carreras had told him the walk through the arroyo would take about forty-five minutes. Their pace was steady and without incident, and not one gust of wind had arisen.

Trust in the Lord and lean not on your own understanding. His faith grew with each uneventful step.

◆ ◆ ◆

Carreras signaled everyone to stop. "This is the spot." He turned his flashlight on and off three times.

Four pulses of light pierced the darkness ahead of them. Carreras turned to the others. "That's our connection. Let's move."

Carlos turned around. Carreras's men had unholstered their pistols. "¿Por qué?"

"We need to be ready for anything," one of the men said.

Carlos turned and sprinted to Carreras. When he caught up to the coyote he tapped him on the shoulder. "Did you tell your men to draw their weapons?"

"You really are *ingenuo*, aren't you?" Carreras opened his jacket and pulled a pistol from a shoulder holster. "Stay a few paces behind."

Carlos's pulse pounded and his leg muscles tightened. He slowed his pace. Carreras opened about a ten-meter lead ahead of him. Carreras turned on a flashlight, then turned it off, slipped his pistol back inside his jacket, and took three, then five, then ten paces. The faint oval of a man's face emerged from the darkness.

Carreras lifted his light and turned it on. Carlos strained to hear what the men were saying to each other, but he could only discern sounds, not words. Then Carreras turned his light off. Carlos could see nothing in front of him. He turned around. Carreras's men held their pistols in both hands, arms extended toward the huddle. Carlos motioned to them to go ahead of him toward Carreras and the shadow man. One went forward, the other stayed to guard the rear.

A strong light shined at them. Carlos was blinded.

"All of you drop your weapons," a voice yelled out. The man who met Carreras got close enough to Carlos for him to see his face and the rifle he was holding. "I said drop your weapons."

Bright lights appeared from the left and the right. A red laser dot appeared on Carlos's chest. Carreras's men laid their pistols on the sand.

The man with the rifle approached Carlos. "Your plans have changed. You will not be meeting Marco Lopez." The man reached into his jacket pocket and pulled out three zip ties. The lights on their left and right moved closer and closer, until two other men brandishing rifles appeared. They picked up the pistols Carreras's men had laid down and kept their rifles trained on them.

Carlos choked back tears and held his tongue. Everything inside him wanted to lash out. He wanted to attack the leader of this bunch, like he had at the canal. He'd be killed, of course. He had to stay alive. Bernal and Salvatierra could not be allowed to get away with their crimes.

The leader of the invaders thrust the barrel of his rifle into Carlos's breastbone. Carlos staggered and fell on his backside.

"Get up," the man yelled.

Carlos stood, and the man yanked him around, pulled his arms back, and tied the zip tie around his wrists. He did the same to Carreras.

"If we wanted you dead you would have already been shot."

Chapter 41

Hancock Park, Los Angeles
2:41 a.m.

Edward's heart raced and his hands trembled from a rush of adrenaline unleashed by the ringing phone.

Jacqui held his arm.

It was Sanchez.

Hope rose. His plan had borne its fruit. "Is Carlos with you?"

"Uh . . . Judge Lamport . . ."

No. It can't be.

"What happened?"

"They didn't make it to the transfer point," Sanchez said.

The words he'd secretly dreaded. The words he wouldn't let himself consider, to not in any way diminish his faith that God would deliver his son into his hands. His arms.

He didn't make it to the transfer point.

Didn't make it.

"Judge Lamport, you all right?"

"Why do people keep asking me that question?" He tried to shake the disbelief out of his head. Didn't work. "Sorry."

Jacqui tugged at his arm. "What happened?"

He turned to her, shaken to his core. "Carlos didn't make it."

He pushed the speakerphone button. "Jacqui and I are on. What went wrong?"

"Marco thinks Carreras got on the wrong side of a drug cartel."

"Who's Marco?"

"Marco Lopez. The man Carreras arranged to hand Carlos over to me."

Edward rubbed his eyes. "Albert. How?"

"Carreras was one of the last of the old guard. We don't know if the guys who intercepted them are connected to Bancomex-ALEXA or from some cartel who's been after him because of his refusal to join them."

"Where are you now?"

"Marco told me to hightail it out of the reservation. I'm on Arizona Highway Eighty-Six, about forty-five minutes south of Interstate Eight."

All Edward could do was sigh.

Another failure.

Another option erased.

Jacqui wrapped her arms around his waist. "I'm so sorry."

"Yeah," Edward rasped. He choked down a lump.

"You have a big day today, Judge Lamport. Let's regroup after you announce your ruling."

Edward nodded. "You're right." He drew a slow breath. In. Out. "Let us know when you're back in LA."

He pushed the Off button on the handset. It was like he'd pushed End on his hopes. He took Jacqui's hand. "No sense going back to sleep now."

She kissed his cheek and stood with him. "Let's have some tea." They moved to the kitchen, arm in arm. Her love and support meant everything right now.

Edward filled the teakettle while Jacqui retrieved tea bags from the pantry. "You want herbal or green or Earl Grey?"

"You pick."

She brought an Earl Grey for him and a green tea for herself.

Edward put the kettle on the stove and turned on the fire. He stared at the flames under the kettle.

Fire.

Burning.

He closed his eyes. He summed his fears.

He stared at the wide blue flame and considered every significant life choice he'd made. Why he'd made it. What had happened after.

Meaningless. All of it. What difference had he made? How had he made the world a better place?

He'd be remembered for only one thing. Breaking the hearts of the two women he'd loved.

The kettle whistled. Time's up. Game over.

He brewed their tea and brought it to the living room. He handed Jacqui her cup and sat next to her on the sofa.

"I can't . . ." His throat caught. He reached for Jacqui's hand.

"It wasn't enough. I didn't do enough. I didn't have . . . Was I wrong the whole time? Did I flat-out misread this whole thing? Why would God allow Carlos back into my life and then let him be snatched away?"

How would he even begin to make sense of this defeat?

It couldn't be over.

What could he have done differently? He was tempted to think he'd been too impulsive, that he hadn't thought his actions and their consequences through as he'd been trained to do and learned to do through his work.

His work.

Justice. The elusive ideal. The one he'd given up his life dreams for, to be part of the solution to the ravages of crime and indifference and . . .

For his son, all his pursuit of justice amounted to was a big fat zilch.

He turned to Jacqui, his eyes stinging. "It's been a waste. The last twenty-five years have been a complete waste. What difference have I made? How has my life made things better?" He buried his face in his hands and exhaled a low groan.

"Ed, please don't pronounce that over yourself. You were a great prosecutor. You set records for convictions. You got justice for a lot of people."

He sat up. "Justice? You mean *revenge*. Punishment. Payback. How does that make anything right? I won a conviction of the guys who hit Gleason and his company, and he's a big-deal businessman, so people paid attention. And it got me a seat on the federal bench. So what?"

He sat forward and hung his head. Shame pressed down and pressed in. Guilt uncurled its tentacles and encircled the remnants of his heart.

Jacqui set her cup down and wrapped her arms around his waist. Her eyes met his, and the tension melted a bit. "What you've done and do now matters. The Prop. Sixty-Eight case wasn't assigned to you by accident. Your number didn't just come up."

She rested her forehead on his and his nose brushed hers. He kissed her lips. He drew her closer and kissed her again. Deep. Warm. They released. She rested her head on his chest.

When was the last time they'd shared such a kiss?

"I've missed you. I didn't realize how much."

He held her. No words. Only comfort and love passing through their embrace.

"I took on the job of judge like I did as a prosecutor. Screw the politics. Ignore the wind." He reached for his mug and took a sip of tea. The warmth soothed his aching throat. "I was gonna set an example. Be the first of a new breed. Get us away from the whims of men."

"Yeah. I felt the same way when I was promoted to local district superintendent."

"You did?"

"Every wrong I'd seen and been hit with as a principal, by golly I was gonna fix 'em all. Then reality set in."

Reality.

He was exactly where he'd aimed to be. The opportunity to fulfill his mission was there.

Then Tuesday came.

And all of his success and his zeal for justice was worth exactly squat.

Jacqui lifted her head. "Maybe Beverley will listen to you now?"

"Not a chance."

His knee-jerk reaction was no, but what did he have to lose? Why not try one more time?

"That's a good thought, dear. You're right." He kissed her lips. "I can't give up. I'll call him after I announce my ruling."

He looked at the clock on the mantel. He needed to be at the courthouse in five hours.

He thought of Padraig Lamport. The despair he'd poured out in the letter to his wife Edward had read the day before. And a seed of strength sprouted. Padraig Lamport would have mustered what it took to get through today.

Was Edward Lamport cut of the same cloth?

Chapter 42

Edward adjusted his tie and smoothed out the pleats in his robe. He moved a few stray hairs into place. Thankfully, the bench in Courtroom Five was far enough from the attorneys and the gallery that they couldn't see the bags under his eyes.

Keep the glasses on.

His veneer was in place. He would show the public and the litigants what they expected. While his insides simmered like an awakening volcano about to blow. He was loaded on caffeine and his stomach was paying the price.

And thoughts of Carlos and what his captors might be doing to him dominated his mind.

As did thoughts of Alana and Foley.

And whether the same brutal men had them all in their lair.

He grabbed his black portfolio, double-checked that he had all the documents he needed, and held it in his right hand as he strode with head high through Judge Kenworth's chambers into the courtroom.

"All rise," the court clerk announced. "United States District Court is now in session, the Honorable Edward J. Lamport presiding. Please be seated and come to order."

Edward took his seat and removed three sets of clipped pages from his portfolio and spread them side by side. He skipped his customary acknowledgments of counsel.

"This court is convened to announce its ruling in docket number C-13-0796 EJL, the matter of United States of America, plaintiff, versus Douglas Robison, in his official capacity as governor of the State of California, Wilfred Johnson, in his official capacity as attorney general of the State of California, defendants, and James Wright, Guillermo Gutierrez, and Yes on Sixty-Eight, official proponents of Proposition Sixty-Eight, as defendant-interveners."

Edward ran through routine administrative procedures, then paused to scan the courtroom. Six deputy marshals were stationed around the perimeter of the two-story-tall, fifty-foot-square space, and three stood at the public entrance at the rear wall. Some in the gallery displayed rapt expressions, others sat with eyes closed in a prayerful posture, and still others looked down. Some would cheer after his announcement, others would weep, and he expected at least a few would shout derisive words about him.

He would tolerate one disrespectful outburst before having any offenders removed from his courtroom.

"Now to the matter at hand. Plaintiff has challenged the constitutionality of the California voter-enacted law, Proposition Sixty-Eight, under Article One, Section Eight of the Constitution of the United States. Plaintiff also challenged defendants' right to enact and enforce Proposition Sixty-Eight on the basis of statutory requirements on the use of federal funds by state agencies."

Edward shifted his gaze between the plaintiff and defense counsel teams. He picked up a single sheet and put on his reading glasses. "In its entirety, Proposition Sixty-Eight, voted into law by a majority of the California electorate, provides as follows:

> *All residents of the State of California shall be required to present a State Services Eligibility Identification Card ("the Card") in order to obtain any state, county, or municipal services, permits, licenses, financial assistance, or other entitlements. The Card will be issued by the California Public Services Bureau ("CPSB"), the establishment of which is mandated by this law.*

> *Valid proof of legal residency in the United States and the State of California must be presented to obtain the Card. Legal residency in the United States may be proven with one of the following: an official copy of a birth certificate issued by a United States county, bearing county seal; federal naturalization documents; federal permanent resident card; H1/ L1 work visa; or other federal visa that grants legal residency status for a minimum of two years. Valid California residency may be established with a current California driver's license or California Identification Card issued by the Department of Motor Vehicles, and a current utility bill from the applicant's primary dwelling.*

> *All persons unable to present proof of legal residency in the United States and the State of California who wish to be eligible to receive services must register with the CPSB to obtain both a Non-Resident California Identification Card and State Services Eligibility Identification Card.*

"Defendants and defendant-interveners dispute the plaintiff's challenge, asserting the State of California is making no attempt to usurp the federal government's power to regulate immigration and grant legal residency in the United States. Furthermore, the defendants claim they are offering undocumented residents the opportunity to qualify for taxpayer-funded services, including those supported with federal funds, by submitting to a California residency verification protocol."

He paused again to scan the assembly before him. He checked his posture to ensure he didn't signal anything with his body language. "Having considered the arguments of counsel and the evidence presented, along with prior decisions of district and appellate courts, this court finds for the defendants on the first challenge, that Proposition Sixty-Eight does not violate Article One, Section Eight of the United States Constitution—"

A loud murmur erupted from the gallery. Members of the public shouted, "How can you turn your back on your own people?" and "Finally, a judge with courage." Edward banged his gavel five times.

"We will have order in this courtroom." Another bang of the gavel. "Order." The assembly fell silent. "May I remind you that the community members and media present in this courtroom are here at my discretion. I will not tolerate another outburst. I hereby instruct the US Marshals to remove all persons who speak another word without permission."

He reached for his water glass, cleared his throat, and took a long sip. "I repeat . . . having considered the trial evidence and the arguments of counsel, along with prior decisions of peer courts and higher courts, this court finds that Proposition Sixty-Eight does not violate Article One, Section Eight of the United States Constitution, nor does it conflict with the body of federal statutes regulating immigration. This court also finds that the plaintiff's claim that the State of California cannot withhold services to illegal immigrants is immaterial to the effect in law and execution of Proposition Sixty-Eight, and is hereby dismissed."

Faces that had been jubilant settled into contentment. Expressions of outrage and disappointment quieted to sad resignation.

"The stay this court placed on Proposition Sixty-Eight's enactment and enforcement at the beginning of these proceedings is hereby lifted. Proposition Sixty-Eight, as passed into law by majority vote of the people of the State of California, shall take effect immediately." He banged his gavel once.

"Copies of the order and opinion of this court in this matter will be available beginning at eleven fifteen this morning at the office of the Clerk of the Court and henceforth during normal business hours."

He paused for another drink. "This concludes the proceedings for the aforementioned case." He paused to move the document containing his personal statement into reading position. "Before I adjourn this session, I want to read a statement directed at the litigants in this case, the residents of the State of California, and all concerned citizens of the United States. This statement shall have no binding effect on either party in the matter concluded before this court." Another drink to loosen his dry tongue. He shifted his weight to relieve pressure on his back muscles.

I'm going through with this. It's now or never.

"This is a message from a concerned citizen to my fellows."

The body posture of the media contingent shifted in near unison, with eyes wide-open and notepads poised. "The matter just concluded by this court received an exhaustive examination of the facts, applicable case precedents, and historical rulings concerning Article One, Section Eight. The rhetoric and debate on both sides of the immigration issue has been and continues to be passionate, sometimes earnest and sincere, and sometimes self-serving. The existing body of law regulating the legal entry of foreigners into the United States is clear and comprehensive, yet enforcement is selective and inconsistent based on the prevailing political climate. As a judge, I must examine cases like this against the text of the Constitution and other applicable laws. My judicial philosophy is to stick to the original meaning of the text as best as can be ascertained."

The journalists were heads down in their notes. Community members shifted in their seats and had quizzical expressions. "I am a God-fearing citizen and son of immigrants. The human dynamics behind the immigration debate did weigh heavy on my conscience during my deliberation and continue to weigh heavy."

A murmur rose, which Edward squelched with two gavel bangs. "May I remind you this court is still in session and disruptions subject you to expulsion." Another sip of water. "As you just heard, I concluded based on the weight of the evidence and precedent and the arguments of counsel that Proposition Sixty-Eight is in fact constitutional. It is clearly the will of the majority of Californians that this proposition become law, and the right of the people of this state to propose and enact laws through the ballot proposal method is guaranteed by the constitution of the State of California and shall in no way be infringed upon by the federal government."

A smattering of applause. One bang of the gavel. "One of the brilliant facets of the American character and our system of government is that while the will of the majority prevails, the rights of the minority are vigorously protected. This is the right and just thing to do in a free society. It's a doctrine established by our founding fathers and deeply rooted in our American tradition and system of laws. This facet of our national character makes us unique among all nations. Because the requirements of Proposition Sixty-Eight apply to all who seek government services or benefits within the State of California, the law does not discriminate against any individual or group. It provides for anyone living in California who is in this country illegally an opportunity to come out of the shadows and receive government services and benefits. And it does not interfere in any way with the federal government's responsibility or discretion to enforce existing immigration laws or jurisdiction over the administration of those laws and resulting processes."

He paused to turn a page and scan the gallery. They seemed to be tracking with him and anticipating his next words. "I found no constitutional reason why Proposition Sixty-Eight should be prevented from becoming law in the State of California. It is an earnest attempt by the majority of the residents to take action that, in their collective wisdom, they believed their elected representatives did not have the will to take."

Applause and murmurs broke through the hovering tension. Edward let it go for a few moments, and it died down on its own.

"I say now, not as a federal judge but as a resident of this great state and a concerned citizen of this great nation, that Proposition Sixty-Eight as conceived, written, and sold to the public, is a bad law."

The murmur returned, louder this time. He banged his gavel twice more, also louder. "This is my final warning. One more outburst and I clear the courtroom." He realized that what he had just said worked against his purpose for reading his statement. But he had to stay consistent in managing his courtroom, lest he lose control altogether.

"I say Proposition Sixty-Eight is a bad law for two reasons. One, I believe it to be mean-spirited. Many disagree with my belief, and it was not a factor in my deliberations. Two, it's a bad law because it doesn't address the real issues. In spite of the claims of its proponents, this law will do nothing to stop the flow of illegal drugs into this country. It will do nothing to stem the rising tide of human traffickers encroaching on our southern border. It does not deter the flow of illegal immigrants from Mexico and Central America through the porous sections of our southern border. And it contributes nothing to answer the question of how to resolve disposition of the people who already live in this country illegally."

His palms moistened as he anticipated reaction to what he would say next. He cleared his throat and took another sip of water.

"Yet in spite of my personal assessment, the passage of Proposition Sixty-Eight *has* accomplished something this country has needed." His hands began to tremble, and heat rose on the back of his neck. "It shined a light on the cumulative consequence of prior decisions, at the district and appellate levels, that were reflections of ideology or political leanings rather than a sound legal foundation rooted in constitutional principles."

A cacophony of applause, cheers, and derisive shouts erupted from the gallery. He banged his gavel repeatedly until the crowd fell silent.

"Each time a judge strays from fundamental principles to inject his or her own views or political leanings into the disputes set before them, the foundation of our society cracks. Every decision motivated by ideology or contemporary politics amplifies the cracks in our foundation, to the point where we not only cease being a government of laws, but we become a government of men and women with the loudest voices, a government of personality and force of will. As one of our distinguished appellate judges in another circuit has written, if changing judges changes law then it is not clear what law is. Ladies and gentlemen, I believe in my core that the passage of Proposition Sixty-Eight, while technically constitutional, is a tangible demonstration of how far we as a society have strayed into the tyranny of the loudest voices."

Applause and jeers again erupted. Edward let it go for half a minute, then banged his gavel until order was restored.

"Justice is an objective reality. It cannot be voted on or legislated or politically wrangled. It does not change with ideological fashion. Neither can a republic governed by laws be shaped by the decision of individual judges who usurp the will of the people, expressed through direct action or through their elected representatives, in accordance with our federal Constitution." The hands of journalists in the gallery zipped across their notepads, and many leaned into their colleagues to compare what they'd captured.

"I urge both parties in this now-concluded contest, along with leaders in every state in our union, to work together to enact reforms that show compassion for the weakest and most vulnerable people in our hemisphere while restoring our foundation as a government of laws, not men. Our country was founded as a republic where the rights of the individual and the minority are protected from an omnipotent majority. Checks and balances were established to ensure that no single branch of government could exert its will over the other two. Faithfulness to the law and mercy for the weak and oppressed are not mutually exclusive."

He paused for water. His last two sentences released a mélange of eye rolls and smiles, head shakes and affirming nods.

"I urge us all to work together to do justice and love mercy, remembering that from the many peoples of the world we are one nation, under God, indivisible. That inside our borders is liberty and justice for all."

He collected and straightened the pages on which his statement was printed. "Thank you, ladies and gentlemen of the media, and thank you, fellow citizens." He banged his gavel once.

"All rise," the clerk said. "Court is adjourned."

The media swarm jumped from their seats and shouted questions at him while the six deputy marshals moved to stand guard at the gallery barrier. Edward shot a long look their way, then at the community members who were filing out of the courtroom. He strode through the door to Judge Kenworth's chambers suite, closed it quietly, and stepped toward the private entrance to the judges-only elevator.

It was done. He'd ruled justly. He'd begun the debate.

And he'd said the words he never thought he'd say in a courtroom, behind the bench or in front of it.

Love mercy.

Yet all he could see were three faces counting on him to live another day.

◆ ◆ ◆

Jacqui sat quietly as the radio reporter droned on about her husband's decision on Proposition 68 and his personal statement. After thirty minutes of listening to a panel of so-called experts amplify the rhetoric on both sides, taking potshots at Edward along the way for airing his personal views, she turned off the blather and got up to make herself a cup of tea.

He'd surprised her. Oh, she wanted him to strike down Proposition 68. But, being honest with herself, his logic for upholding it was impeccable, even brilliant. It forced the higher courts to make a political rather than legal decision in order to overturn his ruling—exactly his point. Something, in retrospect, she expected her husband would do. And his personal statement was a masterstroke. Not only had he dared the higher courts to overturn him on political grounds, he'd fired the first shot of the debate.

He'd acted like a leader instead of a dictator.

She poured hot water from the spigot over a bag of orange spice tea, then steeped her face in the fragrant steam as she sauntered back to her desk. She wanted to talk to Edward. She wanted to tell him he'd handled himself with dignity and done his job the way it was supposed to be done. He'd made it clear he had ruled the way he did in spite of his personal feelings.

More than an hour had passed since he'd announced his ruling. She dialed his mobile phone.

◆ ◆ ◆

Jacqui calling. Perfect timing.

"Glad you called."

"You sound relieved." She hesitated. "I want you to know I'm proud of how you did your job today. I wanted it to come out differently, but I think you made your decision the right way."

"Thanks. That means a lot."

"The journalists are buzzing about your statement. Half are saying you broke new ground, the others are calling for your head because you tainted the appeal."

"Well, it's not over. Justice filed their motion for a stay pending review at the Ninth Circuit Court of Appeals. What a surprise, huh? The government will use my statement against me, of course."

"I think you broke huge ground. You filled a leadership void."

"I can't wait to hear what Marrone has to say."

He expected trouble with Marrone. And right now he didn't care.

Chapter 43

A knock on Edward's chambers door. "Judge Lamport, Chief Judge Marrone—"

Marrone pushed past Rebecca and marched into Edward's chambers and slammed the door. "Have you lost your mind, Lamport? Why'd you throw your colleagues under the bus?"

Marrone's behavior was irrational. Something else was at work here.

"My opinions are my opinions. Some judges write theirs in a book. Others announce theirs on TV or in legal forums. I chose to air mine in my courtroom."

"I told you the other day if you so much as nicked your toe on that knife edge you're dancing on, I'd put you up for sanctions myself." Marrone stomped back and forth, running his hands through his hair. "Where do you come off spitting in our faces?"

"You may not like what I said, but criticizing my fellow judges hardly qualifies as misconduct." Edward sat in his desk chair and folded his hands in his lap. "Lower court judges have regularly criticized the Supreme Court and individual justices. We're not above scrutiny."

"You made it personal, Lamport." Marrone strode to the door. "And it's going to cost you. Big."

"I did no such thing. We are independent from political influence. That includes within the courts."

Edward met Marrone at the door of his chambers. "Michael, what's the real problem here?"

"I took you under my wing when you joined this court. I saw through your maverick ways and found someone I wanted to groom."

"And I appreciated it all."

Marrone glowered at him. "I thought you'd gotten it. I thought you'd understood how the game was played around here." He yanked open the door and stormed out of Edward's chambers.

Game? Game of what? Ideology?

Edward dropped his hands to his sides. He was no stranger to controversy. But Marrone's anger made no sense.

So now his docket was clear. A cooling-off period for all concerned was in order.

◆ ◆ ◆

International Trade Center
12:36 p.m.

"Lamport's ruling doesn't change what we're doing one bit," Gleason said to his team huddled in his office at the ITC. "The borderless labor zone pilot doesn't allow Mexicans to live inside California. It's always been up to the Feds to worry about immigration status."

"Are you sure?" one of the men said. "There's already chatter on the news about your connection with Judge Lamport."

"Relax," Gleason said. "All I did was recommend Lamport's nomination to Senator Corman. He once got me justice, and I always repay those who help me."

Rodrigues poked his head into the meeting room. Gleason waved him in.

"Before I forget, where are we on finding those workers Sanchez interviewed?"

"They haven't clocked in the last two days. I've sent men to their apartments, and it looks like they've cleaned out and left town."

"Keep after them! And make sure we keep a tight lid on everything from here on out." He put hands on hips and scanned the faces in the meeting room. "I wonder if you all realize how serious a security breach is in this complex."

◆ ◆ ◆

Edward called Conrad Beverley's direct line.

He got voice mail.

"Mr. Secretary, this is Judge Edward Lamport. New developments have occurred since our meeting, and I need to speak with you soonest. You have my number."

A knock on his door. It was Rebecca. Her eyes said she was worried about him. "I've never seen Marrone so angry."

"Makes me wonder if something else in his life is off-kilter."

His cell phone rang. Beverley had actually returned his call.

"Would you excuse me?"

His assistant nodded and scooted back to her desk.

"Mr. Secretary—"

"Judge Lamport, this is Mark Blair, Secretary Beverley's assistant. He asked me to reply to your voice mail. He gave me a message to relay and said you would understand. 'Thanks for your call. Regarding our meeting, no further follow-up is required. The matter is closed.'"

He understood, all right.

"Give the secretary my regards."

"I will indeed, Your Honor."

Your Honor in his courtroom.

You're sunk in Washington.

Think, Lamport. Where else to turn? Carlos was in the hands of drug lords somewhere in Mexico. If he was even still alive. He was out of resources, out of options.

Except one.

The president of the United States.

Who wants confrontation with Mexico, not cooperation.

Jessup had to come through. He had to.

Or else.

Chapter 44

Carlos could barely see out of his left eye and his right was swollen shut. The air in the room was dank, and a sliver of dusty light from a gap in the top of the low wall angled to the floor. He willed his right arm to move, but it wouldn't budge. Pain wrapped his body like a wetsuit three sizes too small. For now, lying on his back would have to do.

Whoever had beaten him didn't want him dead. Only close to dead. He had no idea where his mother was. No idea what the men who beat him had planned next.

He'd been sure God would protect him.

He was alive.

He'd been sure God would give him success.

Maybe He had a different plan and Carlos had missed it. Or maybe things were unfolding as He intended.

Either way, Carlos had one choice left.

The knob of the door across the room clicked and turned. Sunlight beaming through the doorway transfigured the man into a dark silhouette.

"Still breathing in here?"

"Why don't you kill me and get it over with?"

"A swift death would not be very sporting, Alvarez." The man walked into the room. His hair was cut close, like it had been three days since he'd shaved his head. He had a full, dark beard and thick brows.

"Señor Bernal will be here in a few minutes to speak with you." The man dragged a wooden chair from the far corner of the room. "Let me help you up."

The man grabbed his arms and pulled up. Fire shot from Carlos's hands to the small of his back. He let out a guttural scream as the man dragged him to the center of the room. He flopped Carlos into the chair. It wobbled under him. He sucked air and heaved it out to endure the searing pain. The man pulled a length of rope from his back pocket and wrapped it around Carlos and the chair back twice, then cinched it tight, slamming Carlos's back against the frame of the chair. Pain gave way to delirium. His head bobbed up and down.

The man slapped his right cheek. "Stay with me, *hombre*. You can't die yet."

He felt nothing from the slap.

"Water," Carlos mumbled. "Water."

The man walked out of the room, leaving the door open. He returned moments later with a metal canteen. The man opened it and put it to Carlos's parched and swollen lips. The water was lukewarm and metallic. He gulped as much as his aching throat would allow.

The man pulled the canteen away in midswallow. "Perhaps Señor Bernal will bring you a more pleasing beverage."

"Where is . . . where is my mother?"

The man laughed. "She is with Señor Bernal as we speak."

"Here?" Carlos groaned.

"That's not for you to know."

"Did you beat the stuffing out of her, too?"

"Señor Bernal prefers to deal with the *señora* in a more genteel way."

Carlos drew in as much air as he could. "Liar! Why should I believe anything you say?"

The man turned and left and closed the door.

◆ ◆ ◆

Lake Arrowhead, California
6:04 p.m.

Edward emerged from a much-needed nap and shower. Jacqui was parked in front of the television watching the local evening news. He joined her on the sofa.

"Did Sanchez call while I was down?"

Jacqui shook her head. He got up to get his phone. Jacqui pulled him back to his seat.

"A story about you is on next. Call him afterward."

"This oughta be interesting."

Jacqui hopped to the kitchen and returned with two glasses of Coke on ice as the report began.

"Federal judge Edward J. Lamport's controversial ruling to uphold California's Proposition Sixty-Eight continues to generate both praise and controversy," the newscaster said. "Today the leader of the Howard Jarvis Taxpayers Association, Benjamin Wyatt, issued a statement hailing the decision."

Cut to a sound bite of Wyatt: "California finally has the mechanism it needs to fully account for how much it really costs all levels of government in the state to provide services to illegal immigrants. This is a big step forward to responsible governance and prioritizing of limited resources."

Edward grabbed the remote and paused the program. "He didn't pay attention when I said Prop. Sixty-Eight was a bad law."

"I got a few e-mails today from the No on Sixty-Eight campaign," Jacqui said. "They liked what you said. Gonna use it to rally a Repeal Sixty-Eight drive."

"That's how it should be! People get involved. Take responsibility."

Jacqui nodded and gave his arm a squeeze. He hit Play.

"The protests that had been taking place across the street from the federal courthouse in downtown Los Angeles have exploded since Judge Lamport's ruling. Let's go to Tim Thornton live on the scene."

He hit Pause again. "This frustrates me. Instead of yelling about the way things are, why don't they organize? Or join Repeal Sixty-Eight. Or march on Sacramento and demand the governor delay implementation, which he can do."

"They wanted you to fix it for them."

Edward hit Play and zipped through interviews with three different protesters. He kept fast-forwarding until a graphic appeared on the screen that said "Judicial Misconduct." He stopped the DVR and rewound to just before the graphic came on screen.

"And in the most extreme reaction to date, the California Hispanic Voters Alliance has filed a formal judicial misconduct complaint against Judge Lamport. Our Vikki Marasco was on the scene when the alliance's general director filed the complaint earlier this afternoon."

Pause.

"Marrone will have a field day with that one." He turned to Jacqui. "I still can't fathom why he was so upset. Plenty of judges have fired way harsher criticism at higher-ups. I didn't name any names."

Play.

"Judge Lamport took an open-and-shut case and dragged it out for more than three months," the alliance director said. "He left millions of Hispanic Californians in limbo for months, only to make his outrageous ruling. We have to take a stand against his irresponsible conduct in this case."

He turned it off. It wouldn't last. People would move on.

And Carlos was still in danger. If he was even alive.

He had to depend on back-room-deal-making politicians to save him. Not good enough. He dialed Sanchez.

"How close are you?" Edward said.

"About an hour. I stopped home to shower and pack fresh clothes."

"Jessup and his squad leader are due here around eight," Edward said. "After we're done here I'm going to round up McCormack and Ross Milostan from HSI and give 'em Carlos's data."

"You going to clue the Feds in on Jessup?"

"No. They need time to deliver."

They did indeed. Edward still needed leverage. Lots of leverage, from wherever he could get it.

Chapter 45

Lake Arrowhead, California
7:15 p.m.

Edward welcomed a haggard-looking Sanchez through the front door of their mountain chalet. "What happened this morning was the greatest disappointment of my life," Sanchez said.

Edward helped him move his gear into one of the guest bedrooms. "You were in the best position to make the call on Carreras."

Sanchez put hands on his hips and looked down. "I was *sure* he'd deliver. I sensed genuine compassion under his hard crust when I interviewed him two years ago. More so when I set up Carlos's move. We had him, Judge Lamport. We had him and he's gone again."

"Don't beat yourself up," Edward said. "We don't give up."

The taunts of failure competed hard in Edward's mind against his optimism and determination. Sure, he'd lost before. And he'd always learned from it.

But courtrooms had rules. And he'd been in charge as a prosecutor—lining up the evidence, preparing witnesses and lines of questioning, aggressive cross-examinations, kick-butt closing arguments.

He still didn't see what losing Carlos would teach him.

◆ ◆ ◆

Undisclosed location near Culiacán, México
8:19 p.m. MST

No one had entered Carlos's dungeon since the man who'd tied him to the wobbly chair had left. His mouth and tongue were leather. Every breath was hard labor. The room would spin, then fade, then spin again. He spread his feet to keep some balance.

"God, You said You were with me." His groan was inaudible. "Where . . . are You now?"

He had neither strength nor breath to speak anymore. Only his heart had voice.

The door to his prison flew open. The dusky light was enough to blind him.

"Your mother and her American friend are here. But you will not see them again. You are defeated, Carlos Alvarez." His tormentor approached and slapped his face.

He felt nothing.

His parched throat seized and he coughed. Blood spattered onto his filthy shirt.

They thought they'd won because they'd gotten his CD. Only he knew that the data that could expose ALEXA lived on in the hands of Sanchez and Judge Lamport.

Still, it was of no value without his explanation.

And Bernal knew it.

Chapter 46

Lake Arrowhead, California
8:00 p.m.

Colonel Jessup arrived sharp on the hour dressed in a crisp tan shirt, navy-blue slacks, and black oxfords. Once a Marine, always a Marine. Next to him stood a man who, by appearance, could be active duty. He stood about Edward's height, six-two, and sported a crew cut and medium-brown complexion. He wore a chambray shirt, faded Levi's, and brown low-cut hiking shoes.

"Judge Lamport, meet Jaime Beltran, your squad leader. Jaime was a first lieutenant in one of my MARSOC units at Pendleton."

Edward shook the special forces leader's hand and welcomed the men inside. "I'm grateful you've accepted this mission, Lieutenant Beltran."

"It's what I do, Your Honor," Beltran said. "It's what I was made to do."

A born warrior. A man who knows who he is. Excellent.

The three men joined Sanchez at the dining table. "Quite a place you have here, Your Honor," Jessup said.

"Our refuge. Shall we get down to business?"

"I'm sorry about the failed extraction of your son," Jessup said.

All Edward could do was nod an acknowledgment. He couldn't allow himself to dwell on failure. "Colonel Jessup said you've prepared a thorough game plan, Lieutenant."

Beltran pulled a stack of pages from a brown leather satchel. "I'll start with my mission assessment. Our success in locating your three targets will be totally dependent on quality intel. The challenge we have is sourcing. I understand your son was last seen at a police station in La Junta, Mexico."

"Spoke to the captain myself. He offered to help."

"We'll need more to narrow down potential locations. I recommend we send an intel team into Guadalajara first. We'll also canvas the town your coyote, Carreras, was from for people who know something about that migration route through the Tohono O'Odham reservation and who else uses it. We can communicate with the La Junta police captain remotely to identify leads, too. Honestly, I'm not optimistic. We have to connect a whole lot of dots."

"We have to take a shot, Lieutenant," Edward said.

"I'm not saying we won't pursue it," Beltran said.

"The captain told me the cartels have moved their operations away from the larger cities."

"*If* a cartel has them. We have all Spanish speakers on our team, and two are retired DEA. We'll use their tribal knowledge as a launch point. Both have said they'd never established any connection between Bancomex-ALEXA and the major cartels."

"When you do find them, what's your plan for getting them out?"

Beltran looked down at his papers for a moment. "Your Honor, our plan is to repatriate Mr. Foley and secure Carlos and Alana Alvarez inside Mexico until such time as you can work out their admission into the United States."

Edward shrugged off yet another kick in the gut. *The law prevents good. Again.* He turned to Jessup. "Permission isn't coming."

"Your Honor," Jessup said, "Beltran is the best man for the job. But we talked this over long and hard, and we're not willing to bring non-cits into the country without authorization."

"Then how are they supposed to apply for asylum?"

"We're committed to locating and protecting Carlos and Alana. We'll secure them until you can arrange their admission."

Edward threw up his hands. "That's my whole problem. No one will cooperate. I've met with Secretary of Homeland Security Beverley and Secretary of State Carlisle. They're not willing to help. They say the president wants confrontation with Mexico on immigration, drugs, trade—"

"I can't count how many times in my career in the Corps we wanted to undertake missions that pushed the boundaries of policy," Jessup said. He stood, hands on hips. "We couldn't achieve our objective unless we got the handcuffs off. Sometimes we won, sometimes we lost. Ultimately, we served a commander in chief who had to make the final call."

"So what are you saying, Colonel?"

"You need the White House behind you. The president is the one who must approve any extralegal operation."

"I just told you—"

"What the administration signals publicly, even inside the government, and what happens in secret is very different. We conducted classified black ops twenty years ago I still can't talk about. They'll go with me to my grave. Don't assume you can't get help."

"I'll need to go through the chief of staff. Whom I don't know."

"The thing to keep in mind is if the president decides he wants to help you he's going to need something to trade with the Mexicans."

And what might that be? Edward stood and paced around the table, working the question around in his mind. He snapped a finger. "The president wants confrontation. What he needs is something to force the Mexicans to bargain on *his* terms. And I have it. Carlos's data."

"I'm not following," Jessup said.

"Bancomex and ALEXA are laundering drug money. Americans are involved. But the data's incomplete, so Carlos needs to explain it in person."

"If the data implicates Americans, that would help you get in the door. But how would it give the president leverage over Mexico?"

"The La Junta police captain said there was a competition between the government, the drug cartels, and the business conglomerates for control of the country. If Bancomex, ALEXA, and one or more of the cartels are aligned financially, they have an enormous power base. Wouldn't the Mexican president want to know what we know?"

Jessup nodded. "Our president leverages theirs to help find Carlos so he can fill in the blanks. Then they go after ALEXA and the bank, and that leads to whoever has your son. And the cartels."

"I need to get the data to HSI." Edward turned to Sanchez. "May I have a word with you?"

Edward and Sanchez stepped into the hallway. "We need to postpone the interview."

"I'm good with that, Your Honor. I'll use the time to follow up on what I learned at the ITC grand opening. I picked up some scuttlebutt about Gleason's relationship with Salvatierra and Bernal and about how the place was built. I asked Gleason some questions. He was evasive. I'll poke around some more, see how he reacts."

"Keep me in the loop. I need as much leverage with the president as I can get."

Edward returned to the table and Sanchez stepped down the hall. "Let's recap our next moves. Sanchez will follow up on what he learned at the International Trade Center grand opening. I'll get with HSI on Carlos's data. Lieutenant Beltran will deploy his advance team."

"We'll muster and move out tomorrow afternoon, Your Honor."

"Excellent. We haven't discussed your fees."

"The team is volunteering its services."

Edward stood. "You'll be in harm's way. I won't have it."

Beltran's face was firm as granite. "We have sponsors, sir."

Chapter 47

Wednesday, February 24
Bancomex Headquarters, Guadalajara, México
9:04 a.m. CST

Bernal was amused by Gleason's fondness for video-meeting technology. Bernal was old-fashioned. He preferred to conduct important business *intiamente*.

Face-to-face.

But he'd learned long ago that pragmatism outweighed preference.

The ultra-HD Telepresence center his younger executives had convinced him to install next to his war room felt like American gimmickry at first. But he was soon impressed with its ability to reveal the subtle body language cues he needed to maintain advantage.

Even the slightest perspiration around men's eyes. That alone was worth many times the cost of equipment and fiber optic lines.

Bernal sat to Salvatierra's right so he would appear on the left in Gleason's screen.

The power position.

Bernal's three executive vice presidents and his chief security officer occupied chairs behind them, elevated-stadium style.

The sixty-inch monitor lit up and Gleason appeared, dressed in a plain blue shirt and no tie.

Casual is careless.

"I have very good news, Señor Gleason," Bernal said. "We have captured Carlos Alvarez and his mother."

"About time," Gleason said. "You got the second copy of the data?"

"He had a CD in his possession," the chief security officer said. "We think he also sent a copy to someone via the Internet but don't know to whom or when."

"Yet," Bernal interjected.

"You haven't gotten him to talk?" Gleason's face reddened. "Bernal, if you didn't have that weak-minded idiot in charge in Mexicali, none of this would have happened."

Bernal waved a hand. "Courage is a powerful weapon. Alvarez possesses a large measure. We have a third person in our custody who was traveling with Señora Alvarez. An American named Joseph Foley."

"Name means nothing to me."

"His phone showed calls to a number in Los Angeles. To a friend of yours."

"Who is?"

"Edward Lamport. An American federal judge."

The redness drained from Gleason's face. "What has Foley said?"

Ah . . . this system was a superb investment.

"We've been brutal to him. He's not talking. We're sending all of them to San Luis."

Gleason smiled broadly. "About time you get the professionals involved. What exactly is in the data he stole?"

"On the surface, only routine transactions."

"If that's true, then why was it so important to find Alvarez?"

Bernal leaned forward. "Someone with inside knowledge could interpret the information in a way that would severely damage our operations."

"So what are you waiting for? Get rid of them."

"Impatience is your downfall," Bernal said. "Until we know to whom he sent the data, uncertainty will linger. Dead men don't speak."

A voice from behind spoke up. *"Perdóneme,* Señor Bernal.*"*

He turned to Daniel Canedo, his young executive vice president. "You have a suggestion?"

"Señor, this talk of torture and death is disturbing and I believe unnecessary. If Alvarez sent anything over the Internet or by e-mail in the last seven days, he left a trail behind. We have the clout to get every Internet service provider in Mexico to give us their message logs by account and IP address. It is possible for the IT team to find what we're looking for."

Gleason chuckled. "Your guy in the back there has some spunk."

Bernal smiled tightly. "Rest assured, Señor Gleason, we will do whatever is necessary to ensure our secrets remain so."

Bernal ended the session and pulled Canedo aside. "Do not embarrass me like that in a meeting ever again."

"But, *señor,* we don't need to make more trouble if there are other—"

"If you are not in agreement with how we do business here, perhaps it is time for us to part ways. Of course, you cannot erase from your mind what you have heard. And when people who work for me show disloyalty, I can no longer trust them. So you see, you've created a most difficult situation for me as well as yourself."

Canedo looked away. His lower lip trembled. *"Sí, señor.* Please accept my apology."

"By the way, Daniel, your idea is good. I will direct our chief technology officer to do what you've suggested."

Chapter 48

Chambers of Hon. Edward J. Lamport
2:36 p.m.

Edward leaned back in his chair and rubbed his temples in an attempt to massage fresh wisdom into his mind. The obstacles he'd encountered and decisions he'd had to make over the last week had melded into a blur, and he felt he'd lost control.

Beltran's commando team would be his eyes and ears inside Mexico and, if they were able to find Carlos and Alana, would provide the best protection he could muster, which might not be enough.

Jessup's exhortation to give the president of the United States a try gave him a much-needed boost, and even though this president was the one who'd appointed him to the federal judiciary, it would still be a long shot to get a meeting with him, much less secure his help to rescue his loved ones.

But he would see his latest plan through. He would do whatever he could possibly do. Leave no stone unturned. Starting with his upcoming meeting with Homeland Security Investigations Special Agent Ross

Milostan and his crack forensics expert, Special Agent Scott Huizenga. Carlos's data would have to tell its story, at least enough of it for the agents and their team to flesh out the narrative.

He stepped to his outer offices, and Rebecca held up a short stack of printed pages. "Your latest Google Alerts, Your Honor."

He scanned the first two sheets. Controversy over his Prop. 68 ruling had grown more intense. He rolled the sheets into a baton and tapped his palm with it. "I'll save the rest for the next time I'm bored."

The security door to his office suite buzzed. Rebecca confirmed that McCormack and the two HSI agents had arrived, and Edward met them at the door and led them into his chambers.

"We ran down the basics on ALEXA," Special Agent Huizenga said. "About seventy percent of their revenues come from their casino properties."

"Gambling . . . cash business," Edward said.

Huizenga opened his laptop and turned the screen toward Edward. "They own six high-volume casinos—two in the Dominican Republic, two in Panama, and two in Venezuela—and a dozen smaller ones around the Caribbean and South America. We were able to identify deposits to Bancomex through foreign exchange markets and bank clearing houses, which we presume came from those operations."

"So the question is where the cash comes into the casinos from," Edward said.

"We converted your PDF to an active spreadsheet," Huizenga said. He highlighted three of the columns. "These are identification numbers of the source of funds—who wrote the deposit check or sent an electronic funds transfer. The second column is the identification of the clearinghouse that processed the EFT transactions. Domestic sources, whether check or EFT, carry the Bancomex number, and international sources have the identifier of the clearinghouse used there."

Huizenga sorted the transactions by source and date. He scrolled through the spreadsheet and pointed out how a pattern emerged. "These all come through the FOREX currency exchange. In order to trace back which currency was exchanged, the source bank's currency exchange department would provide that information. From what I see here, Bancomex doesn't provide that service to ALEXA."

Edward rubbed his chin. "Any patterns that imply money laundering?"

Huizenga scrolled down to the payments section of the spreadsheet. "ALEXA makes regular income tax payments, on schedule. Sometimes early." He scrolled to a cluster of transactions and highlighted the cells showing the payees. "Here are six payments to the Tax Administration Service." Huizenga highlighted another group of payees. "These are payments to foreign government taxation agencies."

"Paying taxes keeps governments off their backs," Edward said.

Huizenga scrolled farther. "Here are the biggest clues. Three payments made from ALEXA's operating account to Ramón Fuentes, director of the Mexican Tax Administration Service. Four payments to Hugo Cortez, director of the CNBV—the National Banking and Securities Commission."

"*If* they're bribes, then they're a Mexican government problem," Edward said.

"I didn't find direct links," Huizenga said, "but when you add up the pieces—high-volume cash business, offshore corporations, facilitation payments—something huge and illegal *appears* to be happening. What I don't see, though, is American financial institution involvement."

Edward's hope for an audience with the president of the United States evaporated. "No smoking gun. This won't get us anywhere." He turned to Special Agent Milostan. "We need to get into Bancomex's system. What would we need to get a hearing at the Foreign Intelligence Surveillance Court?"

"If we can show cause, we ask for a warrant to conduct a communications intelligence operation where we intercept transmissions between parties. International communications intercept ops are usually handled by CIA. It can take days to get one approved. But we may be restricted to intercepting phone and e-mail communications. Penetrating the internal systems of a foreign company could be considered an act of war. NSA monitors the SWIFT international transaction system, and their Tracfin database might have what we're looking for. Not easy to get, though. Our best next move is to trace the ALEXA links to the US side of the International Trade Center project."

"But we *can* pursue the reverse," Edward said. "The law allows the government to require financial institutions to disclose records without notifying the customer if there is probable cause the information is drug trafficking or espionage related."

Edward stepped to his desk and punched a number into his desk phone. "Eriksen, it's Edward Lamport. I need you in my chambers ASAP. I'm with HSI and we need to write a request for a warrant to search financial records. I'll explain when you get here." He ended the call and returned to the table.

"The US Attorney will be here momentarily. I'll sign the warrant and issue any subpoenas you need." Edward turned to McCormack. "We'll include a search of the financial records of the Las Reconquistas group in New Mexico."

"We've had no reports of heightened activity, Your Honor," McCormack said. "On either threat."

"But you can't give me an all clear yet."

"There's no timetable for relaxing our protection."

Edward's intercom sounded. "Mr. Paul Eriksen is here to see you, Your Honor."

Eriksen was Edward's hand-picked successor as the United States Attorney in the Central District of California. He leaned to the formal in his dealings with people. Between his Danish heritage and his Yale Law education, he'd always fancied himself refined. Edward had considered

Eriksen annoying at first but had come to discover ample talent and a warmth beneath the rigid exterior and found both endearing.

Rebecca escorted the US Attorney into Edward's chambers. "I believe you know Deputy McCormack and Special Agent Milostan," Edward said. "Meet Special Agent Scott Huizenga."

"Good afternoon," Eriksen said as he extended his hand to Huizenga. "This gathering is out of order. Process-wise, I mean. You agents usually come to us first, not a judge."

"They're here at my request, Paul," Edward said. "Take a seat."

Eriksen raised an eyebrow as he settled in at the opposite end of the table from Edward. "And why did you go directly to them instead of through my office?"

"This began as a personal pursuit. I have a son in Mexico whose life is in danger."

Eriksen's eyes telegraphed surprise. "I didn't know you had family in Mexico."

"You don't remember I'm Irish-Mexican?"

Eriksen shook his head. "Please continue."

"My son discovered that the bank he works for is laundering drug money, and people want him dead. We've obtained some data that he took from the bank to back his claim, which I've shared with HSI. We need two requests for bank record search warrants. One to investigate all the US entities associated with the International Trade Center project on the border, which I will sign. The second needs to go to FISC—to investigate the activities of the Mexican company my son claims is the perpetrator. He insists the scheme involves American entities, but the data he has doesn't show US financial institution activity."

"Forgive me, Your Honor," Eriksen said, "but why are you involved at this level of investigation?"

Edward shot a glance toward the HSI agents, then at McCormack. "All cards on the table, gentlemen."

He gave Eriksen an accounting of the events of the last seven days concerning Carlos and Alana. And the snub he had received from both Homeland Security and the State Department to rescue them and bring them to the United States.

He kept the lid on his failed smuggling attempt. For now.

"The bottom line, gentlemen, is the only way I can save my son's life is if our government commits some resources to help me. The only way that can happen is if I give the president of the United States something he can use to extract the necessary cooperation from the Mexican government. Whether I succeed or not, I've handed you an opportunity to make a major interdiction."

Chapter 49

Albert Sanchez prided himself on his adherence to best practices and principles of investigative journalism. Truth. Verification. Impartiality. Clarity.

The one he struggled with was empiricism—the belief that you only report what can be observed and experienced. If you want to expose wrongdoing, particularly criminal activity, observable evidence will be hard to come by.

Stanley Gleason was hiding something. He'd seen the kind of evasiveness Gleason had exhibited at his grand opening event, hundreds of times. And Gleason wasn't that good at it.

He didn't know enough about what he was looking at in Carlos Alvarez's spreadsheet to draw any conclusions. But he believed a golden story was hidden in the ore of those thousands of lines of Spanish names and cryptic code numbers.

He took a break from thinking about Gleason and checked the LA newswire. Judge Lamport was still getting a lot of digital ink. The usual array of crime stories—gang activity, homicides, bank robberies, drug busts. One a little off the norm—LAPD arrests three men for selling drugs to undercover cops, and they were illegal aliens from Mexico. He tagged that story for updates and future reference.

It grieved him still that so many young Latino men chose a life of crime over working hard to better themselves, though he understood why they did. He saw and heard and experienced the street-level animosity toward Mexicans and the judgment that if you were Mexican you were here illegally and sponging off the people who work hard and pay taxes.

An update notification came in from the newswire.

The story about the three illegal aliens who sold drugs to cops.

"Police say the three men told them during questioning they were employees of Sotomayor Construction, the Mexican firm that built the Mexicali side of the experimental International Trade Center that straddles the border between California and Baja California. The three men confessed they had entered the United States by making an illegal exit from the ITC complex."

He'd interviewed three men from the construction crew. They'd told him they worked for Angeles Development. If these were the same men, why would they lie about who they worked for?

Gleason had said he hadn't heard about the men and what they'd told him—that there was unusual equipment on the construction site. They said they'd never seen anything like it before. That it kind of looked like a jet engine for an airliner.

He called Will Daley, his source in the Los Angeles Police Department, and asked for the names of the three illegal aliens who'd been arrested. Will obliged.

He checked his notes. Same names as the three men he'd interviewed.

◆ ◆ ◆

Chambers of Hon. Edward J. Lamport
4:19 p.m.

Paul Eriksen handed Edward the application for a warrant to search the domestic financial records of Angeles Development Corporation and Stanley Gleason and associated entities connected to the International Trade Center. He'd attached three sheets of explanatory text to the form.

His name and signature were missing.

"What's the problem, Paul?"

Eriksen crossed his arms. "I had to open an investigation in order to process this."

"Right."

"So it's visible to headquarters."

"The attorney general's office."

"Mm-hmm."

Edward looked at Milostan, then back at Eriksen. "What's going on?"

"The AG ordered me off this. He called me personally."

Will the litany of rejections never end? Edward kept his shoulders straight. "Reason?"

"The White House now considers anything having to do with the International Trade Center a matter of national security. If any investigations are made, they'll be handled inside Washington."

What kind of hornet's nest had Edward poked his stick into? "I take it 'if any are made' means none will be."

Eriksen nodded and sat at the table. "I'm sorry, Your Honor. And I'm concerned about the pattern of events. Something's not right. When's the last time you saw the AG override any US Attorney's investigation?"

"I don't think it's the AG."

"What makes you say that?"

"Did the directive come straight from the president?"

"It normally would, but the AG didn't say."

Edward rubbed his temples. "Based on my conversations with Carlisle and Beverley I'm not surprised."

So much for his strategy to give the president leverage with Mexico. He appeared to be dead serious about his desire for confrontation.

Dead.

If Carlos, Alana, and Foley were going to survive, Edward would have to go it alone.

Unless.

Unless he could convince someone inside of the conflict. The someone driving it.

He had nothing left to lose. If the president was going to say no, he'd make him say it to his face.

Chapter 50

Albert Sanchez and Will Daley each toted a bottle of Cerveza Bohemia to an outdoor patio overlooking Hollywood Boulevard. It was a good thing the general public didn't know how much real investigation work got done over drinks.

"Kinda freaky you'd interviewed the three guys we arrested today," Daley said. "You have 'em on video?"

"Yep. And I have a proposal. I'll trade you a copy of my video for a transcript of their confession."

"No can do, *amigo*. Not before the trial, and only if the confessions are entered into evidence."

Well, he had to try.

"You know the gist?"

Daley nodded.

"Did they give up anything about the International Trade Center?"

"Can't divulge."

I thought you were my friend. "Tell you what. I'll run down the things they told me in the interview, and you tell me whether you heard the same or something different. So far, what they've told you and told me don't line up."

"Oh?"

"Yeah, so I help you in your investigation, you help me in mine?"

Daley took a pull from his Bohemia and looked out at the bustle on the boulevard. "The crowd's changed since I came down here last."

"How long's it been?" Daley was stalling. Okay.

"At least two years since I hung out in Hollyweird."

"Mm-hmm. So, what do you say?"

"I'm game. Same, different, or not at all."

"Fair enough. According to the news release the three men are Mexican nationals who made an illegal exit from the ITC into California."

"We already made that public."

"Humor me, Daley. They told you they were employees of the Mexican company Sotomayor Construction, who subcontracted to Angeles Development, owned by Stanley Gleason."

"Also public."

Sanchez took a swig from his Bohemia. "Right. So they told me they saw some unusual equipment during the construction. Something that looked like a jet engine from an airliner."

"Not at all."

Hmm. "They said workers in their crew were involved in selling drugs."

"Same."

"Good." Sanchez leaned in close to Daley for the next one. "They claimed the ITC was paid for with laundered drug money." They hadn't told him that, of course. Carlos Alvarez believed it, though.

No response.

Score?

"Will?"

Daley picked up his bottle of Bohemia, took a long pull, and held it up toward Sanchez.

"Different."

Sanchez sighed and reached for his beer.

"Not what you wanted to hear, eh?" Daley said.

Sanchez had a choice. Let Daley in on what he'd learned from Judge Lamport and keep pushing him to reveal more.

Which would make things more about him breaking a juicy story than helping the judge.

Or he could spin some theories on the fly and see if he hit on anything.

"We're playing by your rules here, Will."

He flipped through his notes.

"They said rumors were flying around that the ITC was paid for with laundered drug money."

"Asked and answered."

Don't let your feelings show. "I know I'm pushing you and don't want to waste your time. Did you hear anything at all from those men about money laundering?"

Daley drained his Bohemia. "Those guys are Mexican construction laborers who make dirt wages. They're small-time drug peddlers doing some big guy's bidding. I wouldn't give much weight to anything they told you."

Chapter 51

Thursday, February 25
Chambers of Hon. Edward J. Lamport
6:07 a.m.

The White House operator had been surprisingly brusque. Annoyingly so. Nevertheless, she'd routed him to the Executive Office of the President efficiently. The gatekeeper there verified his identity and passed him through to Chief of Staff Carl Bender.

"I'd like a meeting with the president. As soon as possible."

"Is this related to your ruling on Proposition Sixty-Eight?"

"It's a personal matter of grave importance. Threats have been made against my life and members of my family. I'll be straight. Your administration has turned its back on me repeatedly, and in every case they've blamed their rejections on the president's policies. I don't believe them."

"With all due respect, Judge Lamport—"

"Mr. Bender, I'm out of time and out of options. I need the president's help now."

"I'll speak with him at his next opening and pass on your request."

"Time is of the essence, Mr. Bender. I'm as close as the next flight out of LAX."

◆ ◆ ◆

USANews Network Headquarters, Hollywood, California
6:48 a.m.

Rubio Torres was, in Sanchez's estimation, the finest investigative reporter in Mexico. Like himself, Torres plied his trade on a cable news network, FOROtv, owned by the Televisa media conglomerate.

In a country where journalists who got too close to the truth wound up dead.

What he liked most about Torres was that he'd decided years ago to lay down his life in service of his country. He believed his work was as important as the politicians and soldiers—if not more so. He was resolute in his desire to stand up to the corruption and drug cartels tearing down his beloved land.

Why not him? he'd told Sanchez years ago.

When Sanchez had called to ask for help with Judge Lamport's rescue mission, he'd jumped at the chance. Torres's call came earlier than expected.

"Alberto, a mixture of news for you."

"I want the bad news first."

"There is a, *cómo se dice*, consolidation, happening among the big cartels."

"As in bloody?" Sanchez said.

"No, and I'm not surprised. The cartels want to take over the country, and they're forming a federation to compete with the government and the business conglomerates."

Judge Lamport had heard the same thing from the police captain in La Junta. "So which cartels are joining up?"

"Cartelo de Sinaloa, who are already a federation, plus Cartelo de Golfo, Los Zetas, Caballeros Templarios, Matas Zetas, and San Luis, a new and fast-rising group. Sinaloa has in the past received favorable treatment from our government and the US DEA. They used Sinaloa to infiltrate weaker and more stubborn cartels and keep them in line. That all changed when Mexico began the drug war. What no one talks about is that as the drug war damages the big cartels, many more smaller ones arise. Some estimate as many as twenty-five new cartels have formed."

"Has one of them taken the lead?"

"San Luis is the strongest of the new breed. They've modernized the production and distribution of their poison and are rumored to have the most sophisticated system of tunnels under the US border."

Sanchez wrote furiously to capture everything Torres said. "Any insight on whether ALEXA Inversiones or Bancomex has ties to any of the cartels?"

"Ah, *amigo*, the question everyone asks. The cartels generate so much cash, every bank in Mexico has to be a suspect for money laundering. In the past, our government mostly looked the other way. They say they're cracking down now, but the evidence is not there. ALEXA, I don't know. They own many casinos, which are heavy cash businesses. But they also have a large commercial real estate portfolio and long-term petroleum pipeline contracts with PEMEX."

Sanchez was amazed at how Torres had access to more information than any other journalist could uncover. The situation was maddening. Disheartening. Carlos Alvarez and his mother were untraceable. Everyone had speculations, only speculations. Nothing with which to narrow the search.

If speculations were all he would have, he would have to use the best ones he could get.

"If you had to guess which cartel might have a connection to Bancomex, which one would you pick?"

"San Luis, hands down."

Emphatic. Torres wouldn't be without good reason.

"What makes you so sure?"

"They are financial wizards. They profit from their brains and operational sophistication, not muscle and armament. And they're masters of propaganda. Many in our country now call them *el cartelo limpio*—the clean cartel. As if there could be such a thing."

"Where's their base of operations?"

"San Luis Rio Colorado. Near the border where California, Arizona, and Baja California meet."

Chapter 52

Edward was about to experience a first—a morning run through his gated community of two-million-dollar-plus homes with a bulletproof vest under his sweatshirt and a pistol in a pancake holster at his side. He had to wear belted shorts to keep the Glock 27 from falling off while he ran.

McCormack, who would accompany him, had strongly recommended he carry while they ran. LAPD statistics had shown their neighborhood had experienced a few burglaries and automobile thefts in the last three months.

It had been ten days since he'd gone for his usual morning run with Jacqui. She hadn't started back up either, and she had to get to the office for a seven a.m. meeting.

Edward tightened his shoelaces and fussed with the holster until he could twist side to side without it chafing.

"How long you good for?" Edward asked McCormack.

"Three to five miles is in my ballpark."

"Since I haven't done this in ten days, let's do an easy forty-five minutes."

They stretched their hamstrings and inner thighs for five minutes and set out. Edward ran three steps and stopped.

"Forgot my phone." He ran into the house and retrieved it and they hit the road.

He settled into a comfortable pace after a block. He fixed his eyes about a hundred feet in front of him. He was in no mood to talk. Only think.

He should pray instead of think.

Later.

Now he was good and loose and in an easy rhythm. He checked his watch. Eight minutes since they'd begun. He pulled his phone and checked his fitness app. On a ten-minute mile pace. A little fast, so he eased up a bit.

McCormack tapped his right arm. "How are you holding up, Your Honor?"

"My wind's better than I expected." Stride. Stride. "Feeling good."

"Good." Stride. "So how are *you* holding up?"

How indeed. Anyone who'd been in his business long enough threw out "I've seen it all" like a bravado front, as if to say none of it got through to them and they were able to dissociate, stay above or outside the madness.

He once thought that way.

But when you were the one in the middle of the madness, when people you loved were held captive somewhere and were being tortured or God knows what and no one would—

His phone rang and vibrated in his pocket. He slowed his pace and checked it.

Beltran. He stopped and answered.

"Lamport." Breath. Breath. "What do you have?"

"I've split the unit into A and B squads. One ex-DEA in each. A squad visited with the police in Ciudad Obregón. They've scoured a ten-kilometer radius from the taqueria for eyewitnesses. Found none. I sent B squad into Guadalajara. They're gathering grassroots intel on Bancomex connections with cartels and coyotes who've used the Tohono O'Odham crossing. We have a few bites, but most have been afraid to talk. Most of what we hear is *plata o plomo*—you either side with the *narcos* or you end up dead."

Plata o plomo . . . Edward had heard the expression before . . . one of the witnesses in the Ernesto Marroquín trial had said it.

Another call came in.

"Albert Sanchez is calling. I'm going to patch him in."

Three taps and they were on the line together.

"What do you have, Sanchez?"

"Just got off the phone with a journalist friend in Mexico. I asked if he had to pick a cartel that might have a connection to Bancomex, which one would it be. He said the San Luis cartel, hands down. They're one of the new breed that's emerged as an unintended consequence of the Mexican drug war. Their base of operation is San Luis Rio Colorado."

"I know exactly where that is," Edward said.

Something leaped in Edward's gut. He couldn't put his finger on why, but his every instinct told him Sanchez was onto something. "Lieutenant Beltran, find out what your DEA guys know about this San Luis cartel and the size of their footprint."

"Roger that, Your Honor. What Sanchez heard about the new breed of cartels checks out with what we heard on the street in Guadalajara. The propaganda war rages in multiple sectors of the city. Reminds me of Iraq."

Finally. A ray of hope.

"Grateful beyond measure, Lieutenant. By the way, I never asked who's sponsoring you."

"Can't disclose that information, Your Honor."

"Fair enough. Godspeed to all."

"Your Honor," Sanchez said, "I have more to pass along. Can we meet?"

"Come by the house. I won't be in chambers today."

"When did you change your plans?" McCormack asked.

"Just now." He checked his watch. "Let's finish this run. I need to fill you in on some things when we get back to the house."

They stretched for a minute and resumed an easy pace.

Edward's phone rang again three minutes later.

Washington, D.C.

"Judge Lamport, Carl Bender here. Spoke with the president. We're sorry, but he must decline your request to meet with him."

Chapter 53

One step forward, three steps back.

How many more times could Edward come up empty? How many more walls could he slam into before he became a pile of rubble? He hadn't entertained the thought of giving up and wouldn't now. As long as there was the remotest of possibilities to save Carlos and Alana and Foley, he would not quit.

No, his greatest concern now was that he would break down. That his body or his mind or his spirit would cease to function.

The jog back home was silent. McCormack would ask questions and Edward left them to hang in the air. What he needed now, more than anything, was to hear from the Lord what to do next.

He'd never in his life been backed into a corner like the one he found himself in now, pressed on all sides by dense clouds of uncertainty and immobilized by shackles of rejection. The government system he'd dedicated his life to had morphed into an ambition-fueled, ego-driven, pride-directed force to prevent good.

He was meant to save them.

Then it dawned on him.

He'd not paid a high enough price to win their freedom. He'd held on to something he was supposed to let go.

If you try to hang on to your life you will lose it. But if you give up your life for My sake you will save it.

When Jesus was killed, His family and friends were devastated. They'd lost a man they'd loved and the hope of freedom from government oppression. But they didn't fully understand who Jesus was and His life's purpose.

Jesus had set His mind on the ways of God, not people.

Okay.

So, what did that mean for Edward and Carlos?

He unlocked the front door and left it open for McCormack.

◆　◆　◆

Edward and McCormack helped themselves to coffee and settled on the backyard patio.

"I need to change my strategy," Edward said.

"How?"

"I'm going to Mexico."

McCormack stiffened. "To do what?"

"I can't spend one more day here pulling levers to save Carlos." Edward leaned in to McCormack. "I have to put my own neck on the line."

"Your Honor, that's too high a—"

"You say that because your job is to protect me. So as of this morning I'm relieving you of your responsibilities."

"Judge Lamport, that's not a wise—"

"I don't care! It's my life, and I know what I must do."

"But you have a responsibility—"

"To whom? The Central District Court? If I keeled over this second, what would it matter? They'd reassign my workload and carry on. To my wife? I love her with all my heart, but when God makes it clear I need to lay down my life I'm not saying no. Nothing else has worked. My country won't help me. Everyone's either hidebound in laws and rules and codes of ethics or blinded by political ambition and power lust. The law is supposed to restrain and deter evil. Not prevent good. So the only way I have left to save Carlos is to sacrifice myself."

McCormack got up slowly from his chair and shook his head. "What's the point, Judge Lamport, if you go down there to save him and end up dead?"

"The point is sacrifice, Deputy McCormack, for another's good. My choices and actions brought Carlos into the world. If sacrificing myself will keep him alive, then I have to do it. And the only way that makes sense is to know that this isn't all there is."

"What isn't all there is?"

"This life."

"Oh. I didn't realize you believed like that."

Edward stood and joined him. "And what do *you* believe, Deputy McCormack?"

He looked Edward in the eye. "I believe, Your Honor, that the world is a pretty rotten place, and what I do to protect people in your position and what the Marshals Service does to track down fugitives from justice matters. Some days it feels like putting my finger in a leaky dam, but I'm doing something to fight against what's wrong with the world."

Edward left McCormack on the patio and retrieved the pistol and pancake holster from the bedroom. He returned to the patio and found McCormack standing with hands in pockets, his head down.

"I appreciate all you've done for me these last ten days," Edward said.

McCormack didn't respond.

Edward laid the gun and holster on the patio table. "I won't be needing this anymore."

McCormack turned and looked at him, then at the table. "You sure about this, Your Honor?"

"Sure as I can be."

McCormack picked up the holster and slipped it into his waistband.

"Help the other judges, Deputy McCormack. I'm called elsewhere now."

PART IV

BREAKAWAYS

I have always found that mercy bears richer fruits than strict justice.

—Abraham Lincoln

Chapter 54

"What happened to the marshals guarding your place?" Albert Sanchez asked.

"Sent 'em home," Edward said. "I'm going to Mexico. No more managing from the dugout. Time to get on the field."

Looking concerned, Sanchez followed Edward into the living room.

"You a Bible-reading man, Albert?"

He changed from concerned to uncomfortable. "I follow the daily readings of the Catholic Church. Why do you ask?"

"When you read Jesus saying, 'Whoever wants to save their life will lose it,' what does it mean to you?"

"Well, basically, that if you live for yourself you won't have a life at all."

"And what about the second part—'whoever loses their life for My sake will find it'?"

"That living right means we give up what we want and follow Him, live His way."

Edward nodded and stroked his stubbled chin. "You said you had other information to pass along."

Sanchez gave him a blank look.

"Did I misunderstand?"

"No, Your Honor, it's . . ." He pulled a notepad from his jacket. "Anyway. About the ITC. I'd gone down to Calexico a few days before the grand opening with a camera crew to do some advance work. Get the lay of the land, talk to people in the nearby communities on both sides of the border. When I was in Mexicali, I interviewed three construction workers. Heard some interesting things, but didn't give them much credence until I received the e-mail from A. Believer."

"You mean Carlos."

"Yes, your son. So when I went back down to cover the grand opening, I poked around some more. Even talked with Stanley Gleason about what I'd heard."

"Which was?"

"The workers said they'd noticed some unusual equipment on the site during construction. They said one of the machines looked like a large jet engine, like on an airliner. The other thing they told me was that a lot of the men on the job site were selling and using drugs. They complained about the *culturo narco*—the social attitudes that accept the influence of the drug cartels in Mexican society and make it okay to sell and use drugs openly."

"On the ITC job site?"

"On the Mexican side. Before the complex was finished, the border fence remained in place. They didn't allow Mexican workers to cross into the United States and vice versa without special credentials, and they would be transported to and from the job site by government-operated buses."

"Interesting, but how does this help me find Carlos?"

"The three men I interviewed were arrested in Los Angeles yesterday. They'd exited illegally from the ITC. Probably a day or two after I'd interviewed them."

"Have you offered the police your video as evidence?"

"Told my friend at the LAPD about it yesterday. He said it's not relevant."

Edward crossed his arms. "I haven't heard anything that helps me find Carlos. What else you got?"

"A hunch. When my contact told me about the San Luis cartel . . . the proximity of their operations to the ITC is interesting, don't you think?"

Edward bounded out of his chair. "Come to Mexico with me."

"I had the same thought. Before I do, though, I want to confront Gleason one more time. The timing of yesterday's arrest is no coincidence. I've been working on a feature piece on the ITC. The fact that three men were able to escape from a complex billed as ultra secure raises questions, and I want to get something about that on tonight's show."

Chapter 55

Sanchez was ready to poke the bear and find the spot that would make him growl. He got Stanley Gleason on the line after passing through three gatekeepers.

"I want to follow up on our conversation last Friday. Are you aware that the LAPD arrested three men yesterday who made an illegal exit from your International Trade Center?"

Silence on the line.

"Mr. Gleason?"

"I was not."

"They sold drugs to an undercover officer. They confessed they were illegal aliens and that they'd entered California through the ITC."

"To my knowledge no one in our organization has been contacted by the authorities."

Next stick.

"LAPD released their names. They were the same men I'd told you I interviewed before the grand opening."

More silence.

"I'm running part one of my feature series on the ITC tonight. I'll be making mention of this arrest in light of what you told the media about border security systems. Care to comment for the record?"

"No comment. To my knowledge my company has received no official communication from the LAPD or any other government agency on this matter."

"Very well. One of the things I learned from these men had to do with the open sale and use of illicit drugs on the Mexican side of the project. They used the term *culturo narco* to describe social attitudes in Mexico toward acceptance of the drug cartels' influence and power. Were you aware of this, Mr. Gleason?"

"Angeles Development Corporation was not responsible for the hiring or supervision of the workforce on the Mexican side. We were the general contractor and dealt solely with Sotomayor Construction of Mexico at the design and engineering level. There was no standardization of US and Mexican building codes. Each side was built according to prevailing laws and requirements in the respective countries, states, and municipalities."

"So you were not at any time made aware of a problem with the open sale and use of illegal drugs on the ITC job site?"

"The border fence remained up until the very end of construction, once the north and south ports of entry were finished and operational. We covered that at the media briefing."

"Of course, Mr. Gleason. You still haven't answered my question. Were you or any of your management team aware of illegal drug sales and use taking place on the ITC job site?"

"We were not. The cross-border worker exchange was highly controlled by Homeland Security and Mexican Customs and Immigration. We had no role whatsoever."

"One more que—"

"I've given you more than enough of my time, Mr. Sanchez."

"Would you prefer I say on the air that you were unresponsive to my questions?"

Silence.

"Would you, Mr. Gleason?"

"Go ahead."

Last stick.

"I have two sources in Mexico, from very different vantage points, who both say the operative government and business culture in Mexico is *plata o plomo*. Have you ever heard that expression?"

"I don't speak Spanish, Mr. Sanchez."

"It literally means 'silver or lead,' but it's an idiomatic expression that means you either cooperate with the cartels or you die. Have you encountered anything from the people on the Mexican side of the project suggestive of this culture?"

Silence. Long silence.

"Mr. Gleason?"

"Had to put you on hold."

A stir.

"Do you have any comment about this culture impacting the International Trade Center project in any way?"

"I refer you to the US government officials who negotiated the borderless labor pilot treaty. Our role was constructing buildings, not dealing with politics and culture."

He has a handler in the room. Good.

"Mr. Gleason, doesn't every real estate development involve government relations?"

"Angeles Development was awarded the project by the federal government and we are under contract to manage the facilities. There are mirror-image arrangements on each side. We built and manage the

US side. Sotomayor Construction built the Mexican side and ALEXA Investments manages the property."

An open door. I'm walking through.

"ALEXA Investments. I understand that they're aligned with Bancomex, based in Guadalajara."

"Where is this going, Mr. Sanchez?"

"Is it possible ALEXA and Bancomex are part of the *plata o plomo* culture?"

"Again, I refer you to US government officials. There was no commingling of financial assets in the ITC. The only integration was infrastructure. We covered that at the grand opening."

Poke.

"These same Mexican sources, separately, told me that the Mexican side of the project was funded in whole or in part with laundered drug money, and that ALEXA and Bancomex are the orchestrators of the money laundering. I'm offering you an opportunity to comment before I address this in my report."

The line was quiet for a few moments.

"Mr. Gleason?"

"That's a bunch of bull and you know it."

Growl.

"Are you denying the allegations?"

Silence.

His handlers are at work.

"Vicente Salvatierra is a well-respected business leader in Mexico. He played a key role with the Mexican government in the borderless labor zone treaty negotiations that led to the International Trade Center. He also facilitated government relations in Mexico at all levels."

"So you deny the allegations?"

"There's nothing to talk about. Whoever your sources in Mexico are, they've made up a story to stir the political pot and cause me trouble."

"Cause *you* trouble, Mr. Gleason? You said there was no commingling of financial assets and that each side of the ITC is separately owned and managed. How do my sources' stories cause you—"

"I'll tell you how! Stories like that from Mexico will put a stink over the whole project. Tenants will bail. You report that garbage and I'll have my lawyers in federal court tomorrow morning suing you and your network for libel, slander, and monetary damages."

End of interview.

He'd crossed a line.

He didn't have empirical data. Only deductions.

From people on the front lines.

Who knew the truth but didn't have enough hard evidence to prove it in a court of law.

Poke. Growl. Make 'em tell you why.

◆ ◆ ◆

Rodrigues answered Gleason's summons to his office.

"Have you found those guys who disappeared from the site?"

"No."

"Do you know why you haven't found them?"

"What are you getting at?" Rodrigues asked.

"They were arrested yesterday in LA. They sold drugs to an undercover cop. They told the police they made an illegal exit from the ITC. Albert Sanchez is all over it and is going to report on it tonight."

"So what's the big deal? It's not true."

Gleason was quiet.

"What? It *is* true?"

"It's on the newswires. We gotta finesse the security issue. Pronto. Anyway, pack up. We're going back to LA."

"But we're supposed to monitor the first shipments through the sewer."

"Get one of your underlings on it. Sanchez has sources in Mexico who've told him the ITC was built with laundered drug profits. He's running a story on the ITC tonight and says he's going to include what he's heard."

Rodrigues was quiet.

"I told him if he aired anything we'd be in federal court first thing in the morning. We're off to see Ira Abelson."

He sent Rodrigues away and wrote the story his lawyer would include in the lawsuit he would file against Sanchez and USANews Network first thing Friday morning.

Chapter 56

Undisclosed location, San Luis Rio Colorado, México
10:07 a.m. MST

A night and half a day in the back of a truck with plastic ties around his ankles and wrists and a gag in his mouth, bouncing over bad roads and not being allowed to go to the bathroom, had been worse torture than Carlos had endured in the warehouse.

At least he'd been able to share the ride with his mother and Foley. His heart broke every time he looked at her bruised face. Foley, like himself, was battered and scarred from head to foot, but still resolute. His determination to not give in had given Carlos and his mother the courage to do likewise.

They didn't know where they were. Their captors blindfolded them before they yanked them from the back of the truck into yet another dank prison. More of the same. They were kept in separate concrete-walled rooms. There was no light except what managed to peek through the gap between the door and its frame and a gap between wall and ceiling opposite where they'd strapped him to another wobbly wooden chair.

His captors had total advantage. With each breath, he moved closer and closer to accepting that his mission would fail. That the wicked men he'd fought against with everything he had would prevail.

Yet they would not prevail.

God said so.

The wicked draw their swords and string their bows to kill the poor and the oppressed and to slaughter those who do right. But their swords will stab their own hearts, and their bows will be broken.

He wasn't seeing it, but it was better to believe than not.

The door opened. A muscular man of average height stood in the doorway. Sunlight from behind masked his face.

"Hey, *chavo*, you can end this game any time you want. All you need to do is tell us to whom you sent the information you stole."

"I sent it to no one."

The man stepped toward Carlos. He punched him in the face.

And again.

Carlos tasted blood.

Life.

Life is in the blood.

"You will not win," Carlos mumbled.

"Oh, we will most certainly win," the man said. "We always win."

Chapter 57

Ever since he had relieved Deputy US Marshal Campbell McCormack of his duty to protect him, Edward had been trying to figure out how to tell Jacqui what Jesus had asked him to do.

Sure, it was in the Bible.

But it was no metaphor. He meant what He said.

If you lose your life for My sake you will find it.

Edward Lamport could parse text with the best of them. He was a professional interpreter of the law.

Man's law.

When a law enforcement officer said someone lost their life, the meaning was clear.

They were dead.

When church people talked about losing their lives, they thought it meant laying down your conveniences, putting others first, living for the sake of others.

And then there were the few. The missionaries. Who'd taken it to the extreme, particularly those who went to hostile lands. Some paid the ultimate price. Still did.

He'd been called to a mission all along.

Now he had to be ready to pay the ultimate price.

Another bomb to Jacqui's heart.

Oh. Wait.

His father.

Edward had released his pent-up anguish in front of Jacqui and Sanchez the other day. He had spoken the words.

He'd had a hard time forgiving his father. He still did.

But his father had had only seconds to react. Or maybe he hadn't. Maybe what he had done in that moment had sprung from a lifetime of decisions. Or fears. The point was, Edward didn't know. He wasn't and couldn't be in his father's shoes. Only his own.

Edward had to persuade Jacqui hard to come home. Her early meeting hadn't gone well, and taking the afternoon off would tighten the squeeze on her team. Proposition 68 fallout. The survey predictions were happening. Families unenrolled like panicked investors in a stock market crash. Teachers were beside themselves. Financial managers pulled their hair out.

Jacqui's idea to counter the unenrollment problem—defiance through compliance—had been given lip service by the school board, but nothing had been implemented. She'd put together what he thought was a brilliant plan—educate at-risk families about the true requirements of the law and rally them to stand up to the people who wanted to drive them away by applying for the undocumented-status state services ID card. What were they waiting for?

Edward checked his watch.

She'd be home in ten minutes.

Bombs away.

◆ ◆ ◆

Ten minutes had passed like ten hours.

The weather was unseasonably warm, so Edward served lunch for Jacqui on the patio. He set the chicken salads he'd made on the same table where he'd laid his US Marshal–issued Glock 27 earlier that morning.

"Sorry your proposal didn't fly. I thought it was brilliant."

"I don't know, babe. Maybe someone more politically skilled will make it happen. So, things aren't going well for Carlos."

"Hope mixed with more rejection from Washington."

"Ed, you didn't ask me to come home to make small talk. What's going on?"

"The deputy marshals won't be back."

Her face perked up. "The threats are gone?"

"I relieved them of their responsibility to protect me."

Her countenance fell. "Spit it out."

"I'm going to Mexico."

She squeezed her eyes shut. "Mexico. Why?"

"Sanchez spoke with a colleague there who's on top of the drug cartels. He said the one most likely tied with ALEXA and Bancomex is in San Luis Rio Colorado. I'm joining up with Lieutenant Beltran and his men."

Jacqui kept her eyes closed. Her hands trembled a bit in her lap. She mouthed something he couldn't hear.

His mouth and throat dried.

"I have to go."

She kept quiet.

"Whoever loses their life for Jesus's sake will find it."

"So that's it? You justify going after your old girlfriend with a Bible verse?"

"Carlos is my responsibility. I'm his father. I can't sit here in comfort while other men put their lives on the line to save him. I need to be on the field with them. Saving Alana is for Carlos's sake. Not mine."

"I don't want to lose you, Ed."

"Jacqui . . . it's a call. From the Lord. I have to go."

Her expression hardened. "God doesn't ask people to be irresponsible."

Chapter 58

Law Offices of Abelson, Frye & Nichols LLP, downtown Los Angeles
4:06 p.m.

Ira Abelson was a round man with a balding pate and wire rim spectacles. The perfect disguise to conceal the great white shark within. He was the most feared litigator in Los Angeles.

And he was Gleason's man.

The *Top Stories* intro played through Abelson's DVR and fifty-inch television. Gleason set his scotch on the rocks on the side table and focused on what Sanchez was about to say. Rodrigues stood to the side of the office.

"Good evening, USA, I'm Albert Sanchez and you're watching *Top Stories*. Our top story tonight: government-sanctioned money laundering. Could the government of Mexico have brokered a deal to approve the investment of laundered drug money—more than a billion dirty dollars—to fund their side of the historic International Trade Center that straddles the US-Mexico border in California? This reporter has obtained credible information from multiple sources that alleges the tentacles of the Mexican drug cartels have slithered their way into the highest levels of power. Has the United States negotiated an experimental labor treaty with organized criminals? Did they know what and with whom they were dealing?"

Gleason hit the Pause button. "He's running with those phantom sources from Mexico." He stood and paced.

Abelson leaned his ample girth back into his well-padded leather chair. "Except they're not phantom."

"He's finessed it so far. Let's see what else he's got." Gleason fast-forwarded through commercials and hit Play when Sanchez's face reappeared.

"Welcome back to *Top Stories*. Yesterday, the Los Angeles Police Department arrested three men for selling cocaine and methamphetamine to an undercover narcotics detective. Nothing newsworthy about that. The three men were illegal aliens from Mexico. Nothing unusual there either. What *is* news is that these three men entered California by making an illegal exit from the International Trade Center."

Pause.

"Agresta from the PR shop will send spin sheets over here within the hour. We're already getting calls from tenants who haven't moved in yet."

Play.

"When I attended the gala grand opening, Stanley Gleason, president and CEO of Angeles Development Corporation, who built the American side of the ITC, had this to say about the border security built into the complex:"

Pause.

"How much you want to bet he edited my comments?"

Abelson swiveled his chair. "Stanley. Calm down. He wasn't the only journalist who attended. You've already gotten a lot of good press and TV coverage."

Play.

"The port of entry and exit on the north end of the International Trade Center is the most secure crossing on the US-Mexican border. We went beyond the requirements of the treaty to implement three-factor security—passport, fingerprint scan, and a seven-digit code delivered by satellite onto a digital fob or secure smartphone app that changes every ten seconds. No one is permitted to enter or leave the ITC compound on the north port unless they pass all three levels."

Pause.

"He kept that clip clean. Still don't trust him."

Play.

"Two days before the grand opening of the ITC, I spent some time in Mexicali, Baja California, interviewing people on the street, outside the complex and in nearby communities. I interviewed the three men who the LAPD arrested yesterday. Here's some of what they had to say, voiced by an interpreter."

First man: "There's never been as much excitement in Mexicali before as there has with the trade center. This has more promise than the maquiladoras because of the opportunity to work in America for American wages."

Second man: "It was built because of the drug cartels."

Sanchez: "What do you mean by that, *señor*?"

Third man: "He means the cartels are doing more to help the people than the government."

Sanchez reappeared on screen. "I don't know about you, USA, but that sounds like propaganda to me. One of my sources has told me in no uncertain terms that a serious unintended consequence of the war on drugs in Mexico has been to spawn the emergence of a new breed of criminal enterprise, skilled in finance, manufacturing, and public relations, and diversified beyond the drug trade to include extortion, kidnapping, human smuggling and sex trafficking, and even counterfeit pharmaceuticals. The leaders of this new wave of criminality appear to be the San Luis cartel, who've carved out a stronghold in northeast Baja California."

Gleason hit the Pause button. An icy wave flowed down his face and arms, and his chest tightened. "How in the . . ."

"I've heard enough," Abelson said. "We'll file a motion to force Sanchez to release his sources." He turned to Gleason and gave him a stern look. "I think it's time you clue me in on the parts of your business you haven't yet told me about."

"I pay you to represent me and my interests. I tell you what I want you to know, when I want you to know it." He leaned forward to get up from his chair, then sat back. "Look, don't get all Catholic school on me here. If I don't tell you something, it's for your own protection. You can't perjure yourself on things you don't know about."

Abelson furrowed his brow. "I'm Jewish, remember?"

Gleason waved him off. "How soon can you have the lawsuit filing ready?"

"We'll work the night and file it when the court opens at ten."

"Make sure we get Judge Marrone assigned to this case. He owes me one."

Abelson shook his head. "I don't think this is the right case on which to cash that chip."

Gleason's phone vibrated in his pocket. He yanked it out and checked the screen.

Senator Mitchell Corman.

He calculated what he would say, then answered.

"I take it you're watching USANews Network."

"What have you done?" Corman screamed into his ear. "Do you have any idea how bad this makes me look? My neck's hanging out so far I can hardly keep my head up. How could you be so sloppy?"

"Sanchez called me for comment. I told him if he ran the story I'd sue him in federal court tomorrow. I'm with Ira Abelson right now planning our attack."

"I'm not talking about Sanchez. When were you going to tell me about the security breach?"

"Those three guys escaping were—"

"Not that. The transaction data theft."

Heat crept up Gleason's neck. "How'd you hear about that?"

"Carl Bender."

Chapter 59

Guadalajara, México
10:43 p.m. CST

Daniel Canedo watched Albert Sanchez's report on the USANews Network website a second time.

He feared for Sanchez's life.

Journalists in Mexico who dared to report the things he'd just watched ended up dead. One of them was close to him.

His childhood friend.

Sanchez's report had put together bits and pieces of the truth about *culturo narco*. Daniel knew the whole truth. Firsthand.

Bernal. Salvatierra. Beneficiaries, personal and professional, of *los cartelos'* reign of death.

He had not known of Carlos Alvarez before he had ignited the current crisis. When Daniel first heard about what Alvarez had done, he thought him a fool. What could one man do against a colossus of evil?

Now he was envious of Alvarez. He'd done something courageous. Heroic, though no one would know about it.

He closed his laptop and carried it to his bedroom. He sat in the middle of the bed, facing the wall. He fixed his gaze in the center.

At the crucifix over his pillow.

What could one man do against a colossus of evil?

He opened his laptop. Searched for United States District Judge Edward Lamport.

Central District Court of California. The website listed the e-mail address to contact Lamport's court clerk.

Daniel opened his e-mail program, addressed a message to the judge's chambers, and wrote in Spanish:

> *Dear Judge Lamport,*
> *Your friend Joseph Foley and his companions, Carlos Alvarez and Alana Alvarez, are in the custody of the San Luis drug cartel in San Luis Rio Colorado, Baja California. They know Foley is connected to you from his mobile phone, which they confiscated.*

Perspiration stung his left eye. He brushed it away with a sleeve.

> *I was present in the meeting in which this was revealed.*
> *I pray you will find them.*
> *With respect,*
> *Daniel Canedo*

He'd heard it in the same meeting where he'd told Javier Bernal to have Bancomex's IT security team get the e-mail records from every Mexican Internet service provider to determine if Carlos Alvarez had sent the transaction data he'd stolen to anyone. He'd heard Bernal order them to check the last seven days of e-mail traffic. He didn't know if the IT security team would try to intercept future e-mail communications.

A drop of sweat landed on the *X* key of his laptop.

He gazed at the crucifix again.

His sweat fell to the ground like great drops of blood . . .

This wasn't even close to being close.

He read the e-mail one more time.

This may be my last night to sleep in this bed.

Click.

Sent.

Chapter 60

Friday, February 26
Chambers of Hon. Edward J. Lamport
10:52 a.m.

Edward's first day back in his chambers since the Proposition 68 decision was quiet.

The protesters were gone.

The courthouse grounds had returned to their normal appearance, except for double the usual number of federal protective police officers on guard outside the Main Street and Spring Street entrances.

This could be his last day here.

Rebecca's signature knock thumped through the door, and it opened before he could tell her to come in.

"Chief Judge Marrone is here to see you."

This ought to be interesting. "Send him in."

Marrone strode into the room and turned his face to the wall covered with law books. He flexed the fingers on his right hand repeatedly. "You're still a functioning judge in this court. The sanction proceedings haven't commenced yet." He pulled an envelope out of his inside jacket pocket and held it out to Edward. "By the way, the judicial misconduct complaint against you was dismissed this morning."

Edward accepted the envelope and set it on his desk. "Thanks for the news."

"Yes. Well, a new case has come in and I'm assigning it to you, out of rotation."

"Michael, I need more time off to deal with my family situation. Things have escalated and I need to travel to Mexico."

"You have to delay that trip. This is a media libel suit. Given your proclivity for the fourth estate, you're the best judge in our court to handle it."

Out of respect to Marrone, he would listen before he told him his family came first. "Who are the parties?"

Marrone raised the document he held in his right hand to eye level and slipped on his reading glasses. "Angeles Development Corporation, plaintiff, versus USANews Network and Albert Sanchez, defendants."

Hold it right there.

No way could he take this case.

No way could he tell Marrone why.

"Is this about the report Sanchez broadcast yesterday?"

Marrone nodded and thrust the court filing documents at him.

He took the papers. "Tell me more."

"Plaintiff is suing for libel and damages over allegations Mr. Sanchez made on his broadcast last night. They also filed a motion for an injunction against further reports and to compel Sanchez to reveal his sources and turn over all notes and video files on which he based yesterday's report. The complaint reads like their lawyers didn't have enough coffee while they stayed up all night writing it."

Edward flopped the document onto his desk. "I recuse myself."

Marrone took a step toward him. "You'll do no such thing."

"You know I can't take a case involving Stanley Gleason. He promoted my nomination to Senator Corman. Blatant conflict of interest. I'd be shocked if the defendants didn't move to disqualify me."

"Are you saying you can't be impartial?"

"Of course not. I'm saying the defense will make an issue of my connection to Gleason, thin as it is. I also think USANews's competitors will make a circus out of this, which will make it impossible to seat an impartial jury. Plus the wake of Proposition Sixty-Eight is still churning."

"Then convince the parties to make it a bench trial."

Marrone's dismissal of his concerns raised a red flag. "Aren't we getting a little ahead of ourselves here? And why is it so important that I hear this case?"

"We're slammed, and your docket is empty."

"And I still need time off. It's at life-or-death stage."

Marrone relaxed his shoulders. "You have the background to get up to speed fastest. I need you to take this one. At least handle the preliminaries. That'll buy time to sort things out."

"Give the preliminaries to a magistrate."

Marrone shook his head. "This needs to fast-track."

"And what's the compelling public interest?"

He caught a twitch in Marrone's eyes. Something was off. This seemed too personal.

"It's our court's compelling interest, Judge Lamport. We just came off a high-profile case. We need to push these litigants to ADR. You're best equipped to make that happen."

Marrone's shift to formality raised another red flag. Marrone was cunning. Alternative dispute resolution was the court's bias in civil cases.

He knows I'm suspicious.

"I'm sorry, Michael, but I must recuse. You can't force me to take this case."

"Technically, no, but . . ."

Edward moved toward Marrone. "Michael, help me out. With all due respect, three days ago you were in here filled with venom toward me, and now you're working me for what feels like a personal favor. What gives?"

Marrone turned and headed for the door. He stopped as if to say something, then bolted out without a word.

Rebecca poked her head in the still-open door. "Your Honor, Catherine Becerra is here to see you."

His deputy court clerk.

She handed him two sheets of paper. "Your Honor, this e-mail came in to the chambers address overnight. It was written in Spanish. I know you understand, but I translated it for you."

Edward read the Spanish version.

His heart jumped.

He read the English version.

Catherine's translation was perfect.

"Does that e-mail make any sense to you, Your Honor?"

"Thank you, Catherine. You're excused."

◆ ◆ ◆

Angeles Development Inc. Corporate Offices, downtown Los Angeles 11:42 a.m.

"You don't want to hear this, Stanley, but you don't have much of a case," Abelson said.

"Do we have Marrone?" Gleason barked into the phone.

"Marrone said he would assign it to Judge Edward Lamport."

"Lamport . . . yeah, even better."

Gleason congratulated himself. Lamport was a friendly. If he could get the chief judge of the Central District Court of California to do his bidding, subduing Lamport would be child's play.

On second thought, maybe not.

Marrone was on his last lap, his eyes fixed on the more-than-comfortable retirement Gleason's largesse would add to his ample government pension.

Lamport was a man on a mission. With fire in his belly. A more formidable adversary than Gleason was accustomed to defeating.

But he would still prevail. Like he always did.

"We're halfway to a win," Gleason said.

"Don't get too smug," Abelson said. "Lamport recused."

"What? He can't do that. He . . ."

"He what?" Abelson said.

"I was going to say Lamport owes me for giving his name to Corman, but that was my payback for him nailing the punks who shot me and trashed my offices."

"That's why he recused himself. Huge open door on appeal."

"I pay you big money for results, Ira. You failed." He slammed down the phone.

I'll handle Lamport myself.

He went online. Searched for Joseph Foley, Los Angeles.

First listing—*Joseph Foley, Foley Private Investigations.*

Click.

Domestic and international investigations . . . skip traces . . . industrial espionage . . . missing persons searches.

About Joseph Foley.

Click.

He skimmed Foley's bio.

Third bullet point.

Twelve years as a Senior Investigator in the Los Angeles County District Attorney Bureau of Investigation.

◆ ◆ ◆

"Beltran. New intel for you," Edward said.

"Ready to copy, Your Honor."

"The San Luis cartel has them. Got an e-mail from someone on the inside. They know Foley and I are connected. From his cell phone."

"Roger that, sir. We've consolidated the team and are within two hundred kilometers of San Luis Rio Colorado."

"Do you have accommodations arranged yet?"

"The DEA guys got us set up outside Mexicali."

"I'm coming down to join you."

"Come again, sir?"

"I'll be there with you."

"I strongly recommend against that, sir."

"I'm coming down. I want the hotel information straightaway."

"Sir, are you planning to travel with our squad into the target?"

"If you mean do I want to be in on the action, yes."

"With all due respect, Your Honor, you'll be a liability."

"I need to be involved, Lieutenant Beltran."

"We'll need a day to get organized once we arrive. We'll finalize our plans together. I still advise against, sir."

"Noted. Send me the hotel info. I'll be there midday tomorrow."

Edward's desk phone rang as he ended the call with Beltran. Deputy McCormack on the line.

"Good news, Your Honor. Artúro Mondragón has been arrested. LAPD got a lead on him from one of their snitches and it panned out."

"So both of the death threats have now been eliminated?"

"Assuming Mondragón doesn't have a contract out on you, yes."

"That's not funny, Deputy McCormack."

"It wasn't intended to be. We have to be on top of every possibility, Your Honor."

Edward cradled the handset and rubbed fatigue from his eyes. He needed some kind of win right now, and got one.

On top of every possibility.

Edward understood that. Deeply.

Chapter 61

12:43 p.m.

Stanley Gleason calling?

Edward had recused himself from Gleason's suit against Sanchez. So his call wouldn't be ex parte communication. But what could he want?

"Stanley. What's the occasion?" Lame, but he didn't know what else to say.

"Judge Lamport, you know I'm a resourceful man. When I want something done, it gets done."

Gleason was resourceful and successful. And arrogant. "Your track record speaks for itself, Stanley. I'm sure this isn't why you called."

"And you know, firsthand, I'm well connected in a lot of high places."

Edward pulled the phone away from his ear. *What is he up to?* "Your relationship with Senator Corman certainly benefited me. For which I'm grateful."

"That's right, Judge. Say, I've heard through the grapevine your friend Joseph Foley has gone missing. That right?"

What? Whoever has Foley and Carlos and Alana is connected to Gleason?

"How do you know that?"

"So it's true."

"Yes."

"And he was traveling with a Mexican woman when he went missing. His girlfriend."

Foley, you're a master.

"I didn't know he had a girlfriend in Mexico."

"And his girlfriend's son is named Carlos Alvarez."

"Okay. Why are you telling me all this?"

"Aw, c'mon, Judge Lamport, don't you care about your friend Foley?"

"Of course I do."

"What would you say if I told you I know where he is and can help get him home?"

"Stanley, what's this about?"

"You know I filed suit against that con man Albert Sanchez this morning."

"Yes, I'm aware."

"My lawyer is Ira Abelson. I believe you know him."

"Fine attorney. Went up against him once in federal court."

"And lost, as I recall."

Give him more rope. "He's an excellent litigator."

"The best. I only hire the best. Did you know Ira is good friends with Michael Marrone?"

So. It is personal with Marrone. Is he dirty? "I did not."

"When Abelson filed the suit, he made a special request that Chief Judge Marrone take the case, but he assigned it to you. Ira informed me you recused yourself."

"Our connection creates a conflict of interest."

"I'll cut to the chase, Judge Lamport. You wouldn't *be* a judge if it weren't for me."

"This conversation is highly inappropriate, Mr. Gleason. Good day."

"You want to hear what I have to say, *Your Honor*."

"You're seconds away from a contempt citation."

"It didn't take me long to figure out you hired Joseph Foley and sent him down to Mexico to protect Alana Alvarez. Who is the mother of Carlos Alvarez. Who both work for Bancomex. Abelson also told me you've requested a leave of absence to deal with a family problem in Mexico. Two plus two equals you sent Foley to protect Alana and Carlos Alvarez because they're related to you and you knew they were in danger. And they're in danger because Carlos Alvarez stole transaction data from the account of his bank's largest customer. Who happens to be the lead investor in the Mexican side of the International Trade Center. He stole the data because he thinks he knows something. Which is having ripple effects on the American side of the ITC. Which is causing my tenants to bail out left and right. Which is costing me and my investors hundreds of millions of dollars. And then Sanchez runs his hyped-up story based on the assertions of three small-time drug dealers and unnamed Mexican sources."

There has to be a connection between Gleason and the San Luis cartel. How else would he know? Edward would play along to see how much Gleason would expose himself.

"So, what do you want?"

"I want you to handle my lawsuit! I want you to order Sanchez and his network to make a full retraction and reassure my tenants that nothing going on in Mexico affects what we do on the US side of the ITC. I want you to make him cough up the names of his sources so the investors in Mexico can do what they need to do. In return I'll use my influence to get Foley and the Alvarezes into your hands. But you can't ask me how that will happen."

Lord. Is this how you want to save Carlos?

If Gleason isn't dirty, he's dancing with people who are. Happens all the time in international politics.

"I'll take this under advisement and—"

"My offer expires at the end of this call. Take it now or it's off the table."

"May I put you on hold for a moment?"

"You have thirty seconds or the deal's off."

"And what happens to Foley and the Alvarezes if I say no?"

"I have no control over that. This is critical business for me. If USANetwork isn't forced to retract, I'll be sitting on a billion-dollar mausoleum in a sleepy border town."

"All right, thirty seconds."

Edward rushed to the door "Rebecca, in here quick."

Her eyes were like moons. "What's wrong, Your Honor?"

"I need you to call Paul Eriksen, Campbell McCormack, Frank Novack at the FBI, and Ross Milostan at Homeland Security Investigations. I need to see them in my chambers this afternoon. Four o'clock or as close as possible. Don't take no for an answer."

"I'll do my best, Your Honor."

"You always do, Rebecca." He blew her a kiss and closed the door.

He got back on the line with Gleason.

"I need some assurances before I say yes."

"There are no guarantees when you work in the dark."

Gleason had pull with people in Mexico who had sway over the San Luis drug cartel. But there was still the matter of getting Carlos and Alana into the United States.

"Does your influence extend to someone in Homeland Security who will let the Alvarezes enter the country?"

"Can't promise anything."

"You want me to put my neck on the chopping block in exchange for a maybe?"

"There's equal risk for both of us, Judge Lamport."

"Not good enough. My answer is no."

◆ ◆ ◆

La Ferme Restaurant, downtown Los Angeles
1:22 p.m.

Edward had promised Jacqui he'd take her to La Ferme at least a half dozen times in the last six months, so when he called and asked her to meet him for lunch that day she jumped at it. His tone was somber and urgent, so she expected a generous order of tension with her duck confit sandwich. Energized by the ten-minute walk from the LAUSD Administration Building, she followed the hostess to a table in the far corner of the dining room, then texted Edward to let him know she'd arrived and had been seated.

She removed a compact from her purse and checked her eyes. Satisfied, she refreshed her lipstick and folded her hands on the table. An ominous weight settled on her as she replayed Edward's invitation to lunch. She believed things would get much worse for her husband— and her—before a turnaround could come. She didn't like it one bit, but she'd come to accept that the enormity of the odds against Edward ever seeing Carlos alive would only compel him forward, not deter him.

He was driven to make right what he believed was his life's greatest failure—abandoning Alana and their baby.

She didn't see it that way at all.

Of course it was difficult to walk away from them. She knew all too well. Where he saw cowardice, she saw respect. Even if Carlos was rescued, Edward might never change the way he thought.

They'd both made choices as younger people that they now regretted. Heavily.

At least Edward's was redeemable.

He stood at the entrance to the dining room and spotted her. She waved at him and he strode to the table, his face grim. He walked as if he saw no one else in the crowded dining room except her. She lightened inside at seeing him as the gravity of the conversation they were about to share pressed on her chest and stole her breath.

He grabbed her hands and kissed her lips. "Thanks for coming."

"Thanks for picking this place," she said, trying to soften the mood. "I walked here."

"So I can drive you back." His eyes twinkled a bit through the tension on his face. He lowered his brow and thinned his lips. "I just got off the phone with Stanley Gleason."

"I heard about Sanchez's report on the International Trade Center."

Edward leaned in. "He's suing Sanchez and his network. Marrone asked me to take the case. I recused. Gleason tried to bribe me."

She grabbed his forearm. "With what?"

"Somehow he knows about Foley and Carlos and Alana. He said he would use his influence to get them to me if I took his case and decided it his way."

"Does he know Carlos is your son?"

Edward shook his head. "Foley convinced whoever is holding them that Alana is his girlfriend. They connected me with Foley by his cell phone."

"What are you gonna do about the bribe?"

"I have a four o'clock with Paul Eriksen and the federal agents I've been working with. I'm going to lay out the whole story. Everything about Carlos. The coyote. The commando team. And Gleason's bribe."

Her heart palpitated.

There would be more.

"And?"

"Gleason has to be dirty. He has to be tight with the San Luis cartel. How else would he know?"

"You still going to Mexico?"

"Beltran doesn't want me there. I believed I was supposed to go, but . . . maybe all God wanted was for me to be willing. There's another way . . ."

Edward got that look on his face he usually did when he was thinking a big thought.

"I'm happy you're not going." *Am I ever. I couldn't bear losing you.*

"Gleason's desperate. He thinks Sanchez's report will snowball and all the ITC tenants will bail. If we run a sting against him we could crack the money laundering, which would support the president's Mexico policy." Edward took both her hands in his. "I bargain myself as bait in exchange for getting Carlos and Alana into the US with asylum. Same call, different answer."

Her stomach turned rock hard.

He'd kept insisting his quest was about Carlos, not Alana. Try though she did, she hadn't been able to accept it. She couldn't shake the threat of another woman in his life.

Now, death was the bigger threat.

Was it selfish to want him to stop? What was *she* called to do in this situation?

She gazed into his eyes and willed herself not to break down. "I don't know which is more dangerous, Mexico or this."

Chapter 62

"Beltran. Change of plans. I'm staying in LA."

"Roger that, Your Honor. Right choice."

"More intel for you. The San Luis cartel is somehow connected to Stanley Gleason, the man whose company built the US side of the International Trade Center. He knows about Foley and me. He figured out I'd sent Foley to Mexico to protect Carlos and Alana. Bancomex has to be the link. Find out who San Luis's biggest rivals are and talk to them. We need to know who's in charge and how Gleason is connected."

◆ ◆ ◆

4:04 p.m.

McCormack and Eriksen were already seated at Edward's conference table. Milostan was en route from Long Beach and would be late getting in. Novack was two minutes in the car and an elevator ride away.

Time to lay everything bare. Carlos had indeed been onto something. The hard evidence was still scant. But Sanchez's report had shaken Gleason enough to expose his hand.

Partially.

Rebecca escorted Special Agent Novack into Edward's chambers. He sat across from Edward, next to McCormack. Eriksen sat to Edward's left.

"Special Agent Milostan is stuck in traffic on the 710, but I want to get started. All of you have heard some of what I'm about to share." Edward walked them through the events of the past ten days, leaving nothing out.

Edward studied the faces in the room as he unfolded his story. Their demeanors were attentive and professional.

Edward went on to recount Carlos's disappearance, Alana's denied entry into the United States, his conversations and meeting with Secretary of State Ronald Carlisle and Homeland Security Secretary Conrad Beverley, the e-mail Carlos sent to Albert Sanchez of USANews Network, and Foley and Alana's disappearance.

Rebecca escorted Special Agent Ross Milostan from Homeland Security Investigations into Edward's chambers. Edward gave him a quick summary of what he'd already covered with the others in the room.

"So, after Foley and Alana disappeared, I took matters into my own hands. I contacted a retired Marine special forces colonel who helped me recruit a mercenary team to go into Mexico and keep Carlos and Alana alive. I asked for federal assistance to get them here so they could apply for asylum. No one would help. The same people shut me down who look the other way from the millions here illegally."

Milostan asked, "Which retired colonel?"

"Steven Jessup, former MARSOC leader out of Pendleton. They agreed to secure Carlos and Alana until I could bring them in.

Meanwhile, Carlos reappeared in a small town in Chihuahua State. So I made a deal with a coyote to smuggle him across the border."

They didn't need to know Sanchez had facilitated the coyote deal.

He scanned each man's face and saw unblinking eyes and tightly set jaws. "He crossed the border into the Tohono O'Odham Indian Reservation, but was intercepted and taken captive by drug cartel soldiers. At the time we didn't know if the men who intercepted them were connected to Bancomex-ALEXA or from some cartel who'd been after the coyote because he'd refused to join their human smuggling operation."

Silence hovered over the table. Edward shifted his gaze to each of the men. He would say no more until one of them responded to what he'd shared.

Eriksen shifted in his chair. "You just confessed to a crime, Judge Lamport."

"There was no other way." He scanned the faces at the table. "Would you do anything different if you were in my shoes?"

Eriksen was stoic. "Where is your son now?"

"I'll get to that. So we looked into the spreadsheet from Carlos and ran into the mess with the AG shutting down the search warrant request. After that I made a personal appeal to the White House for a meeting with the president. Shut down again."

Milostan and Novack shook their heads disapprovingly. "The boys inside the Beltway . . ." Novack muttered.

"Sanchez broadcasts his report, Gleason sues him, and Chief Judge Marrone assigns the case to me." Edward rubbed his eyes. "I immediately recuse because of Gleason's role in my appointment to the bench. Marrone insisted I take it because of our court's backlog and my media expertise. He said my association with Gleason was no big deal."

Eriksen leaned forward. "What is Marrone's interest here?"

"What I wanted to know. His tone and body language were out of character, like he was under pressure to give me the case." He turned to look at Eriksen. "Gleason got to Marrone somehow. You can add bribing a federal judge to your indictment."

"Right now I need to figure out what I'm going to do about you," Eriksen said. "You've admitted to two felonies—attempted smuggling of aliens into the United States and payment to a foreign national to illegally transport aliens into the United States."

Edward bored his gaze into Eriksen's steely blue eyes. "You do what you have to do. My concern is Carlos's life. Period." He turned to the three federal agents. "There's more."

"Which is?" Eriksen interrupted, peering over the top of his reading glasses.

Edward shot an angry look at Eriksen, then turned back to the agents. "Right after my meeting with Marrone, my deputy clerk brought me a printed copy of an e-mail sent last night to my chambers account. It was written in Spanish." Edward passed out copies of the translated version.

"Someone in Mexico who works for the people who want Carlos dead sent this. The San Luis cartel is holding Carlos and Alana and Foley captive. Their compound is near San Luis Rio Colorado, in Baja California."

Novack turned to McCormack. "You guys running a trace on this?"

"First I'm hearing about it," McCormack said. He gave Edward a stern look.

"Here's the clincher. Gleason called me earlier this afternoon. He knew Foley was in Mexico and that he was with Carlos and Alana. He couldn't have known that unless he's somehow tied with the people holding them. He offered me a bribe—he'd use his influence to get them out of the cartel's hands in exchange for taking his lawsuit and making sure he wins."

Novack sat up straight. "You record the conversation, by chance?"

Edward shook his head. "Here's what I propose. Set up a sting. Wire me up. I'll call Gleason first thing tomorrow and ask for a meeting at

Hancock Hills. I'll tell him I've changed my mind and will take his case if he can guarantee Carlos, Alana, and Foley's safe return. I'll get him to say exactly what he wants in return and who it will benefit. We send that to the director of the FBI, he takes it to the president, and we go from there."

He turned to Eriksen. "I'm putting my life on the line to nail this guy and save my son."

"*If* your proposed sting bears fruit, perhaps I can overlook the fact that you paid money to a foreign national to illegally transport Mexican citizens into the United States."

"Money never changed hands, Paul."

Eriksen stood and paced. "Judge Lamport, I can't in good conscience drop the smuggling charge. How can I, or any of my attorneys, appear before you in court knowing you've done this? You've compromised your integrity."

"Integrity? Please. No one on God's green earth gives a rip about Carlos Alvarez's life except me. I chose to fight for him. To the end. You know there's something you can do to save a man's life, and you don't do it because it's against the law, and you call that integrity. Not me."

He stood and walked behind his desk. "We help each other and do this quick, or you stand on your precious laws—that your own bosses selectively enforce to serve their political ambitions—and my family members die. Your choice, gentlemen."

Eriksen stared at Edward with arms folded. He looked down at each federal agent, studying their faces, then back at Edward.

"Look at the big picture," Novack said to Eriksen.

Eriksen relaxed his arms and slipped his hands into his pockets. He looked down. "I'll go along with it. For now."

Edward strode around his desk and got nose to nose with Eriksen. Eriksen backed up a step.

Edward pointed a finger at Eriksen's chest. "Paul, you don't know the first thing about *real* justice."

Chapter 63

Club Café Juarez, Benito Juarez, México
5:38 p.m.

Jaime Beltran and ex–DEA agent Raul Chavez shuffled into the low-slung diner and spotted two men seated at a back corner table chewing on burritos, swilling *cerveza*, and smoking marijuana. Presumably, they were the two dealers from Cartelo de Sinaloa whom they would talk to about joining their organization. Open drug use in remote towns like this one had become more prevalent since Chavez had last set foot in Mexico three years ago.

"Let me do the talking," Chavez said. "My accent sounds local. I'll tell them you're an *amigo* who's come from California to make some real money."

They ordered *tacos al carbon* and *tequila reposado* and made their way to the corner of the dining room.

"*¿Eres de* Sinaloa?"

Two pairs of bloodshot eyes looked them up and down. "*¿Y tu quien eres?*"

Chavez repeated the phrase the Sinaloa cartel *mulas* they'd met earlier in the day told them to say. *"Sinaloa nunca será vencido."*

Sinaloa will never be defeated.

The two dealers motioned for them to sit at their table. A petite *señorita* served Beltran and Chavez their shots of tequila and told them their tacos would be ready in five minutes.

Chavez put his hand on Beltran's shoulder. "I am Ramon. This is my *amigo* Jorge. He came from California last month."

"I want to make some real money," Beltran said.

"You sound like you're from East LA," one of the dealers said through a marijuana haze. "I was there for a year before *los migros* sent me back."

Beltran nodded. "Olympic and LaVerne. Where did you live?"

"Duncan Street, between Verona and Whittier."

Chavez slammed down his tequila shot. "So I hear *cartelo de* San Luis is taking over Sinaloa territory in BC."

"People hear a lot of things," the dealer said. "Only two matter. Money and guns. Whoever has the most wins."

The man talking was clearly the alpha dog. The second seemed content to smoke his weed and be semiconscious.

Beltran said, "We've heard San Luis has bought influence in high places even Sinaloa has never been able to penetrate."

The spokesman nodded. "They have perfected how they clean their cash from the US."

"You know how they do it?" Chavez said.

"If we did, our *jefe* would copy them. They have help. Big help."

"From whom?" Beltran said.

"People who used to help us. Government people."

"In Mexico?"

"*Sí.* And America."

The food Beltran and Chavez ordered arrived. *"Más tequila, por favor,"* Chavez said. "So where is San Luis vulnerable? How do you fight back?"

The spokesman puffed on his joint. "We have to kill their producers, kill their dealers. We have to get to their leaders and kill them, too."

Beltran tapped Chavez on the leg. "We are good fighters," he said to the spokesman. "We can help. If you get the leaders, the rest will scatter. You go in and clean up. Who are the leaders?"

"Humberto Peña is *el jefe* in San Luis. But we don't think he is *el gran jefe*."

"Who is?" Chavez said.

"We don't know. But we believe he is American."

Beltran nodded as he wolfed down a taco. He wiped his mouth and extended a hand to the spokesman. "I didn't get your name."

He grasped Beltran's hand. "Paco."

"We can do business, Paco."

Chapter 64

Saturday, February 27
US Marshals Command Center, United States Courthouse,
downtown Los Angeles
9:08 a.m.

Novack, McCormack, and Milostan settled themselves at opposite ends of a conference table laden with notebook computers and digital recording devices. Novack had won a minor turf war with McCormack over which agency's equipment and technician would be used for the surveillance and phone taps. The tall and taut FBI technician looked more like a field special agent in training than an electronics wizard. He busied himself with cables and connectors and testing links between devices. Edward landed at the far end of the table to review notes from the previous day's meetings and readied himself to call Gleason.

"We're a go, Judge Lamport," the FBI technician said.

He dialed Gleason's number. He answered on the second ring.

"Judge Lamport. Didn't expect to hear from you again."

"Are you willing to reopen your offer?"

A pause. "What offer do you mean?"

Edward gave Novack a questioning look. He motioned for Edward to continue.

"The one we discussed yesterday afternoon. About Joseph Foley and his companions."

"You mean the one I said expired at the end of the conversation? I'm a man of my word, Judge Lamport. That offer no longer exists."

"I see. What if I told you I could guarantee Sanchez would not only retract the story he ran on Thursday night but issue an apology on the air and meet personally with your tenants to assure them he was led astray by sources who, as it turned out, had an agenda? And all this settled out of court. No messy trial, no more negative publicity."

Silence on the line.

"Do you need time to consider, Stanley?"

"I'm not stupid, Lamport. Why the sudden change?"

"I didn't like the way you served up your offer."

A chuckle. "Well, things are what they are. Ira Abelson informed me last night that Judge Marrone has decided to take the case himself. Seeing how you're dealing with your family troubles and all. I hope that all works out for you. Like I said yesterday, no guarantees when you work in the dark, but chances are I could have gotten your friends back in your hands. Good day, Judge Lamport. See you around the club sometime."

Call ended.

Novack yanked his headphones off. "A start, but we need more." Novack handed Edward a slender padded envelope. "Something for you to wear in face-to-face conversations."

Edward opened the envelope and pulled out a pair of reading glasses. "These are mine."

"There's a transducer embedded in each arm and small holes on the inside of each arm to pick up sound. Can't see 'em without a magnifying glass. With these we don't need to wire you."

Edward tried them on. "Good guess on the magnification."

"Rebecca gave us the name of your optometrist."

Edward slipped the glasses into the case Novack provided. "I have a couple ideas."

"You gotta talk to Marrone," Novack said. "Is he in his chambers today?"

"I'll check." Edward called Marrone's direct line from his mobile phone.

No answer.

"I'll go upstairs. My security card will get me into his suite. Anyway, I think we need Sanchez in on this."

"What do you have in mind?"

"I can convince him to go along with what I proposed to Gleason without any involvement on Marrone's part. If, in fact, he's taking the case."

Milostan said, "I think Gleason's bluffing."

"Could be," Edward said. "He's no garden-variety negotiator. Here's my other idea—tell Gleason that Carlos is my son. Make it personal. Get him to tell me what I'd have to do in return for him delivering my three people."

"I don't see the benefit," McCormack said. "It could provoke him to do the opposite. If he has the influence he says he has, he could use it to harm Carlos as payback for you turning him down. And you'd never be able to prove it."

"You make a point," Edward said. He gestured toward Novack and Milostan. "What do you think?"

"It'd be high risk," Novack said. "But if you can get him to bite, we wiretap his communications, which will link us to who has your son and to the money launderers."

"Mmm. I feel like I'd be gambling with Carlos's life," Edward said.

"I agree," McCormack replied.

Milostan chimed in. "Let's look at the right equation. The risk of revealing Carlos's identity to Gleason versus the risk of doing nothing. I don't see an alternative."

Edward shifted his gaze around the table. Heads nodded all around.

"I'll see if I can get him for dinner at Hancock Hills tonight."

◆ ◆ ◆

10:44 a.m.

"You want me to manipulate the news to bait Gleason?" Sanchez said.

"Wouldn't be the first time it's been done," Edward said.

"But we *know* that what I reported is true."

Special Agent Novack stepped around the table to Sanchez. "Of course we do. We're talking psy ops now. Work backward from the end game. Gleason flashed his hand. The only way he can know about Joe Foley and company is if he's linked to the people who have them. Who are linked to—or are themselves—the money launderers."

Edward said, "What if we start this way. Gleason has agreed to have dinner with me tonight at Hancock Hills. We've agreed on a new strategy to get him to talk. Depending on how that goes, you could be waiting in the wings, and at the right time I'd text you to join us. We go *mano a mano* about your report and sources and how to reckon the truth. See how he reacts."

Sanchez steepled his fingers. "I'm concerned about my colleague in Mexico. He's had rough encounters with the old-guard cartels and survived. But he's still a marked man."

"If you're concerned about your own safety, we'll have undercover agents at the club," Novack said.

Sanchez looked at Edward and nodded. "I'm thinking about what we discussed last Friday." He turned to Novack. "I'm in."

◆ ◆ ◆

Edward called Chief Judge Marrone at home.

Straight to voice mail. He left a message.

According to Gleason, Marrone and Abelson were friends. What did that mean?

The revelations of the last twenty-four hours accelerated Edward's already spinning mind, spreading his search for answers to places he'd never expected to go. Chief Judge Michael Marrone—the senior judge in the Central District Court, the man who had mentored his transition to the bench in spite of their contentious dealings in court—compromised? Could that be the root cause of Marrone's erratic behavior toward him?

The possibility turned up the acid flow in Edward's stomach. He thought back to their last conversation . . . Had Marrone been trying to groom an apprentice who would follow his dark path?

Chapter 65

Beltran, Chavez, and the other twelve men in their squad rolled their caravan of four SUVs over a clay-and-gravel road to a cluster of four low-slung, metal-roofed buildings tucked between sprouting alfalfa and cotton fields. Low dust clouds trailed their vehicles and signaled the squad's arrival to their hosts.

Paco and a half dozen other men met them as they exited their SUVs. "What's all this?" Paco said through an angry visage.

"We are here to help you fight San Luis," Chavez said. "We also have our own objective. San Luis is holding three people as prisoner we want to retrieve. We help you, we help ourselves and the people who want them rescued."

Paco stepped toward the line of eleven ex-Marines and law enforcement agents. "Who are you working for?"

"*La familia,*" Chavez said. "The people we want learned something about San Luis's operations they weren't supposed to know."

"Ah. So what they know may be helpful to Sinaloa?"

"We don't know," Beltran said. "Our job is to find them and get them out of San Luis's hands. What we must do to get our job done will benefit you. You can help us by sharing what you know about your enemy."

Paco swept his gaze across each of the men in Beltran's squad. "El Teniente awaits inside. I will ask if he would like to speak with you." He turned and strode to the largest of the four buildings.

One of Paco's men approached Chavez. "Why should we trust you?"

"We can say the same about you. The only way to build trust is to walk together. Deeds, not words."

Paco emerged with a man about half a head taller than him who looked like he could give Beltran a run for his money on a Marine Corps obstacle course. He strode toward Chavez. "You are the leader of your group, *señor*?"

Chavez extended his hand. "I am Ramon. This is my co-leader Jorge."

"Paco tells me we have a common goal to penetrate the stronghold of the San Luis cartel."

Chavez and Beltran nodded.

El Teniente eyed Beltran's squad. "You have a good-looking group. Military?"

"Private security, *señor*," Beltran said.

"So you think the enemy of your enemy wants to be your ally?"

"We share a common interest and can help each other achieve our goals." Beltran took a step toward him. "We're here to invite you to join us. We are a temporary force. Once we get what we came for, we disband. You have knowledge that can help us, and we have abilities that can help you. Your choice, *señor*."

El Teniente looked at Paco, who nodded. As did his other men.

"Come inside."

◆ ◆ ◆

Guadalajara, México
4:17 p.m. CST

Bernal said to Salvatierra, "We know where Carlos Alvarez sent the data he stole. Albert Sanchez, an American TV journalist."

"You've seen what he sent?"

"No, only the metadata of the e-mail transmission. The contents of the e-mail had been deleted from the server."

"You do not look pleased to have made this discovery, Javier."

Bernal crossed his arms. "I told you last week I suspected one of my young leaders might use the stolen data incident against me."

"I remember you like to spy on your own people. I do it, too."

"I know which one I can't trust. Canedo."

"Your technology genius? Pity. I liked his smarts."

"You won't like what he did. He sent an e-mail to the American judge who is the friend of Joseph Foley. He disclosed their location to him."

Salvatierra ran a hand through his hair. "Then they must be killed."

Bernal raised a hand. "*El gran jefe* wants them kept alive."

"Did he say why?"

"Gleason has been approached by the American judge, Edward Lamport. *El gran jefe* wants to allow their dealings to play out. He thinks they may ultimately be to our benefit."

Chapter 66

Gleason wouldn't arrive until six thirty. Two thirty-something men who looked like professional golfers but were really FBI agents occupied a table in the back left corner of the dining room. About half of the other tables each had two or three couples seated at them, typical for a Saturday evening, and the rest had pairs and foursomes of die-hards who played thirty-six every Saturday and whose wives wanted nothing to do with the club.

Edward donned his FBI-issued reading glasses and pored over the beverage and dinner menu, then turned his attention to his notes for the conversation with Gleason.

"Judge Lamport, your guest, Mr. Sanchez, has arrived," a preppy young hostess announced.

"Please escort him to the Founders' Room. I'll be there in two minutes."

"My pleasure, Judge Lamport."

Edward called Novack. "How's the sound quality?"

"Crystal clear. Keep the glasses on the table or in your shirt pocket when you're not wearing them."

He hung up and strode to the Founders' Room. Sanchez had his game face on.

"I'll text you—one if I want you to join us or two if we punt."

"Talked to my colleague in Mexico a while ago. The San Luis cartel's propaganda machine is running overtime. They just assassinated the local police chief and the regional head of the Mexican Federal Police. They hung their bodies upside down in the town square with their intestines spilling out."

Edward had heard about gruesome displays of violence by the *narcos*, but nothing like what Sanchez just reported. "Didn't you tell me your colleague had said San Luis was viewed as the clean cartel?"

"They're consolidating their power. The new breed's no different from the old."

Edward checked his watch: 6:21 p.m. "Time to roll."

◆ ◆ ◆

"So we meet away from prying eyes." Stanley Gleason stood behind the chair opposite Edward. He sported a blue blazer and a creased brow.

"Works for both of us." He remained seated and shook Gleason's hand.

Gleason removed his jacket and hung it on the chair back, then plopped his oversized frame onto the seat. "Let's order first."

Gleason flagged down a server and asked for a menu. An eager young man showed up in seconds with a leather-bound portfolio. Edward picked up the menu that had been placed next to him on the table and adjusted his reading glasses. He felt calmer than expected as he settled the magnifiers on the bridge of his nose. He chose a grilled chicken salad, then removed the glasses and set them on the table at his right hand. Gleason ordered a twelve-ounce filet mignon, then rested his chin on folded hands, elbows on the table.

"So there's more to the story about Joseph Foley." Edward bored his gaze into Gleason. "Alana Alvarez isn't Foley's girlfriend. She's the mother of my son."

Gleason blinked twice. His mouth gaped.

"Carlos Alvarez is my son."

Edward kept his gaze firm. Gleason sat stone-still.

"Alana and I were in love a long time ago. I got her pregnant. Things blew up with her family, and I never saw or heard from her again. Until last week."

"So you sent Foley to Mexico."

"Alana asked for my help because Carlos's life is being threatened."

Gleason's left eye twitched.

He knows.

"Threatened by whom?"

"He works for Bancomex. They're an investor in the ITC."

"Yes, in the Mexican side."

"Carlos saw things he wasn't supposed to see."

Gleason sat upright. "Like what?"

"Business that looked like money laundering. International. Including Americans."

Edward studied him for body language giveaways. Nothing.

"And you know this how?"

"Doesn't matter. You said you could use your influence to get the three of them into my hands. The people with whom you have this influence are connected with international criminals. I'm not naïve, Stanley. I know our government makes secret deals with dictators and criminals and even terrorists to advance its objectives. I'm sure the politics south of the border would turn the stomach of the most hard-boiled cynic. The Mexicans are at the point where the cartels have more resources and will to fight than the government does."

"You think you know what's going on, Judge Lamport. But you have no idea."

"I don't care what I don't know. What I care about is saving Carlos's life. What you care about is saving your billion-dollar investment. There's a deal to be made, Stanley."

"Judge Marrone is handling my lawsuit now."

"And federal lawsuits are matters of public record. You don't want this to go to trial, and you don't want a judgment. You want this settled privately. USANews Network isn't some penny-ante local TV station. They're owned by a global media empire that can turn public opinion against anyone they want in a matter of hours, if not minutes. How's fighting them in court going to help you?"

"But Sanchez—"

"I told you this morning. I can deliver Sanchez's retraction and public apology and the assurance your tenants need to get your project back on the rails."

"And how do you propose to do that?"

"You first. When and how will you deliver my people to me?"

"You'll need someone in Washington to get your son and his mother into the country."

"I've barked up that tree for the last ten days. They've shut me down every time."

Gleason rested his elbows on the table. "Not surprised. Much bad blood flows between us and Mexico. The Mexicans are ticked off at your Prop. Sixty-Eight ruling. So is our president. He and Congress are battling over whether to suspend the borderless labor pilot."

Oh. So whatever Sanchez offers may be moot.

"Who are the stakeholders?"

"Besides the real estate, the big players are the electronics companies. They've developed breakthrough battery technology, and the favorable labor footprint made possible by the ITC would cut the cost of electric car batteries sixty percent."

This isn't getting me where I want to go.

"So what's it going to take to get Carlos and Alana out of Mexico?"

Gleason laughed heartily. "You are naïve, Judge Lamport. When leaders say Washington is broken, they don't mean special interests. We have three hundred million special interests in this country. Nothing gets done in that town without an exchange. A *personal* exchange."

Edward leaned in. "What's it going to take?"

Gleason locked eyes on him. "I want a sealed judgment in my favor against Sanchez and his network, with the on-air retraction from Sanchez *and* his network bosses. Live."

Edward didn't move a muscle. "That's one."

Gleason leaned in. "And reverse your decision on Prop. Sixty-Eight."

He envisioned Special Agent Novack doing cartwheels in the white catering van parked in the clubhouse loading area. "No way."

Gleason smirked at him. "The Yes on Sixty-Eight people can't compete with the Feds. You reverse your decision, they appeal. The Justice Department overwhelms them with an army—"

Push him. Make him expose his trump card. "Do you have any idea what you're asking me to do?"

Gleason's face flushed. He pointed a finger. "Do you want your son alive or not?"

"If I *were* to reverse my decision, who would benefit?"

Gleason narrowed his eyes. "As things stand now, if the president gets his way, the ITC will become a ghost town."

The president wants confrontation with Mexico. "Who else stands to lose?"

Gleason sat still. Ten seconds. Twenty.

"Who are you beholden to in Mexico?"

"What are you talking about?"

The server arrived at the table with their meals. Edward leaned back and folded his arms. He told the young man to leave them alone until he signaled. Then he leaned forward and put his hands on the table.

"You must know who the real power brokers are in Mexico. Who did you curry favor from to get the ITC deal?"

The corner of Gleason's mouth curled slightly. "There's more to the borderless labor pilot than what's been shared publicly." Gleason picked up his napkin. "Let's enjoy this food."

Edward contemplated his next question while Gleason stuffed several mouthfuls of filet mignon and smashed potatoes into his mouth.

"Who on the Mexican side vouched for ALEXA Investments?"

"What's with all the questions?" Gleason said with his mouth full.

"They're Bancomex's largest customer. Carlos managed their account. What could he have seen to make his bosses want to kill him?"

The veins in Gleason's neck bulged. "How would I know?"

"The same way you know who's holding my three people and who'll release them."

Gleason took another bite of steak. "Remember, you can't ask me how."

"Can you guarantee me their return or not?"

"They come in when I get what I want. Where is none of your business. Once they *are* in, I'll have them delivered to a neutral location of my choice."

"Not good enough. I need them delivered to me in the next twenty-four hours, with Foley. Do that and you'll get what you need." There was no way, of course, that Edward would reverse his Prop. Sixty-Eight ruling. He only needed Gleason to *believe* he would. "Excuse me a second. Phone's buzzing."

He tapped 1 and hit Send.

"It was Jacqui. Asked me to call her when we're finished."

Gleason finished the last bite of his filet mignon. "How will I be sure Sanchez delivers?"

Sanchez approached their table from behind Gleason. "Ask him yourself."

"Good evening, Mr. Gleason. Good to see you again."

Gleason turned and smirked. "Well, I'll be . . ."

"Judge Lamport has filled me in on the situation. What he's asked for violates every principle of journalistic integrity and a few laws, too. And puts my career in jeopardy. But I'm prepared to do it to help him save his son's life. What say you, Mr. Gleason?"

Edward's phone buzzed in his pocket. "Excuse me again."

Text from Beltran.

`Update.`

He pocketed the phone. "Well, Stanley?"

Gleason glowered at Sanchez. "How do I know you won't stab me in the back the next chance you get?"

"It's like the Cold War," Sanchez said. "Mutually assured destruction. We all hold up our parts of the bargain, everyone wins. One of us doesn't, we all lose."

◆ ◆ ◆

Edward ducked into the Founders' Room and called Beltran.

"What do you have?"

"Sir, we've infiltrated the San Luis organization and confirmed they have our three targets."

The weight of the world lifted from Edward's chest. Now they *knew* who was at the end of Gleason's chain. "Great news, Lieutenant."

"There's more, sir. We learned through talks with one of their rival cartels that the head of the San Luis cartel is an American."

"Do they know who?"

"Negative. Still working on that, sir. We've recruited some assets locally who've agreed to help us extract our targets."

"Great. Who'd you get?"

"Rather not say, Your Honor. Best for all concerned."

Beltran and company knew where they were and could secure them, but that wouldn't get Carlos and Alana into the United States.

"Okay. Hold off on the raid until I get back to you. I may have a solution to get Carlos and Alana into California, but I need more time."

Chapter 67

Angeles Development Inc. Corporate Offices, downtown Los Angeles
8:19 p.m.

Gleason returned to his office and found Rodrigues waiting outside his door.

"We're dropping the lawsuit." Gleason strode into his office.

"We're doing what?" Rodrigues said, following.

"We have the perfect leverage. Carlos Alvarez, the guy who stole the data from Bancomex."

"I don't understand. San Luis already has him."

"Alvarez is Judge Edward Lamport's son."

Rodrigues smiled and crossed his arms. "Our friends in Mexico will be pleased to hear this news."

"We're not telling them. Yet. Lamport handed me a key that will open doors we want opened and lock doors we want locked. For a long time."

"How so?"

"Lamport's got moxie. He had Sanchez there with him. We get Lamport his son and his old girlfriend and Sanchez retracts his report and apologizes on air. He said he'd consider reversing his Prop. Sixty-Eight decision, but I don't buy it and we don't need it anyway."

"So you trust Corman to handle the president?"

"Corman and I have a clear understanding. He says he can deliver."

"But what about the missing data?"

"Think, Rodrigues. Alvarez becomes permanent leverage. If the data ever comes to light, all it will take to keep it out of the wrong hands is well-applied pressure on Alvarez, which gets us Lamport, which gets the evidence thrown out. He's far more valuable to us alive than dead."

"What does Abelson think?"

"Don't need him. Go to San Luis and pick up Lamport's darlings. Bring them to the Mexican side of the ITC. We'll move them through the sewer. Sedated, of course."

Gleason's chief of security rushed into his office. "Sir, we have reason to believe Lamport was wearing a wire. The men I had stationed at the club saw him talking with three men who left the grounds in a white unmarked van. They took pictures. We have a make on one of them. A US Marshal assigned to protect Lamport. The other two must have been federal agents."

Gleason muttered a string of curses.

He called Corman.

"We know why Lamport changed his mind about our Sanchez problem."

Chapter 68

"So we give Gleason twenty-four hours to keep his end of the bargain," Edward said. "Suggestions on what we do in the meantime?"

"If Gleason doesn't come through, then your commandos move in, but you still need a way to get your non-cits in," Special Agent Novack said. "I can submit a Hostage Rescue Team request to Quantico. We have HRT and SWAT capability in the LA field office. That would need presidential approval, Judge Lamport."

"We have Gleason on audio. He's confirmed his connection with people who want my son and his mother dead. Isn't that enough to convince the right people?"

Special Agent Milostan said, "The fact that you've already knocked on Beverley's door makes Novack's idea more likely to get support."

Edward shook his head. "I don't know if Beverley has the sway with the president—or the conviction. We're entangled with serious bilateral politics. Why else would things have gone this far?"

No one offered an answer.

Edward turned to Novack. "We need wiretaps. Phone, e-mail, mobile, the works. I'll sign off on it right now."

◆ ◆ ◆

Guadalajara, México
10:27 p.m. CST

"Too many people have gotten too close," Bernal said toward the speakerphone. "We need to discourage further incursions without drawing attention."

"Too late for that," *el gran jefe* said. "The repercussions of the stolen data are nothing compared to what Judge Lamport has revealed to the federal agents. We need a diversion."

Chapter 69

Jacqui was grateful for a quiet morning, her first in days. She hadn't realized how internally disruptive having deputy marshals around twenty-four-seven had been until they'd left.

Edward had gone to the courthouse an hour ago to huddle with the federal agents running the sting against Stanley Gleason. The shock of what Edward had discovered about Gleason still reverberated. As did her fear of losing her husband.

In the stillness of the new day she recalled what Cynthia Thompson had said the night Edward told her about Carlos.

I see a bigger purpose in all this . . . more is about to unfold that we cannot foresee.

More had unfolded that neither she nor Edward would have predicted. He hadn't shared it, but she sensed he felt betrayed . . . The man who had advocated for his judicial nomination was the only man who had shown any willingness to help him save Carlos—for a dirty price.

She looked at the clock on the fireplace mantel. There was still time. Cynthia had invited her to visit her church many times, and she'd always had a reason not to go. Today she had a reason. She padded down the hall to the bedroom and took ten minutes to put herself together. She knew Edward would be in heavy work mode, so she texted him about church with Cynthia and lunch afterward and said she'd call him later in the afternoon.

A strange rattling noise came from the living room. Like something had fallen. She grabbed her purse and shoes and trotted down the hall barefoot through the room's arched entryway. Everything looked in order. Then a masked figure appeared from her left and a black-gloved hand put a cloth over her nose and mouth. The room spun out of control.

Her world turned black.

Chapter 70

US Marshals Command Center, United States Courthouse,
downtown Los Angeles
8:57 a.m.

Edward smiled as he read Jacqui's text.

> *Surprising Cynthia today going to church with her at Angelus Temple. Will send up prayers for you and the agents. Gonna ask her to lunch. Call you after. xoxo*

Edward and Jacqui hadn't begun their life together with fireworks. They'd forged their relationship, honed each other's sharp edges through conflict and wrought acceptance and respect for each other's differences. Alana was his first love, but Jacqui was his tried-and-true.

"What's the word on HRT approval?" Edward asked Special Agent Novack.

"I have the LA team on standby alert, but we're still waiting on Washington. Gleason has eleven hours to keep his end of the bargain."

"And the wiretaps?"

"We're on his office lines in LA and the ITC, mobile phone, business and private e-mails."

"So we wait?"

Heads nodded around the table.

Wait.

FBI on standby alert.

Beltran's squad on hold until further word from him.

There was nothing else to do except wait.

He checked his watch. There was still time to meet up with Jacqui.

"I can't just sit here. I'm going to meet my wife at church."

◆ ◆ ◆

9:24 a.m.

Finding Jacqui and Cynthia inside the thirty-five-hundred-seat Angelus Temple auditorium with its two balconies would be a challenge. He strode through the main entrance and scanned the nearly full lower level and less-populated middle- and upper-level seats. Three sweeps yielded no sighting of his wife. He strolled up the center aisle.

"Edward!"

The voice came from his left. A woman seated in the middle of the third from last row waved at him.

It was Cynthia. Jacqui wasn't with her. He stepped up the aisle and worked his way through the row to get to Jacqui's best friend.

"Lord, it's good to see you here," Cynthia said. "Is Jacqui with you?"

"She was supposed to be here by now to surprise you. She wanted to take you to lunch after the service."

"Then she'll be here. The worship's gonna start. Let's save her a seat between us."

Edward had a bad feeling about Jacqui not being there. She could have gotten lost, or missed the parking entrance, or her car could have broken down.

He texted her.

No response.

He called.

Voice mail.

Cynthia reached for his hand and held it. A pastor on the platform called for prayer, and he bowed his head.

You know where she is. Show me. Please.

The worship band began to play a soft ballad about the greatness of God. As the song built to a rousing chorus, hands rose throughout the congregation. All he could do was wonder what had happened to his wife.

He'd called off the US Marshals' protection because they were getting in his way.

His way.

They were interfering with what *he* wanted. What *he* was supposed to do. He hadn't thought to reinstate their protection. The earlier death threats seemed to be a minimal concern by this time.

He hadn't calculated that laying down his own life would put Jacqui's at risk.

Had he gotten it wrong?

He was in the right place to get an answer. So he asked.

And he heard.

Jacqui needs you.

Maybe she'd changed her mind. Maybe the thought of being with all these people worshiping God was more than she could bear right now. He knew she feared for his life. He hadn't feared for hers. It wasn't her fight.

He leaned toward Cynthia. "Can we step out to the lobby?"

She gave him an understanding look and led the way through standing worshipers out of the auditorium.

"I need to go home. I heard God say Jacqui needs me. Something's wrong."

"I'll follow you," Cynthia said.

◆ ◆ ◆

Edward entered the house through the back door and marched into the kitchen. Cynthia was right behind him. The kitchen was clean. A frying pan, plate, and fork were in the sink, rinsed off. "Jacqui, I'm home." He walked through the kitchen into the living room. Empty. "Jacqui?" He headed for the hallway to the master bath. He walked through the double doors and saw no light coming from there. He poked his head into the vanity area. Not there.

He turned to head for the guest room. Nothing.

He came back to the living room. Cynthia stood there holding an envelope. "This was on the coffee table."

It was sealed. Plain, no writing on it. He ripped it open and unfolded a single sheet of white paper. His eyes grew large as he read the laser-printed text:

IF YOU WANT YOUR WIFE BACK

TELL THE FBI AND THE OTHER AGENCIES

TO BACK OFF

Oh. No.

He'd called off protection. So he could do what he was supposed to do. Wanted to do.

And his wife had paid the price.

"Jacqui's been kidnapped."

The words floated from his mouth to Cynthia's ears. He heard himself say them, but as if reality had been suspended.

How could all of his efforts have come to this? He'd answered the call. He had laid down his life. He had persisted in doing everything he could to save Carlos.

And *Jacqui* disappears?

Cynthia put her arm around his shoulder and prayed. Fervently.

His mind warred with his faith and emotions. What had he done wrong? Did Gleason not have the influence he claimed? It was possible Gleason had proposed the release of his three loved ones and the San Luis cartel had refused, and instead, in their anger, had his wife kidnapped. Which meant Gleason had told them Carlos was his son. Which meant Carlos and his findings were still a threat to the cartel. Which meant they would not only kill Carlos and Alana and Foley, they would kill Jacqui to get what they wanted. Free rein to sell their drugs and launder their money and consolidate their power and . . .

Edward phoned McCormack.

"Jacqui's been kidnapped. Get over here now."

Chapter 71

10:41 a.m.

McCormack and Novack arrived at the house about twenty minutes after Edward called. An Evidence Response Team crew were on their way from the Westwood FBI field office—forensic technicians who would scour the home for fingerprints, a serology technician who would search for blood and other bodily fluid evidence, a field photographer, and a communications technician who would connect monitoring devices to the Lamports' phone and Internet lines.

Edward handed Novack the notice left by Jacqui's abductors. He placed it in a plastic bag and slipped it into an outer pocket of his sport coat.

"What's the time stamp on the text Jacqui sent?"

Edward pulled up his text messages and handed Novack his phone. Novack jotted some notes and handed it back.

The ERT team arrived five minutes later. They spread out through the house with their instruments and evidence collection tools. After twenty minutes, Special Agent Will Walker, the ERT team leader, called everyone together in the kitchen.

"Here's what we have. Impressions in the living room carpet of two bare feet, size eight."

"Jacqui's a size eight," Edward said.

"Two sets of shoe prints, size ten and eleven—smooth sole and heel, like dress shoes. We also found bodily fluid in the carpet and a couple of hairs. We picked up traces of chemicals in the carpet near the footprints. The kidnappers likely surprised your wife and put her out before they took her."

Novack handed the envelope with the note from the abductors to Walker. "Judge Lamport and Ms. Thompson both touched this."

"We canvassed the neighbors," an ERT special agent said. "Only two were home, and both said they didn't notice anything unusual. One said a black Mercedes drove up the driveway around nine, but it looked familiar."

"My husband's car is a black Mercedes E350," Cynthia said.

Special Agent Walker turned to Edward, brows raised.

"The Thompsons visit us regularly," Edward said.

The house phone rang. The FBI team put on headphones, and the comms technician initiated a trace. The tech gave Edward the signal to answer.

"Edward Lamport."

"We know you're listening, FBI." The voice was an electronically distorted baritone. "If you and the judge want to see Jacqui Lamport alive you will call off your surveillance activities and destroy all recorded evidence you've obtained. Judge Lamport, you will issue a permanent injunction to prevent the FBI from opening or reopening any investigation against the principals involved in the International Trade Center, both the individuals and the business entities associated with it. These two demands must be met in the next twenty-four hours or Jacqui Lamport dies."

"Where is my wife?" Edward said.

"I'm not finished. If these two demands are met, then the location where Mrs. Lamport is being held will be disclosed. You will receive further instructions that must be followed to the letter if you wish to see your wife again. If you fail to do so, Mrs. Lamport will die."

The line went dead.

"Call came from a drop phone," the FBI tech said.

Novack spat a curse. "We don't know if this is a crank or legit."

"Their demands make no sense," McCormack said. "How do you prove you've deleted digital files and not kept copies?"

"Same with the court order," Edward said. "As soon as Jacqui's returned, we go after them. They have to know that."

"Which could mean they have no intention of returning her," Novack said.

"No!" Edward said. "We have twenty-four hours. You run the crime scene labs stat. You get a make on the hair and fluid samples and you comb every criminal database—"

"Your Honor," Novack said, "the FBI has the finest crime lab in the world. We'll get it done."

"Sorry, Agent Novack."

Edward walked to the back door and stared into the yard. At nothing. What was his life turning into? The last twelve days swirled and morphed into something beyond surreal.

It couldn't end this way.

He couldn't lose them all.

Chapter 72

Jacqui blinked her eyes three times, then squeezed them to coax some tears. She couldn't rinse away the blurriness. Her head pounded, a deep throb unlike any she'd ever felt. She moved her hands downward and stroked them across what felt like short, rough carpeting, like you'd find in an office. She tucked her knees up toward her chest. Pain shot through her lower back and right leg.

Where did that come from?

She rubbed her eyes again. A sofa and a chair, neither of which looked familiar, lay across the room. She labored to sit upright, gritting her teeth through spasms and pain in her lower back. The fog in her vision gradually dissipated. *Where am I?* The room was maybe ten feet square, like a small bedroom in someone's home. The sofa and chair were clear now. Old and tattered. Between them was a small end table with a lamp. She turned to survey the rest of the room and saw a short, empty two-shelf bookcase. It looked like it hadn't been dusted in a year.

A pole lamp sat in the corner to the left of the bookcase. There was a small metal-framed window high in the wall above the bookcase, with frosted glass, the kind you'd find above the bathtub of a 1960s vintage LA tract house.

She crawled to the sofa and pushed herself up to her bare feet. There was a brown door in the wall opposite the sofa. She stepped toward it gingerly and grabbed the handle.

Locked.

She flipped a light switch to the left of the door. The pole lamp remained dark. She took three steps and turned the switch. Nothing. She peered over the frosted-glass shade. No bulb.

"Where am I?"

Jacqui padded to the bookcase and got on top of it on her knees. She reached for the window. Beyond her grasp. She pulled up one knee to rest her foot on the top of the bookcase and started to push herself up to both feet, but the shooting pain intensified and caused her to lose her balance. She fell to the floor, and the bookcase tipped forward, landing on her ankles. She screamed and writhed on the rough carpet. She breathed deep and fast to get through the pain. She lay scared and disoriented.

After what seemed like hours, a sound radiated through the doorknob, like a key had been inserted. She stared, waiting for movement. The door opened, slowly. In walked two men, one tall and slender, the other short and stocky. Both wore thin black masks that exposed only their eyes and mouths.

"Are you comfortable, Miss Jacqui Lamport?"

"Who are you? Where have you taken me?"

"Who we are and where you are is not important. What is important is that you are here for a purpose."

"Why? What purpose?"

They didn't respond. The shorter man lifted the bookcase off the floor and took it out of the room. He returned, and both men hoisted the ratty overstuffed chair and took it away, closing and locking the door behind them. Voices vibrated the door, though she couldn't make out their words. Then they faded away.

You are here for a purpose. What purpose? Whose purpose?

The two men returned. They lifted the sofa and carried it to the doorway. She rushed forward, pushing through her pain and against the sofa. The shorter man dropped his end, grabbed her arm, and slapped her across the face, knocking her to the floor. "Like we said, lady, you're here for a purpose. If you want to make it out of here alive, you'll do what we say when we say. Don't try another stupid move like that again."

Jacqui dabbed blood from her lower lip as the men hefted the sofa out of the room and locked the door behind them.

A thought bored through her terror—she was a hostage. Her husband had kicked the bear and it had swiped back. She would press her captors for answers.

The door unlocked again and the two men reappeared. The tall, slender man picked up the pole lamp, set it outside the door, and closed it. "All right, Miss Lamport. I'm gonna tell you why you're here. Your husband, the judge, is poking around places he shouldn't be if he wants to stay alive. You're here because you're leverage—with him and with the federal agents he's working with. Once our boss has used you to get what he wants, you'll be released. If you cooperate."

"Who's your boss? Is it Gleason?"

"Our boss's identity is none of your business," the shorter man said. He flashed a lusty, disgusting grin through his mask. "You're a feisty one, Miss Lamport. I bet you'd be a lot of fun to play with."

"Don't even think about it."

The back of the stocky man's hand met the side of her face and knocked her into one of the walls. Both men charged at her. The lanky one grabbed and held her while the stocky one slapped her face again and again until he'd drawn blood from her nose and mouth. Then he punched her in the stomach. She gasped for air as the lanky one released her. She fell to the floor in a limp heap, coughing and desperate for breath.

"That's a taste of what'll happen if ya keep flappin' your lips."

The lanky man grabbed her left arm and jabbed a syringe into her vein.

Her torturers left the room and slammed the door. The lock engaged.

She closed her eyes. And drifted away.

Chapter 73

Hotel Internacional, Mexicali, México
12:40 p.m.

For the first time, Stanley Gleason regretted saying yes to the International Trade Center project. Bernal, Salvatierra, and their weak-kneed lieutenants had, with one bungled security leak, blown apart the most carefully crafted and well-executed political power play of his life. He was no crusader. He didn't care one bit about Washington's policy objectives and their nation-building gambit south of the border.

Gleason was a businessman. He cared about profit. His political influence paved the path.

As did his knowledge of the illegal drug trade.

Of which he had become the undisputed champion.

But someone in Washington had panicked. And now he was caught in the middle. They'd thrown him under the bus in a heartbeat. Edward Lamport had handed them a gift. Sure, Carl Bender and company would have to change strategy and cover a few of their tracks. If they'd taken the long-term view, they would have seen, as he did, that they could have accomplished their objective of changing the government in Mexico before the next election cycle.

And he would have consolidated his grip on the other cartels, shut it all down, and walked away with his billions. His reward for doing the job the American and Mexican presidents knew needed to be done but would not do themselves.

Instead, he had to cover his own tracks.

"Big boss" Bender—*el gran jefe* to Bernal and Salvatierra—had gone too far.

Gleason would not follow orders this time.

He dialed Rodrigues, whom he'd left in Calexico to monitor the shipments through the sewer.

"The first product movement is progressing well," Rodrigues said. "We'll ship twenty million worth tonight."

"Move it out quick. May be the last one for a while. Judge Lamport's wife has been kidnapped and the FBI is going to think I was the one who ordered it."

Silence on the line. "How could they be so stupid?"

"Corman's beside himself. Bender is crazy if he thinks this will get the FBI to stand down."

"Where are you now?"

"On my way to San Luis. Humberto Peña said Bender told him to kill Carlos Alvarez and the other two." Gleason cursed. "I had it set up perfectly. They screwed me. Time to screw them back."

◆ ◆ ◆

Hancock Park, Los Angeles
12:47 p.m.

US Attorney Paul Eriksen arrived at Edward's home and joined him and the team of federal agents at the makeshift command center they'd set up at the dining room table.

"What did the attorney general have to say about the kidnappers' demand?" Edward asked.

"He won't contest."

Edward had expected pushback. "So he's willing to accept a permanent injunction against an FBI investigation without so much as a conference call?"

"He didn't elaborate." Eriksen took a seat. "I didn't push the issue. Something's not right, folks. Got a very strange vibe talking to him."

Special Agent Novack rushed into the room. "We got a hit on the ITC wiretap. Gleason's not the one who ordered the kidnap." He handed Edward an iPad.

He read the transcript of the wiretap intercept aloud.

Carlos and Alana were still alive, but not for long.

Every refusal of help from Edward's own government now made sense. "Senator Mitchell Corman is entangled in this mess." He shook his head. "Is the 'big boss' the president of the United States?"

Eriksen weighed in. "When I told the AG about the injunction, his tone was odd . . . resigned, like it was a fait accompli before I'd called him."

"Did you get a location on Gleason's call?" Edward asked.

"Mexicali," Novack said. "Not surprised he bolted before things got hot."

Edward turned to Novack. "We need your director in on this. Now."

"I need to work it through my special agent in charge."

"There's no time! Do you have his number?"

"I can get it." Novack returned to his laptop and retrieved the FBI director's mobile and home phone numbers. "Try the cell phone first."

Edward dialed the number on the FBI-supplied speakerphone.

Three rings.

"This is Walter Moore."

"Director Moore, this is United States District Judge Edward Lamport calling from Los Angeles."

A pause. "How did you get this number?"

"I'm sitting with US Attorney Paul Eriksen from the Central District of Los Angeles, Special Agent Frank Novack from your Los Angeles field office, Special Agent Ross Milostan from Homeland Security Investigations, and Deputy United States Marshal Campbell McCormack. We have a matter of highest urgency to discuss with you."

"Director Moore, this is Special Agent Novack. I gave Judge Lamport your number."

"Very well, Agent Novack. Judge Lamport, you have my full attention."

For the next thirty minutes, Edward and Special Agent Novack gave the FBI Director a thorough briefing on Edward's efforts to rescue Carlos and Alana, the commando operation, the sting against Stanley Gleason, the revelations of the last twenty-four hours, and Jacqui's kidnapping.

"Sir, the phone intercept we made this morning was the clincher," Novack said. "A high-level conspiracy appears to be taking place that involves the International Trade Center, the San Luis drug cartel in northern Mexico, and people in our government."

"Director Moore, these matters must be brought to the president immediately," Edward said.

"I'm in full agreement, Judge Lamport. The president's at Camp David today. Agent Novack, write up everything you've told me and I'll get on the horn with him." A pause. "Judge Lamport, we will recover your wife. And I'll talk with the president about your son and his mother, too. One caveat, though."

"Which is?"

"If he is the 'big boss,' he'll turn you down. Which would take things to a level I don't want to contemplate for a second."

They ended the call.

"That went—"

The phone rang. Undisclosed number.

Had to be the kidnappers.

"Edward Lamport."

"Your wife is being quite uncooperative, Mr. Judge."

Different voice, different disguise from the previous call.

"The injunction against further FBI investigations on the ITC is in effect. The evidence has been deleted. Where is she?"

"Patience, Mr. Judge, patience. We need to verify that the order is in place. Give me the docket number."

Edward mouthed *inside job* at Novack, who nodded his agreement. He read the docket number for the injunction aloud.

"We will verify that you're telling the truth and that your orders are in place and enforceable. Once we do we will call with your next instructions."

The caller hung up.

"Same as before," the FBI tech chimed in. "Drop phone."

"I don't remember if PACER refreshes real time or daily," Edward said.

"The case management system updates in real time," Eriksen said. "Documents are immediately accessible if you have the docket number. The indexing system needs time to catch up for searches."

"Good to know," Edward said. "So they should call back quickly."

But they didn't.

Fifteen minutes. Nothing.

Thirty.

Nothing.

So Edward sat with Novack and spent the next hour crafting the brief for FBI Director Moore. Satisfied it was complete, they e-mailed it to him along with a request to be included in the conversation once the director was convinced the president of the United States was not Stanley Gleason's "big boss."

Thirty more minutes.

No call from the kidnappers.

Chapter 74

San Luis Cartel compound, San Luis Rio Colorado, México
1:52 p.m.

Carlos marked the time by each cycle of rosary prayers he completed.

I believe in God . . .
Our Father . . .
Hail Mary . . .
Glory be to the Father . . .
Oh my Jesus . . .

He held the black-and-gold string of prayer beads in his mind—the one his mother had given him at his first communion. He touched and counted each polished sphere with the hands of his memory.

He remembered that each round of sacred prayers took a half hour or so. Half an hour reciting words of life out loud, or in his mind. More so in his mind today. The pain in his throat and lungs was excruciating when he spoke even at a whisper. The metallic water his captors would bring him once a day was barely enough to keep his eyes and mouth from drying to a crisp. His teeth were coated so thick he couldn't count them with his tongue anymore.

He marked the time with his prayers from when he awoke to when it was time to let go of the day.

Heaven. Home.

He wanted to go. Now.

He'd done his best. Stood up to evil. Evil had defeated him.

But it would never defeat God.

The door to his prison room burst open. The light blinded him. His eyelids ground away at his eyeballs, and they burned like they'd been splashed with acid.

"Your misery will end soon, Alvarez. The big boss has ordered that you and your mother and your friend Señor Foley are to die."

Die.

Life is Christ and death is gain.

For him.

For Mamá.

For Señor Foley? He did not know. They'd not talked about it.

"When?"

His captor sneered at him. "You in a hurry to die, Alvarez?"

"I need time to prepare my soul to be received by God. And to pray for my mother and Señor Foley."

His captor squinted. "What, you want a priest or something?"

Carlos hadn't considered the possibility. "If one could come, yes."

The man laughed. "Not gonna happen, *hombre*. You're on your own." He kept on laughing as he walked away and slammed the door shut.

Joe Foley fought through the haze of his pain to stay awake and labored to breathe through what was left of his nose. There had to be a way out.

Not only to survive the beatings, but to get Carlos and Alana out of here and to where they belonged.

If he could get out too, great. If not, he'd die for something worthwhile.

The visage of his friend who'd survived Vietcong captivity appeared in his mind. "There was always hope," he'd said. "Always. If they got your hope, they won."

His friend had held on to hope because he knew his brothers in arms would not leave him behind. They would find him and rescue him. Or die trying. And more would come and do the same, until he was free.

Foley was supposed to be Edward's hope. Edward had no one else fighting for him.

Foley had no one fighting for him either. No one who would do everything they could to find him and rescue him or die trying.

So how could he hold on?

He had no one in whom to have hope.

◆ ◆ ◆

Alana no longer dreamed.

Her brain was so starved of nourishment and her soul so bereft of hope she could no longer hold on to the dream that her son would one day know his real father.

She'd confessed to the Lord—repeatedly—that she wanted to be with Edward. She'd renounced the horrid thoughts she'd harbored that somehow Edward would be free to be with her. Horrid because those thoughts meant pain and sorrow would visit Jacqui and Edward so that her selfish dream could come true. She'd pleaded with the Lord to forgive her for wishing ill on another person so she could have the desire of her heart.

Alana no longer dreamed.

To do so would be to spit in another woman's face.

She searched what was left of her heart. She had not truly forgiven her father for driving Edward away and forcing her to marry Guillermo. She had not forgiven Guillermo for treating her as a housemate, not a wife. She had not expressed gratitude for him being a good father to Carlos. She had not forgiven herself for allowing the men in her life to define her.

And she needed to forgive these brutal captors who tortured her son, who raped and abused her, who beat Señor Foley to a pulp as if he were the criminal, not them.

I can't, God . . . I can't . . .

PART V

SETTLEMENTS

Who asks whether the enemy was defeated by strategy or valor?

—Virgil

Chapter 75

Hancock Park, Los Angeles
5:30 p.m.

Four hours had passed since the kidnappers' last call, and Edward was no closer to knowing whether their promises would be kept. No closer to knowing Jacqui's fate.

"Get ready to play offense," Edward said to Novack.

"The director gets in with the president inside the hour. Give him time."

"Isn't there something you can do to position your agents in advance of a go from headquarters?"

"Your Honor, LA SWAT is mobilized and standing by. We have no idea where your wife is. They could have taken her to Mexico."

"Have you contacted the Mexican Federal Police? Are you coordinating a joint task force with them?"

"They said no. I think you know why."

"Then what are we going to do if Jacqui has been taken there?"

Milostan said, "If the president wants something done, we have the means to go it alone."

Jessup had given him a heads-up on how it worked at the presidential level.

We couldn't achieve our objective unless we got the handcuffs off. Sometimes we won, sometimes we lost. Ultimately, we served a commander in chief who had to make the final call.

"The politicians figure it out," Novack said. "We get the bad guys they tell us to get."

The phone rang. The agents scrambled to their seats.

Edward answered on the third ring.

"Congratulations, Mr. Judge. You have passed your first test."

Same voice as last time.

"Where's Jacqui?"

"She is being held in Yuma, Arizona. We will only release her to you. If any Feds or police follow you, she will be killed. Are you hearing me, you agents listening to this call?"

Edward shot a glance at Milostan and Novack. "Done. Give me the location."

"You must drive into Yuma. Do not allow the FBI to fly you in. When you arrive, you will stay at the Sunrise Motel on East Thirty-Second Street, north of the airport. They're expecting you for late check-in tonight. You will call 928-555-7220 from the telephone in your room. You will be given instructions on where to meet a messenger who will give you your wife's location. You come alone, or Jacqui dies. If anyone tries to call that number from any phone other than the Sunrise Motel, she dies. If anyone intercepts our messenger, she dies."

The FBI tech yanked off his headphones in disgust and scrawled a note that he handed off to Novack, who passed it to Edward.

Another drop phone.

"How can I contact you if something happens along the way?"

"You can't. And don't bother locating the number I gave you. It's disposable."

Silence. The line was still open.

"What else?" Edward said.

The caller hung up.

Edward looked up the distance on his map app.

He looked at Novack. "You have five hours to deploy."

Chapter 76

The brown door in Jacqui's square prison was ajar. She stood and ran toward it—the pain in her back was gone—and flung it open. She ran through and slammed into something she couldn't see. Stunned but still conscious, she got up on her knees and put out her hands.

A curved glass wall.

She pounded on it to break through, but it was thick, like bullet-proof glass. Discouraged, she stood and walked back into the room. The small window near the ceiling had grown taller, almost floor to ceiling. She spotted a casement-style window crank, like the ones in her home. She opened the window and stepped through, only to find herself in a large pit with walls at least four times taller than she was. Smooth, slick walls. She turned to go back into the room and saw a man who looked like Edward standing there, smiling, with his hand extended toward her. As she approached him, he morphed into the tall, lanky man with the black mask. She backed away, and the man removed the mask to reveal a snarling, demonic visage.

"When you think there's a way out, you'll find another snare."

Then the apparition vanished.

She opened her eyes and she was on the floor again.

Against a wall.

In a different room.

This one was empty. No window.

And her back hurt worse.

She crawled across the room to a door and grabbed the knob and pulled herself to her knees. Locked.

She was alone with her fears. Alone with her anger toward her captors.

And toward Edward.

He was always so careful. Why hadn't he checked out Gleason better? Hadn't he heard the news? Even a grandstander like Albert Sanchez didn't just make stuff up.

The door unlocked and she sat up against the wall. The tall, lanky man carried a plastic gallon jug of water and a plate with two bologna sandwiches on white bread. The stocky man carried a large cardboard box. Both were still wearing their black masks. "Hungry, Miss Jacqui Lamport?" the lanky one asked.

She was famished, but she wouldn't give these scumbags the satisfaction of knowing. "I might be later. What's in the box?"

The stocky one opened it and pulled out what looked like a green wastebasket with a white lid on it. "This is your toilet, sweetie. Like you'd use camping." He pointed to the food and water the lanky one set in front of her. "What goes in has to come out, right?"

She seethed but kept quiet. The stocky man positioned the camping toilet in the corner opposite where she sat.

She couldn't take it anymore. "Is that the best you can do? Afraid to let a woman you can so easily overpower go to the bathroom?"

The stocky man put hands on hips and looked down on her. Bright green eyes poked through the mask, like he wore colored contacts. "You take what we give you, when we give it to you. Do we need to repeat the lesson, Miss Jacqui Lamport?"

She looked away.

"We'll be back. The big boss is still working on getting what he wants."

Chapter 77

FBI Director Walter Moore turned up the collar of his wool peacoat and paced from his car to the front entrance of Laurel Lodge, the main cabin of the compound officially known as Naval Support Facility Thurmont. He kept stride through the twenty-degree night air with his Marine escort at his left shoulder.

He'd taken a bit of a gamble when he'd forwarded the brief prepared by Judge Lamport and Special Agent Novack to the president as "eyes only," though the attorney general had given him cover. The AG had chosen not to attend this meeting. A curious decision under the circumstances, though not unprecedented during major crimes investigations and hostage rescues.

A Secret Service agent dressed in a flannel-lined blue jacket and jeans met him at the door of the cabin and escorted him down the central hallway to the president's office. He'd expected to meet with President Landon Jeffries alone. Chief of Staff Carl Bender stood to the president's left. They quickly dispensed with the usual pleasantries, and the Secret Service agent who accompanied Moore stood by the door, a required security presence.

As chief of staff, Bender was required to know everything the president did. Moore wondered if the reverse was true with this president. Jeffries sat behind his desk and Moore directly across. Bender settled at Jeffries's right.

"I asked Carl to join us because the situation at hand rubs against a project he's running for me."

Bender sent Jeffries a look Moore had seen thousands of times before, a forced calm that translated to *you held out on me about why I'm here.*

Jeffries addressed Moore. "Walt, this brief says Judge Edward Lamport made a request through Carl to meet with me about what he'd discovered." He turned to Bender. "And he said you spoke with me and I turned him down. That never happened."

"Oh, yes, Mr. President. My call. We get requests every day from people who have a personal need and want an audience with you. We can't possibly accommodate them."

"Carl, a federal judge isn't just another person. Especially one I appointed. And he wasn't only concerned about getting his son out of Mexico."

Bender's face turned smug. "His son's not an American citizen."

"Is that the real reason you turned him down?" Moore said.

The chief of staff inclined his head toward Moore. "I beg your pardon, Mr. Director, but the president relies on me to keep his schedule—"

Jeffries raised a hand. "Carl, let's cut the nonsense. Mexico is a top priority of this administration. What Judge Lamport has bumped into is squarely in the middle of my policy objective—the unintended consequences of their war on drugs have mushroomed beyond their ability to contain and have become a clear and present national security danger to us. We need to force them to clean up their act or we'll end up doing it for them."

Moore had not been privy to the White House's Mexico policy momentum at this level of detail. His immediate reaction was hope for an expanded budget for drug interdiction at the source. A topic for another day, though.

"Mr. President," Moore said, "the choice before you is narrow. The lives of two of Judge Lamport's family members are in danger at the hands of the very destabilizing force your policies are aimed at eliminating." He paused to measure his next words. "Judge Lamport's encounters with your administration are disturbing. There's a clear connection between the disappearance of Lamport's son and the kidnapping of his wife. The nexus point of that connection is the confluence of interests in the International Trade Center. The San Luis cartel—the most aggressive of the new breed of cartels—is the primary actor in both crimes."

Moore shot a glance at Bender. His head was down, as if he'd tuned out everything Moore had said to Jeffries. The president, meanwhile, appeared fully engaged.

"Clearly, I'm not privy to the treaty-making process and the operational realities south of the border with respect to the ITC. But, Mr. President, going after the San Luis cartel now will save the lives of Lamport's family members and deal a mortal blow to the very national security threat you seek to extinguish."

Jeffries turned his attention to Bender. "Carl, Director Moore makes a compelling case. That ITC project has been polluted before it's had a chance to accomplish its purpose. We have to clean it up."

"Mr. President, I respectfully disagree," Bender said. "Now is not the time to upset the delicate balance we're running within. The whole reason to pursue the borderless labor treaty and the ITC experiment was to drive change in Mexico from the inside. If you go in and blow it apart over the lives of two people, you'll set us back twenty years." He placed his hands on the president's desk and leaned forward. "This isn't the first time you've had to accept collateral damage to achieve a broader purpose."

Jeffries glanced at Moore, then back to Bender. "The program wasn't supposed to play out this way. We've had assurance on top of assurance, as recently as when Carlisle and Beverley met with their counterparts at the grand opening. Lamport's decision on that Proposition Sixty-Eight was a wrinkle for sure, but they smoothed it out. What I want to know is, how come we had to find out about these problems this way? Our intelligence community has some explaining to do."

Bender stepped back from Jeffries's desk, hands in pockets. "I'm sure you'll get the answers you want at tomorrow morning's national security meeting."

"I want to know why I didn't have them months ago."

The president stood, signaling the meeting was over. "Director Moore, tell your Los Angeles team I owe them a debt of gratitude."

"Judge Lamport is the catalyst, Mr. President. Perhaps a call to him would be in order."

"Agreed. Carl, get the video link fired up in the conference room. I want SecDef and the Marine Corps commandant online in thirty minutes. We're using our MARSOC forces in California to take care of this."

"Mr. President, you're making a big mistake. You're about to flush years of relationship building and diplomacy. I can't support it."

"So noted, Carl. Now get behind your president and let's get this thing going. And get Jesse Jessup in on this. His country needs him and that team he put together for Lamport."

"I'm sorry, sir, but no. If you insist on pursuing this reckless path, I have no choice but to tender my resignation."

Jeffries looked Bender up and down, like a father dealing with a recalcitrant son. Bender stared at him with arms crossed. "Carl, you surprise me. After all we've been through." Jeffries slipped his hands into his pockets and dropped his gaze. A minute or so passed, and he extended a hand to Bender. "Very well. I accept your resignation."

Bender turned and left the room.

"Director Moore, I want you to investigate Carl and his key staff. Thoroughly. He was on point for me with State, Commerce, and Homeland Security on that ITC project. His resignation is out of left field and irrational."

Jeffries moved straight to his desk and picked up the phone. "Stick around, Director Moore." He commanded his personal aide to get the president of Mexico on the secure line. "Judge Lamport's a good man. We should never have allowed this to go off the rails."

After a few pleasantries and formalities, Jeffries got straight to the point with the Mexican leader. "We have a mutually beneficial opportunity and we'd like your cooperation. We have reliable intelligence that the San Luis drug cartel is holding three of our people in captivity at their compound in northeast Baja California. We intend to get them out. I'm about to order Marine Corps special forces units into the area to execute a raid and rescue. With your cooperation, I'm willing to expand the mission and destroy the cartel's operational base. But we're going in, regardless."

Chapter 78

Gleason stormed into Humberto Peña's office. "Where are the prisoners?"

"In separate buildings at the back of the compound. *El gran jefe* has sent the order to kill them."

"Well, he didn't talk to me first. If we kill them it'll ruin everything. Get them out of there and give them whatever medical attention they need."

"*Señor, el gran jefe* insisted we do it tonight."

"I'll deal with the big boss. You do what I say. As soon as they're able to travel I'll take them to Mexicali and send them across the border through the sewer."

Peña stood and stared at him.

"What do you not understand?"

Peña stayed still.

Gleason reached into his jacket and pulled out a pistol. "You work for me, remember? Get those prisoners out of there now."

"*El gran jefe* warned me you would do this."

Three men brandishing automatic rifles surrounded Gleason.

"What do you think you're doing?"

"Your friendliness with the American judge has become a problem. *El gran jefe* says you have become a detriment to the operation."

"So, what, you gonna kill me? Who do you think built this thing? I'm gonna talk to that idiot now. Get out of my way!"

Peña stared him down. He took a step forward. Peña waved the gunmen off, and Gleason stormed to his headquarters within the compound.

He shoved the door open and dialed Carl Bender. Time for that high-in-the-sky string puller to come down and get his hands dirty.

"Have you completely lost your mind?" Gleason said. "You start killing people when the heat turns up a bit, it's only going to get worse."

"It already has."

"Because you kidnapped the judge's wife! You haven't learned a thing about real influence. I had it all teed up to get the judge's son and his girlfriend back to him. I told him he couldn't ask how I did it and he didn't care. He'd have been happy and no one—"

"They already knew San Luis had them. We needed a diversion."

"How did that happen?"

"Someone inside Bernal's bank tipped off the judge."

"And I suppose that person's dead now."

"Of course. People have to know the cost of breaking—"

Gleason fired a volley of curses into the phone. "When are you ever going to learn? *Money* gets you influence and cooperation. Everyone has a price. Everyone!"

Gleason paced the cramped office and rubbed his forehead. The operation needed fast and decisive action. Their margin for error was gone.

"All right. This is what we're going to do. First thing, you get down here pronto. Second, I call Rodrigues and tell him to suspend the sewer operation and disable the access systems. Then we give these three people to Lamport. Send them through the ITC. And you tell whoever has Jacqui Lamport to cough her up now. No demands, no ransom."

"Now don't *you* be stupid," Bender said. "The president of the United States is about to order Marine special forces to storm your compound. Those prisoners and the judge's wife are your only leverage."

Chapter 79

Jacqui gambled that she was dehydrated enough that taking a long pull from the jug of water wouldn't create a need to use that disgusting commode. She stared at the now-dried sandwiches she'd moved aside and reached for one. She took a bite and immediately spit it out. The meat was rancid and the bread moldy. She grabbed the jug and took a swig to rinse her mouth. Holding her breath, she spit the water into the commode.

She sat down and rubbed her icy feet. She was tempted to loosen her jeans and slide them down to warm them. The stocky man's lust nixed that idea, and she rubbed her feet harder.

The door unlocked, and the tall, lanky man walked in alone. "Things are now in motion, Miss Jacqui Lamport. All will be over tonight."

She perked up at the news. "Now can you tell me where I am?"

"I could, but it wouldn't matter."

"And why is that?"

"Because when tonight's events are over, it's over for you."

A barrel of cold terror doused her soul. "What do you mean, over for me?"

"My orders are to kill you when your purpose has been served."

◆ ◆ ◆

Eastbound Interstate 8 near the Arizona state line
10:49 p.m.

The California Highway Patrol escort the FBI had arranged allowed Edward to zoom his Range Rover from Hancock Park to Indio in just over ninety minutes. The drive down two-lane state roads from Indio to Interstate 8 in El Centro had taken another hour, and after a fuel stop and thirty more minutes driving at ninety miles per hour he'd reached the Arizona state line and was now ten minutes away from his destination, the Sunrise Motel near the Yuma International Airport.

The way Jacqui had looked the last time he saw her—her fresh morning face and her bed-rumpled hair swirling down her neck in an oh-so-sexy way—motivated and haunted him. He didn't remember the last words he'd said to her. Whatever they were, he was determined they would not be the last. No way.

He arrived at the Sunrise and stopped his Range Rover in front of the office. He'd had no police presence with him since he'd entered Arizona. McCormack had returned the Glock 27 to him before he left Los Angeles, and the feel of the holster and firearm at his right hip brought added confidence.

He strode into the office and a twenty-something male attendant handed him his room key and an envelope. "A message for you from a Mr. Novack." He didn't know if that meant Novack and company were staying at the same motel or the FBI had sent an advance team to make sure the place was safe. Didn't matter. He hustled to room 111 and ripped open the envelope. Two notes inside.

One was on FBI letterhead. He dropped his backpack on the floor, flopped himself onto the bed, and read:

- FBI, Yuma police, and Arizona state police on full tactical alert. Every major and secondary artery out of Yuma roadblocked.
- Border crossings at Calexico, Calexico East, Andrade, and San Luis, Arizona, closed.
- When Jacqui's location is revealed, text address to 32485. Immediately delete sent message from your phone.
- FBI and Yuma police will surround the location in a quarter-mile radius.

The second sheet of paper was a handwritten note:

Praying for protection and victory.
Ross Milostan

He'd suspected Milostan was a believer. The way he carried himself balanced Novack's rough-and-tumble affect. A hopeful sign. If nothing else, he wasn't the only one who believed divine guidance was needed.

He picked up the handset on the vintage touch-tone phone and tapped the ten digits that would free Jacqui.

"Lamport, you made good time. And you follow instructions well." The voice was not electronically disguised this time. The Mexican accent sounded authentic.

"Where do I find Jacqui?"

"Drive to Kennedy Memorial Park. Take Arizona Avenue north to East Twenty-Second Street and turn right. The street will dead-end into the park. A messenger will be waiting for you next to the locker building on the north side of the pool. He will be wearing an Arizona State University hooded sweatshirt. Approach the messenger and say to him, 'Are you a Sun Devils fan?' The messenger will say, 'Here are your tickets,' and hand you an envelope. Inside the envelope you'll find the address where your wife is being held. Then go back to the Sunrise Motel and wait for my call giving you the all clear to pick up your wife. What is your room number?"

"One eleven."

Chapter 80

Gleason's patience with Bender had worn threadbare.

The only thing that mattered now was covering his tracks and getting out of the country.

Two hours ago, his security team had crated all files and media documenting the construction of the ITC and sent them through the sewer into Mexico. The Feds on both sides of the border had no clue about the tunnel. Having his men destroy the electronics and motors that operated the concealing walls should delay them until he'd reached Cape Verde.

After that, he didn't care. The funds he had stashed away in Madagascar and Nigeria would provide him with more than a comfortable existence. In a few years, after things blew over and the US government lost interest in him and moved on, he'd build a new organization and amass a new power base. There were suckers everywhere, people who wanted position and status but didn't have the desire or the aptitude to do the dirty work it took to get there.

His sweet spot.

Bernal and Salvatierra would convince themselves with their machismo that they'd be able to carry on without him. But they would fall on their faces. They were in it for the power.

For Gleason it was all about the money.

And he could make money anywhere. The world had changed and opened up so many new places and opportunities. China. Russia. South America. Countries that had asserted themselves on the world stage and begun to build a new economic order that didn't include the United States in its long-term plan.

He hadn't foreseen that the International Trade Center gambit and all that came with it would end this way. Not at all. But plans changed all the time, and he'd built his fortune in large part by being willing and able to stay flexible and execute better than his competitors.

So having spirited assets out of the US government's reach as a matter of good global money management would make it possible for him to start over in short order.

Stanley Gleason, citizen of the world.

Chapter 81

Monday, March 1
Yuma, Arizona
12:18 a.m.

A seven-minute drive from the Sunrise Motel on Arizona Avenue and East 22nd Street landed Edward at Kennedy Memorial Park. He parked under a streetlamp, scanned the area, and exited his vehicle. He patted the gun under his jacket. Just because.

He treaded slowly to the pool area and swept his gaze left and right as he approached the low-slung stucco building. Its pale walls and darker doors reflected a sepia image in the ambient light. He turned the corner to the back side and encountered the promised hooded figure. Slender, about six-one. Male body shape. Back turned. Edward stepped forward. "Are you a Sun Devils fan?"

The hooded figure pivoted and revealed an Arizona State University logo on his hoodie and a black mask with only a slit that exposed both eyes. The messenger pulled a letter-sized envelope from a front pocket. "Here are your tickets," a deep voice said.

He snatched the envelope from the messenger's hand and turned to walk away.

"One more thing, Mr. Lamport."

He wanted to keep on, but he wasn't in charge here.

"I need your cell phone number. When you arrive at the address you'll find in the envelope, you must call the same phone number you called when you got this location. If the phone number on the caller ID doesn't match what you give me, your wife dies."

Edward gave up the number. "Anything else?"

The hooded man turned and walked away.

Edward jogged to the Range Rover and thrust himself behind the wheel. He ripped open the envelope and read the note.

820 EAST 18TH STREET

He located it on the map app. A five-minute drive south from Kennedy Park. But he had to backtrack to the Sunrise Motel first.

Another hooded and masked figure appeared at his driver's-side window just as he started the engine. This one was taller. The baggy sweatshirt disguised both build and gender.

He rolled down his window.

"What are you doing with your phone, Mr. Lamport?" A high, nasal voice.

He held up his iPhone with the directions list. "Finding my next stop."

"I trust you're not sending information to the police or FBI."

Adrenaline pumped up his heart rate. "Doing as instructed."

The hooded figure scanned him up and down, then looked through the side window into his backseat. "Be on your way."

Chapter 82

The White House
4:32 a.m. EST

Walter Moore had participated in plenty of briefings in the White House Situation Room, but this one felt different. He and President Jeffries had bonded in an unexpected way at Camp David. The president had even hinted bigger things might be in store in the not-too-distant future and perhaps Moore shouldn't get too attached to his office at the Hoover Building.

A magnanimous gesture. But Moore was a cop. First and always.

Four people's lives depended on what was about to happen in the basement of the West Wing. Moore and the attorney general entered the conference room together at the opposite end from the president's seat at the head of the rectangular mahogany table. Already seated to the president's right were Secretary of State Ronald Carlisle, Secretary of Homeland Security Conrad Beverley, and the Marine Corps commandant, four-star general Lawrence McCaffery. The first two seats to the president's left were empty. The third seat was occupied by the director of Homeland Security Investigations.

"Director Moore, please sit here next to me." The president had his hand on the back of the chair immediately to his left. The AG settled into the seat to Moore's left.

Moore knew seating position in a Situation Room session was meaningful. But he was a cop, not a politician.

A rear-projection video screen at the end of the room opposite the president displayed images of two uniformed military men whom he didn't recognize and a third whom he did—Jesse Jessup, a retired Marine colonel he'd seen on one of the cable news networks.

Jeffries called the meeting to order. General McCaffery introduced the men participating via secure video conference: Colonel Stephen "Jesse" Jessup, United States Marine Corps, retired, a founding officer of MARSOC brought in as special consultant; Lieutenant Colonel Marcus Mattis, commander of the 1st Marine Special Operations Battalion at Camp Pendleton Marine Corps Base, California; and Major Michael Bryan, commander of Marine Special Operations, Charlie Company, also from Pendleton.

"Gentlemen, an American citizen and two Mexican family members of one of our federal district judges are being held captive by members of the San Luis drug cartel in northern Baja California. I spoke with the Mexican president last night to inform him of the situation and our intent to send American forces into his country to locate and rescue these three people. Given the current tensions between our two countries and the reasons behind them, I made an offer to the president to expand our mission to destroy the operations of the San Luis cartel and apprehend its leaders and operatives. He refused, saying it was premature to launch such an attack for fear of repercussions from the other cartels. But he agreed not to stand in our way for the narrow mission—locate, rescue, and repatriate Joseph Foley, Carlos Alvarez, and Alana Alvarez."

Jeffries turned the floor over to General McCaffery.

"Colonel Jessup helped Judge Edward Lamport assemble a team of retired military and law enforcement personnel to serve as a private force to secure and protect his family members. Their on-the-ground reconnaissance and infiltration of a competing cartel organization, along with some inside information received by Judge Lamport, has confirmed the captives' location. Good to have you on this one, Jesse."

Jessup nodded into his camera.

Moore glanced at the cabinet secretaries seated across from him. Scowls. The president's attention was locked onto his military men, as if Carlisle and Beverley weren't even in the room.

"Any operational concerns?" Jeffries asked the Marine leaders.

Major Bryan said, "Beltran and his team have done excellent work, sir. The armed security force at the cartel compound numbers between thirty and fifty. We're well equipped to overpower them."

"Colonel Mattis?" the president said.

"Mr. President, we have full confidence in Major Bryan's assessment."

"Very well," Jeffries said. "You're authorized to use whatever force necessary to accomplish the mission and preserve the lives of your team and Lieutenant Beltran's squad. Secretary Carlisle, concerns on the diplomatic end?"

Carlisle gestured at the AG and Moore. "Mr. President, why are they here?"

Jeffries flashed him a sarcastic grin. "Feeling a little hamstrung in their presence?"

Carlisle's face said he failed to see the humor.

"Ron, I asked Justice here because there's a connection between this mission and the kidnapping of Judge Lamport's wife, as well as the need to investigate large-scale money laundering connected with the ITC project."

The news of Jacqui Lamport's kidnapping seemed to catch Beverley by surprise. "I know Jacqui Lamport, Mr. President. When was she kidnapped?"

"Yesterday morning," Moore said. "From her home."

"Back to you, Ron," Jeffries said. "Concerns?"

"The Mexican president is right about his country's readiness to handle an escalation of the drug war. This level of aggression has major unintended consequences written all over it."

"Such as?"

"Such as flushing a hundred billion dollars of American direct foreign investment down the toilet. Such as destabilizing the Mexican government."

"I don't see how a surgical strike to extract three people from the clutches of a criminal gang gets us there," Jeffries said. "When I spoke to the president I made it clear we need to change our strategy. We had a frank discussion about Mexico's handling of the ITC and the continued setbacks in their drug war. He said now is not the right time to go after the new cartels because they've built large decentralized crime networks."

"Right," Beverley said. "Build Mexico up from the inside and contain from the outside. We have to see the plan through, Mr. President."

"I made it clear the United States would protect its interests above all. That we would continue to support and train their military and law enforcement personnel, but they had to muster the courage and pay the price now to change their country for the long term."

"Mr. President," Carlisle said, "with all due respect, your view of the situation is incomplete and, dare I say, naïve."

Jeffries glared at Carlisle. "And your plan, Ron, has failed. We need a new strategy." He turned to the Marine commandant. "We move forward with the rescue operation." He pointed at Carlisle. "And I want you to contact the Mexican foreign affairs secretariat and tell them we want to start a new round of talks on economic development and security. This week."

◆ ◆ ◆

Georgetown, Washington, D.C.
6:58 a.m. EST

Carl Bender's first priority was to leave the United States as soon as possible. It would help to arrive in a country without an extradition treaty with the United States. But there wasn't time to be selective.

The ten a.m. flight on Delta from Reagan National to Mexico City via Atlanta would have to do. He had confirmed seats in first class, and he'd have about seven hours to decompress in the Sky Club with the assistance of several spicy Bloody Marys while he calculated his next moves. His first priority was obvious—storm the gates of the National Palace and salvage what was left of the grand plan before he began his self-imposed exile with the friendlies in Madagascar.

Bender printed his tickets and boarding pass, powered down and restarted his laptop in restore mode, and erased his hard disk. He set up a second zero-overwrite pass while he packed his bags. He'd run a DoD-compliant seven-pass erase once he got on the plane.

One final detail before he left for the airport.

He dialed Peña in San Luis.

"I've pulled the plug . . . no time to explain . . . the president is going to move on the compound . . . don't know when . . . it's done. You're on your own. Move forward as you see fit."

Chapter 83

Edward's pulse pounded through his temples as he sat on the rumpled bed and waited for the old beige telephone to ring. Cheap coffee and persistent uncertainty sent acid reflux howling up his esophagus.

He didn't want to imagine the condition in which he'd find Jacqui, but he had to prepare himself. What had these men done to his beloved?

Yes, Jacqui was his beloved. To the core.

His cell phone rang. His heart leaped out of his chest.

Special Agent Novack.

"How you holding up, Judge Lamport?"

"I don't dare sleep. The coffee is eating away at my stomach. You picking up anything on your end?"

"Good news from Washington. The director told me the president has approved the rescue operation. He's sending Marine special forces in. Details to follow, but it sounds like they'll be ready to go by nightfall."

He'd expected to be ecstatic when he heard that news.

He wasn't.

Without Jacqui, Carlos's rescue would be a hollow victory.

◆ ◆ ◆

4:41 a.m.

The red light on the phone flashed as it emitted its muted mechanical ring.

"Now?"

"You may go to the address you received from the messenger."

He grabbed his keys and jacket and bolted through the door, sprinting to the Range Rover as he unlocked it with the remote. He slid behind the wheel and cranked the starter before he even closed the door. He backed out of his parking space and realized he'd forgotten his seat belt. And the text to the FBI. He buckled up, sent the address, and slammed the accelerator to the floor, loosening a spray of gravel from the crumbling asphalt.

He'd rehearsed the route enough to drive to where Jacqui was being held without needing to check the directions on his phone. His heart threatened to pound itself out of his chest as he turned right onto 18th Street and approached the single-story industrial building. He whipped into the parking lot and strained through the dim light to see the addresses mounted over the door of each suite. His target was just to the right of the building's center. He brought the Range Rover to rest in front of the walkway, kicked open the door, and bolted for the entrance that stood between him and Jacqui.

He jumped the two steps leading to the door. As he landed, he saw an envelope taped to the door with his name scrawled on it, the handwriting barely legible. He ripped open the envelope and found another note.

YOU WILL FIND YOUR WIFE IN A FARMHOUSE

AT THE INTERSECTION OF COUNTY ROAD 119 AND E TRAIL.

CALL THE NUMBER NOW BEFORE YOU DRIVE.

He willed his thumbs to stop shaking as he tapped 928-555-7220.

"You have forty-five minutes to retrieve your wife. If you're late, the house she's held in will explode."

"What are you—"

"Come alone. The house is monitored. If anyone is with you we will detonate explosives, and she will die."

Chapter 84

5:11 a.m. MST

If Jacqui moved, her body hurt. If she didn't, it hurt.

She rolled onto her back and scanned what the light seeping through the door frame allowed her to see of the walls and ceiling.

For the first time in her life she was lost and without hope.

The door unlocked. Both of her tormentors entered this time.

"Miss Jacqui Lamport, you will be a free woman forty-five minutes from now. If your husband gets here in time, that is."

She willed her aching body to sit up. "What do you mean, if my husband gets here in time?"

"We've just contacted him. If he doesn't arrive within forty-five minutes this place will explode. There will be nothing left of it, or you."

"So he knows where I am? Where is this place?"

The two men now stood over her. The stocky one produced a thin rope from his pocket. "If he shows up on time, you'll know." He tossed the rope to his partner and grabbed her arms, pulling them behind her with enough force to revive the pain of her previous beating. She screamed and tried to wriggle out of his grip, to no avail. They bound her feet and she felt the cutting force of another rope around her wrists.

"Pull your masks off, you cowards. Look me in the eye before you do whatever you're going to do to me."

The lanky one backhanded her cheek, knocking her to the floor. A shoe thumped her rib cage from behind. She gasped for air. "You need to remember who's in charge here, lady," she heard from behind her. Before she could respond, she felt a pinprick in her left upper arm. The men left and locked the door. The dim light in her prison room faded to black.

◆　◆　◆

35 minutes to detonation

Edward raced to the intersection of Arizona Avenue and 24th Street, where he encountered Novack and his counterpart from the Phoenix FBI field office and four more agents, all wearing blue raid jackets with "FBI" on the back and matching baseball caps. "We need to head east on Twenty-Fourth to Avenue Three-E. It turns into E Trail south of County Road Fourteen."

"We'll escort you," Novack said. He handed Edward a radio. "Let's talk on this. We've alerted Yuma PD and Arizona state police to shift their perimeter south."

"Let's move," Edward said.

Novack and crew led the way, no lights or sirens. They passed out of town and into farm country in ten minutes. "Take the lead," Novack said through the radio.

"Got it," Edward said.

He arrived at the intersection of E Trail and County Road 18 fifteen minutes later and stopped his vehicle. From this point Edward would go in alone. He pulled the Glock from its holster and set it on the seat next to him. "Locked and loaded," he said into the radio.

"Ten-four. Emergency vehicles on the way. Meet us here when you've got her."

"Ten-four, Agent Novack."

The drive down the last mile of E Trail transported him into a surreal realm. Edward was outside himself, filled with an energy and a confidence he'd not known before. His Range Rover reached the intersection of the unpaved Road 119 and he saw the outline of a house on the edge of a fenced-in field. He aimed the Range Rover's headlights at the structure and saw that it was weathered, but, as far as he could tell, in good repair. He shifted into four-wheel drive low and bounced through a hard right turn and random potholes to the gravel drive of the farmhouse. Floored it up the drive, spraying a rooster tail of pebbles. Drifted his ride to the front porch, driver's side facing the front door. He grabbed for the door latch twice before the door would open, and he bounded toward the porch.

Edward tripped over a small boulder and stumbled up the two steps to the front door. He turned the doorknob, but the door didn't budge. Tried a second time, leaning his shoulder for leverage. Still wouldn't budge. He kicked at the door three times and got it to swing open.

"Jacqui! Jacqui! Where are you?"

No response. He felt the walls on either side of the front door and found a light switch. No lights. He pulled out his phone and turned on the LED.

"Jacqui!"

She wasn't in the main room. He darted to his left to the kitchen. Scanned the floor with the light.

Nothing.

He called her name over and over as he walked down a short hallway. Three doors, all closed. He opened the first and aimed the light into an empty room. He opened the second—a bathroom. He rushed in and flung the curtains away from the bathtub. Nothing.

He sprinted through the third door.

She was on the floor, wrists tied behind her and ankles roped together.

"Jacqui!"

She didn't respond.

He got on his knees next to her and shook her twice. No response.

He felt for a pulse. Slow but strong.

They've drugged her.

He lifted her limp body over his shoulder and headed for the door as fast as his weary legs would move them.

He bumped Jacqui's head on the door frame. "I'm so sorry, dear." He shifted her perpendicular to exit the narrow hallway into the main room of the house.

As he entered the living room, he heard a pulsing electronic tone to his left.

He glanced quickly in that direction and saw a black box with a blinking red light.

He bolted for the door.

An intense flash of light.

A concussion of heat and rushing air.

The blast thrust him and Jacqui through the door and over the porch. They slammed into the side of the Range Rover. He landed on top of her.

The world spun, faded out, faded in.

Pain sprinted up his legs and back. He strained to turn his head and moved enough to see the house out of which he'd pulled his beauty engulfed in flames. Intense heat seared his face.

He willed himself to get up.

He could not.

"Jacqui," he whispered.

The world spun again. Faded to black.

Chapter 85

The blast concussion reached Novack and team seconds after a flash of light pierced the night sky. "Move out, now!" he shouted into his radio. Three sedans, two ambulances, and a company of fire trucks lit up and sped down County Road 18 and E Trail, lights flashing and sirens blaring, to the inferno that had been Jacqui Lamport's prison.

The two ambulances led the way up the gravel drive and came to a stop short of Judge Lamport's Range Rover. Flames licked violently as four EMTs sprinted to the side of the vehicle facing the fire, stretchers in hand.

Novack hustled to where Edward and Jacqui Lamport's bodies lay. A pair of EMTs moved Edward facedown onto a stretcher and hustled him away to one of the ambulances. The other pair of EMTs did likewise with Jacqui. Novack ran after the emergency workers to the ambulances as the fire team took their positions and commenced dousing the home with water pumped from a tank truck.

"They're both still alive," one of the EMTs shouted to Novack.

He heaved a huge sigh of relief.

"The judge is in bad shape. He took a lot of debris from the blast. Deep-gash head wound, too. She's unconscious. Appears drug-induced. She had a fresh puncture mark on her left arm. A lot of contusions and abrasions, most likely from beatings. Her husband's body shielded her from the blast."

"Yuma Providence is standing by," Novack said to the EMTs. "Godspeed."

Chapter 86

Gleason paced around Humberto Peña's office, seething.

"Why'd you do it? Why'd you kill the judge and his wife?"

"*El gran jefe* told me the operation was over and to do as I saw fit. Face facts, Señor Gleason. Your new ways of running the drug business didn't work. It's time to go to war."

"With what? Popguns?"

"We are joining with some breakaway cells from Matas Zetas. We will be more than ready for the US Marines."

Gleason shook his head and muttered to himself. What did it matter? He'd already made up his mind to leave this all behind.

"Congratulations, Humberto. The San Luis cartel is yours. I'm out."

Peña flashed a sinister smile. "You are correct, *señor*. You are out and I am in."

Four soldiers brandishing automatic rifles surrounded him. Peña lifted a pistol at Gleason's head. "The last time we danced like this I let you walk away. Not this time."

Peña squeezed the trigger on his pistol. A click. A piercing pain on the side of Gleason's neck. Fade to black.

"Tie him up and throw him in with the others," Peña ordered the gunmen.

Gleason was a large man, and the four wiry soldiers strained to lift the drugged dead weight of their former leader.

Peña spat on Gleason's face. They dragged him away.

◆ ◆ ◆

Reagan Washington National Airport, Washington, D.C.
9:20 a.m. EST

The gate attendant announced early boarding for first-class passengers on Delta flight 1569 to Atlanta, the first leg of Carl Bender's trip to Mexico City.

He slapped his laptop closed and tucked it under his arm and strode toward the gate.

Two men in dark suits and sunglasses stepped in front of him. "I'm sorry, Mr. Bender, your travel plans have changed. You can make this easy, or we can cuff you right here."

Chapter 87

Yuma Providence Hospital, Yuma, Arizona
2:56 p.m.

Edward opened his eyes. Light snapped them shut. He was flat on his stomach. He opened them again slowly. He saw two men and two women wearing white. "Where am I?"

"Yuma Providence Hospital, Judge Lamport. I'm Dr. Lewis, chief of surgery. Looks like you're going to be just fine. You were severely dehydrated and lost over three pints of blood, and you've got quite a few foreign objects embedded in your back and buttocks and the backs of your legs. We've scheduled you for surgery within the hour to remove all the debris, and we have you on a strong broad-spectrum antibiotic to ward off infection."

His head pounded. "Where is Jacqui?"

"She's resting comfortably in a private room on the second floor. They'd injected her with propofol, a general anesthetic. Dangerous stuff in the wrong hands. Thankfully, they didn't give her enough to cause harm. She has multiple lacerations and contusions on her face, back, and limbs, but she's going to be fine."

"Can I see her?"

"Not for a while. We need to start prepping you for the OR."

Edward tried to move his head. Pain forced out a groan.

"How long do I need to be here?"

Dr. Lewis smiled. "We'll need to go deep into some of your muscle tissue to get the debris out. Two days, maybe three, depending on how you respond."

A knock at the door. It was Agent Novack. "May I come in?"

"Yes, of course," Dr. Lewis said. "Judge Lamport is doing fine. I'll leave you two alone." The doctor waved the emergency intern and two nurses out. "Thirty minutes until we prep you for surgery, Judge Lamport."

"Surgery?" Novack said.

"A lot of junk to clean out of my body."

Novack took a seat next to the bed. "The raid at San Luis goes down tonight."

Jacqui was alive and safe, so he could hope for Carlos and Alana again. "Any new information?"

"That security squad you sent down there will be working with a Marine special ops team. Director Moore said the president really went to bat for you."

Went to bat for you.

At last. Someone finally got it.

◆ ◆ ◆

Jacqui tried to shift her weight to her left side, but her arms and lower back protested. She wanted a better angle for conversing with the two FBI agents in her room, Marlene Henning and Chuck Callaghan. Flat on her back would have to do. She raised the upper part of her bed as high as she could bear.

"We'll keep this brief, Mrs. Lamport," Agent Henning said. "What can you tell us about the kidnappers?"

"One was tall and lanky, the other short and stocky—kind of fat, actually. They both wore black hooded sweatshirts and thin black masks with holes for their eyes and mouth."

"Can you guess their height?" Agent Callaghan said.

"The shorter one was a little taller than me, maybe five-eight. The other was a head taller."

"How about their voices?" Henning asked.

"They both sounded young. The shorter one had a tinge of barrio accent. The taller one was probably white. His voice had a surfer-dude ring."

"Where in the house did they hold you?" Henning's eyes softened. Like she knew Jacqui's pain. Intimately.

"Two different rooms, both about ten by ten. Rough, musty-smelling carpet. Floors sagged to the corners, and it felt like wood underneath. Other than that I never got a good look. The place exploded as Edward carried me out of there."

"He's about to go into surgery," Callaghan said. "He shielded you from the blast and debris with his body. Took a lot of fragments in his back, butt, and legs."

Conviction merged with compassion and melted the sear around her heart. "Is it bad?"

"You'll have to ask the doctors," Henning said. "All we know is they have to remove hundreds of fragments, some of them deep. They said the surgery will take hours."

Jacqui exhaled deeply. Her lack of emotion dismayed her. She stared at the ceiling, searching her heart for reasons why. "Any more questions?"

"Give us a minute, please," Henning said to her partner.

Callaghan closed the door behind him.

"I know you've just been through a horrible ordeal," Agent Henning said. She paused to wipe away a tear. "Ten years ago, I was kidnapped. From my home, just like you. Turned out the men who did it had business with my father. He owned his own company that made parts for the aircraft industry. He got involved with some investors who turned out to be connected with the New York Mafia. He wasn't making enough money to keep up with the payments, so they knocked him around some and kidnapped me."

Words that Cynthia Thompson said to Jacqui often—*divine appointment*—came to mind. Still, she was emotionally flat.

"He tried to save me on his own," Henning said. "Without the police. He . . . he liquidated everything he had to catch up on what he owed, and he brought it to them. They said it wasn't enough and they called in the loan. There was no way he could pay. So they . . . killed him. Then they let me go. They said I wasn't needed anymore. I never reported it. I was afraid they'd come after my mom, our house. Things were bad enough without that hanging over our heads. So we moved to California."

"Where were you living then?"

"Queens."

Jacqui tried to take her hand but couldn't move her arm without excruciating pain. She opened her hand, leaving it to the FBI agent to take it or not.

"Your father didn't know what he was getting into, did he?"

"Not until it was too late."

"How did you carry that weight alone all these years?"

"For one, it motivated me to join the Bureau. Someday I'll go back and bring those guys down. New York Bureau has been on them for years. I've talked to the special agent in charge in Manhattan about it. We agreed I would sit tight until the right time."

"What about your mother? She has no closure."

"She died a year later. Never got over losing him." Henning dabbed a tear. "Tranquilizer overdose."

Jacqui wiggled her fingers, and Henning took her hand. "Why are you telling me this?"

Henning lifted Jacqui's hand so she could sit on the edge of the bed. "When it first happened, I hated my father. When Mom died, I vowed I would never forgive him for what had happened. Even though he was dead, I couldn't . . . I wouldn't let myself have any positive memory of him as a dad. I felt for the longest time like he'd betrayed us by trying to be the hero and get out of his mess without getting the police involved. Later on, some friends helped me get rid of my unforgiveness. They helped me realize I needed to forgive my dad for me, not for him. The bitterness inside ate at me in ways I hadn't realized. The other thing they helped me understand was though my dad's actions didn't produce a good result, he did what he did out of love. He gave up everything he ever held dear to protect me and my mom."

Jacqui struggled to wipe her eyes. "You have wonderful friends, Agent Henning."

"Call me Marlie. My dad called me Marlie, and my friends do now. And yes, I do have great friends. My home group from church."

Jacqui thought of Cynthia and the women's Bible study she kept asking her to attend. Maybe she needed to talk to her again about that sooner rather than later.

"You're a brave woman, Marlie. Thanks for sharing. You've given me things to think about, for sure."

Marlie leaned over and kissed her forehead. "What helped me forgive my father was a passage from the Bible: *people look at the outward appearance, but the Lord looks at the heart.* My friends helped me see what God saw in my dad—he was motivated by his love for me and my mom."

"Thank you so much, Marlie. I . . . I know what I need to do next."

Jacqui rang for the nurse and asked her to bring the phone to her and dial Cynthia Thompson's number.

Chapter 88

Edward awoke still on his stomach. In a different room.

He was pain free. Groggy. In no hurry for whatever drugs they'd given him to wear off.

"Judge Lamport, your surgery was a success," Dr. Lewis said. "Took longer than we'd planned. You have more than two hundred sutured wounds."

"Thanks, Doc."

"Pleasure's ours. You'll need to spend the next twenty-four hours on your stomach, except for hourly walks we'll help you take to boost your circulation and speed your healing."

Physical healing, anyway.

He still hadn't talked to Jacqui.

"Is my wife ready to see me?"

"She's not yet able to get out of bed, and we need to keep you here in ICU one more day. We'll put you in a room together tomorrow."

It was strange to know they were one floor apart in the same hospital and yet hadn't even shared a "hello." He had no excuse to be the least bit impatient after all he'd put her through.

And when he did see her he needed to be kind and loving and undefended, ready to hear and receive whatever she had to say.

If the shoe were on the other foot, he would want the same from her.

But it wasn't. It was on him.

Chapter 89

Jaime Beltran felt like himself again.

The turbine whine and rotor chop of the two CH-53E Super Stallion helicopters that had flown to the rendezvous point from Yuma Marine Corps Air Station awakened something in him.

The Marines were first to fight. The most ready when everyone else was least ready. The mind-set would never leave him. He was made to be the first to fight. The sand spray whipped up by the helo rotors made this mission feel like Iraq all over again.

Once a Marine, always a Marine. Now that the commander in chief had given his team and the regulars they'd fight alongside the clearance to bring Judge Lamport's non-cits into America, nothing could stop him.

Two fifteen-man Marine Special Operations Teams poured out the back of each helicopter and merged with Beltran's fourteen-man security squad for their pre-mission briefing.

Major Michael Bryan, Charlie Company commander, 1st Marine MSOC, called the men to attention and handed out pages with satellite images of the objective.

"The compound consists of a main building and six smaller buildings clustered behind the main building in a semicircle pattern. The buildings are all-steel construction, identical to those at the neighboring farms. The compound is surrounded by approximately eight acres of avocado trees. The perimeter is secured with an eight-foot-high iron fence topped with razor wire. There are two entry gates to the property, one north and one south."

Major Bryan motioned to Beltran. "Lieutenant Beltran here and his men will combine with Special Ops Team One as our security element. Half will deploy to the north gate, half to the south. SOTs Two, Three, and Four will be the assault element. Once the security teams disable the entry gate armed guard, half will remain outside the gate and half will patrol the north and south ends of the property. The assault team will enter through the south gate and move straight for the compound buildings. SOT Four will conduct search and retrieve in the six small buildings, and SOTs Two and Three will assault the main building."

"Major Bryan, sir," Beltran called out.

"Go ahead, Lieutenant Beltran," Bryan said.

"I request to be assigned to SOT Four, sir."

Bryan stepped toward Beltran and stopped directly in front of him. "Why is that, Lieutenant Beltran?"

"I made a commitment to Judge Lamport to find and secure his son. I want to honor that commitment, sir."

Major Bryan turned on his heels to the captain of SOT Four. "What do you think, Captain?"

"It would be a pleasure to have Lieutenant Beltran on my team, sir."

◆ ◆ ◆

Humberto Peña turned his ear toward an open window. The night air was quiet.

He was chagrined that Los Matas Zetas had not shown the enthusiasm to join with his San Luis cartel he had expected. Their leader had said he saw a golden opportunity, but he supplied a token force of twenty men armed with pistols and automatic rifles. Coupled with the meager security team Gleason left him with, he had fifty men with which to fight off the US Marines.

But he had a weapon the Marines did not.

The prisoners.

Their precious cargo.

They would want Gleason, too. Alive. Peña would not give them such satisfaction. He would tantalize them with the opportunity to bring a major criminal figure from their own country to justice. And then he would deprive them of what they wanted.

Nine years the Mexican government has fought against los narcos, *with the help of their American advisors and trainers and their superior armaments. They have not defeated* los narcos. *They will never defeat* los narcos.

Peña would demonstrate this to the Marines and their president.

With night-vision optics in place, the Marine units began their movement to the objective. Major Bryan traveled with SOTs Two and Three. Ex–DEA agent Chavez marched with the north gate security element. Beltran's team trailed the main assault group, and the south security element brought up the rear.

Peña huddled with his black-clad soldiers and barked orders to distribute through the avocado orchard, concealing themselves from the

Marines. He would leave the gates unguarded to confound the soldiers and make them vulnerable to the series of ambushes they would face. The Marines could not shoot what they could not see.

"Bring the prisoners out and set them in a line in front of the main building," he said.

Peña's soldiers dragged Foley, Carlos, Alana, and Gleason from the back buildings through the dirt-and-gravel courtyard. They tied each of them to one of the support posts that held up the sunshade over the main building entrance, as human shields against their attackers.

◆ ◆ ◆

Beltran's radio crackled in his ear. "Team Four, stay close until the forward teams break down their second line," Major Bryan ordered.

The north gate security team peeled off and double-timed around the perimeter fence. The other teams held back, crouched behind bushes that lined the dirt road they'd marched over.

"Security team north," the captain said into the radio. "Gate is unmanned."

"Hold your position," Bryan said. He turned and pointed toward the objective.

They ran to the south gate, rifles in ready position. They reached it and Bryan held up his right hand to stop the advance.

"Security team north, this is leader," Bryan said into the radio. "South gate unmanned. Move in. Watch for sniper fire."

The soldiers following Major Bryan streamed through the unmanned south gate with weapons in fire position. Bryan pointed to SOT Three and signaled right and sent SOT Two left. Beltran and SOT Four took the center path. All engaged their night-vision gear and moved out.

Beltran swept his gaze right and left. The danger was high, but he felt *alive*. He was made for this. There was a price to pay to defeat evil in this world.

Five steps. Ten steps. Sweep left. Sweep right.

Staccato and flash. Fire dead ahead. Beltran and company hit the deck and rolled to positions behind tree trunks.

"Report in, report in," Beltran heard through his earpiece. "Anyone hit?"

"SOT One, negative."

"SOT Two, negative."

"SOT Three, negative."

"Security north, hold your position," Bryan said. "Two and three, fan out wide and look for infrared signatures. Shoot at anything not wearing our uniform."

Beltran got up on one knee and aimed his rifle ahead. He focused through his night-vision glasses for movement and anything forward of their position that glowed orange.

"Move forward one row of trees at a time," Bryan said.

"Security south, we got your back."

Beltran crouched and stepped forward, scanning five degrees from center in front of him and trusting his teammates to do the same.

He saw an orange glow to his right. He aimed and squeezed off a round.

Hit.

A flash to his left. A teammate returned fire.

Enemy down.

One more row of trees. Sweep. Clear. Advance.

Sweep. Clear. Advance.

A black-clad figure ran toward the center of the compound. "Hold fire" came through the radio. A second, a third figure ran in the same direction.

"SOT Four, advance. Two and Three, cover us."

Beltran and team followed Major Bryan at double-time pace, then a jog, then full sprint. Gunfire spat behind and around them. *Two and Three are doing their job and doing it well.*

They cleared the trees and approached the main building. Riflemen from Two and Three converged from the flanks. They met gunfire from a line of cartel soldiers and took them out in less than a minute.

A cartel soldier emerged on his knees with his hands up. "Human shields, human shields. Stop shooting or they'll die."

"Hold fire, hold fire!" Bryan barked through the radio.

When the shooting stopped, the soldier stood and spoke in Spanish.

"Carlos Alvarez and Alana Alvarez and Joseph Foley are tied here at the front of the building. And Stanley Gleason, our former leader. Who will be a wanted man in America. Carlos Alvarez and Foley have already been hit by your bullets." The soldier pointed his rifle at the captives. "Lay down your weapons now if you want them alive."

The judge was right. Gleason wasn't just dirty. He was the dirt pile.

A large, burly man dressed in jeans and boots and a light shirt emerged from the shadows, brandishing an assault rifle.

"We know what you want," the man said.

"Your compound is completely surrounded," Bryan said. "We've taken out more than twenty of your men." A pause. "It's over. Tell the rest of your men to lay their weapons down and come forward with their hands on their heads."

The man pointed his rifle toward Carlos and Alana. "You're not getting these two. And you're not getting us without a fight." He raised his rifle and fingered the trigger. Two cracks of fire came from the left and the man went down, screaming and holding his right thigh. Beltran and SOT Four rushed forward and the remaining cartel soldiers dropped their weapons and raised their hands in surrender.

Bryan waved his men toward the man they'd shot and the other soldiers. Beltran knelt before the four captives. Carlos had been hit in the stomach and Foley in the shoulder. Blood oozed from Foley's wound. Carlos bled profusely.

"Air support, move in," Bryan barked through the radio.

A medic team would arrive in minutes. Beltran put the heels of his hands on each man's wound to stop the flow. He looked Carlos in the eye and said, "You're going to make it. Hold on. Trust God." He prayed over him in Spanish.

He turned to a teammate who was tending to Alana and Gleason. "No gunshot wounds in these two," the Marine said.

The heavy chop of the Super Stallions approached. Beltran kept his hands in place until the medics arrived. After they took over, Beltran waved Chavez over to join him.

"Who was that last guy we shot in the legs?"

"Humberto Peña. He's been the local *jefe* of San Luis from the beginning." Chavez pointed at Gleason. "Now we know why he told the judge he could bring his son back to him."

Beltran nodded. "Major Bryan said our orders are to only take Judge Lamport's three people and Gleason. Our new *amigo* El Teniente will have a fine time cleaning up here."

Chapter 90

Tuesday, March 2
Yuma Providence Hospital
5:34 a.m.

Edward opened his eyes. Special Agent Novack stood at his bedside.

"Good morning. Can you help me turn on my right side so I can see you better?"

Novack called a nurse into Edward's room, who helped him rotate without disturbing any of the surgeon's work.

"They got Gleason. He was the head of the San Luis cartel. Can you believe it?"

His worst suspicion was proven correct. "And Carlos?"

"They left his top local guy in Mexico. Part of the deal the president made."

He's avoiding my question. Not good.

"All great news, Agent Novack. What about Carlos?"

"He's in this hospital. So are Alana and Joe Foley." Novack licked his lips. He started to speak, then turned his face away.

Edward had thought he was prepared for what might be said next. Instead, his pulse galloped and his breathing constricted. "Is he dead?"

"He took a couple of rounds in the abdomen. Lost a lot of blood. Shredded up his small intestines." Novack huffed a deep sigh. "Still in surgery."

A wave of grief submerged Edward. He laid his head down.

Novack grabbed Edward's left forearm. The wave pulled back after a time. "Foley and Alana?"

"She was dehydrated and bruised but otherwise fine. Foley took a bullet in the shoulder, and they broke fingers on both his hands. He's gonna pull through."

He hadn't been in the field to rescue Carlos like he wanted, like he had thought the Lord had called him to do. The professionals got the job done. They got Carlos out.

And he might die anyway.

He swallowed hard. Pain. "Could you help me with a drink of water?"

Novack put a straw to Edward's mouth. He gulped the contents of the small plastic cup.

"Have they said what Carlos's chances are?"

"Too early to tell. Doesn't look good."

He heaved a sigh and clenched his chin to keep it from trembling. "Thanks for all you did, Agent Novack."

Novack moved closer. "Gotta hand it to you, Judge. You're one committed man. You cut some big corners to get Carlos out of harm's way. No one does what you did, extends themselves like that." He turned and paced slowly around Edward's bed. "I don't know if I'd do it were I in your shoes."

Edward turned his head toward Novack. "It may all be for naught."

"I don't think so, Judge. There'll be a lot more to the story soon. They airlifted Gleason to LA for booking. I'm heading back in a bit to question him. My gut tells me he's gonna sing like a bird."

"Hope you're right," Edward said as he shook Novack's hand. "Hope you're right."

"Oh, one more thing. No need to worry about the smuggling charge. Eriksen made sure there would be no prosecution against you."

"Well . . ." Edward said. "What changed his mind?"

"You'll need to ask him. My guess is what you said to him about real justice sank in."

A knock at the door. A petite blond nurse poked her head in. "Judge Lamport, you have a visitor."

Edward swiveled his gaze toward the door. "Who is it?"

The nurse wheeled in a man whose head was completely bandaged except around the eyes and mouth. His right arm was in a sling, and he had casts on both forearms, covering his fingers. "It's me, Ed."

Foley! How do I ever . . . I owe him. Big-time.

Foley's wounded visage smashed Edward's last pillar of emotional resistance.

"You're . . ." he said through trembling lips. "I don't know what to say. How will I ever repay—"

"Don't, man," Foley said in a gravelly voice. His lips barely moved. "We got 'em out."

Novack slipped behind Foley's wheelchair and waved. "We'll be in touch."

Edward bade Novack good-bye while he studied every one of his friend's bandaged body parts. Edward had never come close to experiencing the kind of physical torture his friend and his son had endured.

Then the thought hit him—Padraig Lamport. Between Foley and Carlos, he'd witnessed the same kind of unwavering determination his ancestor had displayed. His own wounds, as lifesaving as they had been for Jacqui, paled in comparison.

"How long they gonna keep you in here?" he asked Foley.

"Three, maybe four more days. Gotta make sure I can take care of myself. Occupational hazard."

"I don't follow," Edward said.

"I got nothing except my work, man." Foley paused for a visibly labored breath. "Choice I made, but at a time like this it'd be nice to have someone to go home to."

"Come stay with us. We have room."

"Nah, you guys got your hands full with Carlos and Alana. Who's gonna take care of you?"

"Not a big deal. They'll send me out of here with one of those donut cushions. I'll be doing more standing and lying on my stomach than anything else."

"Can you call the nurse back in here?" Foley said. "Need to do some business."

◆ ◆ ◆

8:44 a.m.

Edward had managed to get the swirl of thoughts about Jacqui and Carlos and Foley and Alana to slow down enough to get a nap in without the assistance of medication. He woke feeling more refreshed than he had since he'd first awakened in this hospital. His bedside phone rang. A moment's hesitation before he answered.

"Judge Lamport, it's Albert Sanchez."

Another man to whom he was indebted. "How'd you know I was here?"

"The news about the Marines rescuing your family and getting Gleason is everywhere. FBI Director Moore gave you the credit for breaking the case open. He said, 'Judge Lamport's persistent pursuit of justice made the difference.'"

"Excuse me a second." He reached for a pillow and stuffed it under his abdomen. "Need to lay on my stomach. Took a lot of shrapnel in the backside. You were saying?"

"Your rescue of Jacqui was heroic, Your Honor. I'm glad I could play a part. I also need to thank you for making me look good."

"How'd I do that?"

"My report about laundered drug money funding the ITC."

"The one you need to thank is Carlos. Pray for him. He's in surgery right now and it's real touch-and-go."

◆ ◆ ◆

3:08 p.m.

Edward returned from his hourly walk feeling vigorous. He did ten laps of the floor without the walker. Pleased with his accomplishment, he was happy to see Dr. Lewis waiting for him in his room.

"Lookin' good, eh, Doc?"

"You're making outstanding progress. The wounds are healing well and there's no sign of infection. We're moving you upstairs with Jacqui."

"That's great." His mood turned somber. "How is she?"

"Well. We have the propofol completely flushed out of her system. And . . ."

"Yes?"

Dr. Lewis beamed. "Carlos pulled through the surgery. He'll need some extended recovery, but he's gonna make it."

He's going to make it. Thank you, God. Thank you.

"I'd give you a hug, Judge Lamport, but I don't want to hurt you."

Edward shook the doctor's hand. "Thank you for everything."

He was giddy as a schoolkid. His son had made it through. He would soon be with Jacqui. He hadn't felt this excited and nervous to see her since their first date.

He was ready. He wasn't ready.

He'd lost count of how many times he'd rehearsed his first words to her. Had no idea what he would face.

"Do I need an escort to my new room or can I go on my own?"

"We'll take you."

A strapping male nurse rolled a gurney into his room and slid Edward onto it from the bed. He winced as sutures pulled at tender skin around his mosaic of wounds. "I need more pillows." The nurse quickly obliged, and they were on their way.

Being nervous was good. He appreciated the empty elevator and the nurse's discretion to refrain from conversation. He wanted to stay focused on Jacqui and what he would say. The nurse seemed to sense that without being told. "Thanks for keeping it quiet," he said as the nurse rolled him to Jacqui's room.

"I know this is a big deal," the nurse said.

They stopped in front of the entryway to his new room. Green curtains were drawn around Jacqui's bed. He offered a silent prayer. "Ready," he told the nurse.

A female nurse was inside the room. "Mrs. Lamport," she said, "your husband is here."

"Thank you." Her voice sounded strong and steady.

The nurse pushed him around the curtain to the right of her bed. He locked his eyes on hers. She looked beautiful. The bruising on her face had faded some. Her hair was shiny and healthy-looking.

The wife of his youth, through the bruises and scars.

His beauty.

"Hi, honey. Can't get around without my friend's help."

"I'm starting to feel like myself. I can move my arms without pain now so they don't have to feed me like a baby." She giggled. "I kinda liked it."

He smiled at her. She returned it. Both smiles faded away in a few seconds. "Honey, I . . . uh . . . can we—"

"Talk about everything? Yes."

Her finishing his sentence was unexpected, and a boost. He reminded himself to take it slow and gentle. "Telling you I'm deeply sorry doesn't satisfy, but I need to start there."

"I agree."

Edward asked the nurse to move his gurney next to Jacqui's bed. "Ring the desk when you're ready for us to help you into your bed, Judge Lamport," the nurse said. He left and closed the door to Jacqui's room behind him.

"I watched USANews today," she said. "You're a hero."

Edward looked down a moment. Why was he getting credit for what so many others did? "The kidnapping . . . how are you feeling?"

She inclined her head toward him and smiled. "Had a great talk with an FBI agent yesterday, Marlie Henning. She helped a lot."

Her calmness amazed him. "What'd you talk about?"

"She'd been through something similar ten years ago. Also the result of a family member's good intentions gone bad."

Ouch. I deserved that.

"How'd she help?"

"I'll get to that. How is Carlos? Haven't heard anything." She looked down. "Or about Alana either."

What was happening here? Evading a question wasn't her style. Especially when the issue was her well-being.

"They're here. So's Foley. Carlos took shots in the abdomen during the rescue. His small intestine got ripped up, but he survived surgery. He's critical but the doc says he's gonna make it. Alana was roughed up but she'll be all right. Foley . . ." He choked up. "They tortured him pretty bad. Bandaged almost everywhere. Casts on both arms. He's a tough son of a gun, though. He'll be fine."

Jacqui looked at him and smiled, then her face turned serious. "Here's where I am." She reached for his hand and held it. "Hearing Marlie's story and talking with Cynthia, I understand why you did what you did. You believed in love. That doing what love required was more important than playing it safe. More important than the law. You got a second chance to be Carlos's father and you went for it."

"I should have told you about getting Alana pregnant. I should have trusted you with it." He cleared a lump out of his throat. "Forget about what I promised her father."

"You acted in faith for Carlos, but not for me. That was the hardest part." She teared up. "But now I have to confess something. And hope you'll forgive me."

Oh.

Lord.

Whatever it is can't be anything close to what I've put her through.

He wanted her to feel his compassion. "What is it?"

"Remember when I miscarried, the doctor said I had uterine abnormalities?"

Why is she bringing this up? "I don't want to, but yes."

She took his hand. "When I was sixteen I got pregnant."

Pregnant.

Someone did to you what I did to Alana.

He strained to put his other hand over hers. The stitches pulled hard. She'd carried an old secret tied to deep pain. Like him. He knew her ache. Immediately. Intimately. He'd spent his adult life keeping the consequences of his choice buried in someone else's reality. He'd chosen. He'd told himself he made a sacrifice for Alana's good. But the truth was he'd copped out. He could have fought. He could have persisted.

He looked into her eyes with all the love and compassion he could muster. "I understand. You don't need to say any more."

She began to sob. "I killed my baby. I killed our babies. It's horrible, so horrible . . ." Her sobs turned to wails.

Jacqui had faced a difficult choice, alone and afraid.

She'd done what she thought was best. Like him.

A nurse walked in.

"What's wrong, Mrs. Lamport?"

Edward beckoned the nurse to let him whisper in her ear. "We're letting go of the past."

Chapter 91

Wednesday, March 3
Metropolitan Detention Center, downtown Los Angeles
8:38 a.m.

The Los Angeles federal jail had not detained someone as high profile as Stanley Gleason since it opened in 1988. Special Agents Novack and Milostan had picked up on the buzz that had spread among the guards and some other detainees who cared about such things.

The agents took a break from interrogating Gleason for a cup of coffee and a sidebar. He'd stonewalled them repeatedly and his lawyer, Ira Abelson, had threatened to end the interrogation five times.

"I think he's ready to crack."

Milostan didn't understand the FBI agent's confidence. "What makes you so sure?"

"He's a pragmatist. He made his fortune by taking care of his self-interest. We have him dead to rights. David Boies couldn't get this guy acquitted. If he'd even take the case."

Milostan gulped the rest of his black coffee. If Novack thought Gleason was ready to crack, he was ready to swing the hammer. "Let's do this."

They returned to the interrogation room. Both agents paced around the table and stared Gleason down.

"You guys like what you see or something? What are you doing?"

Novack sat opposite Gleason and Abelson while Milostan stood to their right. "One more time, Mr. Gleason. You know you're done. Your own people have ratted you out."

"You believe what those Mexican scumbags say? What are you, a bunch of idiots?"

"No, sir," Milostan said. "Your domestic and foreign assets have been seized. We have federal and international warrants to look at every transaction in every account you and Vicente Salvatierra and Javier Bernal own or control. When our president gave Mexico's president the heads-up on what's been going on through the ITC he did the same to Salvatierra and Bernal."

Novack grabbed the baton. "Your so-called security men have tucked tail and are tweeting like parakeets to the *federales* in Mexico. All those documents you spirited out of the country? We got 'em."

Gleason glowered at Novack. "How the—"

Milostan slid a chair from the corner of the interrogation room and sat next to Gleason. "Before you dump another bucket of cuss words into this room—all recorded in pristine high-fidelity sound so the jury at your trial gets every tasty morsel—I'm gonna read a few interesting names we found in your files. Mitchell Corman, US senator from California."

"Corman was a champion of the ITC," Gleason said. "His support was very public."

"That's true. However, his signature is on loan documents as a guarantor. Care to explain that one?"

Gleason was quiet. His legs bounced.

"Why would Senator Mitchell Corman guarantee a loan made to you by, let's see, Vicente Salvatierra?" Milostan said.

Gleason sat mute.

"We've got US Marshals bringing Corman in for questioning as we speak," Novack said. "If you tell us before he does, and it checks out, maybe the prosecution will go a little easier on you."

Gleason bobbed his head, then stilled himself. "Okay." He glared at Abelson and motioned at him to keep quiet. "Corman signed as a guarantor because he got the US government to deposit a hundred million dollars in a surety account in his name. He figured out a way to divert funds allocated for infrastructure development for the ITC. Business gets done very differently in Mexico."

Milostan and Novack wide-eyed each other. "So what you're saying, Mr. Gleason, is that our own government supported the use of laundered drug money and guaranteed your repayment of the loan to Mr. Salvatierra?" Novack said.

"Yes."

"So who made the transfer into the surety account?"

"Commerce."

"As in the Commerce Department?"

"As in Jim Branham, Secretary of Commerce."

Novack smelled blood, and he went for the kill. "And all of this was done in the name of the borderless labor pilot, Commerce's pet project?"

"Yes."

"How high did the support of using laundered drug money go?"

"Way high."

"Come on, Gleason. How high?"

"White House."

"The president?"

Gleason shook his head. "Chief of staff."

"The folks at the J. Edgar Hoover Building will appreciate your cooperation. They have Carl Bender in custody."

Gleason rubbed his nose. Kept quiet.

"Now here's another interesting story. Seems you have sway with United States District Judge Michael Marrone."

"I don't know what you're talking about."

"Come on now, you just copped to money laundering and international fraud and conspiracy to commit fraud." He slipped a sheet of paper in front of Gleason with two columns of numbers. "Isn't it curious that over the last four years there's this pattern of cash withdrawals from your personal checking account and identical cash deposits into the personal account of Judge Marrone?"

Gleason stared at the paper. He said nothing. Abelson reached for it, took a glance, and set it down.

Novack took it back. "I don't believe in coincidences, Mr. Gleason. Do you?"

"I'm not saying one way or the other."

Novack checked his watch. "We've got all day, Mr. Gleason. I know you don't have anything better to do."

"I'm not saying anything because others are involved. That's all you get."

"That's fine, Mr. Gleason. We're a patient bunch when it comes to solving crimes."

"You didn't ask me the reason why the US government would have any interest in guaranteeing a loan made with laundered funds. This wasn't about the money."

"Then what was it about?" Novack said.

"My operation was a convenience to them. Salvatierra and I built a secret tunnel across the border between two of the buildings in the ITC. For me it was all about moving product and cash. Bender found out about it—I never did find out who betrayed me on that—and he said he'd keep it hush-hush if I did something for the government."

"Who in the government?"

"I don't know who, but Carl Bender does."

"And what did they want you to do?" Milostan said.

"Move weapons."

"What kind of weapons?"

"Military. Bender hooked up with that Las Reconquistas organization."

That same group that guy who threatened Judge Lamport claimed he was with.

"The White House chief of staff wanted to help Mexico start a war with America?"

"He's smarter than that. He wanted to use their passion to help Mexico clean up the drug cartels. The big payoff was an exclusive rights deal for Mexican oil. Being in the drug business myself, I saw to it those weapons never made it to their destination."

"Did he know?"

"Nope. I paid off Las Reconquistas to keep quiet. They liked my money more than their cause."

"So what did you do with the guns?"

Gleason looked Novack in the eye. Then he turned his head toward Abelson.

Milostan stood. "Would you like some coffee, Mr. Gleason?"

Chapter 92

Two weeks later

Edward's body was now suture-free except for the three deepest wounds on his buttocks that were still healing. The day after the doctors had moved him out of the ICU into a room with Jacqui, he spiked a fever and they discovered a deep infection in his left gluteus maximus muscle. It had taken four days to knock it out, and though he'd now been home almost a week, he was still weak from the infection and the strong antibiotic regimen and lack of nourishment.

His donut cushion had become an indispensable friend. He could sit no more than thirty minutes a day for the next week. Then he could add thirty minutes each week until the wound was completely healed.

Carlos and Alana had been released from the hospital two days before him. He'd purposely avoided contact with either of them until they were healed enough to be released. Though the infection made his intent moot.

Jacqui came into the bedroom and planted a kiss on his cheek. "Lots of good news came in while you were napping. Ramon Ortiz at CIS called. Carlos's and Alana's asylum applications have been approved."

Her words were a welcome salve. One step closer to meeting his son for the first time.

"Where are they staying?"

"McCormack said the marshals helped them find a place to stay. They're in a two-bedroom suite at the Wilshire Executive Suites. Alana is a wealthy woman."

"Her father and husband were both successful businessmen."

"And we got a letter in the mail today from your cousin Pato. He and Marta are in Costa Rica. They're going to move there if they can get immigration status."

"Need to tell my dad."

"Already done." Jacqui pulled up a chair and sat next to him. "I called Alana this morning."

Edward raised his head and rolled on his right side. "You called her?"

"Mm-hmm. Wanted to know how they were doing. Let her know a lot of people are praying for her, thanks to Cynthia."

"So, how are they doing?"

"Carlos is still on liquids, but he's gained weight and strength. The doctors say he's doing great. Should be no long-term effects."

He heaved a deep sigh. What would it be like to meet Carlos face-to-face? What first words would come out of his mouth? What mattered more was what *Carlos* would say when Alana told him the truth.

Jacqui rubbed his hand. "She asked when you'd be ready to see them. I told her about your restrictions."

"Let's do it today."

Jacqui tipped her head. "You sure?"

"Why not? It's only a mile from here."

◆ ◆ ◆

He'd considered walking the mile from their front door to the Wilshire. A little. The stitches in his backside dissuaded him. Better to go the LA way.

Drive.

He situated himself in the front passenger seat of his Range Rover—the marshals had done a great job of getting it repaired and detailed—and did what he could to prepare his heart. He forced himself to not dwell on what he'd say.

They left the car with a valet attendant and stepped into the ornate lobby of the extended-stay hotel. A ten-second wait for the elevator and they zoomed up to the twelfth floor. The penthouse suites.

Edward and Jacqui strolled arm in arm to the Alvarezes' door.

He knocked.

He held his breath.

Alana answered. He fought the urge to bite his lower lip. The right side of her face was mottled with faint bruises, and a large gash under her right eye had scabbed over and was ringed by suture marks.

Good thing he wasn't alone with her.

"*Hola,* Eduardo."

He reached for her hands. "My wounds still keep me from hugs." They'd healed enough for her to hug him, but he didn't dare. He didn't trust how his heart would react.

He'd expected—hoped for—the same soft touch from her hands that he remembered.

Still there.

He wanted to kiss her left cheek, the one that had escaped abuse from her captors. He restrained himself. For Jacqui's sake.

Alana extended a hand to Jacqui. "Señora Lamport, it is wonderful to finally meet you."

"Please, call me Jacqui." She took Alana's hand. Coolly. Jacqui let no trace of fear or jealousy show.

What's happening inside, honey?

Edward had not anticipated the battle in his heart that now raged. Love and concern and care for his wife in this awkward moment. Awakened affection for the mother of his son.

"*Favor venga,*" Alana said, gesturing for them to come in.

"Carlos," Alana shouted across the spacious suite. "Señor *y* Señora Lamport *estan aquí.*"

Alana escorted them to a plush sofa. "I need to stand," Edward said. "Can't sit for more than half an hour a day until next week."

Her face turned quizzical. Edward pointed at his left glute. She nodded and blushed a bit.

She was still beautiful.

Careful, Lamport. Careful.

Carlos emerged from one of the bedrooms. He was gaunt and his hair was cropped close. Little resemblance to the picture Alana had shown him.

Edward extended his hand. "I'm Edward Lamport. This is my wife, Jacqui."

Carlos shook his hand. His grip was strong, considering what he'd endured. "Pleased to meet you, Señor Lamport. Mamá and I, we owe you much gratitude."

Carlos's English was well practiced. Bulges of bandage wrap showed through his dark blue T-shirt. Judging by appearance, his full healing would take a long time.

Alana brought a tray of chilled bottles of water and crystal tumblers filled with ice and set it on the coffee table. She sat in a side chair to Jacqui's right.

Silence settled in quickly. Edward had let go of worrying what he would say, and now no words came.

"The doctors said you're going to make a full recovery," Jacqui said. "That's wonderful."

"*Sí, señora.* God is good."

"Carlos," Edward said, "you did a great thing. You sacrificed yourself for a noble cause. And you succeeded."

"You and Señor Sanchez did much more to defeat them."

"Your commitment to what's right made it possible. You're a hero to a lot of young men in Mexico. And America. You showed us how one man's courage can change the world."

"*Gracias*, Señor Lamport. "

Edward glanced at Alana. She nodded curtly. Her countenance fell. Silence hung in the air.

Carlos's expression turned quizzical. "Mamá, what's wrong?"

"I have something to tell you, *mijo*." Alana fussed with her blouse. "Señor Lamport and I knew each other when we were young. Before you were born."

His face brightened a bit. "How?"

"Through Pato," Alana said.

"Pato Lamport is my third cousin," Edward said. "He and your grandfather were once business associates."

"*Sí*, Pato told me," Carlos said.

"I met your mother when I visited Pato during a vacation. Her family had come to visit."

"So you were friends?"

Edward shifted his glance between Jacqui and Alana.

"Eduardo and I fell in love," Alana said.

Jacqui stood and moved next to Edward. She grabbed his hand.

Carlos smiled and shook his head. He stared at his mother a few seconds, then turned to Edward. "You were my mother's boyfriend?"

"Yes," Alana said. "It happened quickly."

"We were very much in love, Carlos," Edward said. He looked at Alana, then back at Carlos. "I got your mother pregnant."

Carlos's mouth hung open. He turned to his mother. "Why didn't you tell me?" He stood. "What happened to the baby?"

Silence.

Tears pooled in Alana's eyes.

"What happened, Mamá? Did the baby die?"

"You are the baby," Alana said. "Eduardo is your father."

Jacqui squeezed Edward's hand tight. His heart skipped several beats.

Carlos raised his hands in the air, then dropped them to his sides. His mouth moved but he didn't speak. He looked up, down, at his mother. "I . . . I am . . . *un bastardo*?

"No, *mijo*, you are a son. A true son. Guillermo raised you with honor. You have his name. You will have his legacy. Guillermo loved you, *mijo*. He loved you."

"No . . . no! How could you lie to me? How could you not tell me who my real father is? *Querido* Jesús . . ." He flopped into a chair and buried his head in his hands.

Right there. In Edward's face. The consequences of his choice to give in instead of fight, delayed twenty-five years, had been cut open and laid bare. His son sat before him, rent and trembling.

He'd sent a wound deep into his son's core. In their first minutes together.

Before he'd had a chance to be anything to Carlos.

Chapter 93

The next morning

Edward hadn't had a bite to eat or anything to drink since they'd left the Wilshire. He'd been foolish to think Carlos would receive the news well. He'd never been a wishful thinker before today. His hardened heart, his jaded, cynical worldview, had always told him hope was an illusion and evil would not be extinguished and he had to keep defeating it wherever and whenever he could to keep it from consuming every element of life.

What had Carlos known? What kind of relationship did he and Guillermo have? Alana said Guillermo had raised Carlos with honor. Was that the truth or a mother's desperate attempt to keep her son's heart from shattering?

Of course, it wasn't over.

Of course, his relationship with Carlos would not remain in its current tattered state. It would be hard. It would be painful.

And worth every moment.

The Edward Lamport of five weeks ago—the ambition-driven, law-and-order, full-speed-ahead Edward Lamport—wouldn't have understood what he did now.

"I need to go back," he said to Jacqui.

"I know."

He and his donut cushion climbed into and out of the Range Rover and drove back to the Wilshire. "Maybe you and Alana could take a walk. I need to be alone with him."

Jacqui grabbed his arm. "Are you serious? That would be beyond awkward."

"I know. But it has to be me and him alone."

She exhaled from deep down. "I'll do it."

◆ ◆ ◆

Patchy low clouds filtered sunlight into a soft glow. Jacqui chose a tree-lined side street for her walk with Alana to her favorite morning stop, Cafe Saint Étienne on Olympic Boulevard. Pleasantries exchanged, it was time to ask the hard questions.

Jacqui turned to Alana. "Do you still love my husband?"

Alana faced straight ahead. "I never stopped loving Eduardo. When someone is taken away from you . . . someone you believed you were destined to be with forever . . . I was forced to marry Guillermo. We grew to care for each other, but neither of us was fulfilled."

Stuck in an arranged, loveless marriage. Jacqui searched her heart for understanding. Empathy. Hearing the other side of Edward's story shed more light on his choices. And amped up her fears about Alana's presence in their life even more.

"You believed your father would follow through on his threat to banish you and force you to give up your child."

"Yes!" Alana stopped midstride. "He was ultra machismo. Nothing was allowed to tarnish his well-crafted reputation. His business partners and friends were all the same. My father and Guillermo's father tried to soothe us with their money . . ." Her voice trembled. She drew a breath. "I spent my whole life, until Guillermo died, doing the bidding of men who cared nothing for me, only for themselves."

Jacqui had gotten a taste of Mexican family dynamics in the schools, but she didn't dare presume to understand Alana's life.

She only wanted to know Alana's intentions toward Edward. Needed to know.

How do I ask such a thing?

"What are your plans once Carlos is healthy?"

I hope that was benign enough . . .

"I can't go back to Mexico, if that's what you're asking." Alana's tone turned testy.

They reached Olympic Boulevard and turned right, their destination half a block ahead. Alana's retort hung over them as they entered and each ordered café au lait and fresh-baked croissants. Jacqui stirred a lump of raw sugar into her cup and took a bite of warm, flaky goodness.

"This is as close to the best patisseries in France as you'll find in LA."

Alana's croissant remained on its plate, undisturbed. "Jacqui," she said, fiddling with her necklace. "I'm not going to try to steal him from you. I don't like how my life has turned out. At all. But I must accept what is and go forward."

◆ ◆ ◆

Edward and Carlos sat across the room from each other. Carlos wouldn't look at him. Wouldn't speak to him. Small talk wouldn't cut it, so Edward got to the heart of the matter.

"Son, what happened—"

"Don't call me that. Your sperm may have fertilized Mamá's egg, but you're not my father. A father doesn't abandon his son."

"You're right." He ground a fist into his palm. "You're absolutely right. Your grandfather was a hard man. I was young and immature and afraid. He was going to send your mother to a convent. Make her have you there and give you up for adoption." Bitter bile crept into his throat. He still hadn't forgiven the man. "He was only concerned about his reputation."

The pain of those days returned to Edward. Fresh. Raw.

"Your grandfather hated me. I did what I did to protect your mother."

Carlos looked at him with scorn. "A real man does not give up without a fight."

"I agree. Completely." He stepped closer to Carlos. "Would you look at me?"

Carlos kept his head down.

"Please. Look at me."

Carlos lifted his head.

"You have the Lamport heart. A warrior's heart. The heart of your ancestor, Padraig Lamport."

"Los San Patricios."

Edward nodded. "I didn't have the Lamport heart in my early twenties. I didn't know who I was back then. I let fear and loss and failure define me."

He tossed his donut cushion onto a chair across from Carlos and sat. He leaned slightly right to minimize pressure on his wounded glute. "You don't have to do the same. You have a life of promise ahead of you. Whether you stay here in America or go back to Mexico, you have a purpose. You're meant to discover your purpose."

"I know God has a purpose for me. He wants me to fight for what is right. That is why I took the data from Bancomex. Someone had to stop them. Everyone I worked with accepted corruption and looked the other way. I could not. I had to do something. Especially after Gonzalo died. I had to make his sacrifice count for something."

"The world needs more people like you, Carlos. Your intelligence, your courage, your faith." He drew a deep breath. "I'd like a chance to help you. Help you forgive the past. Help you discover what lies ahead."

Carlos blew out a deep breath. "I am grateful for all you did to rescue me and Mamá." He looked into Edward's eyes. "I meant what I said yesterday. We owe you a debt of gratitude."

"I only did what a father is supposed to do."

Edward stepped to the window and took in the view of Wilshire Boulevard.

The street of dreams.

Pacific Ocean blue defined the horizon.

"Come and look," he said to Carlos.

Carlos sauntered to the window, hands in pockets.

"This road is like the aorta of the city. It connects five major business districts between downtown and the ocean. Through Beverly Hills and Westwood and Brentwood and Santa Monica." He pointed at a building two blocks away. "See that tall building with the angled front? That's the beginning of a district called the Miracle Mile. Got its name from a man who made movies and TV shows. His first production was a hit, and he said, 'These miles create miracles.'"

"Only God creates miracles," Carlos said.

"And you're one of them."

Edward turned from the window. Carlos seemed touched by what he'd said. Edward let silence hang in the air for a time, then returned to the chair with his donut cushion. His pain had lessened. Sitting was more comfortable.

Carlos returned to his chair. He picked at some lint on his T-shirt and then looked up.

"So what do you say? Will you give me a chance?"

Carlos eyed him up and down. Looked away for a moment. Then back at him.

And extended his hand.

ACKNOWLEDGMENTS

Blythe: Your enthusiasm for this story in its early days was wind into my sail.

Jessica: You saw the potential of this work, persisted alongside me, and found it the right home.

DiAnn, Jerry, Doc, James, Steven, Robert: I am forever blessed to have learned the craft of fiction from masters.

Steve, Mike, Gail: Your law enforcement and military expertise added pure gold to this work.

Jodie: Your story development guidance and editing made all the difference.

Amy: Thank you for the opportunity to offer this story to readers everywhere.

Faith: As you took this story over the finish line, you helped me become a better writer.

ABOUT THE AUTHOR

Photo © 2015 Rena Collette Photography

Before penning fiction, Dennis Ricci worked as a freelance marketing strategist, copywriter, and instructional designer. He also mentors aspiring writers, conducts writing workshops, and advises marketing professionals on strategy and content. *Perilous Judgment* is his first novel.

Ricci lives in Thousand Oaks, California, with his wife, where they serve their community through a Healing Rooms ministry dedicated to praying for the sick. He has three grown children.

For more information, visit www.dennisricci.com.